BEYOND THE

RUINED NIGHTS

BILLY DON LOPER

SONG OF CALARINE
BOOK I

Published by BILLY DON LOPER, 2025

BEYOND THE RUINED NIGHTS

FIRST PAPERBACK EDITION. 2025.

ISBN: 979-8-9923254-0-9

Cover and Interior Art by J.A. Wellings

CONTENT ADVISORY

Readers should be aware of the presence of the following potentially upsetting and disturbing content:

Graphic Violence, Strong Language, Exploration of Mental Health, Exploration of Personal Trauma, Explicit Sexual Content, Alcohol and Tobacco Content

DEDICATIONS

To Mississippi, my home eternal.

To my wife Miranda, for her perpetual patience.

To my son, Atticus, who it's all for.

PROLOGUE
An Unwanted Audience

===

The late-winter sun rested its light onto the walls of the keep with a delicacy often reserved for the gray pallet of storm clouds. The street sounds of Varinz below carried into the Tower of the Southern Gate as a soft murmur, just enough to raise the already nervous skin on the man's arms. He, a man whose name cannot yet be given, sat slumped in a fine-tooled chair across the room from an ornate wooden vanity. His eyes rested on a small, gray stone no bigger than his palm that laid on vanity's top, trying to find the will to cross the room and make the call he knew was required. The Emperor's Carrier had provided simple instructions: make the call with haste and then return the calling stone to the courier's office without hesitation. No other means could reach the Emperor, who remained in perpetual warding against magic, and any calling stone could only cast its spell once. But it was no honor to be handed that stone. No honor to hold an audience with the Emperor. It was a punishment reserved only for the worst of transgressions. For treason and heresy and terrorism. A typical precursor to the immediacy of execution.

So, the man sat across the room from the stone, his hands patting his knees, wishing he was anywhere else. Most of all, he wished he was back in Savan, the smells of his farm working their way through his nose. He wished his hands were covered in the sap of the short-growth pines he had spent so long raising. He wished his heels were layered with the shit of chickens and hogs, not the stench of city streets, born of the racket outside. His beard was unkempt, ragged and wilded from his time in the dungeons. His hair, gray flecked and middle-aged, had begun to curl and fight against him. The shining new traveling leathers he wore were stiff and uncomfortable. As he pulled at the neck of the leather jerkin he again thought of his farm. Of the soft worked linen that he had become accustomed to since leaving his post nearly a decade before. His boots, though, were his. Truly and really his. They were worn and ragged workman's boots, the heels driven down to nothing. When the Searchers had offered him new ones, neat and leathered in their fine buckskin make, he had refused. He closed his eyes, the thick band of water oaks that lined the edge of his property filling his mind, and gave a sigh that shook his shoulders. He knew that he could never take a step towards Savan again until he first went to the calling stone.

The weight of it all too much to push away for any longer, the man crossed the room with a loping patience only gifted to those walking to their own personal gallows. He picked up the stone and turned it over in his hands, examining the runes and reading them twice over before he poured his intent into it. He emptied his mind of Savan, emptied his heart of all desire except that of the stone. Of the spell it contained. In a moment it crackled alive and a perfect astral image of the Emperor appeared before him. The man knelt, his forehead resting on one knee, hand still clenching the calling stone.

"My Lord, I am here before you," he said, eyes never lifting towards the shimmering visage.

"Rise," said the emperor. His voice was tenor but booming all the same. He was dressed in fine robes that hung over his wiry frame in a way that made him seem ghostly. The man stood as instructed, his eyes now meeting the unseeing projection's. "You have failed this empire in a way I never believed could be done. Treason from one as decorated as you? It is preposterous. Had the report not come from your own father I would seldom have believed it."

"My lord, I never--"

"Pah! Never? Never what? Never meant to sell lumber to our sovereign enemy?"

"The empire has not been at war with the Western Republics for decades, and I--"

"Quiet yourself before I call for the headsman. It is unheard of for a former officer of my army to sell materials to the Republics. It is inconceivable for one of my most decorated Aetics, the damn son of my commanding general, to do this to the empire. You are lucky that your uncle pleaded with me for mercy. You are quite a bit more lucky that he quelled your father's rage."

"I understand, my lord."

"By the end of this, I believe you will. You will be made to understand, if you ever want to return to that patch of scrub brush you call a farm."

The man paused, his jaw tensing as his eyes watched the shimmering visage. "My lord?"

"I considered it for a long time, do you understand? What could be the closest thing to execution I could level against you? It was your father who finally gave me the idea, and I must commend his brilliance."

"Lord, I'm afraid I don't understand."

"You are to be reinstated to your previous post as a commander of the Aetic Searchers. You are to form a battalion and begin, with substantial speed, searching for the Calarinian Library. A place known as the Belhaven. I am sure you know it."

The man's face twisted. He pulled his lips in until they were nothing but a thin line hidden behind the wild hairs of his beard. "Generations of searchers have tried and failed, my lord. My own uncle--"

"You have two options. You can find the library and claim it in my name, or you can fail. Failure will see you hung and your farm burned to ashes. That place, and the damnable traitor who hid it away, holds the key to our domination. Somewhere in it is the research he stole from us, the way to release the wellspring of all power. That library has the secret that could give the empire command over this world, do you understand? Do you understand that you will find it, or you will die? The song has yet to be sung, and I intend to hold that library well before the final chords are written."

The man's head fell, and his eyes scanned the ground. His fist tightened on the calling stone. "Understood, my lord."

"We here in the Central Line do not have the patience for any more failures from you, accidental or otherwise. Should I feel the need, I will send your uncle to fetch you, and we will speak face to face."

The man swallowed hard, understanding that another audience, a physical audience, would be his last. "Of course, my lord."

With a gasping crackle, the image of the emperor

faded, and the man was left alone, the dead and useless calling stone still clenched in his hand. His fist tightened and tightened until his rage pushed through and flame erupted from his palm and enveloped the stone, charring it, but doing nothing more. He pivoted on his worn-down boot heels and headed towards the couriers office, the sound of his steps echoing through the sparse and aging tower.

PART I
<u>THE BELHAVEN</u>

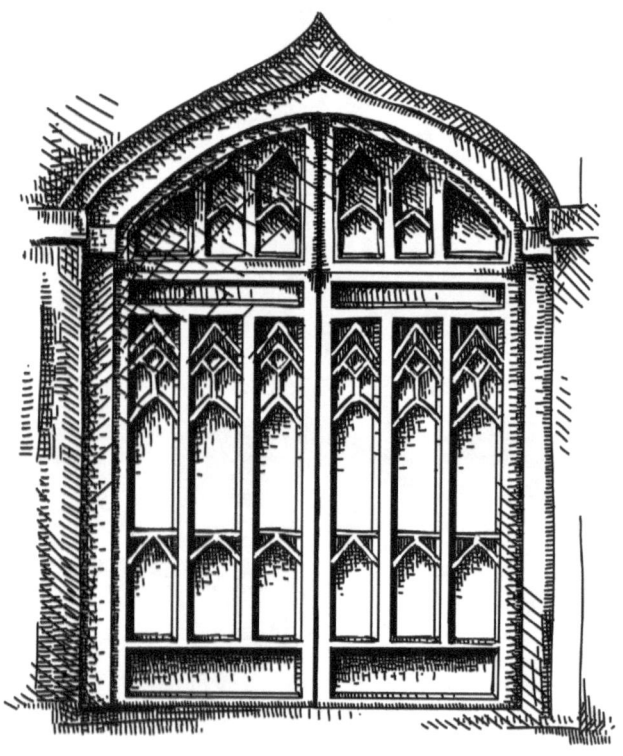

CHAPTER 1
The Paper Falcon

===

The deep ichor of the night clashed with the fire in brilliant bands of orange. Sarah Silvergrove sat on her bedroll, her knees pulled to her chest, and watched as the flickering flames moved along the dry wood in dancing waves. The moonlight couldn't penetrate the tangled canopy of magnolia and oak above, even though she had made her camp just within the edges of the Blinded Forest. Her blue eyes were lit in strange shades of yellow and orange as she stared into the fire. Her mind was far away, as it often was late at night, when there was no movement to keep her from her thoughts. She thought of the southern coast, of her rush north in hopes to outrun what she had left behind in that salty air two years before. She thought of her friends, all of them full of new hate and pushing her away. She thought of her now solitary life, life as a traveler. A nomad whose routine was only broken with the occasional company of strangers, those who had chosen the life of the road. The life she and her friends had taken up, before her world had plunged into the dark below. It was the distinct crackle of leaves that broke her free from her thoughts. Footsteps. She turned to look towards the sound just as a shadowed figure came to the edges of the light.

"There in camp!" a woman's voice called out. "Room for a stopover?"

"I suppose so. Come on."

The woman walked into the camp and laid her things down several feet from Sarah's left before she herself sat on the hard ground with a decided groan. The woman was short with a long, tied ponytail of deep brown hair, and Sarah watched her with cautious eyes as the woman unbuttoned her padded gambeson. She kept it on, but now it was spread open and tucked around the edges of her waist as she sat cross-legged in front of the fire. Sarah sat and watched, saying nothing, as the woman dug through a buckskin bag and pulled out a package of dried meat. She held it out to Sarah and gestured. "Hungry?" she asked.

Sarah shook her head. "Already eaten, thank you."

"I'm Tish."

"Sarah."

"Good to meet you, Sarah. Out all alone?"

Sarah didn't take her eyes from the woman but made a mental note of where her staff rested on the ground to her right. "Does that matter?"

Tish laughed and popped a strip of jerky into her mouth. "No, I don't guess so. You seem a little jumpy, you run into trouble lately?"

"Isn't there always trouble?"

"Guess so, yeah. Seems there's always more the closer you get to the Crown Cities, too."

Sarah nodded at that. "I did run into something in Varinz. A drunkard in some tavern, the Skeeving Fink, I think? He tried to get handsy and, well. He was alive when I left, but on the ground."

"You coming from Varinz?"

"Not directly. I passed through, but…" Sarah trailed off, her eyes following the lines of a flame that reached up towards the black-green canopy above. "I try to stay out of the cities."

"Where're you headed then? Not much on the other side of these woods."

"The Calarine Ruins. I heard there are travelers there. That they've built a haven."

A sudden, choking sound erupted through the quiet night and Sarah saw that Tish was patting her chest, coughing and laughing all at the same time. "Oh god, I'm sorry. I didn't mean to laugh at you, but, well…there ain't shit in those ruins."

"What? But…I heard so much."

"From who?"

"People in Morable."

Tish pulled a canteen from her pack and drank down a gulp. Water ran down the edges of her chin and trailed her neck as she cleared her throat. "Morable is a long way. Salted coast is what? Two hundred miles? How long ago were you in Morable?"

"Two years," Sarah answered, and her eyes now settled on the embers of the fire.

"And you never stopped anywhere between there and here?"

"Well, of course, but…I try not to talk a lot. In the cities, I mean. They make me nervous."

"Two-hundred miles and you never mentioned Calarine to anyone north of Hattin?" The silence hung there for a minute before Tish sighed and ran a hand through her hair. "Look, I'm going north if you want to tag along for a while.

I'm headed to the Northern Line to try and get passage into Canait. I'm going to try my hand at trapping, could probably use the help."

Sarah shook her head and turned her eyes back to the woman. "Canait? Northern Line? Too fucking cold up there for me."

Tish stood and moved closer to Sarah, the firelight now casting them in the same amber hues. She pulled off the gambeson and dropped it on the ground before she plopped down just beside Sarah, close enough then that they could touch. "So what, you're just going to go on to that pile of rubble anyway?" For a moment there was a pause of strange silence between them, and Tish sat looking at Sarah. The firelight, with the two of them so close, cast Sarah in deep shadows. "Hey, red you hear me?"

"What? What'd you call me?" Sarah's face was turned to the fire and her freckles seemed to sparkle in the orange light.

"I called you red. Your hair?"

Sarah pushed a mess of her curly red hair behind one ear and nodded. "Oh, I...right." She felt a heat rise in her face and shook her head. *Stop it.* "Sorry just, can't believe there's nothing there."

"You are, aren't you? You're going anyway?"

"I'm going. I'll be there by the morning, and I want to see it for myself. Have you been? I mean, have you actually been through the ruins?"

"Been around them, never went through. No reason to, really. It's a mess. More forest than city. Certainly ain't a haven, anyway."

"More forest than city. That sounds all right." Sarah

was smiling now, her face pointed towards the toes of her worn boots and her hair pouring around the edges of her jaw.

Tish reached out and pushed at Sarah's shoulder, a bark of performative laughter splitting the air between them. When Sarah looked up, surprised at the sudden contact, she saw that Tish was leaned over, her forearms now on her own knees. Her eyes made their way up and down Sarah in waves.

"I--um, I hope I haven't..." Sarah trailed off, but she didn't look away from Tish. She shifted on her bedroll, unsure what to do with herself.

Tish raised her hands, palms out, and shook her head. "Hey, don't flatter yourself. I'm just surprised someone your age is headed to the ruins. You're what, twenty?"

"Nineteen."

"Close enough. How long have you been traveling?"

"I left the Lake of Bridges four years ago, but I've been on my own for two."

"Fifteen and on the road. That must've been hard."

"There were a lot of us then. I had a group of friends I left with. We met a traveler during a visit to Picaya, and...well you know how it goes."

Tish nodded. "He was all dolled up in armor and toting a sword or some shit and talking about 'the zeal for adventure.' Maybe he had a pretty woman with him. Maybe the pretty woman ran her hand under your chin and whispered in your ear about the freedom of the road and you took off chasing it."

"Something like that. Zeal for adventure, sure enough."

"Too bad they don't tell you the only glamorous thing about the road is the countryside. Rest is pretty nasty."

Sarah shrugged. "I've found a lot in it. Being a traveler,

it's…freeing. I don't owe to anyone but myself." For a moment her mind sent her back to the Morable coast and her friends, their eyes red and hateful and crying. "Now, anyway."

"How the hell have you stayed fed? You don't look like you've struggled much."

"Fished, hunted. I've worked a lot of odd jobs passing through villages, too."

"I've done my fair share of odds. Being a barmaid is never any good."

Sarah shook her head. "No, never worked a tavern. I've worked stables and ranches. I've rode a few posses, too, but never anything serious."

Tish raised an eyebrow and looked Sarah up and down again. Their thin frame was wiry and tight, even sitting. A climber's body. "Well, I hope Calarine is at least something for you. I need to move on, find my own place to bed down. I appreciate the conversation, Sarah." She rolled her gambeson and stuck it under one arm before she stood up and walked back to her things.

"Safe along the road, traveler," said Sarah.

"I hope you find what you're looking for in those ruins."

At that, the woman disappeared out of the firelight and into the shadows of the Blinded Forest, headed north. Sarah leaned back and laid flat onto her bedroll. The fire was still fed well enough to keep any wandering creatures away, and the wind rattled the tangled magnolia leaves above. She placed a hand on her staff beside her and closed her eyes. As she drifted away, she could taste the salted air of Morable on her lips. She felt its sting in her eyes.

The next day, late in the morning but before the sun had reached its noon apex and begun to send the true southern heat down onto the swamped river valley, Sarah crossed through the thin, brushed edges of the Blinded Forest towards the Calarine Ruins. The riverlands were dry in the Spring's drought, and as the sun settled high and hot in the reddening sky, it dried the thick mud onto Sarah's boots. She pushed her hair behind her ears and the tight curls moved and fought against her as she did. The smells of sweet grass and gardenias wafted on the wind, a smell that reminded her of home. A welcome scent after the deep stench of the Varinzian city streets.

That part of the forest was not much. Just a band of hardwoods and pines that gave way to green hedge where the forest met the flatlands that bordered the ruins. As Sarah hiked through the forest, her tall, athletic frame dipped under branches and bramble. Her bag, a leather shoulder satchel filled with everything she owned besides the clothes on her back, snagged and filled the air with a rhythmic snapping as she forced her way through the sporadic bursts of thicket. Her staff, a twisted length of oak cut and shaped by a friend now lost, helped her maintain her footing, and with each step she could feel the anticipation of what was waiting on the other side. The woman's voice from the night before echoed on and on as she hiked. *There has to be something there. This can't have been for nothing.*

She had made her way through the Terovik Mountain

Valley, that small, semi-circle region of the Risen Range, in the days before, but the trek from the Crown City of Varinz across that imagined political line between the empire and the long-abandoned city of Calarine had been much shorter than she expected. Varinz and its swarms of people had pushed her further on, but Calarine had always been the goal at the end of her path. Along that long road she had tried to outrun the ghosts behind her, but even as she found her way across the grayrock bridges of the Pearl River and into the riverlands, they still traveled with her.

On the hundred and some odd miles of blackstone street and blacksteel highway between Hattin and Varinz, Sarah had clung to Calarine as her saving grace. The morning after Tish sat at her fire and told her that nothing waited on the other side of the Blinded Forest, that Calarine was only ruin, she shouldered her pack and went on, unfaltering. But now, as she made her way through the final stands of the forest, she could feel the uncertainty weighing on her. She could feel the ever persistent unknowing of what could wait in a place so long since abandoned by the empire. As she pushed her way through that final band of forest between the Pearl and Calarine, that green border between imperial control and nomadic freedom, Sarah's mind began to swirl with images of what she hoped waited on the other side. She saw communities of disparate travelers, nomads settled into a community far from the prying hands of Crown Soldiers. She saw a place where people did not look at her with the lingering hate of her friends, where she did not see the memories of her failures in the eyes of everyone she met. When the forest thinned to scrub brush, Calarine rose out of the earthen wastes as a final reminder of the road she had traveled between the Salted Coast and Varinz.

Steel towers and sprawling bridges littered the landscape, but unlike those that stood tall and bustling in Varinz, those ancient buildings were the lingering pock marks of a past long left to the annals of history. Many had collapsed and were returning to the earth around them. An ancient creek bed that had laid empty longer than the city itself framed the scene, giving the ruins of Calarine a feeling of deep and total exhaustion. Trees and vines devoured the other structures in the abandoned vastness of the once great city, and patches of hazy smoke shadowed the horizon. Sarah found herself wondering, if even just for a moment, whether the fires were travelers or burning ruins. Whether they were the bonfires of soldiers or camps of raiders. Standing there at the edge of the forest, looking across flatlands towards the city that had driven her from the coast of the Southern Line and into the Risen Range towards one of the empire's most powerful footholds, Sarah did not see her traveler's haven. She saw, instead, what Tish had told her she would see. A great and empty shell more forest than city. She knew that whoever might wait in the ruins would be no different than those she had met along the road north. She knew they would be nomadic ghosts of a bygone time. Refugees not united but forced into diaspora by the actions of the empire.

Still, as Sarah stood propped on her staff and shielding her eyes against the still-rising sun, she saw the way that the flatlands gave way to the once-urban world of the ruins. She saw that the trees, some ancient and towering in a way that felt impossible, broke the skyline and sent shadows cascading across the towers that had once stood as sisters to those in

Varinz. The day young, her heart still hoping that something could lay on the other side, Sarah shifted her staff in her hands and started across the high-grassed field that lay between her and the ruins. A quiet wind sent the unbroken field of grass into a steady slashing dance as Sarah trudged her way through it, leaving a long line cut into the once pristine nature as a she came to the edges of the ruins. At the first of the city's streets, its blackstone paving cracked and sun-stained in its disuse, she heard the heard the hooting of a rock eagle above. She looked to see it resting atop a towering steel pole set into the earth just beside the street, its great horned head twisting nearly all the way around as it saw her. The bird was strange in the daylight, its large eyes made for the night. Its body was light and billowing and that of a pure predator. It hooted again before stretching its wings and taking flight to the broken window of one of the great towers, disappearing into the darkness inside. *A rock eagle in the daylight is an omen* she heard her mother say, but she pushed the thought away and continued on, following the broken street towards the city's eastern edges.

The streets were not laid out in the clear patterns of Varinz and Hattin and the many other cities she passed through between Morable and the Blinded Forest, but instead were a series of strange and twisting serpents that led her on long stretches of meandering paths. She weaved between towers and low-set stone buildings and loblolly pines that seemed to rise beyond existence, stretching into the sky in the ways that the towers once had, long before the war had left them shells of steel and glass and grayrock. As she walked, she rested her staff across one shoulder, her mind easing in the quiet of the forested ruins. The snaking streets gave way to long, straight stretches of blacksteel highway, the towers easing into lower stone structures, some pebbled and some grayrock but all of them hazed and shimmering in the heat.

Ahead of her, cutting through old highway and standing taller than the half-crumbling buildings around it, a visage of dark granite stood out. Its ornate architecture and intricate stone carvings called to her with a voice she did not understand but felt the pull of through every strand of her being. As she reached the building, she saw the words set deep into the front gable high above the doorway. Half worn away by time, they stood out in bold strokes of white against the black granite: THE BELHAVEN. A wave of electricity washed over her. She started towards the building, unable to understand why she continued on even though each step felt heavier than the last. As she grew closer, the pull between her and the building crescendoed. It raised the hair on her arms. It felt as if it should have sent her clothes rippling, but instead it only pulled her ever closer.

Against the vast and overgrown city, the building's preservation stood as a beacon of the power it radiated. The strangeness of the place reminded Sarah of Aetics, the wielders of an old and hidden magic, their faces shadowed and made brilliant by their power. She walked up the steps to the massive oak doors, the brass handles held no signs of age. They shined in the sunlight a brilliant yellow, Sarah's reaching hands casting them in shadows only reminiscent of the aged green they should have been. Her thumbs holding down the latches, she pulled hard on the doors, expecting the wood to have swollen, to have jammed the heavy things home, but the doors swung on their hinges with ease, only the slightest creak announcing any protest. The room beyond cast in strange shadows, she could only make out the faintest silhouette of the scene beyond. Still, she was pulled on. Still, she stepped through. Once her feet crossed the threshold, that feeling of power wrapped her in its embrace. The space around her became one with the crackling aura of magic as Sarah entered the Belhaven.

The building's musty air hit her as a wave. She tried to make sense of the scene cast out before her. Vast rows of bookshelves filled much of what she could see. Books were strewn across the floor, stacked along the walls, and piled all through the aisles. Sarah realized she stood in the largest library she had ever seen. The first floor was filled with tables and a large central desk, books piled in high stacks on every surface. Sarah walked on unsteady legs, looking over the books, overwhelmed by their numbers and uncommon diversity. She picked some up and turned them over in her hands. Their titles, things such as *The Bright Flash Schism*, *The Lost Era War*, and *The Aetics of Mal-Vek* excited her as much as they confused her. Some felt foreign in every way and others ignited moments of nostalgia. Memories of friends, dreams of magic.

The heavy dust in the air cast the place in a thick twilight, light filtering in through high windows and casting sun rays across the dark hardwood floor. She made her way further into the first floor, taking in the library and all its quiet strangeness as she went. She gazed over the dusty stacks of books and long abandoned furniture and more than once thought of the few times she had encountered Aetics during her travels. The strange, unusual magic those scholar-like figures wielded was only a myth to her, but the Belhaven seemed saturated with its presence. At the chest high desk near the center of the room, Sarah ran a hand over a leather-bound book and wiped away the dust. It was a recent book, hand-set and bound in the common way of modern city libraries, instead of the glue and press binding of books from before the Rending. The title, *A Post-Rending Economic History of the Morable Bay* sent a pang of heartbreak through her chest. She clenched the staff in her hands and turned away from the desk.

Near the western wall of the library, flanked on both sides by waist high stacks of books, she found another set of doors. This time they were tall and accented with brilliant frosted glass marked "Library Administration" that would have cost thousands of crowns. Beyond the doors were rows of desks stacked high with books and relics of what her mother had always called "the long ago." Tangles of wire and aging glass marked corners of the room, and near the back was a separate office, the words "Library Director" painted on a plate glass window set into the center of the door. Inside was an ornate desk covered with papers that felt to Sarah like ancient tomes of old stories. The papers talked of Aetics, something called "Great Boroughs," and vague metaphysical theories Sarah did not understand. Unlike the stories of The Lost Era and the vague business of the empire, these papers felt foreign in a way she had never experienced, magical and bizarre. She reached down and shuffled through them, and as she did, she felt a sudden, sharp jab on her hand. As she recoiled, a flutter came from under the desk and a creature landed on a nearby floor lamp. As it settled, Sarah realized it was a falcon, measuring maybe a foot and a half tall, made entirely of paper. Not just paper, she realized, but the pages of books, words dotting its feathers and disappearing into the delicate folks of its paper-crafted form.

"God above! You scared me, bird."

"My apologies," said the falcon. As it shook out its feathers, the sound of crinkling paper filled the room. "My name is Sibella." Sarah's eyes opened wide, and she froze, staring at the now vocal bird. Being made of paper was strange, but the figure of folding and shifting pages speaking had shocked her. She had seen crafted automatons before, coming and going from the imperial ships along the Lake of Bridges, but never one that spoke. Sibella adjusted his position on the lamp and preened his feathers. "It is not polite to stare, daint."

"I'm not a daint, and excuse my staring. Paper birds don't typically move, much less talk."

"I am not just a bird, d--," Sibella stopped himself and adjusted, "stranger." He flew over to the desk and landed with cautious grace. "I am an enchantment, the familiar of this library. Keeper of its words."

Sarah sat down in the leather chair behind the desk and leaned closer to Sibella. She examined him as his folded and placed feathers shifted with each subtle movement. She had seen figures of power before, but often in the form of mechanical marvels working along the dock lines of the southern coast. For a moment her mind wandered back to her home, just as the empire had made its way onto the coast of the Lake of Bridges. Strange mechanical figures in the rough approximation of human form carried crates and goods from imperial ships as the Crown claimed the village and its goods as its own. A hate she thought herself long shed of boiled up inside, and she gritted her teeth against it. When she refocused herself, she noticed, almost to her irritation, that the paper bird seemed unbothered. "Who created you?"

"The previous keeper of this place. A man called the Alchemical."

"He was an Aetic?" Sarah asked.

He turned his head to her in surprise. "You know of Aetics?"

"Just a little," she responded, debating on whether or not to reach out and touch the bird's wing. She decided against it, remembering the sharp peck that had introduced them. "I've seen a few while traveling, but never spoken to one. I know what they are, magicians. Wizards. However you want to put it. I've never actually seen any of their magic, but I know that is what people say about them, anyway."

Sibella let out a sharp kak sound and settled into a more comfortable position on the desk. "The Alchemical was a powerful Aetic. He was a mage of unending wonder and served as the keeper of this place. He found the Belhaven and protected it, using it as a place of research for the Aetic arts. He carved into its foundation great runes that shield it from discovery." Sibella cocked his head. "Curious that you found it."

"It called to me," Sarah said, rubbing at the back of her head as she tried to understand the reality of where she sat, of what, she was talking to. "I know it sounds a little weird, but…I felt drawn here."

Sibella leapt over to her and landed on the arm of her chair, leaning in with his paper beak so close to her face she could feel his breath. It had the same acidic smell as old books. "It called to you?" he asked, a soft tone of discovery in the back of his voice. "What do you mean?"

Sarah shrugged and adjusted in her seat. "It just sort

of…stood out. I was traveling here from Varinz when I saw the place. Closer I got it just sort of pulled me in." As the words left her lips, Sarah realized how strange the sensation had been. How unusual it was that this place called out to her like an old friend. How it had wrapped her up and pulled her in like a beckoning finger.

Sibella let out a breath of sharp, focused air which almost sounded like a "harrumph." A look of strange curiosity in his eyes, he groomed his feathers and went back to the desk. "Very curious. Perhaps the Belhaven has chosen you as its new keeper. The absence of my creator is greatly felt in these dusty old halls. So, what is your name, then?"

Sarah's jaw muscles worked and made the corded muscles in her neck stand out. Her stomach churned. "My name's Sarah Silvergrove, but…well, I don't think I'm qualified to be the keeper of anything."

"I can't imagine anyone would be. Since the city was abandoned, only my master has served as this place's keeper. Now he is gone."

"What happened to him?"

"The Alchemical disappeared." His voice was dry, his answer curt. Hurt loomed over the bird in an invisible miasma, but Sarah's mind rested too deep in its own internal diatribe to notice.

"How long ago?" she asked, more of curiosity than caring.

For a moment Sibella looked uncomfortable, struggling to answer the question. "A long time ago. Long enough that I doubt he will ever return."

"Is anyone else here?" Sarah asked, even though she

had known that answer as soon as she crossed the threshold. As soon as she opened the door.

The falcon shook his head. "Just me and the books, I am afraid. And you, should you choose to stay."

Sarah stood up from the chair and paced in small circles around the office. Her pack swung on her hip, the worn lines of her leather cuirass making soft noises with each step. It fit her lanky, athletic frame in a way only the most well-worn of traveler's clothes could. "I'm just a traveler, what would I even do here?" Her dreams of peace and solidarity began to swirl in her mind, and for a moment she imagined the library becoming the traveler's haven she had thought all of Calarine to be. She pushed those thoughts out, feeling a little ashamed of the grandeur in her mind. Feeling ashamed she would ever dream of something like that again, even after all it had cost her before. "What am I supposed to do with a library?"

"Whatever you want," Sibella answered. "It will be yours to tend."

"Aren't you the keeper of the library, anyway? With the Alchemical gone, I mean."

Sibella shook his head, almost seeming to smile. "No, I am not. I am only its familiar. I know its words better than anyone else can ever know them, but I can never protect it the way that it might one day need protecting. You, though…well, perhaps you could. It must have called to you for a reason."

Sarah's eyebrows, two thick streaks the color of cooling embers, knitted together, and her blue eyes darted from the falcon as she struggled to keep her composure. Her mind was sent back to the ghosts that had chased her from Morable. The whispering specters of failure, of lost friends and failed obligations. The darkened reminder of the last time she had claimed responsibility for anyone but herself.

"Are you all right?" asked Sibella.

She looked up, her face still tight with worry and the delicate lines of her lips drawn in. "This is just a lot. I expected to find…well, I didn't expect to find a talking papercraft asking me to protect a library, anyway."

"If you're no daint, I'm no papercraft. Sibella will do just fine."

"Sorry, right. It's just a lot."

"If it was a little I cannot imagine you would have felt yourself pulled to this place."

Sarah rolled her eyes and ran a scarred, deft hand through her hair. "I just meant that I didn't exactly come here looking for this kind of responsibility. Or to be lectured, as a matter of fact.

Sibella lowered his head and preened at his feathers. Again that sound of rustling paper filled the air. "Of course, I see. I apologize. I have been alone for quite a while. This place is protected with runes and only I remain inside of its walls. To protect it would not be much responsibility, beyond any you might want to put upon yourself, that is."

Sarah nodded and wondered if she was being given an opportunity at redemption. An opportunity to pay for the failures of her past, two years now gone. The years of solitude weighed heavy on her mind, and the walls around her, unlike the busy streets of the Crown Cities, felt safe. The library quieted even the echoing vastness of the Calarine ruins. Its silence, unlike the silence of the roads, did not feel oppressive. Instead, it reminded her of the warm sounds of the lake shore just south of her home. Of the Morable coast just before everything had fallen apart. She thought that perhaps that place, not the ruins, but the library, could be her haven. Sarah stood up from the chair and stretched at the tight muscles in her shoulders. A renewed look of certainty settled into her eyes. "All right, then show me around, Sibella."

The falcon took flight and Sarah grabbed her staff, following close behind.

Sarah followed Sibella through the library to the second floor where the falcon perched on the arm of a tall statue. The beautiful, imposing bronze depicted a cloaked man, his arms outstretched in a stance of defiant certainty. The statue's face held intricate detail, its soft lines and delicate features seeming to hide a power unlike anything Sarah had ever seen.

"Do you know this man?" asked Sibella. Sarah, half distracted by the vastness of the books around her, shook her head. The falcon snapped his beak and flapped his wings, kaking until Sarah turned her attention back to him. "This is Goraln, the first Aetic and a member of the Warriors Who Fought the Sun. He is said to have created the bridges between this world and the Great Boroughs long ago. In that time before memory, when the world was rebuilt."

"The Great Boroughs?" asked Sarah. Sibella had her full attention now, and she stood watching the Falcon, her arms crossed and staff resting against her shoulder.

Sibella cocked his head at her and chittered. "I thought you said you know of Aetics? Did you learn nothing of the

Great Boroughs and the Rending on your travels?"

"I saw Aetics, I didn't learn about them. I only know a little about the Rending from stories I've heard. I know that the world used to be different than it is now, and that some relics remain from that time. Things like batteries and the steel towers and old electro-posit machines. My travels were solitary, for the most part." Sarah thought for a moment about the nobles she'd seen in Varinz just days before, their arms heavy with scrolls and books. She thought about the Aetics, their eyes focused and sharp underneath their strange hoods. "I've never had anything to do with the empire. I've stayed out of the cities as much as possible. You don't find many Aetics in the wilds. Most casters there are witches or sages, nothing more."

"Isolation is never good for the mind, Sarah."

The falcon's words cut through her like a cold wind. She started to tell Sibella that companionship had cost her more than solitude ever had, but instead she just motioned for him to go on. The scared index finger of her right hand swirled in a motion she had picked up from her mother, always impatient with the long-winded stories of the patrons of her tavern. "Tell me about the Great Boroughs. Tell me about everything."

Sibella glided down from the statue to a table nearby, his paper feathers crackling in the wind as he did. As he started in on his lecture, he paced back and forth on the oak tabletop. His talons, though they too were made of paper, clacked in a steady rhythm. "The Great Boroughs are distant places that were once cut off from this world. They are unique worlds, complete and living like our own, though different in ways none of us can comprehend without ever truly visiting them ourselves."

"What do you mean, different? I mean, if we can't go there, how can we know they're different?"

"It is like the sea floor, I believe. It's possible to know that there are things there at the bottom, past the reach of sunlight. We can know it, but can we ever understand it? How can you or I ever know what it is to exist beyond the sunlight?" Sarah paused, thinking of the whales she had seen cresting above the breaks along the horizon off of the Salted Coast. Their size impossible, incredible. Leviathan. She motioned for the falcon to carry on. "How were they connected to us?"

"Long ago, an event most call the Rending brought havoc into our world. No one alive truly knows what happened, what might have caused the sudden rearranging of so much of our world, but it is known that great horrors found their way into this world. The skies were torn asunder and change ripped this world apart. Chaos spread across the land and with it came beings of unbelievable power. Creatures with no name, no form, no understandable purpose besides destruction. Few then survived and those who did could not recognize the world that remained. Cities changed names. Mountains rose where there once were none."

Sibella paused just long enough to be sure Sarah was still paying attention. "The Warriors Who Fought the Sun protected the world from the chaos that came with the Rending, ensuring that it was rebuilt in the image of good, or at least stability, and not that of the chaos that had torn it apart. When the world was rebuilt, the barrier between this world and those beyond softened." Sibella pushed a pile of ragged papers on the table out of the way. He scratched a vague map of many worlds onto the tabletop, between them lines that connected one to the other. He tapped at the connecting lines and gave a soft kak of satisfaction.

"When this barrier softened, Goraln created the bridges. This forged a metaphysical connection between our world and these others, Places he named the Great Boroughs." There was a long silence, and Sibella kaked so loud Sarah flinched. "Are you paying attention to me, girl?"

"Sorry, I just…this is a lot."

"You certainly say that often, don't you?"

Sarah rolled her eyes and thought she saw the falcon start to smile, just a hint curling at the edges of his beak. "So what does all this mean for an Aetic?" she asked. "Is there a Great Borough for particular powers? Is that what you're getting at?"

"That is a very simple explanation, but yes. That is how the scholars who wrote these books understood it, anyway."

"Then how does someone become an Aetic?"

"Many have the power to become an Aetic inherent in themselves. If this library truly called you here, all it might take for you is a little curiosity and determination. Though, if my master was to be believed, the empire would have you think it is a much more complicated process. In reality, access to the correct reading materials is all it takes to unlock the power and magic of the Aetic arts. That and determination."

Sarah closed her eyes and rubbed at her neck, tension radiating down her shoulders. She thought of the powers in the stories that had guided her life, tales from ancient old books she'd found on the road. *The Wizard of Earthsea, The Lord of the Rings, The Wheel of Time, The Dark Tower, A Song of Ice and Fire.*

Her favorite, the only book she still carried with her, *The Left Hand of Darkness*. So many stories of beauty and evil and horror as it called people to their destinies. Stories of magic and power and glory. Stories she had chased for so long, carrying her friends with her along the southern coast, until everything had gone wrong and she found herself alone and hurt and full of hate. She thought of the promises she'd made to those long gone. The friend she'd lost who's staff she now carried. The friends who had pushed her away because of her failure. The world swirled around her, and she swallowed her anxieties down to that same place she had hid them for so long. She nodded her head at the paper falcon, eyes absent and far away. Sibella waited on the tabletop and watched her with a curious, observant expression.

"I want to learn," Sarah said, "but I don't know how easy it will be. I'm just not sure about all of this."

Without a word of warning, Sibella took flight, leading her into the rows of bookshelves that surrounded them. They weaved through the shelves, each one piled so high with books that there was little room for more additions to the library's collection. Sibella came to rest on the top of one of the many shelves. He pointed out a wood plaque which read TRANSFORMATIONS   TRANSMUTATIONS, TRIANGULATIONS in embossed black typeset. He leapt down to the third shelf and pecked at a book before he flew to a table in the aisle and waited. Sarah grabbed the book, saw that its cover read *Rudimentary Transformation Magic*, and carried it to the table where the falcon was perched. She sat down in a dusty leather chair and opened the book. Its intricate illuminations leapt out at her with their bright flashes of red and gold.

Sibella hopped over to the edge of the book and motioned to it with one wing. "Many of the books on this floor are instructional manuals, once used in Aetic teaching academies and such here in Calarine. This place was once the center of the empire's mystical education efforts, before the war, of course. Afterwards, Varinz took that title from the city, like it did most things."

Sarah thumbed through the introductory pages, reading over the table of contents. The titles of spells and techniques poured into her. Each new page seemed a challenge, and each challenge seemed a confrontation. Those same conflicted feelings of her past and the new power laid out in front of her once again rose into her throat.

Sibella placed his wing over her trembling hand. "Do not focus on what might or might not be in these pages. Just see if any of these spells call to you. See if they speak to you in the same way that the Belhaven did. There are three pillars that you must achieve. You must read and understand the spell, you must be open and reveal your emotional core to the Great Boroughs, and you must be headstrong, certain in the spell you want to cast." Sibella seemed to stare through Sarah with his strange, knowing eyes. They seemed to contain the eons and epochs of the library's collection. "Do you understand what I mean, Sarah the traveler? You must know what you want before the words leave your mouth. Uncertainty is tantamount to failure."

Sarah nodded, closed her eyes, and thought through the openness that the magic required. About how the fabric that made up her being felt, at least to her, so opposed to the idea. "That's not as easy as you're making it sound, you know.

Certainty might come easy for paper falcons, but not for me."

The falcon raised his head and considered her, his eyes staring through her as he did. "To find out one way or the other, you must first try. Breathe from your soul. Breathe from the bottom of your being and with that breath push the conflict away. Cast it out and replace it with the power of the spell. When you are an Aetic weaving magic, you will have no past. No anxieties. You will have only a connection to the bridges and the Boroughs beyond. That is what you must be, what you can be. Only the power itself."

Sarah looked at Sibella, her eyes full of wonder as her excitement for this newfound potential overtook everything else. She looked back at the book. The drawings of spells in the margins seemed to swirl and move on the page. As the excitement overtook her, so too did it overtake her past. I can see the wonder in your eyes echoed in her mind again, but this time it did not bring with it pained memories.

I am certain, she said to herself. *Maybe not of everything, but I am certain that I want this. That I've searched for this, and now here it is. I have my opportunity to take it.*

Holding on to that certainty, she clenched her eyes and searched her mind. She felt for the draw of the Belhaven, for that crackling, moving power that had brought her to the steps of the library. In a moment it came to her, a pulling at the back of her mind that felt as much like a rising headache as it did the gentle movement of the Gulf. She followed that feeling into her arms and down to the tips of her fingers, where she thumbed through the book, stopping when she felt the sensation had reached its peak. When she opened her eyes, she saw she had stopped on a spell titled "From Stone to

Ligneous." Sibella hopped up and landed on her shoulder, reading the book from his new perch.

"What you must do now is read. Read and let the magic flow into your being."

Hands shaking and eyes wide, Sarah held the book and began reading its instructions. She worked out its meanings, with phrases like "words of power" and "emotional resonance" falling into place one after the other. Sarah read for a long while, lost in process and absent of other thought. Consumed in the world of magic and power laid out in front of her. Finally she stopped, closed the book, and leaned back in her chair.

Sibella let out a small kak. A thing so full of mirth it sounded like a laugh. "I hope you are not tired already, that was supposed to be the easy part. You have to open yourself up to the Great Boroughs. Open yourself to the powers that lie beyond this place." In a flash, Sibella took flight and in just a moment he returned with a small stone and dropped it on the table.

Sarah picked up the stone and turned it over in her hand. It was a nondescript piece of granite, one of a million in the library that had tumbled down from somewhere in the great, aging structure. She sat it back onto the tabletop and focused. The words of the book echoed in her mind, and she raised her hand to the stone. In her mind's eye she visualized it transforming, opening herself up as Sibella and the book had instructed her. She latched onto that certainty, the confidence and absolutism she knew the spell required, and pushed everything else away. In that moment there was no Morable. There were no failed friends, loss, or betrayal. There were no lofty promises and ambition let slip. No insurmountable responsibility given out in the wake of her mother's passing. There was only the stone and the spell. There was only Sarah Silvergrove and Sibella the falcon. There was only the now, then had never come.

In a flash of green light the rock began to shake and change as oak limbs sprouted from it, folding in on themselves again and again. When it stopped, Sarah picked up what was now a ball of solid wood. A half dozen small, leafed branches sprouted from it, as vibrant and alive as the oldest trees of the wilds.

CHAPTER II
The Wilds of the World

==

The echoing halls of the library became her home in such a swift moment that Sarah did not realize how comfortable she had become. In those early days she explored the library, organizing the books and straightening the furniture as she went. She worked her way through the Belhaven's books on history, politics, and magic with a ravenous fervor, still hardly making a dent in the massive collection. This new opportunity for stationary study sank deep into her being, and Sarah found herself losing track of the hours and days for the first time in a long time. A week passed, and she spent nearly all of it buried in the studies of her new world.

Sarah devoured the magic guides and spell books as fast as she found them. In those early moments, the spells came slow, the mechanics of it all still fresh and exciting, though often as confusing as they were illuminating. As she sat one afternoon, the taste of salt-jerky and rice still lingering in her mouth, reading over the books on simple conjuration Sibella had pointed her towards, Sarah thought back to her mother. Of a time when she was just a child, maybe four or five years old, before the cancer first took hold in her mother's lungs and started that long decline. As she sat thumbing through those books on strange and incredible powers, all of which, at least according to Sibella, rested at her fingertips, she thought of one of the thousand times her mother had read to her of magic in far away lands. Someone had brought a stack of books into her mother's tavern "for the girl," and Sarah had begged and pleaded for her exhausted mother to read them all, one after the other, over and over for a week on end. Most of the time the stories people brought were old, tired things, but that time one of the books grabbed hold of her. It was longer and lacked the brilliant illustrations of the others, but it took her to new places, to strange worlds. In the time that followed her mother read *The Hobbit* to her a thousand times, and she read it a thousand more until the copy finally disintegrated from the constant abuse. She still remembered the simple magic of the story, the power it held over her, and the strangeness of everything within.

Sitting there, the conjuration book in her hand, her mother's voice reading Tolkein to her from some far away memory, Sarah stopped and read the spell open in front of her, almost on instinct. It was called "magelight," a short entry on the conjuration of a ball of concentrated light. She read over it, read how the ball did not hover, but could be moved and thrown just as any other solid object. She leaned back in the chair, pulling her long and curling hair back and tying it off with a short length of leather cord she pulled from her front pocket. She thought of all the time she'd spent straining to see into the library's storage rooms, and the time spent reading the spines of books in half-shadow, the tall stacks casting a near perpetual gloom over the place.

She had asked Sibella once, why more lanterns were not hung across the library, and he had only pointed out the ancient electric lights above, long since non-functioning. She'd gone that day, to find a way to conjure up some sort of lamp, but found the magic too far beyond her grasp, too complicated. But there, thinking of her mother and Tolkein and The Hobbit, Sarah saw in magelight a solution within her grasp. So she thumbed through the pages, reading over the spell again and again, internalizing the lessons Sibella had given her since that first taste of the power beyond. The spell was simple, taking up not even half of a page, and its clear purpose resonated in Sarah's mind. As she closed her eyes and focused on the spell, on the intent it required of her, of her need for light in the library, she again felt that well of power open. When she opened her eyes, a ball of brilliant light was clutched in her closed fist, no bigger than a common river stone, its light cast out across the table. It illuminated the lines of Sarah's smile.

A week later, Sarah then sat on the first floor studying over books on transformation magic, hoping to build the skills she needed to provide permanent lighting to her new home. A length of wood, salvaged from a busted chair found hidden away in one of the library's many storage rooms, laid on the table. It was marked with the burned scars of failed spells. Sibella had begun the day at Sarah's side, but before long he had grown bored and flown into the exposed joists of the library's vaulted ceiling. He had lived so much of his life alone, to be there high above was his natural state. The noon sun settled into its high-skied home, and the ache of the hours of practice settled into Sarah's hands. She moved the books out of her way with a reckless sweep of her forearm, frustration lapping at her neck as she felt the heat rising into her face. Red climbed into her high-set cheekbones, and her jaw clenched in a rhythmic snap-unsnap pace. She placed the length of wood in front of her and held her hands above it, just close enough that she could feel it but not so close that they rested on it. She closed her eyes, the edges of her freckled face tight and creased in concentration. She focused on the spell, pulling up from the well of power she had felt grow so steady. She sent the power into her hands and visualized the transformation of the broken length of worked wood into an unbroken chair leg. She felt the magic begin to form at her fingertips, the static sensation racing across her palms. All at once the magic surged from her hands in streaks of white and green, but as it contacted the length of wood a deafening crack echoed through the Belhaven. When the hazy smoke rising from the wood settled, Sarah saw that nothing had changed. The only notice of the attempt was another burn.

Her day filled with one failure too many, she shoved the charred wood across the table and let out a long, whistling yell. Just as her frustration started to bubble and crack in the back of her throat, she heard a short, clearing kak from behind.

"Having trouble?" asked Sibella, his voice curt and mocking in a way that sounded, at least to Sarah, amused.

Sarah forced the rest of her anger out in a ragged sigh, her eyes rolling as she did. She turned to face the paper falcon, who was perched on a sconce hung high on a pillar nearby. Strands of her curly hair hung in her face as she glared at him. "Thank you so much for your pointed observations, Sibella."

The falcon ignored the indignation in her words, and instead glided down from his perch to the table, where he looked at Sarah's charred experiments in the Aetic arts before he turned his attention to the book. He saw the page was turned to a spell titled "Simple Transmogrification of

Inanimate Objects," and cocked his head in confusion.

"What exactly are you trying to do to this piece of banister?" he asked.

Sarah reached across the table and grabbed the piece of wood. As she turned it over in her hands it left smudges of soot along the creases of her palms. "I'm trying to use that transmorgif--mogif," she broke her words off in a sigh and tapped the page with the end of the chair leg, "that fucking spell to turn this broken chair leg into a not-broken chair leg."

"Chair leg? It looks like a piece of a banister to me. Do you mean you wish to turn it into a chair leg or that it already was a chair leg? Prior to its current broken status, I mean."

"It's a chair leg. The whole chair is busted."

"Well, therein lies your problem. Transmogrification spells, as their name might suggest, transmogrify. If you want to fix something, you want to mend it. Not turn it into something else."

Sarah stared in disbelief as the falcon used one of his hooked talons to flip the pages of the book. Now the spell title along the top read "Mending Simple Objects."

"I believe this spell would better serve you," he said, unable to help the grin that crept into the corners of his mouth. "Mend not 'mogrify, you know?"

Still dumbstruck, Sarah gaped at the falcon, her blue eyes tracing over his small face. She looked at the words that lined his paper form. The way the dotted type scrawled along the soft, cream paper. The way the folds of his form gave way to a an ethereal look. A look that, when mixed with the expression of child-like mockery set in Sibella's small, dark eyes, felt like a dream. At first, Sarah thought she might swing the chair leg at him, but then all at once she broke into a string of laughter and hung her head. "I've been doing this for hours. Where were you when I messed this up the first time?"

"Chasing a lizard along the ceiling's edge, I believe. I would recommend a substantial break before you try the proper spell. You're going to burn yourself." Sarah nodded and rubbed at the corners of her eyes. As she did, Sibella's eyes followed the deep, knotted scar that ran from the first joint of her thumb to the tip of her index finger. "What is on your mind? You have not made a mistake like this before."

Sarah dropped her hand and looked at him. "What do you mean, 'like this'?"

Sibella settled himself on the table. "I mean that you have not failed to do something as simple as read the spell before. If your mind is somewhere else you will have trouble casting spells you are familiar with, much less ones you do not even understand. Certainly it is true that you might allow your mind to wander when a spell is commonplace, but when you are learning it you must focus. You must read and understand the text of the spell. You must become the power."

Sagging into the wood framed chair, Sarah rubbed at her stinging forearms. Her taut, climbers' muscles stood out on them. "This is all just still very new, you know? I'm just... tired."

Sibella nodded. "Yes, well. You have learned a lot in your time here already. You have already acquired a near-mastery of magelight, but, if I might be so frank, you will never be able to advance if you do not shed away that weight you carry."

"What are you talking about?"

A look something akin to exasperation, or the nearest approximation a paper crafted falcon could manage, filled the creases and folds of Sibella's face. "This magic, being an Aetic, requires you to be certain, headstrong in what you want. So often you are. I can see the excitement and exhilaration in your eyes. I can see the deftness in your hands, but…"

Sibella trailed off, and as he did, Sarah straightened in the chair. "But what? Spit it out."

"But sometimes I can see the haint in your eyes. I can see your hands tremble. I can see them twitch at the places where your fingers are knotted with scars."

Sarah's mouth tightened into a thin line. "We've all got burdens to carry."

"Yes, we do, of course. I just mean that, to really be free to study, you have to free your--"

"I know that. I'm not chained down by anything, Sibella. I'm fine. I'm perfectly capable of managing a few spells, I'm capable of managing myself just fine. I just misread the spell, that's all."

Sibella watched the way Sarah's ember eyebrows trembled against the sternness of her face. "Would you tell me how you got the scars on your hands? Just that. Lift just that weight today."

Unable to hold onto her defiance any longer, Sarah's face fell and her eyes left the falcon. She rubbed at the scarred places along the knuckles of her right hand. The thick, knotted scar was pink and stood out against her well-traveled tan. "I was overzealous exploring a cave with some of my friends along the southern coast. We were just south of Morable looking for a place where a cave was supposed to have something in it. Treasure or magic or a weapon. Something like that. I forget exactly what it was now…what came after has sort of pushed all of that out."

"And what came after?"

Sarah tightened the knotted knuckles and closed her eyes. To Sibella it might have looked as if she was trying to remember something far away, but Sarah just hoped she could stave off the tears she felt wetting the corners of her eyes. She took a deep breath and exhaled so hard it moved the ringlet curls that had fallen to the sides of her face. "Like I said, I got overzealous and one of my friends…they fell. I grabbed their tether but they were too heavy for me. The scars are from rope burn."

"And you blame yourself? For your friend's missed step?"

Tears came now, closed eyes or not. "I think I'm done with this."

"All right."

"I've been doing this all fucking day and nothing. I'm done. Talking about this isn't going to make me any better at this."

"All right, yes. Perhaps a break is needed."

Sarah slammed the palms of both hands onto the table and then pushed her fingers into her hair. "What else do you want from me?"

"Blaming yourself does not supersede the certainty needed, only cowardice does."

Sarah looked at the falcon now, unworried about the tears that had reached her chin, distorting the outlines of her freckles. Through the shimmered haze, the falcon did not look like paper. He looked like a falcon, sandy and yellowed feathers, but a simple falcon. She opened her mouth to question him, but just tightened her jaw instead.

"Holding that pain does not mean you cannot cast a spell. It just means that in the moments you cast, you cannot be that person. The person you see as having failed, I mean. In the moment of the spell, you are Sarah Silvergrove. Librarian. Aetic. Keeper of the Belhaven. You are not Sarah Silvergrove, traveler and failure of friends."

Sarah stared at the falcon, unsure if his frankness was a tactful tool meant to disarm her, or the accidental ineptitude of a bird who had lived alone for so long. His words ringing in her ears, Sarah glanced past him to the book that still laid open on the table. Drying her tears with her shirt sleeve, she reached out and pulled the book across the table. Without a word to Sibella, his dark eyes still watching her, she read the spell on mending.

That evening, she moved the now repaired chair into the lobby. There were no charred marks which remained.

Resting on the first floor after a long day, Sibella and Sarah lit the candles and oil lanterns they had placed around the admin offices as the light from the windows grew faint. The flickering cast shadows throughout the room as Sarah rummaged through the desk drawer where she had stored her food.

"Sibella, do you eat?" she asked as she leaned back in her chair. She tore at the tough meat and chewed. Using just her feet she slid off her already-unlaced boots and propped her stockinged feet up on the desktop.

The falcon perched on her desk and preened his wings. "I do, just as any other falcon. The spell that gave me life dictated that I will live as any other. There is plenty here to satiate me, but I expect you have no interest in mice. Or lizards."

Sarah grimaced. "No, I don't guess I do. I'm going to have to go out and find supplies soon. I can manage conjuring water skins, but I'm not exactly able to summon up a fresh-killed rabbit. Do you know the layout of the ruins?"

"No, not beyond what I have learned in the books. I have never left the walls of this library. Master rarely left, and I never went with him when he did."

"I'm going to get up early and go gather some supplies. At least enough to last a few more weeks. Do you want to come with me?"

Sibella took a step back and shook out his feathers. "Me? My place is in this library. The master never would have allowed it."

Sarah leaned forward in her chair and tapped the falcon on the beak. Sibella jerked back and snapped at her finger. "I'm not the Alchemical," she said, "and you told me that I am the new keeper of this place, didn't you?"

"Well yes, bu--"

"But nothing, if I am the keeper then I make the rules, and I say you can come with me. I may be gone for two days. I could use the company."

Sibella brushed a wing over his face, almost as if he was embarrassed, and nodded his head in agreement. "Why...thank you." His eyes looked towards the ever-fading light that came through the high-windows, dusted and stained with years of abandon. "I have always wondered about the ruins. I must say, I am quite excited."

In the morning Sarah and Sibella stepped out of the doors of the Belhaven and into the wilds that surrounded it. The metal towers and great stone structures glimmered in the hazy dawn light in a way that mesmerized Sibella. The paper falcon took flight, climbing high into the air and swirling above Sarah as she made her way to the blackstone road that ran in front of the library. Looking around, she could see the skeleton of a once thriving city resting beneath the reclaimed architecture and grass-pocked streets. To the east, towards the old city center, she saw the brilliant copper dome of the old capitol building nestled in the abandoned towers, its once shining top now tinged a dull green with age. In a moment Sibella came down and landed on her shoulder. She shifted her staff to her right hand and leaned onto it. The sun shining down on them, Sarah reached up and scratched at the bird's neck. His paper feathers crinkled as he stretched out his wings and gave a sigh.

"See anything interesting?" she asked. The sun was reflected off of the buildings around her and she shaded her eyes.

"The ruins seem to go on forever," answered the falcon, awestruck. "I have no idea where to begin."

"We'll head towards the city center then. If anyone's here, that's where they'd be." The rising sun to their back, they headed west from the Belhaven, towards the tarnished dome of the old capitol. As they hiked, the signs of the old city rose like scars of ruination, and with them so too did the signs of scavengers and travelers. Sarah wondered if those travelers had come looking for a haven as she had. Broken windows littered the faces of the abandoned buildings, and remnants of campfires marked the blackstone streets. Old Calarine seemed to exist on two planes, the one which hid away the once great stature of the city, and the other which showed a corpse, picked over and desiccated.

"These ruins feel almost oppressive," said Sibella, looking up at a growth of vines that had overtaken a metal tower. "The old and the natural--it is a juxtaposition I feel most uncomfortable with."

Sarah shrugged and adjusted her bag across her shoulder. "I've seen a lot of places like this. They all feel the same after a while, cold and empty." Sarah swallowed hard at her words, knowing that they were true, but unable to deny that she had hoped Calarine would be different. She kicked at a piece of the loose blackstone and it tumbled in front of her, crumbling into hot, tarred gravel along the path ahead.

As the roads turned to city streets, they rounded a corner and were hit by the strong, obvious smell of smoke. Sarah tightened her grip on her staff and listened. "We may have friends," she said and eased down the street. As they neared the edge of the stone building to her right a small camp came into view. Three men, two carrying large swords across their backs, sat around a small fire with bottles of liquor scattered across the ground. She watched as the men paced around half-shouting at one another, the stench of alcohol wafting in the light breeze that had weaved its way into the city. The men were building a camp around a fire that burned just under the eave of one of the towers. One of the men, big and broad shouldered, started to turn in Sarah's direction and she felt her heart leap into her throat. She stepped back on her toes before she spun around and ran from the camp, putting distance between them and the men as fast as she could. Once she felt they were far enough away, she slowed her pace and stopped to rest beside an ornate fountain in the courtyard of a destroyed building.

Sibella shook out his paper feathers, which the ride on Sarah's shoulder had ruffled, and fluttered down to peck at a smattering of insects around the fountain. "Why did we run?" he asked. "They might have had goods to trade, advice on where to look." As his question left his beak a spider skittered across the side of the fountain and he caught it in one lightning-fast peck.

Sarah rubbed her hands over her face, wiping away the beads of sweat that had broken out on her forehead, and put her hands on her narrow hips. "Those weren't scavengers, they looked like soldiers or mercenaries. On top of that, they were drunk. Doubt they would've been anything but trouble, and three big men like that is more than I can handle alone."

"Trouble?" the bird asked, his attention broken from the bugs. "What would make you think they are trouble?"

Sarah ran a hand through her hair and sighed. For a moment, she thought of how the falcon might have been right. She thought it might have been her anxiety causing foolish decisions, panic. But then she thought of the men who had come in the night as she camped on a ridge outside Varinz. The sounds of moving grass and tumbling rocks waking her just as the three men eased into her camp. As she thought of the drunk men camping under the eve, she thought of those near Varinz and their hungry, wanting eyes. Bird's been locked in that library too long. She took a breath and shook her head. "No point dwelling on what is done. Quit chasing bugs and let's get going."

Sibella let out a short kak and scratched at the stone fountain. He seemed to have already moved on from the men and their camp. "Where are we going now?"

She looked out across the eastern horizon and shielded her eyes against the bright glint of the sun. "As far southeast as we can. I'd like to get to the other side of the Belhaven since this way didn't do us any good. We'll either find an abandoned market or make it to the other side of the city and then we can scavenge the forest."

"Could we not just go around the men?"

Images of men in the night mixed with the drunks again and she only shook her head, never looking at him. "Southeast is better. Little chance of running into them if we're going the opposite direction."

Taking that as his answer, Sibella flew into the air. As the falcon soared overhead, Sarah turned her attention back to the road and headed southeast.

East of the fountain, the desolate city streets showed little sign of travel. Vines swallowed the entirety of some of the buildings, and trees broke through the stone sidewalks, climbing towards the sky in a perpetual, green defiance of what had come before. Once gray concrete was littered with flowers and the brown of dead leaves. Sarah thought of the blackstone streets of Morable and Varinz, their stone tended and kept in the presence of the empire. There in the far-spanning Calarine ruins, fed by the persistent flow of the Pearl River and framed against the foothills of the Risen Range, the wilds seemed alive. Time had outrun itself and nature had claimed its own.

As the sun reached its peak, the blackstone streets amplified the oppressive heat into a searing ray. As Sarah walked, the sweat grew along her hairline and ran down her jaw into the collar of her cuirass. The cotton shirt she wore underneath was damp. Even Sibella grew weary and shielded himself from the sun. Sarah pulled her canteen from her bag, taking a long drink as she stopped and surveyed the area ahead of her. The broken wastes stretched on for miles, and greenery and tarnished steel fought against one another for claim over the horizon. She poured a little water into a cupped palm and held it up to the falcon, who drank it in the quick, chittering way of birds.

"How have you managed?" Sibella asked. His eyes squinted against the sunlight, and his breath came and went in a quick, harried fashion. "Traveling like this for so long, I mean. This heat is near unbearable, and I can only imagine the summers are worse. Cold of winter? Almost makes me thankful for my sheltering inside the Belhaven."

Sarah wiped the sweat from her brow and put the canteen away. As she tucked the hide-covered canister into its spot in her bag, she pulled a length of leather cord out. She pulled her hair back and tied it into a messy, high ponytail, pulling the thick mess of curls off of her neck. "It's not so bad. It's better than where I grew up anyway. A nasty fishing village is not fit for much of anything."

"You did not like your home?"

"Well...I guess it wasn't all bad, at least not in the beginning. The Lake of Bridges is beautiful just at sunset. I used to go to Mandeville Station and sit on the trusses of Low Bridge to watch it. The way the red-orange light seemed to bounce between the Dead River Wall to the north and the Old Gulf to the south? It was breathtaking."

The falcon said nothing, but instead turned his endless gaze to the west, where miles away the Dead River Wall's Warren Gate waited. Sarah watched the falcon as he looked across the wastelands, the brilliant sunlight that baked at their shoulders casting glints through the greenery and rust. Silver star lights seemed to rest on the horizon as rain-worn steel glimmered across the heat lined sky. She could see the longing, a low, drooped look of faraway wanting, along the edges of Sibella's face. She started to speak, to try and comfort the falcon, but her mind wandered to all the times she had found herself caught inside of her own thoughts.

The times in Carnd when she had wished for something new. The times in Morable when she begged to take it all back. She thought of just a few weeks earlier, when she had stood against the red bricked outer wall of the General Goods store in Varinz, the oppressive force of the crowded city street bearing down on her. The bustling herds of people, many dressed in fine clothes and carrying the tools of rulers and leaders, had represented the agony of the great cities. The anxieties of crowds. When in Varinz two of them strode past her in padded armor, the scrolls and books of Aetics in slings across their backs, they had clipped Sarah's shoulder and sent her tumbling forward. The shop keeper, a big man with long knotted hair, had been the one to catch her. He'd smiled at her and patted her on the back and walked her across the bustling street to the tavern, a grimy place called the Skeeving Fink. Be careful lass, his words echoed in her mind, folks're apt to run you over if you stand around like a lost rabbit. He hadn't called her a daint, not like the others always did. She thought it was because he had seen her scars and the haint in her eyes. Because he knew she was no noble.

Sibella kaked and pulled Sarah from her daydream. The feeling of being back in the then and there almost dizzied her. "Sorry," she said, adjusting her staff in her hands, "got lost for a moment."

Sibella eyed Sarah, but said nothing.

"You all right?" Sarah asked. She saw the falcon's chest fall into a deep exhale, but if he had sighed, she had not heard it.

"There is so much I have not seen. Things from the books, those written of our world, anyway, that I always thought impossible. The snow-capped cities of the Northern Line. The foaming tides of the southern coast. Triplet bridges across a sea-sized lake. A wall that hides away a dead and empty river, beyond it the vastness of another world."

"You have time. We have time."

"Do we? You're the keeper now, so yet again am I eternally tied to the library. My mind is connected to its every tome. I possess the knowledge, but it seems I understand so little of it. Have you ever thought of that, Sarah?"

She adjusted, leaning her weight onto her staff. "Thought of what?"

"What it would be like to have all the knowledge in the world just beyond your conscious mind, but no idea what any of it really means. What would I be without that connection? What else besides a lost child?"

Sarah said nothing, but instead just reached up and placed a hand onto the falcon's taloned foot.

The falcon sighed, this time loud enough to be heard, and gave his head a brisk, jarring shake. "I'm sorry, Sarah. I suppose I just feel overwhelmed with the enormity of the horizon. That's enough navel-gazing for today, don't you think?"

"For both of us," she said, and with that the pair started back onto the road again.

They traveled in silence, no longer lost in thought, but instead hoping to find somewhere to escape the sun. In a moment Sarah stopped and her head snapped alert, certain she had heard the sound of running water. She headed towards it, half running in hopes that she wouldn't lose track of the sound. Sibella leapt from her shoulder and took flight just overhead. As they crested a low, rolling hill, they were met with the overgrown landscape of a beautiful creek, which ran through the western part of the city.

Sarah walked to the clay bank, which was almost eight feet above the creek, and looked across the swift water. Sibella landed on her shoulder and gave a soft kak, urging Sarah on towards the water below. Together, the duo started working their way down the steep bank towards the creek side, with the red clay soil shifting under Sarah's feet. Her staff dug deep into the slick earth, leaving gouges and popping as she pulled it free from the mud with each move. As Sarah made it to the edge of the shallow creek, her foot slipped, and her leather boot slid in. The frigid water poured through the laces and soaked her foot in an instant. She let out a gasp as a bolt of ice shot down her spine. Sibella chuckled as Sarah jerked her foot back from the water.

"Not funny," she said, half laughing herself. She shook her wet boot, trying her best to get as much of the water out of it as possible, and then squatted next to the river. She couldn't help but laugh as her boot squelched.

"Is it safe to drink?" asked Sibella, now scratching at insects on the ground.

Sarah looked down the creek bed at the plants growing along its banks. She noted the animal tracks, marks of deer and fox and raccoon, embedded in the muddy soil. She made note of the algae, settled neat along the creek banks in bobbing brown-green waves. "Should be. Plenty of growth and animal sign, no dead animals. Whatever we pull out of here will be safe to eat, anyway. We can take some of the water home and filter it, see if there's anything nasty in it." She took a handful of sand and closed her eyes, focusing her mind into the palms of her hands, and in a short, bright flash of light a water skin formed in her hands. Sibella let out a short chirp of congratulations as Sarah uncapped it and filled it with running creek water.

After the water skin was full, Sarah replaced the cap and hung it from her pack with a length of leather cord. "We still haven't found any food, and as fast as this water's running we'd be lucky to catch enough fish to eat on the way back."

Sibella craned his neck and looked up towards the darkening sky. The orange-red haze of dusk had settled in around them, and the shadows grew longer with each passing moment. "Perhaps so, but it is getting dark. Maybe this is a good spot to rest? We could continue on in the morning."

At the thought of a true, long rest, Sarah's rubbed at the small of her back. She surveyed the creek's edge for a dry spot, only finding soggy clay and wet grass. "Too wet here, but I think back on top of the bank would be good."

Sibella fluttered onto the bank and watched as Sarah scrambled against the soft clay. Her wet boot let out quiet-but-irritating squeaks with every step, and her face was lit up in a wide, laughing grin when she reached the top of the bank. She sat her bag and staff down and walked over to the edge of the forest that ran between the creek and the ruins. She gathered an armful of sticks and dry grass before coming back, where she arranged them into a campfire.

"I'll light that when the sun gets a little lower," she said as she took off her boots, turning the wet one upside down to let the last of the once-trapped water drain out. She took her socks off and wrung the wet one before sitting everything a few feet from the prepared fire. She undid the buckles along the ribs of her cuirass and laid it near the head of her bedroll. Her cotton shirt was cool and stuck to her thin frame. The heat still heavy in the air, she let out a long sigh as she pulled the shirt off and laid it beside her as well. Underneath she wore a wrap of thin linen that ran from her chest to her waist.

The paper falcon paid little attention to her and instead reveled in his time underneath the unbroken sky. He scratched out a cool spot on the ground, weary from his first day outside of the Belhaven, and pulled the cool earth onto his feathers with quick flaps of his wings. His face was tired but still carried its typical wonder. The sunlight growing ever dim, Sarah pulled a flint and steel from her pack and lit the fire with a brief flash of sparks. She stretched out on the ground, propping up her head with a rolled shirt from her pack and let out a long, exhausted sigh. She didn't worry with her camp pad. The ground of the bank was cool underneath and soft enough to let her sleep. The smolder of a fire crackled and grew as the dried limbs caught. As the fire flared, Sibella recoiled at the flicker of the flames.

Sarah raised her head to look at him. "I didn't even think of that. Will you be okay with the fire?"

Sibella gave a nod and settled back into his cool spot. "Yes, as long as I do not touch it, of course. I'm not quite as fragile as regular paper, but fire is fire. I learned that the hard way."

"The hard way?"

"I burned myself not long after I was made. I didn't understand what it was and--well I got too close I suppose. Sparking embers fell on my wings and burned them."

Sarah raised her eyes, and they glimmered in the light of the fire. "But you look fine to me."

"The Alchemical repaired me." Sibella seemed to shake the conversation away as he settled in, now more comfortable in the flickering firelight. "Is a fire wise? Could it not draw attention? You did not want to interact with those men earlier, so why is a fire fine now?."

"We have to take our chances. Sure, someone could see the fire, but this far away from people it's more likely that some beast would find us, and a fire will keep them away." Sarah's mind went back to the men outside of Varinz and how she had slid down the ridgeline as she fled, one of them unconscious on the ground. "Besides, if anyone bothers us I can take care of them, don't worry." Sarah started to speak again, to go on, but instead, she let the crackling of the fire and the sounds of the creek ease her tensions. As the night grew long, it swallowed them with an intense and sudden haste. A sound, dreamless sleep took them both.

As the sun rose and warmed Sarah's face, she stirred to find Sibella perched in a tree along the creek bank. A brilliant sunrise illuminated his paper feathers in a way that made them seem near-transparent. They were a soft cream glimmering against the rich amber hues of the morning sky. She watched him as he gazed out across an endless stretch of ruins and growing forest, the smoke of the night's fire casting him in a haze. After a long while of watching the falcon and the sunrise, Sarah put her socks and boots back on before she whistled to Sibella. He swooped down, landing with grace on the ground nearby just as she buckled her cuirass over her now-dry shirt.

"Good morning," he said. His voice had a bright and excited timbre. "Sleep well?"

"I did," she answered as she slung her pack and the water skin over her shoulder. With the toe of her right boot, she sent her staff into the air and caught it with one effortless motion. Sibella fluttered up to rest on her shoulder and crooned. He stretched out his neck and rubbed at the side of

Sarah's face. Her kit accounted for, she surveyed the horizon along the creek bank. The sun cast bright beams of light along the wild grasses. Water oaks and loblolly pines dotted the area in clusters, their thicket casting strange shadows along the path. About a hundred and fifty yards ahead, Sibella and Sarah both locked eyes on a buck. His velveted antlers cast a beautiful silhouette against the morning sky, an emblem of the wilds. He had just topped a small hill ahead when they saw him. Almost as fast as he appeared, he spotted them and bolted over the sloping hills ahead in rapid leaps and bounds.

"Should I follow it?" Sibella asked. "We can track him."

Sarah shook her head. "Spring is a bad time for deer. A lot of them are covered in wolfs and disease. Rabbits and squirrels and nutria will all be much the same, but that's a little easier to dress out if we have to. We're going to follow this creek. It's got to come to a deep spot somewhere, and deep spots mean fish."

Sibella grimaced. "Wolfs? Do you mean wolves? Wolf-worms?" His mind filled with images from outdoorsmen books, those ancient, pre-Rending books called Foxfire. Worms burrowed deep between the shoulder blades of rabbits, squirrels. It made him feel sick.

"Right, and I don't particularly feel desperate enough to spend the evening digging them out."

Sibella shuttered. "Please, let's not."

Sarah laughed, scratching the bird's neck as they followed the creek's snaking path through the ruins of the old city. The creek cut southeast through the ruins, running a wide bend around the area where Sarah and Sibella had first heard its babbling waters, and then turned to a true southerly path. Its banks lowered from the high bluffs to even, silt-soiled plains where the presence of once-urban structures became ever more uncommon. Before long, the fallen towers and stone buildings gave way to abandoned stone slabs, large stretches of unending blackstone street, and steel poles more than twenty feet tall. Vines devoured these once-purposeful poles and created towering masses of vibrant green that echoed the oaks and pines around them.

"Do you know how long it has been since Calarine fell to the wilds?" Sarah asked, looking out across the horizon.

Sibella sighed and squinted, his mind working through his preternatural connection to the library's collection. "Something in the area of fifty or sixty years, I believe. After the founding of the empire this city was claimed and named Calarine, sister of Varinz. Both names come from old families whose stories existed long before the Rending. After a few decades of politics and greed, it fell and the citizens that survived fled."

Sarah nodded and thought for a while about the way the world had changed so much in such little time. *Sixty years ago my grandfather was alive,* she thought, *he was alive when this city fell but it's been overtaken. So little ever changed in Carnd.* Before her thoughts could crystallize, the rush of water began to fill the air. They picked up their pace, and as they crested a small hill along the banks of the creek they saw the source of the sound. A hollow opened up and the creek spilled into a natural pond. A small waterfall gave way as the creek tumbled into the pond, which was no more than a half-acre. Sarah took off her pack, pulled out a braided fishing line, a small amount of dried meat, and a treble hook. She dropped her pack to the ground at her feet and prepared the line. Sibella watched as she hooked the dried meat and threw the line into the deep water at the base of the waterfall.

The swirl of water sucked the line in, and Sarah let it run through her fingers, stopping it when she felt that it had traveled deep enough into the pond's churning, muddy water. The steady pull as the pond fought against the tension on the line shook the bait as she kept a steady feel of it. In just a few seconds the line jerked and Sarah pulled hard with both hands. She fought against the catch on the other end, the tight, worked muscles of her arm stretched against her wiry frame. The years of travel showed clear through her build as she braced herself against the bank and pulled at the line. After a short fight, Sarah wrenched the line to the bank, pulling with it a large catfish, close to ten pounds. Sibella let out a short kak in astonishment as the fish flopped on the ground. Careful to pull it far from the freedom of the pond, Sarah reached into her bag for a long hunting knife and, in one quick chop, removed the fish's head.

Sibella watched as Sarah separated the meat from the needle-like bones and placed it in bags of salt. She left only a handful, a single night's meal, in a separate, unsalted bag. She tied the bags of fish to her pack and put it back across her shoulder. In careful steps, watching the water for any signs of movement beneath the surface, she moved to a different part of the pond and cast the line out again. Sarah fished like this for more than two hours, catching all manner and sizes of catfish, bass, and other pond fish, until her salt bags were filled with fresh meat. After she bagged the last of the fish and closed them up inside of her pack, she put away the line and wiped her hands on the cuffs of her pants.

"I think that'll keep us for a little bit," she said leaning over and picking her staff up from the creekside. For a moment she watched Sibella peck at the ground before she whistled and patted to his spot on her shoulder.

The falcon turned his head towards her and nodded before coming to her. "Back to the Belhaven, then?" he asked. He preened at his feathers and gave a few soft kaks, watching the sun all the while.

Sarah nodded, and the two headed back down the path along the creek's edge.

"You know," said Sibella, "I believe I understand what I would be without the knowledge of the library."

Sarah raised an eyebrow. "What's that?"

"A paper falcon."

Sarah stopped dead in her tracks, her face locked on the path ahead. Her body started to shake so hard that it almost jostled the falcon loose from his perch. Her laughter came in full, galing breaths. "You certainly wouldn't be anybody's jester."

"Hey," he said, "you laughed."

"You know," Sarah said, dusk settling around them, "I expect I'll sleep like a hammer tonight."

Sibella kaked and scratched at the ground. They had stopped at the same place they had camped the night before. "I expect I will as well."

Sarah reached down and patted the bird on the head,

putting a hand at the small of her back as she did. She ached from the weight of their water and food, and her hands were chafed from the hours spent fishing. She took off her pack and started another fire on the banks of the creek, just as dusk began to give way to dark. The soft whispers of cicadas and blackrun crickets filled the air. Sibella again made a small nest in the cool dirt, and Sarah stretched out on the ground, the fire's flicker highlighting her hair. The familiar sound of the creek babbled in the night's soundscape, clashing with the chirping bugs and the soft wind against the loblollies nearby. As the cool earth and warm fire cradled her, Sarah thought of Morable, not of the failures, but of the place. Of the salted air and soft silt beaches. Sleep took both of them with ease, the cool earth and warm fire holding her against the soft sounds of the creek.

In the dark of night, the sound of crackling brush pierced the air and Sarah's eyes snapped open. She eased up onto her elbows and looked around in the fire-lit night. The dancing silhouettes competed against the bright white of the moon and cast a shadow play of strange, moving figures. At the edge of the woods between the creek and the ruins, Sarah saw the green glow of eyes. She reached over and with a gentle touch woke Sibella. As the falcon stirred, she pointed towards the tree line.

"Wolf?" he whispered. He watched as the creature crept toward them. Its gangly, bizarre visage danced in the fire.

Sarah shook her head and watched as the creature craned its long neck to look back towards the forest behind it. She focused her mind into her hands, calling a ball of bright, white light and tossed it towards the creature. As the area in front of the monster brightened, the beast gave a guttural growl and stood up on its hind legs. Sibella hopped backwards, watching as the thing seemed to stretch and recoil away from the light in a corkscrew. Its body seemed longer than should have ever been possible, and the unnatural shape of its frame sent Sibella shuffling to the back edge of the camp. It looked something like a coyote, but stretched and pulled like the confectioneries of taffy shops in the great cities.

"Go!" Sarah shouted, tossing another ball of light towards it and careful not to hit the creature. She knew that if she did, the creature wouldn't be afraid of them any longer. Just in case, she brought her staff into her other hand and readied it. "Go, get out of here!"

The area around the thing, a beast Sarah knew as a fang walker, was then fully lit. Its red-spotted fur glared as the light illuminated its oily coat. Its legs seemed to shift and change as it twisted back and forth from bipedal and four-legged. Sibella receded further into his cool spot on the ground, covering part of his small, narrow face with his wing. The creature lurched forward, landing back on its front legs, and as it did, it landed on one of the mage lights, extinguishing it with an audible crackle. As the light disappeared, the creature craned its neck towards the ground in a motion of cracking bones and stretching sinew, its shoulders never moving. Sarah's breath hitched as she watched the monster study the space where the light once was, her knuckles clenched white on the shaft of her staff. Behind her, she could hear Sibella's hesitant, shaky breaths. The creature's eyes shifted from its paw to Sarah, and then, all at once, its form flattened to the ground. It began to slide towards the camp, stamping out the mage lights as it came.

Sarah brought her left foot back and braced herself, waiting for the creature to come to them. With each movement it stamped out another ball of light with a crackling thud, and the light of the fire cast deeper and deeper shadows. The thing seemed to twist and change and grow until it was impossible to track. Sarah's eyes followed it along the ground and in the air and all around them, until finally it was in the light of the fire. The fang waker's mouth hung open in a gaping snarl. A maw of endless black teeth hung around a writhing, horrible tongue the color of intestines. Sarah brought her staff in a short, hard arc and struck the monster in the neck. Its body shifted as she did, but it still stumbled away and gave Sarah the time to adjust her footing. Without its body ever moving, or seeming to move, the monster's neck stretched in a sudden, sweeping snap. Sarah brought her staff up just in time, and the creature's jaws clamped closed around it. It gnashed its teeth, rows of sparkling ebony hooks, and they seemed to shift in its mouth as it did.

Sarah brought her right leg up and, putting all of her earned climber's strength and all of the weight her thin frame could muster into it, kicked the shifting mass of fur and teeth. The creature tumbled backwards, and this time it was Sarah who moved first. She brought her staff down hard in an overhand strike and hammered the monster. It yelped, a thing that sounded near-identical to a coyote, but then roared with a screech that made Sarah wince. Again the creature lunged, but this time Sarah was not fast enough. The monster's weight knocked her back, and she struggled to bring her staff up to block another of its gnashing, writhing bites. As its teeth wrapped around her staff again, her feet slid, and she could feel herself toppling over. The monster's body extended and stretched and slid until all of its paws were on the ground, and then it launched itself forward with all of its weight. The creature contracted into itself, its weight now concentrated on Sarah's chest, and began trying to rip the staff from her hands. She clung on, her hands white and hurting and tearing, knowing that it was all that stood between her and the endless rolling teeth inside the monster's black, volant maw.

The monster's hot breath bore down on her, seeming to come in waves. The fang walker began to roll its neck, twisting its endless, incorporeal joints into a corkscrew. Sarah struggled to keep her grip on her staff, her elbows and forearms feeling the racking tension as a sick, squelching sound filled the air with each ratchet of its neck. Sarah began to groan against the twisting she felt in her arms, and then as the monster raised its body, twisted and taffy-like, she began to scream. The pressure reached her shoulders, and she tried to hold on.

Just as she felt her fingers losing their grip, a shadowed blur slammed into the monster, wrenching its grasp on Sarah's staff free and sending it tumbling along the ground. As Sarah scrambled to her feet, a series of ear-splitting screeches filled the air around her. Sarah saw that the sounds did not come from the monster, but instead from Sibella. The falcon was on top of the fang walker, his long paper talons dug into the creature's hide and his beak ripped at the monster's flesh. She saw long, sinewy strands of flesh torn and thrown to the side as Sibella flapped his wings, screeching between each tearing bite. Sarah rushed to them and swung her staff down hard on the long, still twisting neck of the monster, and it let out a baying howl. Sibella released his talons and swooped around the creature before landing on the ground nearby.

The monster's shifting eyes went back and forth between Sarah, Sibella, and the fire behind them. Blood dripped from its matted coat, and without a sound it seemed to return to its original form, looking much the same as any coyote. As it edged its way back into the darkness, the fire cast the beast as a dancing, laughing monster along the silhouetted trees ahead. As quick as it had appeared, the monster disappeared into the forest, leaving Sarah and Sibella trembling in the darkness.

"Sibella, are you all right?" Sarah still stood, watching the tree line.

"Yes, I am all right. Are you?"

"Yeah, I'm fine. Get back to the other side of the fire."

"But--"

"Sibella, now. I'll watch the tree line tonight." *He was almost hurt. He could have been torn apart. To pieces.*

"I would much prefer--"

"Stop arguing. Go, now."

Sibella did as he was told and returned to the far side of the fire. Sarah sat down, her back to the fire and her eyes watching the tree line, every rustle of leaves pulling her focus. She watched the trees for an hour waiting for the creature to return, but after a while the heavy weight of the night found her again and both she and Sibella fell back asleep, though the sleep was light and fitful. When the morning sun struck her face, Sarah woke to find Sibella near the forest line, scratching at blood-splattered ground. She stood up, stretching her sore muscles, and walked over to him.

"What are you doing?" she asked.

He stopped digging and let out a sharp, frustrated kak.

"I am looking for sign of that monster," he answered.

"No need for that. Even if you can pick up any sign, you won't be able to find it." Sarah scuffed her boot on the clay ground, sending powdered dirt over a thin line of black, tar-colored blood.

Sibella kicked at the ground and sighed. "What was that creature? In all the books I have read, the histories and bestiaries, no horror like that was recorded. At least...not in reality, anyway."

"Horror is a good way to describe it. I've always heard them called fang walkers. They are afraid of light, but...well, you saw how it attacked us. Vicious and hungry. I've encountered them a couple of times. The men in my mother's tavern used to say they had migrated from Canait, so they might have come to Calarine after the books in the library were written. I'm not sure."

Sibella nodded, his eyes far away. Their sparkling eons gazed out into the world with a palpable hesitance. "I do not like not knowing, Sarah."

"I know. It's all right, we dealt with it. We won't run into it again."

He fluttered up and landed on Sarah's shoulder. "Where to now?" His voice was still filled with frustration.

"Back to the library," she answered, reaching up to scratch at the top of the falcon's head. "Let's get the camp packed up and head out. I don't want to be in the wilds another night."

Sibella nodded, but as Sarah packed up the camp and made sure the embers of their fire were dead, he watched the trees. His eyes seemed to bore through to the other side.

CHAPTER III
A Measure of Faith
=======================================

Another week passed, and Sarah settled into her life at the Belhaven. One quiet evening, rain tapping at the windows, Sarah came across the library catalogs on the first floor. She discovered that the library's previous denizens, those that had come before the Alchemical, had abandoned the systems of logic and organization laid out in the book. So, to pass the time, she began to collect, reorganize, and re-catalog the books in the library, being sure to gather all those strewn on tables and in the aisles. She spent much of her days that way, sometimes working well into the night. Once, she found herself enraptured by a collection of pre-Rending speculative fiction, and she read on and on. She placed books where she believed they belonged as she finished them, creating categories within categories. She lost herself in those moments, reading and sorting and placing the books. She lost herself in the omelas and big brothers and children of time but there were never any failures. Never any salted Morable coasts.

As Sarah worked through the collection, she sat some of the books aside for her own research. She collected books on spells, Aetics, and metaphysical mythology and put them on the empty shelves in her office. At night, as candles flickered around her, Sarah read through the books with Sibella sleeping in the joists above. She took notes on the scrap papers that littered her desk. Many of the spells held in the tomes were strange and foreign. They utilized new concepts and required unique materials and as she read through these ancient books, she realized how much there was that she did not understand. She peeled back the layers of the Aetic arts a little at a time. Between the books on minor fire conjuration she came across a large book, bound in purple leather, with the title *A Treatise of Communication* embossed in gold on the spine. Sarah sat the book aside on her desk and stretched in her chair, the late hour catching up with her all at once. She laid down on her pallet, the last remnant of the traveler's lifestyle she clung to, and slept. She dreamed of the library's future, grand ideas fading in and out of her mind.

When Sarah woke, she found Sibella perched on her desk, reading over the cover of the treatise she had set aside. She stretched, yawning and shaking out her mess of red hair.

"Communication spells?" Sibella asked, not looking up from the book. "Is there someone you need to contact?" The falcon's voice seemed far away, unfocused.

Sarah cocked her head, and as she did her hair fell across her face, hiding one eye. "Tired?"

"A little, I still have not adjusted to a more consistent schedule after having been alone for so long." Sibella shook out his feathers and tapped at the book with one paper talon. "Now what is this about a communication spell?"

Sarah ran her fingers over the cover, the rope-scars and road weary nature of them a rugged contrast to the neat ink of the typeset. "This one just stood out to me last night, but I was worn out. Thought I would give it a look today."

"Well, what else is there that you have planned for us today, Librarian?" The falcon's voice seemed to have returned to its normal brightness. His unusual eyes watched Sarah as he waited for an answer. They seemed both avian and endless at the same time. His face contained an unsettling cosmic shimmer.

Sarah glanced around the room, her mind reeling with ideas. "Get yourself some breakfast," she answered, now grinning at the bird, "We have work to do."

Sarah and Sibella both readied themselves for the day. The sun started to creep into the high windows, which were hazed and stained from the years. They filtered in a shimmer of soft light, casting streaks and shadows in strange places along the Belhaven's walls. Sarah left the communication book on her desk, the idea of what it might mean still lingering in the back of her mind, and climbed the sprawling staircase to the third floor. She started on her day's work, carrying the books on history and politics back and forth on a repaired cart.

As she moved the books, making notes of titles, authors, and contents, Sarah reflected on how little she knew about the world she had spent so long traveling, how little of it she had ever actually seen. She thought of the villages and cities she'd stopped in, and she thought of the crowds suffocating her in their intensity. She thought of the nights she had spent staring at the same stars in different places, the complex angles and shapes they created the only comfort she'd found. Most of all, she thought of the people she had met, the ones she had lost. Those she had left behind. All at once, the great weight of the collection fell on her shoulders, and the library, eerie and unusual in its emptiness, settled into her mind. The dancing shadows of the filtered light felt like ghosts.

"Sibella," she called out, and the falcon came over to the table where she had stopped to rest, picking at the feathers on his wings as he listened. "What made the Alchemical hide this place?"

The falcon thought for a moment, rapping his talons on the tabletop. "He was afraid of losing its knowledge, I believe. He was terrified that the armies of the High Order would come to take it. The empire and its Aetics often try to," Sibella tilted his head to the side as he paused, considering. "They have a tendency to suppress knowledge about magic and history. Especially knowledge from the Rending. They've all but cast that time into the void. Why, exactly, I am unsure." Sibella grew quiet for a moment, his mind seeming to veer off into another direction. "I am afraid I cannot explain much more than that about his motives. He was a private man. He struggled with himself."

She nodded. If anyone could understand, it was her. She knew what it was like to feel guarded, closed off from those around you. "Why would he need to hide it from the High Order?" she asked, hoping to bring the conversation away from Sibella and the Alchemical's past. "It seems like the government hasn't been anything besides an aether in Calarine for a long time. If they would have wanted something from the library, they could have taken it before the Alchemical ever got here, right?"

Sibella flew over to another table, this one in front of a large tapestry map that hung on the western wall of the third floor, and Sarah followed. "That," he said, his tone much happier than before, "I can provide some clarification on. How much do you know about the High Order? About the political past of the Southern Line?"

"Not much, just what I heard growing up and the little I've seen on the road. Carnd, my hometown, was taken over by the Imperial Navy just after my mother died. But...well, I didn't really get involved with them, you know? Just left because they changed it."

Sibella stretched his wings and turned to face Sarah. He paced on the table as he spoke, his talons clacking with each short, wobbling step. "The Crown Emperor, who I am sure you know is Josiah Fane, is the third of his name. His grandfather, Dovin, founded the empire through conquest. In the wake of the Rending, with the barriers weakened, Dovin Fane founded a core of soldiers meant to make use of the power Goraln had left behind. Those warriors became the first true Aetics, and they used the magic of Goraln, the magic that had saved this world from destruction, to exert power over the lands east of the Dead River."

"So magic defeated the Western Republics?" Sarah asked. "I remember spending sunsets looking across the Dead River to the wall, but what lay on the other side never really settled in for me, I guess. Always sounded like a myth, that there could be a half dozen countries beyond that wall. Countries where magic was still wild."

For a moment she saw a brief flash of contemplation rise in Sibella's eyes. "I would say it stopped the Republics, not defeated them. The Aetics and the firearms of the Western Republics became impassable forces. Neither wanted to fight a war of attrition, and crossing the riverbed was arduous. Treaty was met and the wall was built along the west bank of the Dead River. But it was indeed those first Crown Aetics who mastered Goraln's raw magic. With that power, they conquered the small city-states that had appeared in the years since the Rending, and they unified it under their new empire. That empire consolidated the knowledge of the world and divided us into the Lines. You know this as well as anyone. In the world of the High Order, you are either 'Of the Crown,' or you are forsaken. This city flourished in the early years of the new empire, a shining gem alongside Varinz, and it, not its sister, was the capital of the Southern Line. As wealth consolidated in Calarine's merchant elites, and skirmishes pushed the limits of the Crown's control, the empire squashed it, cutting it off at the stem. Just after the war for Calarine, the Alchemical found this place. It was already abandoned, but the dust of war had yet to settle. He always said he believed it had served as the city government's research repository, likely home to the city's Aetics. He believed that when they left, they had taken some of the knowledge with them."

"So, he had been here a long time then? Before he disappeared, I mean."

"Fifty-five years," answered Sibella.

"Then you're?"

"Fifty-five."

"So then…was he searching for that knowledge when he disappeared?" She regretted the question as soon as it left her mouth.

"I'm tired, Sarah," said Sibella. His voice was weak, far away. "I'd like to rest if I may. This much recollection has worn me out."

Sarah nodded, not wanting to upset him any further, and returned to her work. Throughout the day, she thought about the differences between the world she knew and the world Sibella had described. The differences between Sibella's empire and the world her mother, despite their poverty, had raised her to believe in. Stories of freedom and opportunity echoed in her mind. Like a shadow box theater, the days she had spent sitting at her mother's feet listening to her read grand tales of knowledge and adventure played in her mind. For the first time since she found the Belhaven, she found herself thinking of *The Left Hand of Darkness*, her copy still resting in her pack.

Memories of the first time she had read it moved through her. Of the first time the magic words from a world before her own and the story of a place so different and alien from her own touched her mind. She wondered if the spark of fascination the book had created in her as a child still burned somewhere inside, if it had survived Morable. Survived her running. Thinking on this, and of the many other stories she had devoured in her days on the road, she worked the daylight away. Those stories swirled in her head until they created a thunderstorm of frustration around her. As Sarah returned to her desk on the first floor, the still contemplative Sibella joined her. With her new friend sitting on the table, she opened the treatise on communication.

The sun came through the windows and with it brought a soft heat onto Sarah's face. She had slept in her chair, her head hung back and a stack of books in front of her, a sight that might have been familiar to many of the Aetics who'd called the library home before her. She rubbed at her eyes with a clenched hand, the treatise still open on the table. As Sibella made his way to her desk he looked it over, noticing it was left open on a spell titled "Mass Communication."

"Good morning," he said, watching as Sarah stood up from her desk and straightened her clothes. Her leather cuirass rested in an empty chair nearby, and her cotton shirt was wrinkled and twisted from the night's sleep.

"Morning." Her mind wandered back to Sibella's pained voice the night before. "I'm sorry about yesterday."

"No need for any apologies. The Alchemical is just a bothered nerve, I suppose. I see you kept studying last night after I turned in."

She looked down at the open book and ran her fingers across its yellowed pages. "A little. I mostly thought about this place, I guess."

"Oh?" Sibella's head was cocked to the side as he watched Sarah, a strange expression on his face.

As Sarah spoke, her eyes never left the book. "What if we made this place a sanctuary for travelers? I came here, to Calarine, looking for one and all I found was ruins. So, what if I just made one?" As the words tumbled out of her mouth, her mind screamed against itself. She could still see the hate-filled faces of her friends on the Morable coast, but she pushed them away.

The falcon sighed and looked up at her, his eyes scanning the lines on her face. Scars accented the sun-marks and tight freckles. "My creator worked hard to hide this place away," he said, meeting Sarah's gaze. "I used to think it was to protect it, to protect its knowledge."

"Used to?" she asked, now looking at him. The falcon had spoken of the empire as if it were still at the gates yesterday, but now doubt layered his voice.

"You are its keeper now, even if only by default. What you do with its contents, its knowledge, is up to you. It called to you, not me. My master hoarded its knowledge, and now he is gone. What he did, tried to do, no longer matters. To me or anyone else."

"Are you sure about this?"

Sibella seemed to struggle with his words. "I am not sure which of the Alchemical's words were real. I do not know if the reasons he claimed to hide this place were legitimate, if this place ever really was in any palpable danger. So, I cannot tell you if it is the right thing to do. That is a decision you must make yourself. I'm old Sarah, sure. Older than you, yes, but... I," he paused and took a ragged breath. "I don't quite understand the world outside of this library. I have not seen it. I should not be the one to make decisions on how the Belhaven fits into a world I do not know."

Sarah nodded but was not sure that she understood the world any better than he did. She had seen the empire in Carnd, its orders and decrees. She had been robbed blind in a Morable inn. Accosted by a drunk in the Skeeving Fink in Varinz, a man who had laid convulsing on the ground as she fled the city, his blood still on the end of her staff. She began to feel dizzy, overwhelmed with how fast things had changed, how quick it had gone from nights under the stars to obligations for a place she had only been for a short while. Her knees trembled as she gripped at the back of her chair and sat down.

The communication spell was simple, something she was sure she could do, but the weight of what it meant was enormous. She tried to speak, to rattle off something akin to *I don't know what I want*, but her tongue seemed too big for her mouth. She closed her eyes and worked her hands. As she clenched her fist, her knuckles shone white and the thick scars of her past radiated a mocking pink. A knotted and permanent reminder of how easy it was to let responsibility slip through your fingers. The anxiety swirled in her body before it came to rest at the pit of her stomach.

"Are you okay?" asked Sibella. "I did not mean…I just." The falcon stopped. His eyes traced the table.

Sarah looked up to him, her blue eyes meeting his endless face. Her mind quieted as she saw the longing it held. The worry. The familiarity. All at once she understood the kind of person who could hermit theirself away in a library for sixty years, and she wondered if he too had red hair. Maybe even a past's scar on one of his hands. "Yes, of course I'm okay, Sib. I'm just…overwhelmed."

"Thinking about Morable?"

Sarah swallowed hard. "Yes, I guess so."

"Worried that this time will be like the last?"

Her face grew hot, but she was unsure if it was embarrassment or anger. She started to lie, but then all the energy to pretend faded out of her body. She just nodded instead. Nodded and ran her left hand over her scarred right.

"As am I."

Sarah's eyes came back to his. "What? What is that supposed to mean?"

The falcon looked surprised, not shocked at her anger, but confused that she didn't understand. He didn't answer, but instead just looked Sarah in the eyes, his endless gaze peering into her without remorse.

"So what? You think I shouldn't do this? That I'll just end up letting more people fall?"

The falcon had no jaw to clench, no teeth to run his tongue over. Instead he stood on the table an unmoving statue, his eyes still gazing into hers.

"Say something, god dammit!"

"It does not matter what I think."

"What?! What the hell does that mean?" Sarah leaned forward in her chair now, trying to tear the falcon's gaze away from her soul.

"It means that it does not matter how much confidence I have in you, you must have confidence in yourself."

Sarah swallowed again, collapsing back into the chair. She sat silent for a moment, hoping the falcon would go on, but knowing he wouldn't, before she stood up and buckled her cuirass on without a word. "I think I'm going to take a walk," she said, taking her staff and slinging her pack over her shoulder. "I'll be back before dark. I have to think this through, and I think that's something I need to do away from here."

Sibella said nothing, watching as Sarah walked away. As he heard her footsteps echoing through the vast building, he thought back to the Alchemical, and a tear the color of wetted ink rolled down his cheek.

Sarah stepped into the wind and sun and stopped for a moment on the granite steps of the library, surveying the landscape in front of her. The towering metal structures that filled the city seemed to call to her, and she headed out, this time going deeper into the abandoned ruins of Calarine. She saw with refreshed eyes the vibrant green that swallowed the aging steel towers and abandoned markets. For a moment she could see, underneath it all, the sanctuary that might have been. The long sense of wandering that had filled her for the better part of four years eased into the back of her mind as she made her way down the blackstone streets. The aging roads seemed to wind and twist in a way they had not before. This time she didn't go towards the old city center, instead following along the periphery. As she made her way through the ruins, she came to the steps of one of the many towers. Through the empty doorway she found a tattered, long abandoned storefront. Ragged tapestries hung on the wall, and empty plasti-steel shelves stood along the edges of the room. In the corner, hidden behind a counter, she found a set of stairs. Unsure why, she began to climb, drawn towards the top of the tower by a feeling she knew she had felt before.

The second and third floors of the tower still had remnants of life. Old furniture and clothes made them seem like abandoned homes of people who had left in a frantic race. Beyond the third floor, the stairs seemed to go on forever. As she climbed the tower walls grew ever more bare. By the tenth floor the remnants of occupation gave way to clutter and destruction. By the fifteenth floor the walls were bare, revealing the steel and stone structures beneath. By the twentieth, the tower was more natural than steel. Ivy and vine and green seemed to support the stairs and walls. As she reached the top, she came to a metal door, heavy and well set in against the blank, haunting wall of the ruined tower. Its handle rusted, its frame marred with age, she reached out, expecting the door to be sealed by time, but to her surprise the handle turned with only a slight groan.

As the door swung open, hot sunlight filled the stairway and a brilliant sunbeam forced Sarah to cover her face. Her vision sparkling against the light, she took in the roof of the tower. A waist-high wall of stone, what kind of stone she was not sure, bordered the edge of the roof on all sides. It held intricate carvings of beasts and vines, each inset a different depiction of a strange fantastical world. Vines edged over the wall, almost covering some of the designs. As her eyes adjusted, she saw a silhouette against the horizon, and, before she could react, the shadow moved. A man, dressed in brown canvas with vibrant blue stitching, came into view.

"Ah, hello daint," the stranger said, just as Sarah came into his line of sight. "Have you come to take in the view of old Calarine as well? Well, come on then. I don't bite." The man wheeled on his heels, his body seeming too light for his tall frame, and walked away from the door. His shadow danced in sharp strides. Had Sarah paid closer attention, she might have sworn his shadow moved in its own strange way. He was a tall, dark haired man with bright olive skin and a heavy huntsman's beard. Sarah kept her grip on her staff, following him to the edge of the roof where he stood, hands behind his back, looking across the horizon. Her heart pounded in her chest, but the longer she looked at him, the more her mind eased. His long frame and stiff, upright posture was disarming in a way she did not understand. The world seemed at peace and natural in the ravaged state of the horizon. The wind swept in harsh bands across the tower, seeming to cut through Sarah like ice.

"So daint, what are you doing here?" The man looked at her. For a moment he stared at her eyes, their blue reflected white in the sunlight, and smiled. "No, you're not a daint are you?" A glimmering light glowed on the man's face, and he seemed to look into Sarah's mind. The stone-colored irises, deep set in his dark face, cut through the air between them. "Many miles of road on you, and so young. What brings you to a place like Calarine?"

"I'd always heard there was a sanctuary for travelers here," Sarah answered, unsure why. She turned to look across the horizon. "You can see how that turned out."

The man smiled, the wind tossing his beard in a way that made him seem like an ancient wizard from the stories of Sarah's travels. "Those legends might have been right, at one time, but what does sanctuary even mean?" The man chuckled and scratched at his beard. "What's good for the goose, I'm afraid, is not always good for the gander. This place has been a tangled mess of vines and travelers for some time. Longer than you've been alive, anyway. People come and go. Some make good homes, some do not. Some fight one another, some live in solitude. It is the way of the wilds."

"I suppose the western border hasn't gotten word." she said, kicking at the stone wall.

"Knowledge travels slow in this world," the man said, his voice changing for a moment to a much more somber tone. She fell silent, and together the two of them stood there, as the wind whipped the growing forest in a dancing rhythm. After a moment, the man turned away from the horizon, Sarah shifted on the balls of her feet in his shadow. "What is ailing you traveler? Why've you climbed all the way to the top of this tower? Certainly not just to watch the day whittle itself away?"

Sarah looked at him, his soft gray eyes watching the gears in her mind turn as she processed the decision that had brought her into the wilds. The fear that had chased her to Calarine. "I have a decision to make, but--"

"Oh? What kind of decision?"

"I have a chance to start something here. To make something that might help turn Calarine into a real sanctuary, but that...that'll mean taking responsibility for others for the first time in a long time." Sarah sighed and rubbed at the corners of her eyes. "I don't know if I can do that again." She ran a hand over her neck. She felt flushed, unstable. As the fog of panic tried to settle in, she tried to understand why she felt so comfortable to share everything with the stranger. *Maybe it's because he is a stranger. Maybe it's because I can tell him I am a coward and then never see him again.*

The man turned on his heels and walked towards the door, his hands behind his back. "The world sometimes issues us challenges," he said as he stopped and turned to face her, "but the world isn't a fair place. It never has been. Whether guided by the Faith of Seven Lights or the Old God or even just blind luck, challenges are seldom easy. They almost never make any sense in the moment. But when we are called to something, when that force pulling you towards action is so strong that you feel terrified, you know it is a challenge worth taking." A wide, impossible grin appeared on the man's face, and he looked up to the sky. "I often find that once the task is begun, it is impossible to stop. I've spent a lot of my life alone, traveling the wilds. You know as well as I do, it is less like a stoic solidarity and more like perpetual longing." The man looked back to Sarah, his face framed with a beautiful intensity. His eyes seemed to swirl and move, the deep blue color of cool lapis. "And you know that that longing gets tiring, don't you, Sarah? That it cuts a good bit deeper than any failure ever could. A fall from a mountain top isn't as bad as being alone."

Sarah crossed her arms, the corded muscles of her forearms standing out. Her mind reeled, but she still felt herself being drawn to the man. She could feel him demanding her attention with his silence. She looked up when she heard the scuff of his boot heels just in time to see him halfway through the stairway door.

"I'll leave you to your thoughts," he said. He was looking at her through his windswept gray hair. "Good luck, Sarah Silvergrove. May the road be light beneath your feet." He turned and headed down the stairs. Sarah listened as the clack of his heels echoed in the stairway.

The man now gone, Sarah stood alone on the rooftop. The wind still whipped, catching along the edges of the abandoned towers as it howled against the steel. She sat down on the wall, her feet dangling over the edge, as she thought about the stranger's words. She watched the sun ripple across the horizon. The heat of its spring light sent mirage lines across the skyline. She thought of the communication treatise, the spell that lay within, and all the ways it would change her life. The ways it would change her, unsure if it would be for worse or better. As she did, a thought lingered in the back of her mind. She could not remember telling the man her name.

Sarah walked through the doors of the Belhaven just as the sun began to creep beneath the horizon. Sibella saw that her face was lined with sweat as he welcomed her. The closing of the heavy doors shook dust from the library walls, and the light caught the specks of passed time as they fell, filling the air with twilight. She took off her pack and sat it on the front desk, propped her staff beside it, and stretched her back. She ached from the trip up and down the tower, but her mind felt alive, electric. Sibella fluttered over and perched on the edge of the desk, but the falcon said nothing. Instead, he just watched Sarah and examined the wild smile on her face.

"We need to get some rest," she said, running a hand through her tangled hair. The wind had stirred in a way that made her look manic. "Tomorrow, we'll be calling out into the wilds." Sarah's face was stern, contemplative. She felt unsure of how she had left the falcon that morning, but behind the rest of it she felt a steady nervousness. An apprehension towards the task at hand.

Sibella nodded. The suggestion of a smile edged to the corners of his beak. "Very good, Sarah. So you think you are ready for this, then?"

Sarah reached out and scratched at the bird's paper-feathered head. "I think so." She paused, her eyes far away. Not all the way to the Morable coast, they had receded a little in their introspective wanderings, but they were still away. "I really do."

The next day, Sarah ate a breakfast of dried fish and tiger owl eggs in quiet contemplation at her desk, the stranger's words whirling in her foggy mind. As she finished her food, she closed her eyes and sat for a moment, working to prepare herself for what lay ahead. She reassured herself that this was the right move, that it was her challenge to overtake. That it was, above everything else, a chance at redemption. She opened the communication treatise on her desk and flipped through the pages. She took in its illuminations and gilded lettering. Her eyes stopped on a spell named "Mass Communication" and read it once, twice, three times, each time making careful notes of the spell's expectations, its rules. Sibella flew down from the joists and perched on her shoulder, reading along.

"Ten-mile radius," she mumbled under her breath. "It wouldn't reach Varinz. It should be safe." Sibella said nothing. Sarah reached up and scratched at the paper feathers on his neck. "Get ready," she said, placing her hands flat on the desk. Sibella hopped from her shoulder to the desk and watched as Sarah closed her eyes and focused her thoughts. She fixated on her intent, working to still her breathing and ensure that the purpose of the spell was clear through her words. She visualized the library as a traveler's haven. The thoughts of her lost friends along the Southern coast were a thousand miles away. In the void behind her eyes a call leapt forward and into the world, echoing for miles.

Travelers, refugees, nomads, I call to you. I call to those who seek shelter, a home. Those who seek community in the darks and dangers of the wilds. Together a home can be built, a place made for those who the world rejects and the wilds overwhelm. I call you to Calarine, to help me build a place where all are welcome. I am Sarah Silvergrove, and I call you to my library.

ʆєʌςħɱʌʅς

Miles away, near the outskirts of the spell's radius, a hooded figure hiked through the wilds towards Varinz. A cat, as large and dark as the night, weaved between his legs. Its form was shadowed in an unnatural haze. As a rush of energy poured over the man, he heard the sounds of a young woman calling out into the world and stopped. His eyes flashed a bright violet as he turned them toward the Belhaven

PART II

<u>A CITY OF PURPOSE</u>

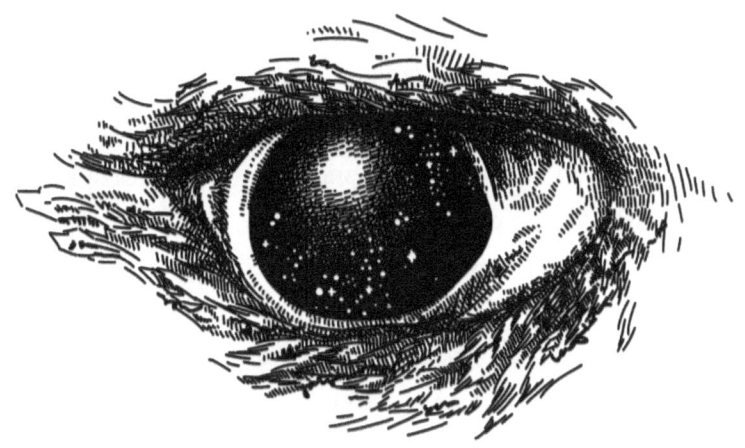

CHAPTER IV

A New Weight

====================================

A week passed before any travelers answered Sarah's call, and she spent that week in a state of constant anticipation. She prepared the Belhaven, turning parts of the first floor into sleeping space with both Sibella's help and an ample amount of magic. She worked to restore the abandoned kitchen used by the workers of the library long ago. When she first saw its ancient stove, she thought for sure it was ruined. It was covered in a heavy layer of dust, and the wires that ran from behind it were coated with cobwebs. She followed the wires to a set of old electro-posit batteries from long before the skies split open and the Rending came. At the batteries she found a set of cables running up the wall and into the ceiling.

Sarah traced the edges of the batteries and followed them to a control box mounted on the wall above. She cleaned the dust and cobwebs away from the controls, revealing an array of metered readouts and switches. "Any idea what charged these batteries?"

"I cannot say for sure, but I can say that there are solar panels on the roof, left here by the denizens of Calarine. But the Alchemical never fooled with such things, so I do not know if they work."

To Sarah's surprise, they did. By some stroke of unimaginable luck the ancient things hummed to life when she flipped the switch and powered on the batteries. The readouts lit up, showing fluctuating levels of energy going from the panels to the batteries. The stove, it turned out, worked like a charm.

As she worked, turning the library into a place for the travelers she hoped would come, she also studied to further her understanding of the magic that now surrounded her. She began to conjure greater and greater items, but at the same time she learned the limitations of her ability. She found herself more than capable of casting any spell she set out to, but they often tired her, wearing on her body in a way she did not really understand. A thing beyond fatigue, rooted in her bones. In the moments where that exhaustion drew closest her spells would die and crackle at her fingertips. But despite the exhaustion, Sarah labored to prepare her new sanctuary for any that might find their way to her door.

It was while she was high on the ladder in the first floor's fiction section, moving books from what was now the living quarters, that Sarah heard the soft, timid knock on the door. At first the thuds caught the attention of neither Sarah nor Sibella, the falcon busying himself chasing moths in the rafters. In a moment, the sound came again, louder and sterner, and Sarah's head snapped to the door. She came down the ladder and Sibella met her near the front, perched on the lobby desk. She opened the heavy oak doors and was met with four cautious faces on the other side. She stood there, the door half open, looking them over. Sibella came to rest on her shoulder, and the strangers across the threshold said nothing.

"Hi," Sarah said after a long silence, still stunned. "I'm Sarah. You can come in. Please, come in." She pulled the door the rest of the way open and the travelers filed in, looking around in awe at the library's high ceilings. It was then, with the visitors now in the soft light of the Belhaven's torches, that she recognized how real everything had become. They were all road-worn, carrying an array of bags and wearing traveler's clothes, their faces pulled tight from the sun. For a moment Sarah wondered how long they had been on the road, where they had been when they heard her call. She wondered how they had felt when they heard her message come across the wilds.

Sarah gave a soft, nervous smile, closed mouth and more anxious than placating, and closed the door behind them. "So," she said, clasping her clammy hands together in front of her, "you heard my call?"

A man, kind faced and stocky, his hair peppered with gray, stepped forward, pushing the eyeglasses on his face up as he did. "Yes, we did. I'm Michael Cokin, this is my daughter Jane." He pointed to a short blonde girl standing halfway behind him. "This one here with the half-cask strapped to his back is Tony Bavritt, and that is Ri. Me and Jane met them on the way here from the Eastern Plains." He pointed first to a stern-built black man, his head totally bald, and then to a broad shouldered, muscular person, their hair short and chopped. Both of them nodded, the choppy-haired one rubbed their hands over the stomach of their padded traveler's shirt. For a moment Sarah found herself distracted, eyes locked on the blonde one's frame, thinking that they looked more like a soldier than a traveler. Gambeson and all.

"Well, welcome. I'm happy y'all're here, and of course you're all welcome to stay--to call this place home for as long as you want. I've made part of this floor into a living space, if you want to take a look."

"Are you an Aetic?" asked Jane, coming out from behind her father. A bright face of youthful wonder looked up at Sarah, wild brown eyes waiting for an answer.

Sarah smirked and started to answer, but Sibella shifted on her shoulder and gave a gentle, amused kak. "She is," he said. All four of the visitors took a step back. Ri's eyes grew wide with cautious alarm. Sibella kaked again, shaking out his feathers. "Nothing to be afraid of. I am the library's familiar. A magic enchantment, that is all."

Ri took a step forward and looked the bird over. "Are you...made of paper?" they asked.

"I am made of enchanted pages from the books held in this place, brought together and given life."

"Did you make him?" Ri asked, now looking at Sarah.

Sarah shook her head and reached up to scratch Sibella's neck. "No, my predecessor created him, a man called the Alchemical. Sibella was here when I found this place. He's been my guide in these early days."

Tony slipped the half-cask off his back and sat it down near the door.. Now free of the weight he seemed to grow six inches. A tall, powerful man with deep-set eyes and the beginnings of a stubbled beard on his face, his body was lean but tight and hard. It was a fighter's body. He spoke in a tone that seemed far too gentle for the power he carried in his eyes. "Seems you've been busy. How far've you come?"

"A long way," Sarah answered, looking around the lobby of the library, "I was born at the Lake of Bridges, but I traveled here from Morable. This place was abandoned for ten years before I arrived just a while ago. So, what's in the barrel?"

Tony grinned and gestured toward it. "Mead--finest you'll ever taste, to pat myself on the back a little."

The idea of joining friends in a drink filled her with an unbridled joy. The pangs of remembrance she had expected in those moments were nowhere to be found. She pointed out the sleeping quarters. "Why don't all of you go and get settled? I'll cook some lunch and then we can all get more acquainted."

Sarah and Sibella went to the kitchen and began preparing a meal of cured fish and rice as the travelers settled in.. Michael and Jane claimed the bunks closest to the western wall, while Tony and Ri each found their own places. The new visitors looked over the thrown-together cots and sleeping quarters, and as the smells of salted fish wafted from the kitchen the group began to stir, hungry from their long years of scavenging. In a moment, Sarah came out carrying a tray of plates, setting them down at the table nearest the cots as the new arrivals made their way towards the smells of salt and starch. They ate without speaking, taking huge bites and chewing the tough, salted fish with a ravenous fervor.

Sarah looked them over again. The soldier-like sun spots of Tony, the tired-but-kind face of Michael, they all told their own stories. Stories Sarah hoped she could, would, be a part of. She tried to remember the last time her mind had been so calm, but couldn't. The past two years of her life were filled with running and regret. Still, there at the table watching as the new arrivals ate her food as if it was their last collective meal, she did not think of Morable, she thought of the library. She did not think of herself as her failures, she thought of herself as the librarian.

"Was it good?" she asked as Jane sat her empty plate down, the last of the newcomers to finish their food. "I'm not a great cook, but I did my best."

"Daint," said Tony, rubbing his stomach with a wide grin on his face. "I think that's the best meal I've had in years." He leaned back in his chair, rocking on the back legs.

The freckles at the corners of Sarah's mouth disappeared in a self-satisfied smirk. "Thank you," she said, "but don't call me daint. My name's Sarah, Sarah Silvergrove. If you feel like you need to call me by a title, call me the Librarian. I'm no noble, no daint, no lady. I've never been anything but a fishmonger's daughter and a traveler." An image of lost love flashed through Sarah's mind and for a moment she almost lost the jesting smile on her face.

Tony nodded, setting the front legs of his chair down. "Sorry, meant no offense. Where along the lake do you come from? I've only been there once, when..." He trailed off, running a hand over his stubbled cheek. "Well, it was a long time ago. Along the southern end of the place, near Old Shieldsboro.

"Small fishing village called Carnd, but I haven't been to the western edge in a long while."

"I come from the Western Hills," interjected Ri, finishing off their glass of water. Their voice was reserved but held a surprising sternness.

Yet another mark of a soldier? wondered Sarah. "I came through a village in the hills, a place called Roxie I think. Sad place, nearly empty."

"Been there only once. We were hill folk. Ma and Da were hermits, so we only went to town once a year."

"What happened to your parents?" Sarah asked. As she did, she saw Tony's eyes scan the ground, his cheered demeanor growing serious.

"Crown Guards killed them. They burned our home too. Had come to collect tithe to the Crown, we had no money to give. Da refused to give over the crops." There was no reservedness in their voice. No anxiety about their past. Sarah felt the slightest tinge of envy at that.

"They let you live?" Sarah asked, her ember eyebrows raised and creating broad lines on her forehead. "Or did you escape?"

"I escaped," answered Ri, their voice dry, curt.

Sarah noticed the deep scars along their arms and left the topic alone. The thick air of pain hung heavy around them, and for a long while the conversation stalled. It was not until Sibella flew down from the rafters and landed on the table that the energy among the newcomers renewed.

"I hope you all do not plan to sit here at this table a great lot of gloomy fools," said Sibella. "There is plenty of room here for everyone. There is a courtyard behind the Belhaven, which we have yet to begin renovating, and three stories of library materials. You all, as long as you wish to stay, have free reign."

"Yes!" Sarah said, her eyes bright and smiling. "Will y'all be staying? I know you're here, but...well we haven't discussed specifics."

Tony looked to Michael, and the two of them nodded at one another. "Yeah," said Tony. "We discussed everything on our way here and decided that if this place was real and you seemed welcoming, then it would be nice to call somewhere besides caves and shacks home. For a little while, at the least."

Sarah clasped her hands together in excitement, looking at Sibella who seemed to almost grin. "That's wonderful! No need to say how long you'll stay. I'm happy to have you for however long you want to be here. Get settled, explore. We'll discuss details of what it'll look like tomorrow. Look through the books. Anything you want to read, feel free."

The group looked at each other, and then each made their own motions of recognition before they started to stir. They spread out through the library, exploring it as Sarah imagined those that explored the world after the Rending must have done. Sibella took flight to the rafters as Sarah returned to the administration offices. For a moment, she fiddled with the papers at her desk, attempting to appear unbothered and busy. She knew, though, that Sibella could see through it to the anxiety beneath. Not the anxiety of remembrance that had been with her since she arrived, but an anxiety of anticipation. As her hand came to *The Left Hand of Darkness* where it rested on the desk, she stopped and sat down. She sat in silence for a moment, turning the ragged book over in her hands. The yellowed edges of the pages were brittle against the pads of her fingers, and she thought of the day her mother gave it to her.

"It's real now, huh?" she said aloud. "No turning back, no turning into someone else and disappearing onto the road." Sarah sat the book down and leaned back in her chair. The open joists above were cast in erratic shadows. She sat there for a long while, listening to the sounds of sliding chairs and pattering feet.

"These people are unlike any I've seen before," she said, still talking to no one but herself. "These people feel tired, road worn. They're going to depend on me. I just hope I'm ready." Just as Sarah started to ease from excited nervousness to genuine anxiety, the sounds of whistling wind echoed from above, and in just a moment Sibella landed on her desk, a green lizard in his beak.

The paper falcon ate the creature in a single, snatching gulp and then shook out his feathers. Traces of the running red blood of the small anole were still on the edges of his beak when he began to talk. "A pensive lot of people. It appears to me that they have been through a lot." Sarah nodded. Sibella's words created echoes of her own worries. "You will be a good guide for them, Sarah. There is a long path ahead for all of you, I believe."

Sarah's head snapped to him and her face faltered for just a moment, her shaking eyes revealing her uncertainty.

"That book, what is it from?"

Her mouth tightened, she had forgotten she was even holding it. "What do you mean?"

"That book, where did you get it? I believe we have a copy of that particular fiction here on the first floor, but you had it with you when you arrived. It has sat on your desk for days, and I often see you turning it over in your hands, but I've never seen you read it."

Sarah's gaze was far away. She looked not at the book in her hands, but through it. Into the miles it had traveled with her. "I've read it a dozen times already. I keep it more for memory now."

"Is that why it looks like it was half-eaten by a wild animal, then?"

Sarah chuckled and turned to the falcon. The faintest

hint of a grin curled at the corners of her freckled lips. "It almost was, once. I lost my bag running from some men outside of Varinz, and a raven grabbed it."

"So it is from Morable then?" The falcon's voice was cautious.

Sarah shook her head, her eyes now back on the book's gray-blue and tattered cover. The edges of its yellowed pages were deckled with time. "No, my mother gave it to me. It was the last book she gave me before she passed."

Sibella nodded and his eyes again seemed to glimmer with cosmic enormity. Sarah realized what he was doing, where his mind went when a look like the night sky came over him. "I see. Well, it is a fine book, a fine book for a mother to give a young girl. If perhaps only one of LeGuinn's broader, denser works. Have you learned from it?"

Sarah's eyes drifted back to the falcon. "I don't know. I like to think so. I like to think that I understand that the world looks different for different people. That othering is wrong. That it takes work to understand experiences, lives. But…I don't know if I always have that in mind, you know?"

Sibella tilted his head and let out a single, soft kak. "Yes, of course. Perhaps knowing is often enough, then. Let us go see how the others are doing."

Sarah sat the book, that centuries old story of rootlessness and tolerance, back down on her desk. The weight on her shoulders felt just a little lighter.

CHAPTER V

Changes, Strangeness

===

Sarah woke in the early morning, the sun still easing over the horizon in the first red-lit moments of dawn. After she dressed for the day, she stood in the main administration offices where she found Sibella sleeping, perched on a rafter above. "Wake up!" she called to the bird, who stirred with a reluctant sigh before he came to sit on her shoulder. "Did you sleep well?" she asked.

"Once I slept, I slept well," the falcon answered with a yawn. His paper crafted beak snapped shut with a decided, and un-paperlike, clack. "Our new friends explored quite a bit last night. It seems they are just as anxious to be here as you are to have them."

Sarah chuckled. "Well, I guess that makes me feel at least a little more at ease. All of this is going a might easier than I expected it to, anyway."

"I would say much of that is because well-worn travelers answered your call. It could have been quite different. A bunch of ineffectual children, or a band of raving lunatics."

Sarah gave an irritated, side-eyed glance and blew a stream of focused air up past the bridge of her nose, jostling the long ringlet of red curl that rested just above her eye. "Thanks a lot for the vote of confidence, Sib."

Sibella only gave a defiant kak in response, and together

they walked from the administration offices to the living quarters. There they found the travelers talking together, laughing as they stretched away the night's aches. As Sarah and Sibella came to join them, Ri looked up and gave a welcoming wave. At the scatter of kind faces, Sarah's anxiety dissolved into a reassured feeling of anticipation.

"Good morning, Sarah," said Ri. Their face was wide and alert, a soft light in their eyes despite the haggard signs of the road that framed them.

Sarah's hand reached down to her waist and straightened her cotton shirt with a subconscious motion. "It's good to see everyone getting on so well! I have a lot I want to talk about, but breakfast first. I don't know about anyone else, but I'm starving."

"Need any help?" Ri asked. Tony and Michael were chatting away in the background, neither of them seeing the way that Ri's eyes locked on Sarah or the way Sarah's breath hitched.

"I'm sure I can find something for you to do." She scratched at Sibella's feathers who, used to the routine, flew up to the joists and began his own morning rituals. She was grateful he was gone. She could feel the heat rising in her neck and didn't trust the falcon not to comment on it.

Ri trailed just behind Sarah as the pair headed to the kitchen. They were broad built, marked from the road in the same way as Sarah, but an obvious gap in strength stood between them. As they stood together in the modest-but-still-cramped kitchen, Sarah looked them over. The lines of Ri's back stood out against the thin, linen tank top that hung over their shoulders.

"How did you end up traveling with Tony?" Sarah asked as they both worked to put together breakfast. Hoping to distract herself from the rolling feeling in her stomach.

Ri stopped. Their face grew serious, and their jaw worked as they turned to look at Sarah. "We met a week or so before we heard your call." They said and ran a hand over an old scar that ran from the top of their hand to their elbow. It seemed like a subconscious motion. "Tony helped me get away from a…group I was stuck in."

"What kind of group? Were you military?"

Ri's eyes darted to the ground and their jaw tightened. "Not the voluntary kind," they answered, almost in a whisper.

Sarah's face dropped and she turned back to the task at hand. She had heard of the collections many villages operated, some called menageries and some called brothels, but she knew that no one who went into them came out the same. She'd heard of other groups strewn across the world, too. Things like cults and mercenary press gangs. Sarah started to ask which of those groups had been Ri's fate, if they had been prisoner or soldier, but she stopped herself. The age lines on Ri's face, the scars on the top of their hands, all at once made sense to Sarah. She didn't have to ask. "I'm sorry," she said.

"It's all right. Let's get the food finished up. I'm sure everyone is wondering what's keeping us." A grin crept onto their face. "Wouldn't want them getting the wrong idea this early." They grabbed as many of the plates as they could carry and turned to leave the kitchen. Sarah stood for a moment, feeling the hot flush filling their cheeks before snapping out of it and grabbing the rest of the plates.

As the pair came out of the kitchen they saw that

Sibella had joined the others. He rested on one of the table tops, spinning tales of long-ago legends and Aetics since forgotten. Michael sat starry eyed as he listened to the Falcon's stories, but Tony and Jane squirmed in their seats, struggling to feign focus as their eyes darted around the room towards every distraction. Tony's big hands were drumming on his thighs in a persistent rhythm. Sarah and Ri sat the food down in front of them and they all ate together. Small snippets of conversation interrupted the sounds of clanking plates, but the newcomers still all ate with a fervor that shocked Sarah. Her mother had taught her to cook, and because of that she had managed to eat well enough. *I even used to cook for others once before,* whispered a thought in her mind. But she didn't latch onto it. Instead, she ate with the others, the relative silence a welcome friendship.

Wiping at his mouth with the back of his hand, Michael placed his plate in the growing stack at the center of the table. "Another fine meal. The cooking alone might keep me around." His kind eyes and salt and peppered hair framed a simple, closed mouth grin in a way that reminded Sarah of home.

Putting her plates with the others, Sarah returned his smile and started to reach out and grab the stack of dishes, but Ri stopped her. They picked up the plates and headed towards the kitchen with a wink. Sarah fought the urge to turn and watch them walk away.

"I'm happy you've all started to settle in," she said. "Michael, where are you from? You don't seem much like the traveling type."

"Lorolel, in the Center Line. Along the Risen Range much like this place is, as a matter of fact. I was a mill worker there."

"Really? That's hard work, isn't it?"

"No harder than traveling, I suppose. My father and my father's father were both lumbermen, but I haven't got a taste for heights. Well, except for a sour one, anyway."

Sarah laughed and relaxed in her chair.

"This is a fine place," Tony said, once again rocking on the back legs of his chair. "Lots of interesting bits here, lots of old books. Lots of stuff I used to hear the old folks talk about. Poe and Lovecraft, Faulkner and Lee, Jackson and Sanderson. Good stuff--good reads. It's been a long time since I've been around this sort of thing."

"There's more here to read than I could ever hope for. I'm happy y'all have at least found some books that interest you."

"Jane has taken a liking to the books on magic," Michael said. The girl had left the table almost as soon as she had finished eating. "She's been reading through those books and talking about becoming an Aetic." Michael's brow furrowed and he scratched at the top of his right hand. "There's nothing dangerous about that, is there?" Before Sarah could answer they both heard Sibella gliding toward them. The falcon landed on the table, filling the air with the sound of crackling paper as he did.

The falcon kaked and preened as he gave a huff of clear exasperation. He had been outwitted by a salamander and was not happy in the least. He turned his attention to Michael just as Ri returned. "There is danger inherent in everything, but there is nothing to be concerned about. She is in no more danger exploring magic and the Aetic arts than she is exploring the library."

"Right," said Sarah. "There's no real way she could hurt herself, at least not without us knowing she was planning to attempt something dangerous, anyway."

Michael nodded. His jaw tightened, but he did not argue. "Thank you. I guess I am just concerned. All of this is so new."

"I will let you know if her studies become worrisome," said Sibella.

Tony looked the bird over and seemed to try and read the words printed on his feathers. "I still can't get used to a talking bird, much less one made of paper. I've seen mechanoids and mechanicals in the greater cities, but none that weren't at least mostly metal, and none that talked like you, either. Well not that weren't Bellumites, anyway."

"I am a falcon," said Sibella, "but you can call me by my name. You do not have to call me 'bird'."

Tony laughed and smacked a hand on the arm of the chair. "You're a snarky one, I'll give you that. All right, Sibella. I apologize."

"It is quite fine. Seeing me as a falcon will likely aid you in getting 'used to me' as well, Mister Bavritt."

"Tony, please."

"See? Irritating to not get your wanted name when you expect it, isn't it?" Sibella kaked, and Tony's face exploded into a grin.

"All right, Sibella, all right. Point taken."

"What did you say about Bellumites?" Sarah asked, her bony elbows now rested on the table.

Tony hesitated, if only for a moment, before coughing

and adjusting in his seat. "Bellumites. Mechanoids the empire uses as enforcement in their armies and ships. They can talk a bit, but not much that makes any sense."

"When did you meet something like that?"

His eyes left Sarah's and he traced the grain of the tabletop with one finger. "Lot of road between here and the Northern line."

Sarah started to push on, to ask more, but feeling the tension of Tony's averted gaze, she instead just shifted in her seat and stretched. "Well, I'm going to get back to work on the library's collection. Take some more time to get settled in if you need it. I'll be spending the day here on the first floor if any of you need me."

"If it's all right with you," Tony started, his vigor renewed as he drummed his knuckles on the table, "I think I'll drag Ri with me to start cleaning on that back courtyard. It'd be a fine place for a fire."

"That sounds fantastic! I've been so overwhelmed with everything here that I haven't had time to get to the courtyard."

"I'd like to help with the books," said Michael. He was pushing his glasses up the bridge of his nose.

"I can use all the help I can get."

TONY

From Sarah's words, Tony had expected a mess in the courtyard, but what he and Ri saw as they stepped through the big french doors still shocked him. Hedgebushes had taken root all throughout the courtyard, stone fixtures and barrier walls were left abandoned to the wanton whims of nature. Near the center, not quite set in the middle but offset enough to cast the scene in a surrealist lean, a pine tree as big around as a flaggan and twenty feet tall stretched towards the half-blocked sun above.

"Goddamn, this might be more work than we thought," Tony barked, already feeling the ache in his back.

"I'm going to go out on a limb and say you don't have an ax, do you?" Ri asked.

Tony feigned a face of mild irritation, and then trotted back to the library. He went straight to his claimed cot, grabbed his pack, and unstrapped the long-handled woodsman's ax from the side.

When he got back, Ri was already moving stones away from the right-hand edge of the courtyard. They stopped, a stone larger than a young hog cradled in their arms. They showed no signs of effort as they shifted the rock onto their right shoulder. They stood like that, one leg cocked out in front, and looked at Tony. "Well, that's the first good news since we got out here, but it looks like in-between every hedge is a pile of rocks."

Tony nodded and headed towards the pine with the ax. "Well, come over here and clear these rocks around the pine. We'll drop it first."

Ri shrugged the stone off of their shoulder, and as they stepped away, the stone crashed to the ground, embedding itself a half-foot deep into the earth. "So what do you think?" they asked as they started carrying stones away from the tree.

"Of what?"

"Everything. This place, Sarah."

Tony positioned himself in a wide stance in front of the tree and paused. "Well," he said, then swung the ax. He spoke between blows as Ri carried rocks. "I think this place is just fine. I'm tired of fighting. I know you are too. This place is more a commune than a settlement. The low profile? I think it'll be nice. No wars. No captains. No fights. Fine by me. Kumbaya and flower crowns."

Ri dropped the last of the rocks out of the way and turned to face him. Sweat ran down their face and into the neck of their shirt. "What about Sarah?"

Tony paused, chunks of the tree already missing. He looked at Ri and raised a single, dark eyebrow. "What do you think of her?"

"Not funny."

"I'm not laughing. She's nice. A little goofy, sure, but nice. Seems to have an idea of what she wants to do with this library, and...well, look, I wouldn't want to go to war for her, but I don't plan on going to war for anyone. That's what all this is supposed to be, right? Fresh start for both of us. No war, no fighting. Peace on the road."

"She asked about...where you found me."

Tony clenched his jaw and swung the ax back into the tree. He was well passed halfway through. "And?"

"I didn't tell her anything. Just that you'd found me somewhere I didn't want to be."

"If you're going to keep blushing like that you'll need to tell her eventually."

"Tony."

"Shut up your 'Tony'-ing and come over here. Use those muscles to push this tree away from the walls.

As Tony sunk the ax into the tree again, they both heard the french doors shut behind them.

SARAH

As Tony and Ri dealt with the stones and hedges of the courtyard, Sarah walked Michael through her new organizational systems. She showed him her methods and her processes, and all the while the bespectacled man nodded and watched, never once stopping to ask for clarification. Before long, the two worked in perfect unison.

"So" Sarah asked, sitting a stack of books onto a nearby table, "what made you leave Lorolel?"

Michael grew still, a handful of books in his hands. "My wife left me and Jane a long time ago." His voice was not cold, but it still seemed distant. Like he was remembering something from another life. "With her gone, I couldn't stand to be in that place anymore. So Jane and I took to the road. 12 years ago now." He went back to moving books, no hitch in his step. His hands were quick and deft and Sarah could see the millers precision working through them.

"Oh my god I--I'm so sorry." Sarah stumbled over her words, hating herself for the way she kept pushing people to talk.

Michael smiled at her and gave a slight nod. His eyes seemed to hide behind his glasses in a way that made him seem mythical. "It's fine. It was a lifetime ago, or it feels like it was anyway. Jane has never known any other way to be. It's just something that happened, and I'm too old to be worrying about how hard I've had it. Maybe she's living a good life out there somewhere." A wild streak of laughter echoed from the courtyard.

"That sounds like Jane," Sarah said. Michael had

stopped and was looking towards the back of the Belhaven, smiling.

"She must have joined Tony and Ri in the courtyard."

"You know," she said, searching for the right words in hopes of not stirring up any more ill feelings before lunch, "I don't really think there's any reason to be worried about Jane. These powers, the magic, it's exactly what you make of it. There's no danger in learning. She can come to me if she wants to talk about it."

"It doesn't matter if I am worried. She's her own person, headstrong and absolute, just like her mother. You try and tell any kid not to do something and it just makes it worse, but you try and tell Jane not to and you're really in for it." Michael had stopped and was looking at Sarah, his face holding a knowing grin half buried in thought. And as far as the coming to you part, you can probably hang that up. The girl confuses the hell out of me. She's headstrong as anyone I've ever met, but shy as a wild rabbit when it comes to asking for help. When, if, she comes to you, it'll be after she's pushed herself as far as she can alone."

Sarah laughed and nodded, a touch of remembrance clouding her eyes. "I'm closer to her age than I am to yours, so trust me, I understand. Let's take a break. Go see what the others are getting into."

Tony and Ri, with a little help from Jane and the others, worked well into the twilight evening clearing the courtyard. What had once been filled with stones and hedges and a single clawing pine, was now a mending courtyard with a pile of cuttings near the center. As the night sky began to shroud the ruins of Calarine, Ri built a fire and Tony drew two canteens of mead from the half-cask. He and Ri had stacked stones into a fire pit, and arranged some of the bigger stones and lengths of pine into a seat for every person.

"Good mead is a must-have after a hard day's work" Tony said, a wide, toothy grin on his face. He handed out some glasses gathered from the kitchen and poured each of the adults a brimming cup of the sweet honey brew. "I was a brewer, you know. If we can find something to make alcohol from, I can try and keep us all well and sloshed."

Sarah took a drink, it was sweet and wild in its flavors. She had had mead once before in a stand along the southern coast, but it tasted nothing like what she then held in her hands. The two drinks were as far apart as port and the wine of a king's table. "If we can find some honey in the ruins, I think that sounds like a fine idea."

"This is fine mead," said Michael, drinking down his glass in one bid swig and then passing it back to Tony, refusing another. "I'm enjoying the company, but I have to get some rest." He stood up and looked around the courtyard for his daughter. "Jane!" he called out, and in just a moment the scrawny girl came jogging up. "Get around, you need rest too."

The others watched in amusement as the universal sign of adolescent hard-headedness knotted Jane's face. Sarah almost laughed when Jane rolled her eyes, arms crossed and jaw hard set in defiance, seeing more than a little of herself in the young girl's face. "Come on. I'm not even tired."

"No arguments, I'm not making these people watch

you."

"What?! I don't need to be watched!"

Michael, his wide, stocky frame slouched and frustrated, ran a hand across his forehead. "Jane, last time I left you alone like that you tried to steal tiger owl eggs while the owl was still on the nest." Behind him, he heard Tony stifle a laugh. If he had looked, he'd have seen Sarah and Ri doing the same.

Jane, though, wasn't amused at all. "Dad, that was three years ago! I was just a kid!"

More stifled laughter, this time even a little from Michael himself.

Sibella, who had been chasing a mouse in a nearby hedge, flew over and landed at Michael's feet. "Michael," he said, looking up at the man with small, sparkling eyes, "if you trust me, I am happy to keep an eye on her while you rest. I'll ensure she does at least get to sleep at a reasonable hour."

"For what it's worth," Sarah chimed in, "Sibella never leaves the library without me. He'll keep her safe, and he'll come get me if she gets out of hand."

Michael sighed and threw his hands up in the air, looking back to the others with a halfway grin. "Well, I've been beaten I guess. Be good for Sibella, okay?" Jane nodded, her blonde hair tossing in the air as she did. Without another word she ran back towards the Belhaven, Sibella following behind. Michael turned to the others and waved a tired hand. "I'm going to sleep, don't burn the place down."

The others told him goodnight and laughed as Tony refilled their cups with mead. "Sarah, I'm telling you we should build a brew house! Why, we might even start pulling a little coin in! Untaxed by that damnable bunch in Varinz. The Free

City of Calarine, built on brews and books!"

Sarah took a drink and pulled the leather cord from her hair. She shook out the curls, glancing at Ri as she did. To her disappointment, Ri's gaze was locked on the flickering flames. "We'll have to try and find the things for it, but I'm sure we can with time. Isn't that a two-person job though?"

Tony waved a hand at her. "For a fool maybe! 'Sides I have Ri don't I? They'd make a damn fine cask-toter any day."

"If you don't watch it," Ri said through a half-laugh, "I'm going to leave the rest of this courtyard to you." They drank down the rest of their mead in a single gulp.

Sarah watched the firelight flicker on Ri's face and for a moment lost herself. She felt her face flush and was thankful that the shadows hid it.

They drank and laughed through the night until the canteens were empty, and once the mead was gone Tony stirred the sparkling embers in the fire and kicked some dirt over them. "That'll keep," he said, his speech slurred and well lubricated. Together the three of them half walked and half stumbled back into the Belhaven where they found Jane asleep in her cot, Sibella resting at the foot of the bed.

"Little guy is true to his word, huh?" asked Ri.

Sarah felt struck by how rosy the brew had made Ri's skin. The soft red-pink hue contrasted with the blonde of their hair in a way that made Sarah feel dizzy. For a minute she thought of taking Ri by the hand and leading them to her office, but she fought those feelings. The idea embarrassed her, or, at least, the idea of failing at it did. The idea of making a fool of herself, of having built something up that was only her's, not their's. She felt certain it was the mead swirling those feelings around in her mind and was thankful Ri couldn't see her flushed face and trembling eyes. "Yes he is. I'm going to go to bed. You two sleep well, and hope that I don't bust my ass halfway to my office."

"Need a hand?" Ri asked.

Sarah stared into Ri's green eyes, trying to understand their words. "I'm sorry, I think my ears are ringing."

"I asked if you need a hand to your office."

Sarah raised her eyebrows, bit at her lip, and realized that Tony had already gone to his cot. Does he know what she asked me? Does he know what I see? She still wasn't sure she understood Ri's words, not sure if the mead had really been that strong.

"You okay?"

"Oh yeah."

Ri shook their head and took Sarah's forearm. Without another word they began leading Sarah across the first floor to her office. As they walked, Sarah could feel the heat rising in her. She imagined Ri standing in her office, or even just the empty-besides-books administration offices, and then only grew warmer. "Oh no, Ri, I'm fine."

"You can stop being weird, Tony knows."

Sarah's head bobbed with each step, but she still managed to look at Ri, her mouth pulled tight and thin. "Knows what?"

Ri just glanced at Sarah. A wild grin was on their face. Sarah's thoughts began to race as Ri chuckled, but when Ri lifted their hand and pushed Sarah's hair out of her face, and in turn her vision cleared, Sarah's entire face turned red. "I'm sorry you had to walk me over here, I didn't realize that I'd drank so much."

"It's fine. Don't worry about it."

Ri reached around Sarah's waist, and as their fingers grazed Sarah's thigh, her heart thrummed. When she heard the knob turn and the door creek open, she met Ri's eyes. "Thanks, I, uh--I appreciate it."

The open door to Sarah's back, Ri glanced through and then brought their eyes back to Sarah's. Blonde hair half-covering one eye, they stood taut and radiating, their body only a few inches from Sarah's. Their eyes wandered to Sarah's cheek and then they lifted their hand. "Be still," they said, brushing a thumb across Sarah's cheek. Despite fighting not to, Sarah sucked in a sharp breath of air when Ri touched her. "Sorry," they said, "you had soot on your face. Ash must've fallen on you."

Sarah closed her eyes and forced herself not to lean into Ri. "Oh, thanks. I had no idea."

Ri lingered for just a moment before they gave a slight nod and took a step back. "See you in the morning, Sare."

Sarah stepped through the administration door and headed to her office. Once there she undressed and laid uncovered on her bedroll for hours, heat radiating from her body. Ri's flushed face and quiet eyes hung in her mind like a sunrise.

The next morning, Sibella woke Sarah with three sharp kaks. She squirmed in her cot, the restless sleep of the previous night still hanging over her head.

"Get up!" Sibella kaked even louder. Impatience seeped from his words. "There is someone at the door. It is time to get up, librarian!"

Sarah sat up, squinting against the sunlight. "Fuck," she mumbled, scrambling out of bed and grabbing her clothes. She finished getting dressed and stumbled out of the offices to see everyone waiting at the front desk. Only Michael and Jane looked like themselves. The others were standing near the lobby desk, dark eyed and squinting against the light. Sarah thought for a moment she could almost hear their heads pounding. Except, she noticed, that Ri seemed unbothered, except for the dark circles hanging beneath their eyes. They shared a quick, lingering glance before another set of knocks interrupted it.

"Someone's at the door," Tony grumbled. "For love of everything make the racket stop."

Sarah put a finger to her lips and opened the doors. Tony cringed against the loud creak that bellowed, or seemed to bellow, into his pounding head. On the other side stood a gray-haired woman and a tall, lanky boy no older than thirteen.

"Hello," said Sarah, doing her best to put on a happy voice as her mind still lay half-asleep in her cot. "My name is Sarah Silvergrove." She gestured for the two to come in, and they stepped over the threshold, taking in the building's ornate design as they did.

"I'm Finch Grett," said the woman in a raspy, strained voice. "This is my son, Pinn."

Sarah shook hands with Finch and noticed the wrinkles and sunspots on her hands. The others came to stand nearby, smiles and gentle looks on their faces. Tony still seemed to squint against the world around him, but he held a narrow smile all the same. She introduced the others one at a time, and to each introduction Finch and Pinn were polite, if only a little quiet.

"Michael, would you show them around the library?" asked Sarah. "I'm going to get started on breakfast."

"Of course!" Michael answered, waving for Jane to join him. "We'll show them around, no problem." Together, Michael and Jane led Finch and Pinn through the library as Ri and Sarah went to make breakfast. As Michael and the others walked towards the living quarters, they could hear Jane and Pinn chatting away.

"It'll be good for her to have another kid around," Sarah said as she stepped through the door to the kitchen, holding it open for Ri.

"Don't let Jane hear you call her a kid," Ri said, half laughing as they walked through the kitchen doors. They lingered close to Sarah as she closed the door, no mention of the previous night on their lips.

The clatter of the kitchen covered the sounds of the others, but occasional laughter still broke through. Sarah lit the stove, and her eyes stopped on the knotted scars on her hand. The rope that had left them felt a thousand miles away.

CHAPTER VI

A New Wrinkle, A New Man

==

Finch and Pinn settled into their new lives at the library without much hesitation. Pinn and Jane became fast friends, spending their days exploring the library and lounging in introspective angst as young adolescents are wont to do. Finch settled into her own quiet life, helping Michael and Sarah move books throughout the library's collection.

One evening, the sounds of the slow, persistent rain casting a placid aura around the library, Sarah, Michael, and Finch worked through the history collections of the third floor. Michael, in one of his many wandering tangents into the library's dark storage rooms, had found a stack of wooden crates, so the three of them had spent most of that day stacking mis-located books into the crates with the intention of relocation. Sarah was moving a handful of magic study guides from a back shelf to the crates, when she heard a sudden, rattling crash.

"Shit on a goddamn bicycle!" shouted Finch. The crashing half-covered her words, but her panther's yowl was clear enough.

Michael stepped out of one of the aisles, giving Sarah a confused glance. When they rounded the corner to where Finch had been reorganizing books on the top shelf, they found her standing, surrounded by fallen books. She had one hand on her hip and the other rubbed at the side of her head just above her ear. When she looked up and saw Sarah and Michael, she raised a finger to cut them off.

"If any more of these fucking books fall on my head, I'm going to throw every goddamn one of them outside."

Michael, stifling laughter, pushed his glasses up his nose. "Well that just sounds like more work, you know?"

Sarah couldn't help but smirk, and when Finch's eyes twisted into a wrinkled, sun aged rage, Sarah had to bite her tongue to keep from laughing.

"You two keep on and see if I'm kidding." Finch, unlike her two compatriots, showed no signs of amusement.

"All right, Finch," said Sarah. "What exactly happened?"

Finch waved a hand towards the top of the shelf and then towards the ladder nearby. "I climbed that ladder to stick those damn old Southern History books at the top with the rest of the classical history stuff. Stuck 'em up there, started down, and then the sonofabitches all fell on top of my head. I'm lucky they weren't all that heavy, otherwise you'd have found me dead."

"Are you okay?" asked Michael, less amusement in his voice than before.

Finch's jaw slacked in abject surprise. "What in the hell kind of question is that?"

"Can't win for losing. I'm going back to my section."

As he started back towards the area he had spent most of the day on, a large collection of memoirs from called "The Great North American Leaders," Finch stuck her tongue out at him, the general tension on her face seeming to ease.

Sarah, though, paid neither of them any mind. Her eyes

had locked onto that top shelf the moment Finch said the books, all of which were no bigger than any other book on the shelf, had fallen. She bent down and started picking up the scattered books and stacked them out of the way. "Here, help me get these out of the way and then bring that ladder back over here."

Finch did, but not without a string of mumbled, rasping complaints. As the books were stacked and the ladder brought back, Sarah climbed until she could see the top shelf. Pushed to the back, just out of view from any perspective but the highest, was a large set of plasti-protect covered paperbacks.

"Hey!" Sarah called out. "Hey Michael! Bring one of those empty crates over here." As she heard the sound of Michael's footsteps on the hardwood floor, she started handing the books down to Finch.

Each book's cover showed an iterative version of the same idea. A white background with a nature scene in the foreground. Superimposed between the two, a long-haired woman, person, or alien in the arms of a bare chested, brawny man. The authors, names like Steele, Capritole, and El' Katier, were familiar, but more than anything the covers were iconic. Sarah had seen a hundred like them in the bookstores in Morable and the half-dozen abandoned markets she had happened across in her travels. "Harlequin Romance," the signing always read. She hadn't expected to find a substantial collection of smut novels in the third floor history stacks, but even more surprising was Finch's face when she saw them. Finch had stacked the books separate from all of the others and held one of the El' Katier books in her hand. Sarah saw the cover, a man with arms the size of trees holding a delicate-looking alien with green-blue hair, skin like the color of sea foam. The title, from what Sarah could make out in-between Finch's calloused fingers, read *Ravager of Worlds*.

"Where did all these come from?" Finch asked. She flipped through the book, stopping occasionally to read. There was no flush in her cheeks, but the temporary widening of her eyes told Sarah that the book did include at least a little ravaging.

"They were shoved up top, behind a bunch of other books. Sibella told me that the Alchemical never really did anything with the books, so whoever stuck them there must've done it at least sixty years ago."

Michael stepped into the aisle, the wooden crate in his hands. He glanced over Finch's shoulder and, having not seen the covers and not knowing what to expect, dropped his mouth open and stepped back. Unlike Finch, there was blush to his cheeks. "Where in God's name did you find that trash?"

"If you would, mister morality, sit that crate down right there." She closed the book and tucked it into her back pocket. "Could I keep these? I mean, not permanently, but--"

"Of course," Sarah cut in. "Keep them as long as you want 'em."

Finch dropped to one knee and began packing the books into the crate, and then picked it up and carried it out of the aisle, cradling it like a precious treasure. As she left the row of shelves, Michael glanced at Sarah and the two of them shared a wide, self-satisfied smile.

A week after the discovery of Finch Grett's exclusive collection of harlequin literature, Sarah's stock of dried meat was no longer able to keep up with the needs of their growing community.

"Well," Tony said in between bites of his breakfast early one morning, "If you know of a creek, I figure that'd do for most of it. Then we could make our way into the city and find somewhere we could scrounge up some rice or flour or something."

"What about this place?" Finch asked in her raspy voice. "What about the kids?" She sat, one leg propped on the arm of her chair and a book, titled An Embrace from Outer Space, in her hands. Her plate was empty and cleaned in front of her.

Jane's head snapped to Finch, a look of insulted defiance on her face. "What does that mean?" She started to go on, but her father's stern gaze told her to settle down.

"Now that much I do know," Sarah said, tilting her head and shrugging at Jane. "You and Pinn will be staying here. We can't keep up with both of you out there."

Jane started to protest, but her father's eyes once again settled it.

"I think the best way to do this is Sibella, Tony, Ri, and myself will go out to scavenge, and the others stay here, if that sounds fine."

Tony and Ri nodded in agreement.

"Sounds fine with me," said Finch. She picked at her teeth with her fingernail as she flipped pages in the book. "I have had my fill of the road for a while anyways. I think I'll sit my happy ass around and smoke and read for a few days. When we passed through Varinz I bought enough tobacco and papers to last months."

"Michael, you'll be in charge while we're gone. Shouldn't be more than a couple days."

"Why me?' he asked. His eyes were filled with concern and hesitation. "Shouldn't Sibella stay and watch over everything?"

Sarah gave Michael a pat on the shoulder. "I need Sibella to help scout. You'll do fine. Biggest job will be overseeing meals."

Michael rubbed at his neck, his thick and sun-spotted fingers scratching at the nape of his neck as he did. "all right, I guess. What if something happens to all of you while you're out there, though?"

"You don't have to worry about us," Ri interjected, their green eyes hidden behind their smile lines. A single sweep of blonde hair was halfway over one eye. "Between the three of us, there isn't much short of a garrison that could give us any trouble." They flexed their right arm to show the thick, corded muscles just beneath their pale skin. They gave a wink, and for a moment Sarah's breath hitched and she darted her eyes away.

"When will you be leaving?" Michael asked through a half-laugh.

"Soon as we finish breakfast and get everything together," Sarah answered. Her eyes wandered up to the joists as she heard Sibella's talons clack against the wooden beams. "You'll do fine Michael, I know it."

SARAH

Breakfast behind them and the noon sun above, the four of them waved goodbye to Michael and left the Belhaven. Sarah led them along the blackstone streets towards the creek, and they walked along its clay bluffs listening to the sound of water babbling over soft stones in the ancient, silt creek bed. Sarah carried her staff tight in her right hand, using it to manage the sometimes rocky banks of the creek. The others followed close behind, their own packs across their backs. Sarah noticed a long, leather case tied to the side of Ri's pack, but before she could ask about it Tony broke the silence.

"Spent a long time alone before I came across Ri," he said, "but I never thought I'd end up in a commune before the summer."

Sarah and Ri both laughed.

"This place has grown up faster than I thought it would," said Sarah. "I wasn't sure anyone would even answer the call."

A questioning "hmm," came from Ri as they scratched at the back of one forearm, which rested on a long, narrow hunting knife hanging from their belt. "Come to think of it, how have you gotten so lucky that no one with bad intentions showed up?"

"That's a good question," Tony interjected. "Not to step on your toes, Sarah, but I'd say that there's more bad than good out here."

'Haps I could tell you all about 'em somewhere a bit more private, hmm? Replayed in Sarah's mind, the man's breath thick with alcohol and the sounds of the Skeeving Fink distracting anyone who could've seen. "Despite my sore toes," she

answered, "I'd say that's right. I suppose I've just been lucky. So far, anyway." She looked up at Sibella, who was flying circles above them, and felt a pang of guilt. *So far I haven't failed any of you. So far, so far, so far.*

"We've had very different experiences, it seems," said Ri.

Sarah started to speak but could not find the words. Her tongue felt heavy in her mouth, the hot breathed images of Ri standing just inches from her outside of the administration offices filled her mind. The scars along their arms, the weight their eyes seemed to carry. The gentle brush of their arm against hers. She wondered how anyone could hurt them when they seemed so impassible.

"Whatever comes our way," Tony said, snapping Sarah out of her daydream, "I'm sure we can handle it. We're a tough bunch. Worst comes to worst and we can sick the falcon on them anyway."

Now, they all laughed together. The tension eased and the sounds of the creek beginning to fill the air around them, Tony regaled Sarah and Ri with stories of his time as a brewer, the strange characters that had made their way into his tavern.

"It was a wild day," Tony said, recounting the time he was trapped in a bar fight as he tried to force three drunk soldiers out of his tavern. "I didn't want to be there, but I couldn't get out the door without playing my part, besides my wife would've clobbered me if I left the tavern to the mercy of those belligerent hoosiers. I've never seen three men fight so hard they swung on each other too!"

Ri raised an eyebrow and scrunched up their nose in a way that drew Sarah's attention. "What did you just call them?"

Tony laughed. "Hoosier. It's an old word. No idea what it might've meant before the world fell apart, but nowadays in the Northern Line it means thug, jackass."

"Well," said Sarah, "I can't say me and my friends didn't raise our fair share of hell. I'm sure we gave some poor brewer just as much trouble, at some point or another."

"You used to travel with others?" asked Ri. "I thought you've been alone this whole time."

"Not the whole time," Sarah answered, her voice steady but eyes set and hesitant. "I didn't start out alone, spent the first while with friends from Carnd. We traveled east. Had plans to go all the way to the Burned Coast and get a ship to the Irradiated Isle, but...well, then I started towards Varinz alone." *Then you dropped him and then the rest of them hated you. They hated you so much they tried to kill you and then you ran and ran and ran.*

"What happened to them?" Tony asked, his words tact. He could see the haze in Sarah's eyes.

And then I ran. "We all went our own way after a while."

Tony and Ri both nodded, but said nothing else about it. *They are questioning you now,* said the hate inside Sarah's mind. *Will you fail them too? Will you drop Ri down a cave and lose them forever too? Will Tony hang you from the rafters for convincing him you could carry them up a mountain? Will--*

All at once, a low, baritone hum cut into Sarah's thoughts. At first she thought she had finally gone mad, that her failures had caught up with her and broken her mind, but as she glanced at the others she realized that the hum came from Tony. His big hand thumped on his chest in a steady, percussive rhythm.

"The clouds might sail the ocean sky

From east to thundering west,

Their shadows racing cross the clay

To chase the sun to rest. "

Ri joined in then, their own voice whispery and soprano in a way that, to Sarah, felt angelic. A sunset contrast to their scared and muscled body.

"But none could run like Luther, son,

A rambler born to ride.

They say each road has known his tracks

Across the countryside."

Sarah watched them, the old Rending-Era folk song filling the air as they walked. Only Tony's drumming hand kept beat at first, but before long the three of them stepped in steady rhythm to the music.

"But none could run like Luther, son,

A rambler born to ride.

They say each road has known his tracks

Across the countryside.

But none could run like Luther, son,

A rambler born to ride…"

They sang like that for a long while, working their way through the "Ballad of Luther Dotson", "Songs to Sing as Men go Crazy", and even ancient songs, strange and unusual in their rhythms, like "Shady Grove", "Arkansas Traveller", and "The Times, They Are a Changin".

Soon, just as their voices tired and the songs died out, the sound of rushing water grew louder, and Sarah jogged ahead as the pond came into view. She took off her pack and pulled out the fishing cords she had prepared for the group and a small bag of dried meat. Sibella rested on the ground nearby, watching close with wanting eyes. Before long, they all began to pull in fish after fish. Sarah kept careful note of how many they pulled in, their sizes and their sexes, hoping to keep the fish population healthy in the way her mother had taught her when they fished the Lake of Bridges. She had never understood how two women with hand lines could over-fish a lake that seemed to stretch on for an eternity, but each time she cast a line into the water, her mother's words echoed in her mind. *We must be stewards of the land, for it is the only one we can ever have.* Still, she could not help but give in to Sibella's gazes. More than once she fed him a fish too small for their meals.

Tony let out a quick chuckle and cast his line into the pond. "If you'd told me ten years ago that I'd be fishing in the ruins of Calarine I'd have called you a fool." He twitched at the line as Sarah pulled in a fair-sized catfish.

"What were you doing ten years ago?" Sarah asked. "Were you a traveler then?"

"I was still in Tinkret. Left there almost six years ago." He paused for a long while, his hands working the line and his eyes far away. "I've been a lot of places between then and now, was a...I led a different type of life for a while, but the road takes us all at the end."

"What made you leave Tinkret?" Sarah asked.

"The Creep took my family."

Sarah held her line in her hand and looked at Tony. "The Creep?"

"Plague from the North Country," Ri interjected. "Nasty stuff. Never made it past the Center Line. The High Order put an end to it. All you'll find here now are Sicks, folks that survived it."

Tony was watching the ground, half paying attention to his line in the pond. His jaw worked into tight knots.

Sarah turned her attention to Ri. "How did they stop it?"

"They did what the empire does." Tony answered, and underneath his voice was a growl, a subtle rage.

Sarah thought of her little fishing village and how it changed when the empire's navy sailed in, claiming it and all it had as their own. Her heart felt heavy in her chest. "I'm sorry. Losing your family and your home like that...I'm sorry."

Tony nodded, and the three of them fished for a while in a thick silence. Sibella, who had been spending time begging for fish and chasing the field mice, came to Sarah's shoulder. "We need to make a fire, hmm?" he asked. The falcon flicked the leaves and grass from his feet as he rested on Sarah's shoulder, waiting for an answer.

Sarah nodded and together Ri and her gathered wood and prepared the fire. They spoke little to one another as they did, sharing quick glances and wry smirks. Sarah, more than once, watched the way Ri's body moved as they stooped, gathering bundles of firewood into their broad arms. She thought about the way she had stood in between the door and Ri and had her chance. *Lost your chance.*

"No, not lost," she said out loud, not realizing it.

Ri stopped, having just come back from taking wood to the burn pile. "What was that?"

Sarah froze, her back straight and stiff and the realization falling as the heat rose into her neck. "Nothing, sorry, talking to myself."

She gave a nervous smile and tried to turn away. Ri walked by her towards the tree line, but as they passed they brushed against Sarah. Just the tips of their fingers grazed Sarah's ribs, but it was enough. Sarah paused in her tracks, her mind reeling as she tried to convince herself to turn around. When she did, Ri was already twenty feet past, almost to the tree line. Sarah watched them walk the rest of the way.

As the sun began to set, Sarah lit the fire and the three of them made their places around it. Sibella scratched out a cool spot of earth near Sarah, and as they all settled in, Tony drew Sarah's attention as he knelt down at the foot of his bedroll and prayed. She watched him as he kneeled, long and silent, the movement of his lips barely visible in the firelight. Once he finished, he laid back on his bedroll and stretched his legs.

"You keep the Old Faith?" Sarah asked and almost at once she hoped she hadn't offended him. Once a wide, knowing smile broke out on his face, though, she knew she hadn't.

"I do. Have for a while. You have to pick your way to keep the light burning, whatever it is. Old faith is mine."

Sarah nodded, sitting up with her arms around her knees. "I wasn't raised around it. We didn't have a church in Carnd, but I think some of the old folks might have practiced in private."

"Many do."

"I've always just tried to follow where the stories lead

me. At least since I left home."

"Faith of the Seven, then?"

"No, nothing that formal"

"We all try to make sense out of this world when we're alone. Most travelers I meet are at least a little religious. Most of the soldiers I knew were very religious. Proximity to violence breeds it, I guess."

"You were a soldier?"

"In a way. Soldiers come in a lot of forms, I guess--"

Sarah watched as the words caught in Tony's throat. She then saw Ri shifting, uncomfortable on their bedroll. The strangeness of everything settling in, Sarah saw that Tony stared at the ground and dropped the subject, unsure what Ri's uncomfortableness might mean. Unsure what else to say, or how to say anything in the silence, Sarah laid down. The three of them settled into the quiet night around them.

The night was cool. A soft breeze wafted across the banks of the creek, and before long Tony slept hard, his snores echoing through the empty wastes. As the sounds of the wilds mixed with the rumblings of their friend, Sarah and Ri stirred, both unable to sleep in the lingering tension. Ri sat up and looked out across the moonstruck creek, their eyes watching the light dance across the gentle waves of the pond. Sarah glanced at Ri before rising herself.

"You okay?" asked Sarah, careful to whisper to keep from waking Tony.

In the moonlight she saw Ri nod, their hands rubbing at their knees. "Just restless," they said, still looking across the pond.

Sarah half-crawled across the thin patches of grass

along the bank and came to sit beside Ri. "What's going on? We didn't upset you with the religious stuff, did we?" Sarah tried to watch Ri's face in the dual shadows of the moonlight and flickering fire. All she saw was far away contemplation.

"No, you didn't. I'm just thinking." Ri ran a hand through their hair. Its ragged ends had started to grow out since they arrived at the Belhaven.

"About?"

In the shadows, Ri looked at Sarah and glimmering streaks danced under their eyes in the strange night light. A bizarre mix of stoicism and anxiety seeped into the air around them. "I've lost family before. I've lost friends before. I don't want to do it again."

Sarah gave a soft smile and reached out, putting a hand on Ri's arm. She had expected them to be trembling, but instead she found them stern and strong and cold. "I'm not letting this fall apart, don't worry about that." Sarah closed her eyes and fought to keep her mind clear, to stay present.

The firelight behind them created dark contrasts as the moonlight highlighted the water's surface. The hard lines of Ri's face were framed in the long hanging strands of their hair and accented their dark, deep set green eyes. Sarah felt the chasm between them then. Her years on the road and anxiety pulled away from Ri's tired, stoic nature. Sarah had stopped talking, and she felt the tension crackle between them. There was a dance of light in the space between their eyes as the moon glimmered in its transient sky. Ri leaned in and their lips touched for a moment that seemed to exist in its own realm of time. Neither of them spoke afterwards, their eyes still set on one another and the sounds of the creek seemed to push away everything around them.

Then, without a word of hesitation, Ri stood and walked away. Sarah watched in a state of confused confliction, unsure what to do. Her own mind reeled with the suddenness of everything that had happened. The kiss. Ri's soft, warm lips. The little scar, white and neat and imperceptible, that Sarah hadn't known rested just along the edge of Ri's bottom lip until her's had touched their's. She watched Ri sit on the bank further down the creek, staring out across the darkness away from the fire. Sarah stood up and went back to her own bed, resolved that it was not a good idea to press Ri, to try and pry away whatever it was that had caused Ri to walk away. She laid awake in the long stretch of night. The taste of Ri's lips still lingered on her mind.

MICHAEL

As Sarah and the others made their way to the pond, Michael wandered through the library, listening to Jane and Pinn on the second floor. He thought about climbing the stairs to check on them, but heard Jane bark at Pinn to go downstairs and get a spare blanket and decided against it just as the sound of the boy's moccasins echoed down the stairs. Jane and Pinn came and went from the second floor, building what Michael would have called a fort despite the insult the childish word might carry for his defiant daughter. All the while, Michael worked on the first-floor fiction section, moving books and shifting collections the best he could alone.

Finch sat down at one of the tables where she pulled out a pouch of tobacco and a stack of papers. Another of her romance novels was stuffed into her back pocket. "Need any help?"

"I think I've got it," Michael answered. "Where'd you get that poison?"

"Bought up a bunch of it in Varinz on the way here." Finch rolled the cigarettes one after another, never taking her eyes from her task. "Where're the kids?"

"Coming and going from the second floor. I think they're building a fort."

Finch raised her eyebrow and gave a half-grin. "A fort? Ain't much a teenager needs for a fort besides--"

"Once they're settled in I plan on checking on them to see exactly what they're up to, don't worry."

Finch nodded, still smiling, and took out a pack of matches and started to light a cigarette.

"Woah, woah. Can you do that outside? Let's not smoke up the books, okay?"

Finch stopped with the cigarette halfway to her mouth and gave a dejected, sarcastic chuckle. "Are you serious?"

"I am."

"Who gives a shit?

"Me, first of all. I would hope that you would care, considering you live here now."

Finch rolled her eyes and put the matches into the front pocket of her shirt. She groaned as she left the table, walking with heavy, frustrated steps towards the courtyard doors. Michael shook his head, wondering to himself if Sarah realized how resistant Finch was to becoming a member of their little community. He pictured Finch's bronze face scrunched in aggravation as she sucked down the thick tar one pale stick after another, mumbling to herself about his "fucking nerve."

As Michael heard the doors to the courtyard close he went back to moving books, assigning them to their correct places just as Sarah had taught him.

As he worked, Michael noticed a book bound in red on the top shelf. It stood out, brilliant and crimson amid the lines of white and black and gray. He worked a ladder into the corner that bordered the staircase and started to climb. As he reached the fifth rung of the ladder his knees began to shake, his mind focused on the ever-increasing height. He stopped and wrapped both arms around the ladder in a bear hug as he clenched his eyes. He could feel the frames of his glasses pressed against the wooden rung as he trembled against it.

"Come on, move dammit," he said, praying his arms loose and forcing himself further up.

Knees still trembling, he looked up and focused on the red book. As he neared the top of the ladder, he stretched and clawed until his fingers found their mark. He gripped the book and pulled but felt a strange mechanical click, and the book refused to move any further. It hung, balanced half off of the shelf as the gentle sound of grinding stone came from below. Unable to look down into the heights, Michael instead made a cautious descent, only turning around once his feet rested on solid ground.

As he turned, he saw that a small doorway had appeared in the stone wall beneath the staircase. He walked over and ran a hand along the opening. He saw the outline where the stone had slid into the floor. The doorway was small, so small that as he stepped in he had to duck to avoid edges of the entryway. The smooth walls gave way to a narrow cobblestone staircase that spiraled downwards into the depths of the library. As he worked his way around the tight turns he wondered if Sarah had forgotten to tell them about a basement. It wasn't until the light dissipated from above and floating orbs of blue light illuminated the way that he wondered if Sarah knew about the stairway at all. He stopped on the stairs and looked ahead, unable to see where they ended. He worried about Jane and Pinn, or Finch for that matter, finding it and following him. But the path ahead called out to him, and he was compelled to continue on. He followed the cramped staircase as it wound further into the world beneath the Belhaven.

After what felt like hours, Michael came to the bottom of the staircase and a bright array of blue magelight almost blinded him. It was the same light that had illuminated the stairway, shining orbs of brilliant blue light much the same as those Sarah had thrown at the fang walker, though Michael had no way of knowing that. They felt, at least to Michael, totally inhuman. Ageless in a way that reflected not an Aetic's hand or the careful crafting of spell books, but stardust. As his eyes adjusted, he saw that the room was a shrine, its walls made of a bright white limestone and the floor was painted, smooth-ground stone arranged in an alternating pattern of blue and white. At the center of the chamber was a large round table, and on that table stood a small statue, no more than a foot high. As Michael crossed the room, he realized it was a statue of Goraln made of white marble. He adjusted his glasses and looked it over, never noticing the way that the magelight had begun to dance around him.

Deep set in the tabletop was an array of gems arranged in a circle around the statue, each one a different hue of blue.

As Michael studied them, he ran his hand over them and wondered where so many blue stones could have come from. As he came to the darkest stone, its color like that of a deep, unending pool of water, a wave of energy filled the room. An invisible fount of power poured into him, and he braced himself against the table to keep from dropping to his knees. As the energy quaked through him, he felt an intense burning erupt in his palm and he started to scream, but the sounds became lodged in the back of his throat. All he managed was a single, near-silent rasp that tore at the cords in his neck. He felt the heat in his hand climb up his arm and into his chest, and for a moment he wondered if his age had caught up to him. He wondered if the feeling was not magic but instead a great beast of a heart attack come to rend him from this world into the darkness of the void beyond. But that fear faded as the heat reached his eyes.

He felt as if he was transported to a new world. His vision filled with swirling imagery. Beautiful washes of color shifted and rolled through his mind. A bright flash of startling silver interspersed with vibrant hues of red and white that danced and danced in the searing stage of his mind. At the back of his thoughts--or what he thought were his thoughts, even though he was unsure what anything was in that moment--rested a writhing mass of black and purple. Huge and tendriled and terrifying. Those dark colors seemed to watch the other dancing images of paint with a menacing intensity that curdled the blood in his veins. As the colors began to dissipate, he felt a spark of brilliance at the back of his mind, the words *You might be the one I need* seemed to dance across his vision as if crafted by great calligraphers with the pens and ink of a long-ago age. As his vision returned to normal and the burning retreated from his body, he pulled his hand from the table. He collapsed onto the patterned floor and sucked in long, whistling breaths.

"God above," he said aloud, his voice weak and tired, "what the fuck was that?" He ran his hands through his mess of gray hair and looked around the chamber, still sitting on the floor. All at once a strike of panic and confusion hit him. He didn't know how long he had spent there. He scrambled to his feet and bolted from the shrine, racing up the stairs as fast as his exhausted body would carry him. The hovering magelight transitioned to natural light and his heart eased. He realized that the light at least meant the hidden door was still open. As he came to the top of the top of the stairs and through the narrow doorway, he saw the first-floor fiction section remained unchanged. The sounds of his daughter and Pinn echoed down the main stairs, and, hoping he had enough time, he climbed the ladder towards the red book above, each step up punctuated with a whispered "fuck," until he reached the top and shoved the crimson tome into its home. As he descended the ladder he heard the soft grind of stone and when he turned around, the doorway was gone and in its place was the stone wall.

Michael let out a sigh and rubbed his eyes, his face gaunt and exhausted. He heard footsteps and whirled on his heels to see Finch walking through the stacks.

"God have mercy," she said, a confused look on her face. "You look like death, what happened?"

"How long has it been?"

Finch shook her head, not a no, but instead a motion as

if she was trying to shake Michael's words from her ears. "What?"

"How long since you went to the courtyard?"

"Ten, maybe fifteen minutes. Mike, are you okay?"

Michael ran a hand through his hair. He took off his glasses and hung them from the collar of his shirt with a shaking hand. "No...yes...I don't know. I think I overdid it is all. I don't do well with heights."

Finch placed a sympathetic hand on Michael's shoulder and led him over to a table where he sat down. "Wait here, I'll go fix you some water."

As Finch walked towards the kitchen Michael glanced behind him towards the empty corner that he now knew hid a deep secret. Flashes of paint danced in his mind.

SARAH

Sarah stood along the pond's edge, the soft morning sunlight warming her back. She tied her hair up, already feeling the sun and its heat driving sweat down her chest. As she looked out across the water she found herself lost in thought. Her mind pirouetted between Morable and the creek bank. With each spinning return to the creek she could taste Ri on her lips, feel their hands on her. Each step of her mind's eye ballet sent her heart into a lurching, reeling soar. She looked back to the camp where the others were clearing the fire and packing their things. Ri was closing their pack, all the while chatting with Tony. The two shared a quick glance, but a stab of tension forced their eyes from one another.

"We should get back towards the city," said Sibella. He had spent his morning skittering along the creek banks searching for crawfish, but now he was at Sarah's feet. "We are running quite low on rice and such things, and I do not think we'll find that in a creek."

"Rice?" said a voice unfamiliar to all of them. Sarah's head snapped towards the sound, and her eyes scanned over the stranger. He was a tall, broad shouldered man with gray-flecked hair, standing just a few feet from Sarah's bed roll. Sarah rejoined Tony and Ri at the camp and they watched the man, nervous expressions on their faces. Ri's hand rested on their hunting knife.

"Who are you?" Sarah asked. Her eyes looked the man over again. His traveling leathers were ornate and tailored.

"Bolivar Jackson, and you must be Sarah Silvergrove." His voice was a deep baritone that oozed confidence. His face was hidden behind a thick, close-cut beard, but his smile still shined out from underneath.

She studied the lines on the bearded man's face, the newness of his clothes. His boot heels seemed worn, the creases and lines of his tunic seemed dinged, but overall the clothes seemed fresh in a way that felt unnatural. "Do I know you?"

"I'm a traveler," he answered, giving a wide, fox-like grin. "I heard your call about the library. I was headed that way when I saw smoke and came to see who could be camping so close to my destination. Turns out, it was you."

"Your clothes are a might clean for a traveler," Ri prodded. Unease seeped out of their voice. Their hand tightened on the knife's handle.

Bolivar gave a laugh, his neat beard jostling with the movement of his head. He paid no attention to the placement of Ri's hand. "I stopped in Varinz on my way from the Center Line and bought these clothes and this bag." His answer seemed careful, planned in a way that would have taken days to perfect. He was patting the palm of his right hand on a fine satchel slung across his right shoulder. Ri looked at Sarah, tense. Bolivar had not taken his eyes from Ri. "What kind of warrior are you? I can see that fight in your eyes."

"I'm no warrior. Just a traveler."

Bolivar flashed a knowing smile and looked at the others, seeming to expect more interrogation.

"You don't seem like a traveler," said Sarah. Her fist now clenched tight on the shaft of her walking stick. "I've traveled a long time. Seen a lot of people, and many were well kept and smiling like you, but they were all from the cities. Most of them wore Imperial Regalia or Aetics' robes."

"Well then, I suppose you have me nailed down pretty well, daint. I'm not what you'd call road-worn just yet. I've only been traveling for six months. I had made it to the eastern bank of the Pearl River when I heard your call. What do you think me, a Tranlor shapeshifter? I hope I don't look that out of place."

"You're not a Tranlor, I can tell that much, but what were you?" Tony asked, his face stern and arms crossed. The words rolling off of his tongue in a thick Northern dialect layered with anger. He didn't have a hand on his ax, it was already tied tight to the side of his pack, but his feet were set and ready to move.

Bolivar's face knotted up in confusion and he tilted his head. "Sorry?"

"What were you before you started traveling? What was

your trade?"

"Ah, I see. I was a teacher. I taught mathematics in Rinz, a burbish outside of the Capitol."

Tony scoffed and clenched his crossed arms. "A burbish? I guess that's one way to look at it. More of a training ground for young militants."

The same fox face had returned to Bolivar, his eyes tight and peering over bushy cheeks. "I suppose that's right. The imperial military has a strong presence there. That's why I left. I lost the taste for military education."

Sarah glanced at Tony, who's eyes seemed to search across the creek bed, uncertain. She closed her own eyes for a second, working through the whirlwind of thoughts in her mind, unable to find a reason to turn the man away. "Well," she said, rubbing a hand on her heavy freckled cheek, "like my call said, we've made a home for travelers at my library." Sarah thought she could feel the hesitation coming from Ri and Tony in waves, but as she looked into the man's gold-brown eyes she felt a sense of conflict she could not vocalize. As he looked at her from underneath his heavy, hooded brow she could not decide if she wanted to run from him, fight him, or welcome him into her arms. She thought of the men along the ridge outside of Varinz. The man in the Skeeving Fink. Their smarmy, slurring faces, different from Bolivar's only in his relative lack of alcohol. Still, she also thought of an old friend, one of the many who had pushed her away along that salty Morable coast. Deep set and kind eyes always searching for a challenge. She didn't know which resemblance unsettled her more.

"Well, I hope you have room for me there. I've come a

long, long way to get to this place."

"Of course, like I said in my call, 'I call to those who seek shelter.' If that is what you're looking for, then I have no reason to turn you away."

Bolivar smiled. This time, though, it seemed innocent and real. It was like a switch had been flipped, and in the place Sarah had once seen a fox's sly deceptions she now saw earnest, genuine happiness. A twinkle of light, just the slightest glimmer of kindness, came from his eyes as he reached into his satchel and pulled out a large bag of white rice, marked in the clear labels of the Varinzian markets. "I think you were saying that you needed rice, right? It just so happens that I picked this up in Varinz. Comes from the fields of the Broken Coast, if the merchant is to be believed."

"Well," sarah said, turning to the others, "let us finish packing up, then you can follow us back to the Belhaven. It isn't far. Once we're there, we can get better acquainted." As she turned away, an excited Bolivar dropped the bag of rice back into his satchel. Sibella came to rest on Sarah's shoulder and brushed his paper crafted face against the side of her head, but she paid no mind. She was back on that salted coast.

CHAPTER VII

A Shrine Unknown

==

It was early morning when Sarah and the others arrived at the Belhaven, Bolivar in tow. Just through the doors, Michael greeted them with a happy smile and flailing wave, his hands full of books.

"Finch, kids!" Michael called out. "Sarah's back." He wiped his hands on his pants and stuck one out to Bolivar, who accepted it. "Who do we have here?"

The library buzzing around its newcomer, Finch and the kids came filing in, looking Bolivar over as well. Sarah placed a cautious hand on Bolivar's right shoulder and smiled at Michael.

"This is Bolivar Jackson. He heard our call, and we met along the creek east of the library."

"Well, welcome!" Despite his smiling face and excited voice, Sarah saw the exhaustion in Michael's eyes. Dark circles hid in the space behind his glasses. "It's good to have you here, and good to have everyone else back."

Finch gave a nod to Bolivar, her eyes scanning over him, his tall, impressive frame creating the slightest smile at the corner of her lips. "Good to meet you." Her rasped voice seemed strained towards something more personable.

"Dad we're hungry," a snarky voice broke in. Sarah looked to see Jane standing behind Michael, her arms crossed in an impatient stance. Neither she nor Pinn seemed concerned with Bolivar's presence.

Michael gave a glance to his daughter and smiled. "Well, let me fix some breakfast while you show our new friend around. Jane, Pinn, you two come with me and help me cook so that everyone doesn't have to wait all day."

As Michael and the kids headed towards the kitchen, Sarah led Bolivar to the living quarters, the others close behind. She could hear Finch talking to Bolivar, telling the story of how she ended up in the library. She heard the tobacco-tinged rambling but could not bring herself to pay attention to the conversation outside of the bloated, giddy chuckles. Instead, even on the short walk from the lobby desk to the living quarters, she found herself trapped in a cycle of worry and frustration. While the others talked and carried on with their normalcy, Sarah felt an ever-growing weight on her shoulders.

"Here's where everyone sleeps," she said as they reached the row of cots. "We've got a free bed, it'll be up to you if you move it around."

"I take it you don't sleep here with everyone else?" Bolivar asked. His big arms were crossed, and he leaned back just enough to make it seem as if he was waiting for the punchline of a bad joke.

Sarah pointed to the administration offices, squinting at him. "I have a private office. It's in the back of that room over there, if you ever need me." *No one else has asked that question.*

"I will say," Tony chimed in, "these cots are a lot more comfortable than they look. Best sleep I'd had in a long time."

"Did you make them?" Bolivar asked, now looking at Tony.

Tony smiled and shook his head. He almost looked

embarrassed by the question, like it was a compliment. "No, I'm about as good with a hammer as I am a politician's podium. Sarah made them, I believe."

"Not like you might think, though," said Sarah, pushing a long curl out of her eyes. "I used magic to do most of the work."

Bolivar raised an eyebrow and scratched at his beard. "Magic, hmm?" He started to ask more, but the sound of the swinging door and smells of breakfast broke everyone's attention.

"Come on then," Michael called out from the tables nearby. "I hope you people did manage to get some food, because this is the last of the meat."

"We did," Ri answered as they sat down next to Tony. "Plenty of fish and a few eggs too."

Everyone took their seats as Michael moved back and forth bringing plates of fish and rice. The last of the others seated with their food, he sat down across from Bolivar and gave a nod as everyone started eating. "Hope it's good, this is the last meal I hope to cook for a while. Typically Sarah and Ri do the cooking, and they're a lot better at it than I am."

Bolivar gave a wide, toothy smile and shrugged. "Tastes fine to me, friend. Fine to me. Thank you."

"Our friend here was a teacher," Sarah said, pointing to Bolivar. "In Rinz, I think he said."

"Rinz?" Michael asked between bites of fish. "How'd you end up in a military town?"

"I was born into that world," he answered. The words rolled from his mouth like honeyed wine. "Grew up in the Capitol, entered into an apprenticeship as a mathematician when I was a young man. I ended up as a teacher to young soldiers from there because it was the job that paid the most. Coin doesn't matter much to a traveler, but it is everything in that world. Specie is wealth, hard and fast."

"We all know that well enough," Ri interjected. "None of us were born travelers, you know, except the kids. We've all scrounged for a little coin before."

"Why'd you leave that life?" Tony asked as he polished off his breakfast. "I can't imagine leaving the cushy life of a noble."

"Wasn't as nice as you think, I'd wager. It was like living in confinement. Surveillance twenty-four hours a day, rhetoric of my entire life eaten up by propaganda and imperial speech. Military tradition dictated my schedule, the empire dictated my job. I was expected to buy full stock into every drop of it." Bolivar was picking at his front teeth with his pinky nail now, his chair leaned back on its hind legs.

"That right?" interrupted Ri from the other table.

The vitriol in their voice surprised Sarah. She noticed the muscles on their shoulders standing out, tense and aggravated. A look of discontent rested on their squared face, the thin lines of their lips working to hide the frustration apparent in their eyes. Sarah thought for a moment that maybe it was Crown Soldiers who had taken them; that Ri hated Bolivar because of the world he represented. Their stern face cut through the air, but Bolivar showed no interest.

As he looked at Ri with a gaze of near-total disregard, the gray flecks in his hair glimmered in the morning light. "That's right. That's why I left. I helped with efforts in Rinz and the Capitol to fight back against all of that the best I could, but they started to get wise. So, I took my money and I left."

Ri, still doubtful, started to speak up, but Bolivar had captured the imaginations of Michael and Tony, who now leaned against the table and listened close to his words.

"What do you mean you helped fight back?" asked Tony. His demeanor had shifted to a more positive one, but an air of caution still hung around him in a haze.

"Oh, nothing grand. No freedom fighting. No paramilitarism. All I did was provide resources to those that did the actual fighting. I tracked down medicine, arranged shelter. That sort of thing."

"Well, I imagine that was more help than you ever knew," said Michael. "What made you stop?"

"Someone I trusted came to me and told me that I'd been found out. I left as fast as I could and started traveling South."

"How long ago was that?" Sarah asked. She searched his bearded face with desperate eyes for something to wash away her doubt.

"Oh," Bolivar said, thinking for a moment, his eyes watching Sibella fly through the joists above. "Six months or so ago, I couldn't tell you an exact time. I've been more focused on staying hidden than anything else. Haven't kept up with the days, you know."

Ri gave an exasperated sigh and stood up, walking towards the administration offices. Sarah tuned out the rest of Bolivar's broad-chested boasting and instead listened to the sounds of Jane and Pinn jabbering in the background. Her mind wandered, and she thought of the way things had changed in just the short time since she'd come to the

Belhaven. Before long, she thought of the previous night, and with it she thought of Ri. She glanced over her shoulder and looked to where they stood scanning the books stacked in half-organized piles near the offices.

"What do you think, daint?" Bolivar asked. His voice cut through her daydreams.

"She's titled the librarian," said Michael, "but we typically don't go for the noble titles here."

"Like Michael said," said Sarah, shifting in her seat, "there's no need for all the glamor. Now what did you ask? My mind was somewhere else."

"I was asking what you thought about expanding the building. Maybe building a separate wing for housing?"

"We have plenty of room as it is."

"For now, but it might be worth thinking about in the coming weeks."

"I guess we'll deal with that when we get to that point," Sarah said as she stood up. "If you'll excuse me, I have some work to do. Bolivar, feel free to explore today. Get adjusted."

Just as Sarah walked away, she heard the sound of scraping chair legs from behind and turned to see Michael trotting to catch up with her. "Everything okay?" she asked.

"Oh, of course!" Michael ran a hand through his hair and Sarah could tell he was lying. He was nervous, exhausted. "This Bolivar guy seems all right, huh? A bit of a blowhard but a nice guy."

Sarah glanced over Michael's shoulder towards the table where Tony still sat with Bolivar. "Michael, what's going on? You look like you're a hundred years old."

Michael's face fell and he nodded. His eyes searched the

floor for an escape before he looked back to Sarah and took off his glasses. He rubbed at the corners of his eyes and sighed. "I just wanted to ask you if we could talk later tonight. I have something to show you that I think you'll want to keep between us. For now, at least."

Sarah's brow knotted and she feigned a smile. "Is everything okay?"

"Yes, yes everything's okay. Just find me tonight after dinner. We can meet at the front lobby."

Sarah nodded and Michael gave a forced smile as he turned around and walked back to the table, re-entering the conversation with Tony and Bolivar before he sat down. Sarah made her way across the first floor towards the administration offices, where Ri still stood half-scanning the piles of books nearby.

"Is he finished running his mouth?" Ri asked, never taking their eyes off of the books.

"Not really. Does seem that they are warming up to him, though. Michael likes him well enough."

The light of the library hung around them like a cloak, and when they looked at Sarah, they glanced, just for a moment, towards the group still sitting at the table behind them. "I'm sorry about last night."

"What's there to be sorry for?"

Ri stopped in their tracks and looked at Sarah, their green eyes shone like brilliant emerald flames. "Are you kidding? You're our leader. You're the one who called us here. You started this whole thing, and I jumped on you."

"Don't be ridiculous," Sarah snapped back. "It's not like I have some great power over you. And hell, it's not like what you did was exactly jumping on me. We kissed. Don't flatter yourself."

"Yeah, well that's not--" Ri cut themselves off. Sarah could see the physicality of them stopping their tongue behind clenched teeth. "Sarah, come on. There's a dynamic here that you have to understand. I wouldn't be Ri anymore. I wouldn't be Tony's friend or a member of the community. I'd be reduced to 'the leader's lover', and you know that. Maybe not at first, but that's where I'd end up. One way or the other. Your guardian, your soldier, or your toy. Their pick."

"You think I need protection?"

Ri closed their eyes and took a long breath. They pushed their hands, the broad-knuckled and calloused hands of a workmen, along the edges of their face. "Look, as much as you might want it to be, it's not an easy situation. Even if you think Michael won't think less of us, what about Finch? We don't really know her. And better than that, what about Bolivar, our new friendly visitor who just oozes imperial machismo. What about the people that come after him? The Old Faith preachers and northern traditionalists that might come with them? You can't tell me you're that short sighted. I hope you're not, since you called all of us here."

Sarah clenched her teeth, her frustration growing ever closer to anger. "So what are we supposed to do? I know you can feel all this the same way I do. Are we just supposed to tip-toe around it? I didn't realize when I sent out that message that I was signing up to be a fucking clergyman."

Ri said nothing. Their eyes again scanned the books with names like, King, Kipper, and Knight. They wore the same stern look of absolutism that they had at the pond. Sarah started to speak up, to ask Ri again what she was supposed to do, when the soft sound of fluttering wings broke the silence. Ri and Sarah both looked up to see Sibella perched on an unused sconce nearby.

The falcon shook out his feathers and gave a soft, almost inaudible kak. "Bolivar seems to have settled into the group well, hmm?" Noticing the concern in Sarah's eyes, he came down to be closer to the two of them. "Neither of you trust him, do you?" His strange, ethereal eyes looked over them both in careful motions. The worlds contained within screamed out, demanding answers from the two anxious figures in front of him.

"I don't," answered Ri. "I've seen too many like him, and they're never honest. Do you trust him, Sib?"

"I do not see any reason not to, at least not yet. It is fair to say he is an unknown, but all of you were to me."

"Ouch," said Ri, a grin on their lips.

Sibella did not seem to notice the sarcasm. "Sarah, what do you think?"

She ran a hand through her hair, still knotted in the early morning, and looked to Ri. "I think that he casts a different shadow than the rest of us, but he may just be fresher on the road. I know he's more educated, high bred. I feel like I need to put him in a position where I can keep an eye on him, at the least."

"He has military experience, if his tales are to be believed," said Sibella. "Perhaps he'd be well suited to security, whatever of that there is to do here. Placing him in a position of responsibility and direct, consistent subordination will allow you to keep track of his actions, would it not?"

"What do you think," she asked, looking at Ri, trying to ignore the tension that still crackled between them. "We haven't really messed around with titles here. Not yet, I don't guess."

Ri smiled, but to Sarah it almost seemed like a haggard expression was hiding just underneath the surface. "I think that it's your call, but I can tell you I don't want to do any security work. And I can't imagine anyone will have anything to say about him getting a title. All of this is new, so there's no reason anyone should have any expectations."

Pacing in little semi-circles there between the stacks, Sarah's eyes were hazed and hidden deep beneath the edges of her brow. As she stood, scarred thumb resting on the delicate edge of her chin, the chin her mother had always called the last remnant of her vagabond father, she tried to find some answer, but found nothing. Just a deep-down, lingering anxiety, the sound of falling somewhere behind her in a place she could not see. She let out a long, frustrated sigh and then brushed her thumb over her nose, trying to bring herself back into reality. "I'll talk to Bolivar later on, Sib. I think it's a good idea. It'll let me keep an eye on him, get to know him better. There may be nothing to worry about, but better safe than sorry, I guess. We could call him Peace Officer. That should clarify the role beyond any misunderstanding."

"Well, I will leave you to it then. Seems you have other worries as well." With that, the falcon flew back to the high joists above, leaving Sarah and Ri alone.

"Well, I have other things to do today," Sarah said, turning back to Ri. "When you've finished thinking this through, we can talk about it again. But I want you to know, I don't care what anyone else t--"

"It's not about what anyone else thinks." A noticeable pain coated Ri's words, but their face still held, stoic and placid as before. "I just...don't want to be the reason this whole thing falls apart. You're just starting to build this, and maybe it could be something. I don't want to ruin it."

Sarah, unable to help herself, gave a short, choked laugh. "I'm sorry, but get over yourself. If you think I'd let that happen, or...or that I would ever mistreat you if something happened, then maybe I need to do a little more thinking about this myself." *You've done it before. You've done it before, and you could do it again. Drop Ri deep down into a salt lined cave where the rocks wait.* Sarah struggled against herself. She knew that no matter what she felt, Ri, the broad shouldered and stern-faced Ri, needed certainty from her.

"I--I didn't mean that. I never thought you would do that or that...Fuck I don't know what I meant. I'm just afraid of losing you...this. Everything. I've lost shit like this before and I'm tired of losing. I'm tired of a lot of things."

"What's the difference between losing everyone and never having anyone? And if you think you're the only one here with loss in your past you need to take a longer look at the rest of us. Even the falcon has his own loss, Ri. I've lost people, more than you know."

Ri opened their mouth to speak, but closed it without a word. The two of them stood there for a moment, looking at one another. Sarah felt a pang of guilt sweep through her chest as she saw Ri's unmoved, placid expression.

Just as Sarah began to think that Ri might have been made of stone, their eyes darted to the ground and they folded their arms. "You don't know what I am, Sarah. You don't know what I've done. Stop acting--"

"Can you stop acting like you know shit about me?"

Ri's eyes cut into Sarah, but they said nothing. They stood as if a monolith, eternal and unmoving in their struggle, but beneath it Sarah thought she could see the glimmers of feeling. Of the same smiling, wanting face that had kissed her along the banks of the pond. Sarah ran her hands over her face and met Ri's eyes.

"I killed my friend, you know? I told them I was strong enough and it was a lie and they died. My other friends, one of them I had been in love with for years, pushed me away. One of them...threatened to kill me. I deserved it. I had failed them and--"

"Sarah, I'm sorry. I didn't--" Ri had taken a half-step forward, but still stood apart from Sarah, the echoing void between them seeming to go on as Sarah spun further and further inward. Inwards towards her own salted caves.

"I failed them and I hurt them and it was my fault. I was in love, I was scared and a kid. I just wanted to prove what I was. I called myself the leader of my own band of merry men, and we were supposed to do so much together, but I failed. I dropped them and it just...The rope went right through my hands." She held up her scarred and knotted hand, the pink reminder of her past almost shining. "Sometimes at night I can still feel the blood running off of my fingers."

Without warning, Ri took Sarah by the shoulders and pulled her in. They were close in height, Ri only a few inches shorter, but Sarah collapsed into Ri's arms all the same. Knees buckled and eyes red and streaming, Sarah looked up and saw that Ri was no longer a stoic figure, but now a stern and certain guard, a watching expression held in the corners of their eyes. Sarah put a hand, the rope-scarred hand of Morable, on Ri's face and traced the lines of their lips. They kissed, the sounds of the others, of Bolivar, still in the air around them.

That night, the taste of Ri's lips still on her mind, Sarah met Michael at the front desk. Everyone else, their bellies full of dinner and hands grasping cups that contained the last of Tony's mead, sat around a fire in the back courtyard. Even through the walls and heavy doors the laughter echoed through the Belhaven, a bouncing announcement of weary backs left to rest. Bolivar's laugh rang out the loudest of them all, bright and shiny like an old barfly might laugh as he tried to please his providers.

"We should move quick," Michael said. As he came to the desk, he looked over his shoulder with frantic, confused eyes. "No idea how long they'll stay occupied out there, and they may miss us if we're gone too long."

"Get going where? What is going on?" Sarah was whispering, even though she had no idea why.

"Come on, over here." Michael led her over to the corner where the non-fiction shelves met the staircase. The ladder still stood in the same place it had when he first discovered the shrine. He pointed to the red book on the top shelf. "Can you go up there and pull at that book?"

Sarah raised an eyebrow at him. "Can't you do it?"

Letting out a dejected sigh, Michael started up the ladder. This time, with hopes to outrun his fear, he raced up as fast as he could and pulled at the book before coming back down. As his feet plopped onto the ground, he wondered how ridiculous he had looked from Sarah's perspective, but the soft groan of stone drew her attention. As the hidden door disappeared into the floor, Sarah's eyes grew wide and she gaped at the entryway that appeared along the wall.

"Holy shit," she said. She turned back and forth between the hidden doorway and Michael, who just stood there, cleaning the nervous sweat off of his glasses. Sarah walked over to the door and peered down the stairway. "When did you find this?"

"The day you and the others left."

Sarah looked down the stairs and then back to Michael. "Did you go down there?"

Michael nodded, staring into a middle distance, his mind far off. "I did. We can go if you want, but I'd rather not."

"Why not?"

Michael ran a hand over his forehead. When he brought it away, he saw that it was damp with sweat. He gave it a hurried wipe on the hem of his pants. "The stairs go down beneath the library," he started, and then recounted the rest of his story. He told Sarah about the strange way the stairs grew dark and the magic that illuminated them as the natural light faded away. He told her about the shrine to Goraln, the stones wild and beautiful in their somber blue hues.

"I had a vision," he said, trailing off.

"A vision? What kind of vision?"

"Have you ever seen any of the artists that perform in the cities like Varinz? They're like…public painters?"

Sarah nodded. She remembered the one she'd glimpsed

just outside the Skeeving Fink on her way to the ruins. His canvas splashed with wild, animalistic veins of color that seemed to hold no reason or method.

"It was like that. I saw splashes of color and paint. It didn't make any sense, but I know in my heart it meant something, I swear on it."

"Have you had another one? Another vision I mean."

When Michael shook his head, Sarah looked back at the open doorway. Its endless staircase almost taunted her. She climbed the ladder and put the book back in its place, descending to the soft sound of stone sliding back into its rightful home.

"Don't tell anyone else about this," she said and placed a hand on Michael's shoulder. "Not Tony, Not Ri. Not even Jane."

CHAPTER VIII
Things Left Behind

===

SARAH

Sarah woke frustrated and exhausted. She had slept in fitful, disconnected bursts. Though the morning was filled with the joy of her and Ri, the evening's anxieties bore their way deep into her mind. Her dreams had warred with one another, ebbing from the gentle lines of Ri's face and the hidden shrine. She wondered if Michael had become the victim of some old curse or if it was something grander. Something important. Something powerful. A new challenge laid at her feet--the fate of the Belhaven laid in Michael's hands.

"Maybe it was just a magic deterrent," she had said to herself in the night. "Not a vision, but something like a poison dart meant to scare him away."

All at once a thought struck her and she scrambled to her feet, half stumbling, half clawing her way out of her bedroll. *The Alchemical,* she thought through rushing breaths and hurried to put on her clothes. "Sibella!" she called out as she hopped into her other pants leg. "Sibella, come here!"

As Sarah pulled on her boots, Sibella flew down through the joists and came to rest on her desk. "Is everything okay?"

Now dressed, Sarah leaned into Sibella, her eyes wild and frantic. "Don't mention a word about what I'm about to tell you, all right?"

Sibella nodded.

"Did the Alchemical hide a shrine underneath the Belhaven. A shrine to Goraln?"

Sibella cocked his head to one side. "No, not that I was ever made aware of. Did you find something?"

"Not me, Michael. Found it while we were all out at the creek and said that when he touched part of the shrine it gave him...a vision."

"Hmm, strange indeed."

"The whole thing is hidden. Switch is in a book in the non-fiction section near the stairs." Sarah sat at her desk now. Her brow tightened into thought-filled knots, her hands writhing over each other in a nervous cadence.

"Well, that answers that then. I've already told you before that the Alchemical never did anything with the books outside of the second floor, he never would have found that switch."

Sarah gave a long, whistling sigh and dropped her head into her hands. She felt like a popped balloon. "Well, there goes that I guess." *They're slipping.* "This's got me worried. Michael finding this just after Bolivar got here? I don't know, it feels... prophetic."

Giving no sign he had heard what Sarah said, Sibella turned his head up to the rafters and stared, silent and statuesque for a long while. "The others will wonder where you are if you sit around here much longer. I am certain there is time to figure out the shrine. Until then, the secret is sealed."

Sarah stood up, balled fist drumming against her thigh. As she left her office and headed out into the Belhaven, all she thought of was the salty air of the Morable coast. She saw those stairs, windings down beneath her library, and at the bottom, a cave floor, framed with broken memories. Unable to push the anxieties away, she made her way across the library, seeing the others stirring near their cots, the morning not yet shaken off. Despite knowing breakfast needed making, despite knowing that she should be checking on Michael, talking with Bolivar, Sarah felt herself drawing inward and instead went into the courtyard, closing the big french doors behind her. The morning light was at its full birth, but the high walls that surrounded the courtyard still filled the place with long shadows that danced against one another as the clouds above made their way across the sky.

As she walked across the courtyard, Sarah tried to focus in on the reality of the world around her, to ground herself in the there and then. She watched the way the grass disappeared beneath her footfalls, the edges of it curling up and around the soles of her boots. She listened to the crack of stray twigs and dead leaves as she walked. Standing by the fire pit, looking down at the way the ashes inside sat unstirred in the still air, Sarah tried to push away everything else, to find that grounding, but she could not. Despite her clawing efforts, she could not push the thoughts of Michael and his shrine away. She could not free herself from the agony of what to do with Bolivar. The thoughts swallowed her, and she stood, eyes locked on the fire pit but looking at nothing, perceiving nothing of the world around her. She did not feel the tears that pooled unbeckoned at the corner of her eyes, and she did not hear the door open behind her or the quiet movement of feet across the courtyard.

When Ri placed their hand on Sarah's shoulder, the sudden shock of being pulled back into reality caused Sarah to almost jump out of her skin, and Ri pulled their hand back, a thin, concerned look on their face.

"You all right?" Ri asked, putting their hands in their pockets, eyes watching Sarah without moving.

Feigning a smile, eyes still cloudy and unfocused, Sarah nodded. "Yeah, just had a rough night. Didn't sleep great. Came out here to try and clear my head."

"Well, if you want to clear your head, we could take a walk. Go out and look around in the ruins or something. Stir up a little trouble." Ri reached out and pushed at Sarah's shoulder, a smirk on their lips.

Before Sarah could answer, the doors opened again and Tony and Michael, smiling and laughing, came into the courtyard. The two were still stretching the night's sleep away, and as they came to stand with Ri and Sarah, Tony motioned back towards the doors.

"The children are asking about breakfast," he said, "so we were sent out here to inquire on its status."

"Never let anyone convince you you're in charge as a parent," Michael added, rubbing at the back of his neck.

"Right, sorry," said Sarah. "Came out here to catch my breath, got distracted."

"No, don't mean to rush you. We can handle it, no problem."

"Please, no," said Sarah, unable to help but laugh. Michael was smiling himself, still rubbing at his neck. "I appreciate it, but I don't want that and neither do the kids. Jane had to suffer so long before y'all came here. I can handle breakfast. Ri, want to give me a hand?"

"Just lead the way."

"Hurry," said Tony, taking on a mocking, concerned look, "the children might stage a coup if we keep them waiting much longer."

At least some of the tension melting away, Sarah laughed and jabbed Tony in the shoulder, following Ri out of the courtyard and towards the kitchen. As they passed Jane and Pinn sitting at the table nearest the cots, the kids stopped their chattering and pointed at Sarah.

"Come on already!" said Jane. "We're starving here!"

"We're hurrying, we're hurrying," said Sarah, her mind finally clearing enough to manage an honest smile. "Take it easy, neither of you will starve."

"You don't know that," said Pinn.

Waving a dismissive, mocking hand, Sarah continued on to the kitchen, and once there her and Ri put together a quick breakfast. They made a simple dish of eggs and rice, returning to the others with Sarah carrying the steaming skillet and Ri carrying the plates and a pitcher of water behind her. No sooner than Sarah sat the food down, Jane and Pinn fixed their plates, grabbed a glass of water, and clamored towards a table of their own. Finch, one leg thrown over the back of the bench at the main table, turned to look at the two kids.

"Hey," she said, her eyes halfway-squinted in an aggravated glare, "y'all say thank you to Sarah and Ri. If I had my vote we'd have left you to starve."

"Ha ha, mom," said Pinn, his face scrunched in youthful embarrassment.

"What did I say?"

Michael cleared his voice and shifted in his own seat to look at his daughter. "Jane?"

"Thank you," said Jane, no ounce of hesitation, eyes watching her dad until he turned back to his own plate.

"Thank you," said Pinn, Finch lingering just long enough to make both of the kids squirm in their seats before turning back and fixing her own plate.

Watching the whole thing, Sarah couldn't help but smirk behind her glass. She could remember her own mother frustrated and furious at her for the pure willfulness she sometimes managed to summon. She could remember her aunts, long after a cancer had taken her mother, screaming at her as she fled into the alleys near their small, dockside home, avoiding her chores again, knowing the fury that would wait when she got back. Despite how far away it all felt, it hadn't been that many years ago.

"Well?" asked Ri, and the sound of their voice pulled Sarah out of her reminiscence.

Hesitating only for a second before giving into the obvious, Sarah cleared her throat. "Sorry, I was daydreaming."

"Ri was telling me that you two were wanting to go on a walk," said Tony, leaned back in his chair, his eyes cutting towards the end of the other table where Bolivar and Finch were chuckling amongst themselves, "and I told them that I need a few things, construction odds and ends, if you two want to go to Varinz for us."

"And then I," said Michael, "said there were a few things I could use, too."

"I can conjure pretty much anything that any of you need, I think. At least, if you give me time."

"No, I don't think so," said Tony. "I'm needing some brewing things, pipes and such, and it would be harder for me to explain it than it would be for me to just walk to Varinz."

"And I would like a proper coffee pot so we can stop drinking hard boiled sludge," added Michael.

"What do you think?" asked Ri. "I wouldn't mind the trip."

Unable to help herself, Sarah smiled at Ri. "Fine with me, as long as Tony and Michael are okay holding down the library."

"Don't worry about us," said Michael, "we'll get on fine without you two."

"Okay, let me go grab my things and we'll get moving."

The rest of them stayed at the tables, Bolivar and Finch still chattering, the kids still off on their own, and Sarah and Ri both went to gather their things. Standing in her office, those thin strands of light coming from the high-set windows along the walls, Sarah stood and looked at her satchel laid open on her desk. She heard Sibella fluttering overhead, the first she'd heard of him since those earliest moments of the morning. The falcon came to rest on a sconce on the central pillar of the offices just as Sarah started sorting through her clothes, trying to be careful in her picking of the spares, trying to leave room for whatever they might be dragging back with them.

"Should I be preparing to go as well?" Sibella asked, preening at his feathers, the soft crinkle of paper catching the gaps between the sounds of Sarah's packing.

"Well," said Sarah, pausing with a folded cloth wrap full of dried fish, hand scratching at the back of her neck, "I don't know, Sib. Do you think you'd be okay waiting outside of the city? I feel like you'd draw a lot of attention if you were with us inside. I mean, talking and paper and all that."

"I don't exactly relish the idea of being stuck hiding the entire time, if it is just the same to you."

Walking over to the sconce and reaching up, halfway on the tips of her toes, Sarah scratched at the bird's chest. "Sorry we're leaving you behind, buddy."

"Yes, well. I do expect you to bring me something back."

Before she could tell him that she would, a knock came at the far door to the offices. "Come in!" Sarah called out.

As Sarah turned back to her packing and Sibella took flight back to the joists above, Tony came through the door.

"There anything I can help you get together?" he asked.

"No, I don't think so. Just getting together some rations, then I'll be done. Can you be sure Ri grabs some food too?"

"I think they've already got some packed, but I'll be sure to check. Thank you for taking Ri. I think this trip will be good for them."

Pushing a loose strand of curls from her face, Sarah looked up to where the light came through in dust-lit bands. "I think it'll be good for me too, Tony."

Sarah and Ri met at the front doors, packs slung over their shoulders, a winding of rope and bedroll tied to the bottom of Sarah's. At the bottom of Ri's pack, Sarah could see their own bedroll and a canvas tent. Sarah held her staff, leaning on it as Michael and the others came to see them off. Everyone chattering among themselves, Ri stood adjusting their pack on their back and their feet working back and forth in a kind of anticipatory shuffle. Just as Sarah was about to say they should be off, as much over the anticipation of getting on the road as in hope of easing Ri's apparent anxieties, Bolivar and Finch came to the front of the group, the big man pointing at Sarah, his beard hiding what looked like a toothy smirk.

"Hey, Sarah!" Bolivar called out, his big, booming voice louder than normal. Finch had her arm threaded through his. "Bring me back news of the state of it all, yeah? These city man's bones are aching for that bustle."

"Of course," said Sarah, trying to smile, but worrying that her face gave way to what was pulling at the back of her mind. That feeling that something wasn't quite right.

"We're burning daylight," Ri cut in, more than a tinge of irritation in their voice.

"You two take care, and try not to get in any trouble in town, yeah?" said Tony. In his outstretched hand he held a folded piece of scrap paper and a small cloth bag. Taking both, Sarah stuck the bag into her satchel and passed the list to Ri. "That should be plenty for everything," he said, nodding at Sarah as she opened the door.

Outside of the library, they stood at the foot of the massive stairs, looking out across the empty ruins at the sun, hanging high in the sky and ever closer to noon. Sarah started to say something, to poke fun at Bolivar, but as she saw the still-clenched jaw of Ri she decided against it, instead turning to face the path that led on towards Varinz. Those winding streets she had followed towards the library those few months before.

"We'll follow the streets along to the western edge of the ruins, and eventually we'll be able to see the Blinded Forest. Ready?"

"Lead the way, o' fearless leader," said Ri, some of that previous tension seeming to have eased.

Starting out along the blackstone street, Sarah rolled her eyes, unable to keep from smiling at Ri. They moved quick through the streets that led out of the ruins and towards the forest, with Sarah moving much quicker than she had on the day she came to Calarine. As she made her way back along those blackstone roads, the weeds taller now than they had been, the green devouring the ruined city still vibrant and stark against the rusting steel of the towers around them, Sarah could not help but see the lives left behind in the empty shell of a city. The people, like her, who had come searching for home, belonging, but finding nothing. It struck her, in the whirl of everything since she first sent out that call, that she had made that place for herself. Behind her, Ri's footfalls created the echo of her own, twin sets of crunching steps. They did not speak for a long while, Sarah turned inward and Ri watched the far horizons, looking over a city that it seemed they had never seen before.

"Did you and Tony come from Varinz?" Sarah asked, breaking the silence and sending a small flock of songbirds into the air not far from the road. She watched them as they fluttered into the empty windows of the towers nearby.

"No," said Ri, adjusting their pack, "we were further to the northeast when we heard your call, near the foothills of the Risen Range."

"This place isn't what I expected. What I had hoped."

"Really? The library, or?"

"Everything, I mean. The city, the ruins. I had no idea the library was here when I got here. It was hidden by runes, at least that's what Sibella told me. We don't have any idea why I could see it when no one else ever had."

"What happened to the runes? We didn't have any trouble finding it, once we heard your call."

Sarah stopped, holding her staff in one hand and looking at Ri, a confounded expression on her face. "I, uh. I have no idea. I haven't even thought of that."

"You didn't check to see if the runes went away after you sent out that call?"

"I never even checked to see if they were there to begin with."

Standing in the abandoned street, the field that ran between the forest and the ruins just within view, Ri burst into a cackling gale of laughter. They doubled over, thin tears forming at the corner of their eyes as Sarah stood, half-smirking and red faced, a hand absently rubbing at the nape of her neck. "Sarah, my god. We really are all flying by the seat of our pants."

"There isn't a manual for this! Cut me a break." Despite the bright heat flushing in her face, Sarah was starting to laugh too. "I can't believe I never even thought to look for them after I sent the call out."

"It's not just you," said Ri, catching their breath and putting an arm around Sarah's slumped shoulders, pulling her close. "I mean, me and Tony hadn't known each other but for a month when we heard your call, and we came anyway. We're all desperate for someone to trust, to depend on. Your bad luck, huh?"

Trying to feign a smile, Sarah nodded and shrugged Ri off her shoulders, pointing towards the field with her staff. "We need to get moving, cross the field and get into the forest. I want to camp on the far side." Ri just nodded, still struggling to keep from laughing, and as they walked on towards the field and the woods beyond, Sarah thought of Ri's words, of her bad luck. Of the bad luck she'd left behind so many miles to the south, where salt licked the air.

They moved through the forest with ease, Sarah mostly silent until they were well beyond the scrub brush and low-stand trees along the edges. Her mind was trapped in itself, the salt fresh on her tongue. She thought she could see Ri watching her from the corner of their eyes, a thin hesitation since the laughing in the street. A new uncertainty. As they moved into the heart of the forest, the old oaks and short-leaf pines around them casting heavy and unbroken shadows, Ri put a hand on Sarah's shoulder, stopping her.

"Hey, I'm sorry if I upset you back there. I didn't mean anything by it."

"It's fine, really."

"It isn't. You're doing fine. As the Librarian, I mean. You took us in. You gave me and Tony and Michael and those kids somewhere to be. To exist without, fuck...I don't know what I'm trying to say. Just, thank you, Sarah. Really."

"Thank you," said Sarah, swallowing down the relief she could feel making its way into her throat, trying to rattle her voice. She reached out and pushed at Ri's shoulder. "Now, stop killing time. We need to keep moving."

"Yes boss, of course, boss."

Reaching out and pushing at Ri's shoulder again, Sarah gave a mocking chuckle. As she stepped forward, her foot caught on a root, and instead of just pushing at Ri, she tumbled into them. The pair of them fell to the ground in a tangled heap. As they did, they crashed into a knot of hedge bushes, only just missing a thicket of greenbriars. Sarah let out a yelp that sent the birds nested in the hedges scattering into the air, the sound of their wings lingering in the air long after the sound of their fall had quieted. As they lay there in a tangle, Sarah's staff on the forest floor, her hair tangled in the bushes, they watched as the birds, a pair of titmice, came back to rest in the low pine branch just above them.

Without warning, Ri's hand shot over to Sarah, who was already halfway in their arms, and grabbed at Sarah's breast while yelling out, "titmouse!"

Cackling, writhing to get untangled from the bushes, Sarah slapped at Ri's arms. "You jackass," she said, finally managing to stand up. She leaned down to help Ri up, the birds overhead taking flight again.

"Sorry," said Ri, straightening their clothes and pulling the hedge leaves from their hair, "I couldn't help myself."

Sarah pulled her now-tangled hair back and tied it off with a length of leather cord. "Fuckin' tease," she said, bending over to pick up her staff. No sooner than she had it in her hands, she felt Ri pinch her ass, and not subtly. She shot upright and spun, whacking Ri in the shoulder with the end of her staff. "Quit that!" Sarah's own hand jerked out and she reached around, pinching at Ri's chest, who yelped, and as they did Sarah started running through the woods, dodging bushes and brambles as she did.

She heard Ri chasing after her, the pair of them laughing, cackling, as they ran through the Blinded Forest, the woods filled with cracking limbs and the sound of their laughter. As they came to a little clearing, a place where a massive, ancient magnolia stood broadleaved and eternal at the center, casting its impenetrable shadow to the forest floor, sending away all the brush that might hope to live beneath it, Sarah turned, staff held out in front of her, trying to talk through her gasping laughter. Ri never paused, dodging the staff and grabbing Sarah around the waist, falling to the ground with her in their arms. As they landed, Ri let out a sigh, trying to catch their breath, struggling to ease the laughing, and Sarah collapsed into their arms, her own breath just out of reach.

"You're pretty damn quick for a big one," said Sarah, reaching up and squeezing Ri's arm.

"A big one? Excuse me?"

"Oh kiss my ass, you know what I mean."

Unable to stop the smirk from creeping across their face, Ri squeezed at Sarah's arm before standing up and helping Sarah do the same. "Kiss you ass?" they asked, pushing their hair out of their face.

"What are you talking about?" Sarah asked, looking up from her satchell and seeing Ri's face.

"*Kiss your ass?*" Ri asked again, now grinning, their dark eyebrows raised.

Eyes widening, face flushing, a near match to her hair. "Tease."

Adjusting their own pack on their shoulders, Ri ruffled their hair and shrugged. "We'll see. Shouldn't we get moving? You want to camp on the other end of the forest, yeah?" Looking up at the canopy above, seeming to watch the gaps where the sky and sun peeked through the magnolia's canopy, Ri started off due west, on towards the edge of the forest.

Sarah stood for a moment, watching them walk, watching the way their body moved, their blonde hair caching the scant rays of light from above.

There along the edges of the forest they made their camp, close to where the treeline broke away to low brushes and field grass, dusk-tinged sunlight coming through in the spaces between. Ri stepped through the brush and towards the field beyond as Sarah unpacked her bedroll and settled her things, dropping her staff just beside her bed.

"What are you doing over there?" Sarah asked, scanning the interior of the forest for good firewood.

"Checking for rain. Sky looks clear, so unless you're antsy we don't need to put up the tent."

"I'm fine with the open-air. That's how I've always done it before."

"There's probably an hour or so left of daylight, we can leave the fire unlit for a while," said Ri, stepping back from the edges of the forest and unpacking their own things.

"Sure, yeah. I'll go ahead and gather some wood, but we can light it later. You worried about someone following us?"

"No, I don't guess. Just habit."

"Well, go ahead and get your stuff laid out, I'll get the rest of the firewood."

As they made their camp, with Ri placing their own bedroll just beside Sarah's, the forest moved and breathed around them. In those lengthening dusk shadows, the pair of them settled at the edges of the Blinded Forest, Sarah sitting cross legged on her bedroll, flipping through her copy of *The Left Hand of Darkness*, finding the pages she had marked in the years before, and Ri lounged, picking at their fingernails with a short skinning knife pulled from their bag. Stopping her reading, putting a finger on the page to hold her place, Sarah looked at Ri, hesitating for just a moment, before fully closing the book and turning to face them.

"So, I'm thinking about giving Bolivar some sort of position at the library."

"Right, yeah. The Peacekeeper stuff?"

"Peace Officer, I think? I don't know about any of it. I'm nervous that there's something going on. That I'm playing into something I don't see. That I'm gonna fuck it all up."

"I already told you to take it easy, to not overthink it."

"It's just," Sarah tossed her paperback aside and leaned forward, laying on her stomach, elbows holding her up and now eye level with Ri, "you've already said how seat-of-the-pants I've been running this thing, and…fuck I don't know. This doesn't seem like a seat of the pants kind of thing, you know?"

"Look," said Ri, stopping the work on their nails and looking Sarah in the eyes. Their own face held a sudden solemnness, a faraway reflection, "Don't let us fucking around about the runes get to you. It's funny, it's not a big deal. Now isn't the time to doubt yourself. I'm trusting you, Tony's trusting you. I'm not trusting the Belhaven's Keeper, I'm trusting you, Sarah."

Running her hands over her face, Sarah tried to believe what Ri told her, but her mind reeled and folded back towards that long ago coast. Sarah just nodded and dropped her head onto her bedroll. Ri reached over without a word, putting a hand in her hair, rubbing at the nape of her neck, saying nothing, only being there, in the moment. As the dusk-born shadows grew longer, Sarah raised her head to look at Ri. Their bright blonde hair was a monochrome light in the shadows, and, at first leaning into their hand, still held tight in her hair, Sarah pulled away, sat up, and shuffled half-squatting over to the unlit fire. Pulling a flint and steel from her front pocket, Sarah lit the fire and breathed life into it. Satisfied its glow would last, Sarah went back to her bedroll, laying back half-resting on her bag, her legs towards the fire. Once Sarah was settled, Ri too moved, coming closer to her, their head rested in Sarah's lap, legs stretched across her bedroll and into their own.

For a moment, Sarah's breath hitched as she watched Ri's movements, waiting. She waited for Ri's hands to move, to make good on their taunt from earlier, to make their way to her hair, to her chest, to her waist. But they didn't, and instead Ri just lied there, eyes watching the flames, head resting in Sarah's lap. Sarah just ran her hands through Ri's hair, her eyes watching their chest as it rose and fell with each careful breath. She watched as Ri's hands went back to the skinning knife, returning to the cleaning of their nails. Deft, defined hands making careful moments, never slipping, never pausing. It was then, as she watched in a near-mesmer as Ri lay in her lap that they turned their head to face hers, eyes all in shadows, but the brilliant whites shining out just the same. As their eyes met, Ri rose up on one arm, their other hand going to the back of Sarah's head, and kissed her. Again, Sarah felt her breath catch in her throat, her heart pick up its pace in anticipation, but instead of feeling Ri's weight shift onto her, instead of feeling their hands sliding beneath her shirt, she felt Ri ease back down, putting their head back into her lap.

"What did you do before this?" Ri asked, their voice a sudden knife through the heat and tension Sarah felt running across her body. "I mean, all of this. Everything."

"I'm not really sure. Nothing, really."

"I just mean at home. Before you took to the road."

"I mean it, nothing. I grew up along the Lake of Bridges. Mom owned a tavern. Dad was a fishmonger, supposedly, but I never met him. Mom died before I turned twelve, so I moved in with my aunts in the same little village.. They weren't...I don't know. I don't think they were bad people, but I hated them. I ran away as soon as I could." Sarah put her hand back in Ri's hair, eyes back to the fire. "You were a farmer, yeah?"

"Yeah, for a long time. I left home when my folks died. Meant to be a traveler, but...well. Things were different for a long time."

"That all I'm going to get?"

"Yeah, probably. For now."

Feeling the muscles in Ri's jaw tighten, Sarah let it go and instead ran their hand down the edges of Ri's neck, feeling the tightness there relax. She felt the scars there, too. Old things, knotted and unseen, just below the surface. Her hand lingered on those hidden scars for just a moment before moving on, before easing further down. She found her way to Ri's collarbone, staying there for only a moment before slipping beneath their tank top and resting her hand on their chest, fingers working slowly. Ri's breath quickened, their own hands laying the knife to their side before reaching up and resting on Sarah's waist, but that is as far as it went, where it stayed. The pair of them lay together, the fire warming them, as the forest grew ever darker. It was there they slept, the dusk of the forest ever deeper as it emptied into the ichor of night.

TONY

The night dark and full of stars, a fire burned bright in the Belhaven's courtyard. Along the fringes where the light was scant and casting strange and dancing shadows, Pinn and Jane sat tossing stones back and forth to one another, laughing, talking about things that meant nothing to anyone but the two of them. There around the fire, Bolivar sat on the ground, his long legs stretched toward the flames. Finch sat beside him, head half-leaned on his shoulder. Just to their right, Tony and Michael sat side by side on one of the lengths of the big pine Tony had hewed out with his ax, turning it into the closest thing to a bench he could manage. Somewhere overhead Sibella chased the lizards that lived along the eaves, white-orange things that seemed to Tony to barely have any consciousness. As he sat watching the light of the fire dance, he noticed in the corner of his vision that Bolivar's eyes scanned the upper edges of the library, the man's jaw tight, thinking.

"What's on your mind, Bolivar?" Tony asked, not turning from the fire. Beside him Michael near-startled, apparently somewhere far away in his own thoughts.

Bolivar's eyes turned to Tony, the fire catching in them and turning them to a deep, burning orange. "What's that?"

"I saw you watching the edges of the roof. If you're trying to catch sight of Sibella, it's a waste of time. He's damn near invisible in this night."

The big man chuckled, running a hand over his beard and readjusting in his seat. "Ah, no, I wasn't looking for the falcon. I was just looking along the edges of this place, those high spots where the third-floor windows are. Thinking about what sorts of things this place is still missing."

"Missing?" asked Michael, seeming to be back into the same reality as the rest of them.

Gesturing towards the dark, near where the edges of the high stone walls give way to the roof, Bolivar scratched at the side of his face. "Back before the Rending when this place was built, it wasn't built as any kind of fortress. I mean, it might not have been a library then, who knows, but it certainly was some sort of official thing like that, yeah? I mean, those high walls, no balconies on the upper windows. They don't even open."

"Sure, but what are you getting at? It isn't a fortress now."

"Well, sure. Not yet. I mean, if Sarah plans to keep this place, she's eventually going to have to fight for it."

"Sooner rather than later, you ask me," Finch cut in, picking at her front teeth with her nail.

"I think if we added some balconies to some of those upper windows, fixed them where they can open up, that would give us easy roof access. Make it easier to build some ramparts or something up there. It's a pitched roof, so it'll take some doing, but I think me and you can manage, yeah Tony?"

"I don't see why it would be a problem," said Tony, his eyes back to the fire, his mind somewhere far away. The words came as if from beyond him, a thing of instinct. He could feel Michael on the other side of him, back to his own world. He could hear the kids beyond even that, Pinn telling Jane about the time that he and his mom had lived for a while in Hattin. Above it all he could feel Bolivar's dark eyes watching him, and he swallowed. "Between me, you, and Ri, I imagine we can manage about anything that needs doing."

As the night carried on, as the sounds of the courtyard perpetuated one another, the flickering of the fire, the chattering of the kids, the soft breathes of Finch, Tony thought of the life he had left behind. Of the weight of a sword on his hip, of the way the steel felt in his hand. He thought of the smells of the battlefield, and more than anything he thought of the faces of the men he had once stood with. He thought of how their eyes always seemed to carry that cunning hunger, like a fox on the trail.

CHAPTER IX

Old Habits

===================================

SARAH

The edges of Varinz stretched on for nearly a mile around the city walls. It was a sight that still took Sarah aback, despite having seen it before. It was a twisting, knotted nest of farms and craftsmen who had made their homes there just outside the seat of the Southern Line. Those small farms, little huts with scant and struggling gardens in front of them, reminded her of the ones along the lakeside in Carnd. Thatch roofs and daubed walls and full of tired, overworked people. The craftsmen seldom fared better, most of them simple carpenters and farriers who made their money more from the farmers than from those within the walls, those who could afford the works of guild artisans. When they first crossed into the ring of settlements from the east, Ri stopped, Sarah not noticing until she had gone a good ten feet further on. When she finally felt Ri's absence, turning back to see them standing and looking towards the open door of one of the farm huts, she walked back to stand with them, seeing what had brought them to a stop. Through the open doorway she saw a family, seated at their table, bread half eaten in front of them, all of their faces thin and bare and exhausted. In the field before the house, the crops starved for rain, wilted and dying.

Unable to pull her eyes from the family, who either from the benefit of the angle or from the importance of their own situation had not seen either of them standing in the street, Sarah put a hand on Ri's shoulder, feeling the tension there, the subtle tremble. Had she looked, she might have seen the blind, brilliant fury on Ri's face, but she didn't, so she didn't. Ri said nothing, and did not take their eyes from the family. Instead they shrugged away Sarah's touch and stepped across the street and through the little wooden gate at the end of the family's garden. With careful steps, eyes watching the crops that remained, following the already well-trod footpaths packed into the sandy soil, Ri came to the doorway of the home. Sarah still stood in the street, not following but propped on her staff and watching as Ri seemed to work to lessen their frame. They drooped their shoulders, they held their hands at their sides, never raising an arm any higher than their middle. They were welcomed in, after some hesitation, by a man with scant hair and dark circles under his eyes. For a moment Ri just stood talking, words inaudible across the distance, but in a moment they dropped to one knee and unslung their pack from their back. Sarah watched as Ri pulled a folded cloth bag out of their pack, at first unsure what it could be until the man unwrapped it, pulling a piece of the dried fish out and looking it over. Ri reclosed their bag, standing to face the man, now not drooping, not trying to seem smaller than they were. The man talked for a moment before he was pushed aside by a woman, her eyes just as dark as his. The woman wrapped Ri in her arms, and when she let go Sarah thought she saw the woman wipe at her eyes, but before she could be sure Ri had started back through the garden.

"We should probably keep moving," they said as they came back to stand beside Sarah in the street. "We don't need to keep standing in the road rubbernecking at strangers."

Seeing the look in Ri's eyes, the thin wisps of something refused in their corners, Sarah just nodded and started on down the blackstone road toward the South Wall Gate and the city that lay beyond it.

The crowds around the gate milled as they filtered through and into the city beyond. Sarah and Ri stood, letting the crowd move around as they took in the wall, its massive, solid-stone structure towering over them to a near forty-foot height. Ri watched the ramparts near the top with a curious kind of intensity, but Sarah knew what the wall meant to her, what the city beyond it was. She realized, standing there on the blackstone street, looking up at the city wall as the heat of the crowd around her sent sweat rolling down the bridge of her nose, that she had somehow kept the city and its crowds in the distance. That on the road there, she had focused on the path, on Ri, on their task. Never on what would wait at the city, on what would be there, the crowds, the milling people, the constant eyes and inescapable, deafening noise. With her mind spinning ever inward, Sarah gasped when Ri placed a hand on her shoulder and motioned toward the gate, toward the crowds. Sarah swallowed hard and tried to at least seem confident in her steps. Ri's eyes were again watching the guards, the ramparts, the gates.

When they came closer to the gates, they could hear the sounds of the stables to the right. A huge building with high vaulted roofs and gilt-worked doors. People in fine dress and soldier's garb moved in and out in a steady stream. Sarah could remember few common people in her life who had owned horses, even fewer who would have dared to ride into the stables of a Crown City with no way to track the animal's lineage, to show proper ownership.

"The kings and their horses," said Ri, their eyes on the stables too, and Sarah saw that the two of them must have been thinking of the same thing.

Pausing to watch as the animals stirred in the pens and stalls outside, Sarah turned back to the gates, not wanting to be further devoured by the crowd. "Did you ever own horses? When you were a farmer, I mean."

"No, my parents never tried to get sanction for horses. We had work mules a few times, but a good ox was what we kept, most of the time. I think one horse would have cost us more than my family saw in my entire life."

Through the gates, Sarah pulled Ri aside and out of the crowd, pointing down the scant, bricked city street. "The mercantile is just over there, let's give the crowd a moment to catch its breath, and then we can head in. I hate this shit."

"The city?"

All Sarah could offer was a nod, her mind ripped away from Ri as she had to dodge around a crowd of guffawing men who paid her no mind, her staff catching eyes, getting in the way. She found herself carrying it more than using it. "Yeah. It's more people than I can stand. Come on, let's go before I have a conniption."

They crossed the busy brick roads in a hurried jog. The crowd seemed to thin the further they got from the gate, people moving on towards the keep near the city's center.

There on the far sidewalk, Sarah slowed her pace, letting herself walk beside Ri, the grayrock sidewalk cracked and stained and crumbling in places, but a freer space than the streets where the morning masses made their way in.

"Have you ever been here before?" she asked, able to manage a clear mind for the first time since they came to the city walls.

"Once, a long time ago. You came through before getting to the ruins, yeah?"

Weaving around a man in a long, patchwork robe with paints and a canvas taking up most of the sidewalk, the canvas already holding a part-finished rendition of the city's skyline, the street artist's patron undoubtedly the Empire itself, Sarah just nodded. Further up the street the main road gave way to a series of twisting brick and cobble paths that wove through the Varinzian cityscape, the crowd thinned to nearly nothing, and that was the form it held when Sarah and Ri finally made it to Beatty's Mercantile. It was a squat, wood building attached onto the side of one of the old grayrock, three story things from before the Rending. It's sign, a big, unfinished pinewood thing with only the word BEATTY painted in bright white, hung just above the door. The clerk behind the desk, a massive man with a white beard that came almost to his waist, raised his eyes from his book as the little cluster of silver bells hung just above the door announced their entrance.

"I'll be, I never figured on seeing you here again, red. Been near on a couple months now, ain't it?"

"Something like that, yeah," said Sarah, unable to help the smile that was creeping across her face. She remembered the clerk, his beard that waggled when he talked, his far south accent and the way it poured out of him like molasses. "I'm surprised you remember me."

"Can't forget a mess of red curls like that, no ma'am. I'd dare say it's nearer curlier'n my own." The clerk ran a hand over his bald head and shrugged. "Well, than my own used ta be, anyway. You've a hanger-on today, too. Headed back the way you come, then?"

"We're actually just here to get some supplies," said Ri, pulling the scribbled list out of their front pocket. "Odds and ends."

Taking the list and looking it over, the big man ran a hand over his beard and looked Sarah and Ri over, his eyes squinted and fixed in consideration. "These things here, paper rolls, pens and inks, a coffee pot, those'll be no problem, but these other things? Red, tell me, are you'n your friend lookin' to build a still?"

"A brewing cask, for mead. Why?"

"You haven't heard then?"

"Haven't heard what?"

"It came down in decree just a week ago, I guess, so if you've been out on the road I suppose you wouldn't've heard atall. The government, the Empire, I mean, seems to have a growin' concern over the sobriety of its fine citizens. If'n you want to run any alcohol makings, you have to get the proper paperwork, leave from the empire to do so. I'm sorry, but I won't be able to sell you these things. It's not for any particular state-born love, you understand, but this is all I have." He raised a hand to gesture at the space around them, at his mercantile.

"It's fine," Sarah said, glancing at Ri who gave a shrug.

"Yeah," they said, "don't worry about it. We'll manage fine without it."

"Alright, give me a moment here and I'll get your things together."

"Add a bag of sugar, some flour, and a half-bag of jerky into that, too, then."

"Five pounds of sugar plenty?"

"More than enough, I'm sure. Oh, do you have any skins? Maybe a fox?"

"Sure I do. Gray, red?"

"Whichever is cheaper."

"Sure," he said, though in his accent it came out closer to shore. "Gimme just a minute here."

At once, the big man started moving about his store, grabbing the pens and things from the shelves behind him, stepping to the side and picking up the bags of flour and sugar. He had their things gathered and stacked on the counter in front of Sarah before she had even found where the pen's had originated from on the wall of shelves.

"Alright," he said, resting an elbow on the counter and looking everything over, "all accounted for, you've got somewhere 'bout fifteen crowns."

Pulling out the little bag Tony had sent them with, Sarah fished out ten of the little silver coins and handed them to the shopkeep. As the man looked them over, she counted the ones that remained and glanced back at Ri.

"We've got enough to get something to eat before we head back," she said, dropping the bag back into her satchel. "I could go for something besides fish and rice, huh?"

"Sure," said Ri, unslinging their bag from their back and

putting in some of the supplies as Sarah grabbed what she could carry.

"Ah, speaking of," said the merchant, "if'n you intend to hang around, I'd find somewhere to eat beside the Fink, huh? That Cooper feller you whopped in the head last time you were here has been stirring it up. Scarce let anyone forget that he got accosted by some tramp, to hear him say it."

As Ri slung their pack back over their shoulders, they looked from the merchant to Ri, a wash of confusion across their face. "What's he talking about?"

"Nothing," said Sarah, clasping their satchel closed and smiling at the clerk. She shifted her staff out of the crook of her arm and tapped it on the thin, wood floor. "I'll tell you later. Thanks for your help."

"No worries. Keep the rain away."

"Same to you," and at that, Sarah turned to the door ushering a still perplexed Ri out. They hadn't even both made it all the way through the threshold when Ri stopped and put a hand on Sarah's arm.

"Hey, come on. What was he talking about? Cooper?"

Letting out a long sigh, Sarah gestured with her staff across the road toward a little place, halfway rundown and jutting out of the bottom of an abandoned building. "That place, it's a bar called the Skeeving Fink. Last time I came here, on my way to Calarine, I stopped there to eat before leaving the city, and…a guy tried to push himself on me. I hit him in the head with my staff before getting the fuck out of town. That's it."

Raising an eyebrow, a near prideful kind of smirk at the edges of their lips, Ri cleared their throat. "What, did you break his jaw?"

"What? No, I don't think so. When I ran he was screaming, so I doubt it, anyway. Look, we need to find somewhere to eat. Hang on."

Without giving Ri a moment to keep prodding, Sarah opened the door and stuck her head through the threshold. "Hey, sorry. Where else is there to eat?"

"Best place would be The Gold Coast, right near the city center. You'll be able to see the gates of the Keep from it, can't miss. Only other option'd be C.S.'s, though, I wouldn't suggest you'd go there. Cooper's likely to be there as he is the Fink."

"Thanks." said Sarah, stepping back outside and letting the door clack shut behind her. "All right," she said to Ri, now leaning on her staff and grinning, trying to force the memory of the man from her mind, trying not to see the strange look in Ri's eyes. "He said that the best place to go would be The Gold Coast near the keep."

"Probably a good idea to be away from this part of town and towards the center, anyway. In case that guy is around."

Just offering a nod, Sarah looked down the street, towards the milling people and the keep, its four ancient towers rising in the distance, their glass windows catching the light in bright flashes. Taking her staff in hand and offering a glance back to Ri, the pair of them moved with the crowd, working their way towards the city's center.

The closer to the center that Sarah and Ri got, the more the crowd of people dissipated. As the streets weaved and branched off to the different parts of the city, towards the merchant's ward and the residential areas, the more the people too shifted their paths, and the more Sarah found she was able to breathe and move among the towering walls and strange, stone structures. It was near the first major divergence, the two of them carrying on straight ahead, that Sarah heard the man's baleful calling.

"Oh, my poor Southerners," he called, Ri seeing him first, standing on the wooden crate. His eyes were scarred, his cloak strange. A solid red thing that came to his ankles with a thick collar that covered his shoulders. "Oh, you poor, diasporic people. You poor creatures, so far from your Emperor, so far from the watchful eyes of our faith. Fear no longer, want of direction no longer, for we of the Cardinals have come at once, finding our way to you at last."

The man's strange, trembling voice stopped Sarah and Ri in their tracks, and they stood in the street listening to him preach. Their expressions held the entirety of themselves, Sarah confused, an almost mocking smirk at the edges of her lips, and Ri's eyes tight, mouth flat and severe.

"In the blessed vision, the Cardinals have begun their journey southward to you, to your salvation. Fear no longer, want no more, for Eld Keahey has begun his pilgrimage to you, for he rests now just briefly in the Center Line, and soon he will find his way to you, journeyed so far from beyond us to you, to your salvation and eternal prosperity."

"Come on," said Ri, putting a hang on Sarah's shoulder and squeezing. "I'm tired of listening to the nut, and I'm starving."

"But Ri," said Sarah, turning to go, raising her staff in a mocking tremble, "my salvation."

"I'm going to leave you," said Ri, and there was little hint of mirth in their voice.

"Right, yeah. We should probably go eat and get headed back, anyway."

Leaving the raving preacher behind, Sarah and Ri continued on towards the city center, the keep, and The Gold Coast. Long before they came to the square that surrounded the keep, they could see it. Four great steel towers stood at each of the keep's corners, their metal frames cleaner, more tended than any others in the city, the glass windows long gone and now framed with wood and stone. The stone walls that brought the towers together were whitewashed, and the great imperial banner of the Crown and Snake hung from almost every rampart. Above the southern gate, the sign above read CITADEL KEEP, scrawled in flowing red letters. Huge double doors of heavy oak, each as wide as a horse-drawn coach, stood open, guards on either side. A scant few soldiers and nobles moved in and out, and on occasion, as Sarah and Ri made their way down the street, an Aetic could be seen. Their leather cuirasses were covered with pale beige robes, some of them with harnesses full of scrolls across their backs. Once, Sarah saw a woman with raven-black hair, her features so stark, so startling, that Sarah could not help but stare, seeing that Ri felt the same. She was tall, beautiful beyond reason, and older, much older, than either of them. She wore a uniform similar to that of the other Aetics, but instead of the beige, her robe was a deep, navy blue, the thing thrown over one shoulder, giving it the appearance of a long and trailing scarf. On each hip was a long, curved dagger, the handles turned inward, never more than an inch from the woman's hands. As Sarah and Ri stood for a moment and watched the woman cross the courtyard toward the gate, they could tell even across the distance that every movement was hers and hers alone.

"She's a Searcher," said Ri, having seen that Sarah was staring at the woman too.

"A what?" Sarah had to tear her eyes from the woman.

"An Aetic Searcher. They're supposed to be some kind of special force, but I've never seen one in person. I know that robe though, my--uh…some of the people I used to know always talked about that robe. They must've had run-ins with the Searchers before, I guess."

Catching the stumble, hearing the rising tension in Ri's voice, Sarah watched their eyes, but said nothing. The pit of hunger in her stomach made it difficult to focus on much of anything, much less another of Ri's eccentricities.

"Well," she said, "let's go eat."

Across the courtyard from Citadel Keep, The Gold Coast stood out among the grayrock buildings and towers. Its once-red brick front was painted a faded yellow-gold, the sign hanging over the door just saying G.C. in red lettering, the paint flecked and revealing the wood beneath. In front, standing just above a little shrub that seemed neglected, if ever tended at all, was a carved wooden sign, a blue background with the raised letters painted a sterling silver. As Sarah and Ri came to the front of the place, they both stopped for a moment, looking the sign over before they headed in.

THE   GOLD   COAST's
name is in reference to the
historic   GOLD   COAST
GAMBLING   DISTRICT
supposedly   maintained   on
the far side of the Pearl
River in the centuries before
The Rending. According to
historical   texts,   gambling,
drinking,   and   murdering
were   commonplace   along
that far edge of the river in
a   County   Court   named
Rankin. According to period
maps,   this   area   was   in
approximately   the   same
location as the current day
Calarinian Ruins.

Interpretation Provided by
the Historical Association of
Imperial Scholars.

"Shit, this place is named after the ruins?" asked Ri.

"Apparently. 'Far side of the Pearl River,' I think that would be just the other side of the grayrock bridge we crossed over on the way here, so just between the Blinded Forest and the bridge."

"Hell, that's not particularly close to the ruins, is it?"

"I guess they mean it was part of Rankin Court? I don't know. I don't imagine many members of the Historical Association of Imperial Scholars make it to the ruins. Let's get inside. I'm starving."

Offering only a nod, paying the sign and its imperial scholars no more attention, Ri started for the door with Sarah following close behind. They were swinging doors, closing behind the two of them just as fast as Sarah let them go. Inside, the place was bustling. The walls were exposed brick, in a few places the mortar was painted white, golden tapestries hanging on some walls, the imperial Crown and Snake hanging on others. On the far side of the room ran the long, wood-topped bar. Tall stools sat along it, a brass rail at the bottom, and beyond the bar a huge mirror lined with bottles and glasses. Above it all, as if to mock the very ideals of symmetry, hung three whitetail deer with massive, malformed antlers. Their racks twisted and curved in ways completely unnatural. Seeing no seats at the little mismatched tables that filled the room, Sarah and Ri both headed across the space to the bar, taking the last two stools. Between them, Sarah propped her staff against the bar and then looped one leg around it to keep it out of the way. Almost as soon as they had climbed into the high stools, the broad-faced woman behind the bar saw them, raised her hand, and headed to them.

"What'll it be?" she asked, leaning on the bar with her palms. Her accent was strange, something akin to Tony's own Northern Line-speech, but tighter, clipped. It seemed to cut through the sound of the place without any struggle. "Special today's hamburger steak, ground come down from Center Line, though. No local stuff 'round right now, sorry for it."

"I can't imagine I would be able to tell the difference," said Ri, "so one of those and a beer would do just fine."

"The same for me, I think," said Sarah.

"Think or know, sweetie?"

Sarah flushed, dropping her eyes and giving a half-hearted chuckle. "I'll take the same, thanks."

The barkeep rapped her knuckles on the counter, spun on her heels, grabbed two mugs, and filled them with a thin, frothy brew. Before either Sarah and Ri could start talking, she came back with the beer and handed it over. "I'll put your food in, all counted you're looking at a half crown."

Sarah pulled another of the silver marks from the pouch and handed it over. In just a moment, the barkeep handed a brassy coin back before moving on to the next customers.

"She's a real piece of work," said Ri, watching Sarah from the corner of their eyes.

Nodding, Sarah took a big drink of her beer. It was thin and warm. It made her miss Tony's mead. "This place is definitely livelier than the Fink."

"I can imagine," said Ri, downing their own beer before sliding backwards off their stool and gesturing toward the far corner. "She gets back, grab me another beer, I'm about to piss myself. You'll be okay?"

Unable to help but scoff, Sarah took a drink of beer and nodded. "I managed by myself for a long time, I think I'll make it okay for a couple minutes."

"Har har," Ri said, tapping Sarah on the shoulder and heading for the far corner and the alcove that led to the outhouses beyond it.

There in that living, bustling place, Sarah sat and drank. As she finished her own beer, the waitress came and Sarah ordered two more, passing the brass mark over and getting a dull copper one in return. It was there, the full beer in front of her and Ri's seat empty beside her, no time at all passed since they had stood and gone to the outhouses, that Sarah felt the small, sharp pressure just at her lower back. Above the bustle of the crowd, she could hear the rapid, slurred speech of a man in her right ear, his stinking breath wafting around her.

"You're gonna act just like we're old friends, or you'll die. Smile, stand up, and walk outside. You ain't seen me in months, happy to see an old barmate. Tickled fuckin' pink, understand?"

Saying nothing, Sarah reached over and took her staff with as gentle a touch as she could manage. She smiled, slid sideways off the bar stool, and took a half-step back, hoping the man took it as what it was, a signal for them both to start towards the door. As they turned, the man was careful to keep the knife hidden and pressed at the small of her back. She caught a glimpse of the man out of the corner of her eye, the left side of his face swollen and bruised. Just below his eye, his cheek was split and a jagged black scab was weeping. She knew him at once, had known him when the pressure first appeared at the small of her back. She could feel the steel trying to slip through the fabric just beneath the break of her leather cuirass. As they headed across the bar and towards the door, her eyes drifted to the far corner where the alcove passed into the alley and towards the outhouses. She hoped for Ri, but they did not come, and in the span of just a single breath the man was ushering her through the swinging doors. She could hear his face creaking with the feigned smile as he patted her on the shoulder, giving his own facsimile of a friend. There in the courtyard, she felt a sudden blind foolishness that she never learned any spells that might have aided her in a fight. No ways to sling fire or stone with the flick of her wrist, only mending, only the summoning of feeble light.

Feeble light. Sarah clung to that thought as the man pushed her around the edge of the building and into the alleyway beside it, a dark, muddy place that ran between The Gold Coast and some unmarked official building beside it. By the time that the man, the man the merchant at Beatty's had called Cooper, had her deeper into the alley, she had decided on a plan and moved all at once, her muscles tight, jaw clenched. She wedged one end of her staff against the brickwork to her right and twisted it, using the wracking leverage to push away from the man, at the same time spinning on the ball of her right foot, halfway dropping to one knee and managing to wrench herself free from the man's grasp. She shot her left hand out, palm outstretched and slamming towards the man's eyes. She called magelight into her hand, hoping that the light would be bright enough to blind him, but as she sent her palm out, his free hand snatched it from the air, the big knife coming toward her. In the terror of the moment, she flinched and the spell sputtered and died in her hand, Nothing more than a crackle of faded white managed to escape. She barely managed to jerk her neck backward to avoid the man's knife, but it no longer mattered. He jerked her arm forward and in a single motion wrapped her hair into his clenched fist, pulling her down to her knees and placing the knife against her outstretched neck. Her heavy satchel clattered against her, the weight of everything from the mercantile pulling on her as she struggled in the man's grasp.

"You fuckin' bitch," he spat, white and foaming spittle at the corners of his furious mouth. "Drop the god damn stick, or I'll fuckin' bleed you. Do it!"

Sarah did as she was told, seeing the wild in his eyes. She could feel the steel at her throat. It wasn't cold, as she expected, it was hot hot. Warmed by the time at her back and by the rage that emanated from the man's hand.

"Do you see what you did to me, you cunt?" he asked, never taking the knife from her neck, his eyes never leaving her face. "Maybe I'll give you one to match, huh? Maybe I'll ruin your stupid, bitch face and see what you think of it."

Tightening his grip on her hair, the man pulled the knife from Sarah's neck and rested the blade just below her ear. His face consumed her vision, his eyes locked onto her. All she could hear was his breathing and the pounding of her own heart. Neither of them were aware of the world around them, the man consumed with his vengeance and Sarah with what was be wrought down onto her. When Ri's arm shot around the man's neck, it was more shock than anything that made him drop the knife in the fraction of a second before they pulled him away. For the first step back the man tried to keep his grip on Sarah's hair, but Ri tightened their grip around his neck with one arm and grabbed at his wrist with their free hand, wrenching it free with no effort that Sarah could discern. In what felt like an instant, the man was away from her and flying toward the right-hand wall, landing head-first into it. Sarah back peddled toward the opposite wall as Ri stepped over her legs, never seeming to see her. Their eyes were locked on the man across the alley.

In a single stride, Ri crossed the space between them and grabbed him by the head. They sent his head smashing into the wall, pausing to grind it against the brickwork, the man's legs flailing as he struggled against their grasp. Sarah watched as Ri lifted the man, never having relinquished their grasp on his head, and brought their knee into his stomach, sending a thin stream of blood and spittle out of his mouth. Again, Ri sent his head into the wall, this time letting go as he slumped to the ground. He folded in on himself, babbling the incoherent language of the dying. Ri did not pause, did not step back to survey the severity of their work, and instead over him, their legs straddling him and half-braced against the wall. They put their hand over his chest as a counter-balance and beat down onto him with all of their weight. A massive one-time farmer's fist sailed into his mouth, blood flying with each draw of their arm. Sarah scrambled to her feet and half-stumbled over to them, putting a hand on Ri's back, trying to call out to them, to tell them to stop, but Ri seemed to hear nothing. The man's eyes were gone, swollen in the bloody remnants of his face, and Sarah put both hands onto Ri's shoulder and jerked.

"Ri, stop! That's enough, please that's enough."

Arm drawn back, prepared for another blow, another strike against the man crumbled and bleeding beneath them, Ri turned and looked at Sarah with wild, unrelenting eyes. Sarah drew back, confused at the way Ri seemed to look at nothing and everything, at the way she felt like a speck in their vision, but as that look softened, returned to the blonde-haired farmer she knew, Ri dropped their arm. Bracing against the wall, they stood, standing over the man before hocking a thick stream of spit into his bleeding face and turning to look at Sarah.

"You okay?" they asked, not seeming to hear the low groans coming from the heap beneath them.

"I, uh…yes. I'm okay. Just shaken."

Only offering a single, curt nod, Ri walked towards the back of the alley where it gave way to the outhouses where a rain barrel stood against the wall, a gutter downspout pointing towards its top. Sarah stood, looking down the alley at Ri trying to ignore the dying man. The man who had attacked her, who had intended to cut up her face, to kill her, if not something far worse. Yet still, all Sarah could see was Ri, face wild with a blank and terrifying fury, beating the man until he could no longer be called anything near living, despite the slow breaths that seemed to rattle out of him. There at the rain barrel, Ri washed their hands and face in dirty water, returning to Sarah with faded stains of red still on their skin.

"We need to go," Ri said, their voice the same softness it had been as long as Sarah had known them. Their eyes were back to that gentle, strange kindness, despite the blood stains at the edges of their jaw, the blood along the front of their white shirt. They had their pack in their hand, Sarah having no idea where it came from. They pulled a clean shirt from it and changed, stuffing the bloodied thing into the bottom of the bag. "We need to go now, before someone takes a closer look at what's going on here."

Able to offer only one more worried glance at the man, Sarah nodded and followed behind Ri as they left the alley. Her heart still pounding into her ears, they left the courtyard, leaving their food uneaten on the bartop in The Gold Coast. As they keep moving on through the city, toward the southern gate of the city wall, towards those failing farms that surrounded it, Sarah could not help but wonder which person was really, truly Ri. The gentle farmer, giving their food to those starving in their home, or the great and raging beast standing astride the bleeding man deep in an unseen alleyway.

MICHAEL

"I have no idea," said Michael, standing near the sleeping quarters. Finch, Tony, and Bolivar all sat around the tables nearby. "Really, I can't tell you. I'm not some scholar of pre-rending fiction."

"God, Mike," said Finch, brandishing one of her romance novels, this one with a long haired, muscular man standing at the bow of a ship, a woman with a torn dress in his arms. "I'm just asking you to tell these two meatheads that these books have merit!"

"I haven't read them."

"Of course you haven't," said Bolivar, his beard failing to hide the wild grin on his face, despite all his efforts to not let Finch see it.

Finch does, of course, see the smirk, and she smacks Bolivar on the shoulder with the book. "Quit laughing at me! These are good books!"

"Michael," said Tony, wearing his own smile in the open, watching Bolivar and feeling some sort of relief at the way the man seemed so relaxed, "be careful picking sides in this kind of thing. We could find ourselves amongst a right and true war."

"I won't be picking sides in anything."

"Daaad!" Jane called, and Michael turned around to see her standing at the foot of the stairs.

"Yes?"

"Need your help!"

Turning back to the others, Michael gave a wry glance to Tony, a look of relief and avoided irritation, and headed to the stairs to meet his daughter. As he walked to the stairs, Bolivar shifted the conversation, asking how Sarah found the library in the first place, and Finch started to tell her version of the story. Michael did not stop to listen, seeing his daughter growing ever more impatient.

"Yes, dear?" Michael asked, ruffling her hair, smiling at the quick turn towards aggravation on her face.

"Need your help with a ladder up there," Jane said, pointing towards the top of the stairs.

Following behind Jane, Michael raises an eyebrow and glances between Jane and Pinn, who was now standing at the top of the stairs, waiting. "These ladders aren't that heavy. They have wheels."

"You told us not to touch the ladders," she says, irritation pouring through her words.

"Did I?" Michael asked, the two of them now with Pinn at the top of the stairs.

"Yes sir," Pinn cut in, "I believe your exact words were 'I'd rather not find out if Sarah has a spell for mending broken bones,' or something like that."

Giving the thin teen a flat look, Michael ran a hand over the back of his neck and sighed. "You have your mother's memory don't you? Alright, well. What do you two need help with?"

"Moving a ladder," said Pinn before Michael could stop him.

"Yes I know moving a ladder, but--ah, just show me. Take me to the ladder you need moved."

The pair did just that, leading him into the tall stacks and to a ladder that rested at the edge of the long rows of shelves.

"We're trying to get that book up there," said Jane, pointing toward the top of the shelves near the end, "because it looks weird. Like it doesn't go with all these magic things."

Michael could see the book that she was pointing to, its painted and colorful spine standing out amongst the gilt and leather bound volumes, so he pushed the ladder over to it, made sure it was locked and secure, and then stepped back. "There," he said, a slight grimace at the thought of the heights, "one of you two climb up there. Call it ladder-use observation so I don't have to do this again."

Without a moment of hesitation, Jane flew up the ladder, stopping at the top for a moment and then grabbing the book and the one next to it before clamoring down. "I knew it," she said, holding up the book with its painted cover, "this one is fiction, not magic stuff. The one next to it was too, both of them are L books, so I guess somebody got confused or something."

"Seemed to have happened a lot here, taking Finch's collection into account," said Michael, "let me see them." Jane handed both books over and Michael turned them over in his hand. The one with the painted cover showed a bird in flight, a falcon or something like it, against a backdrop of blue, the title *A Wizard of Earthsea* across the top. Michael handed it back to

Jane. "It's a LeGuin book. I think Sarah likes this writer, must be something good to it." Looking at the other cover, he knew it from just a glance. The flat-painted tree against the maroon background brought back a flood of memories, and he couldn't help but smile. "Ah, this one is Lee. To Kill a Mockingbird. Jane, this book was--"

"Mom's favorite. You've told me before."

"Right well," said Michael, "it is fantastic. Read it. Read them both. Hell, read everything. We're all lucky to be somewhere like this, you know."

"Thanks, dad," said Jane, no longer paying her father any attention, turning the book over in her hands.

"Yeah, thanks Mister Cokin," said Pinn, taking To Kill a Mockingbird from Jane and turning it over in his hands.

Michael watched as the two of them headed toward the tables nearby, listened as they chattered, listened as their voices mixed with those from downstairs. He turned, heading back down the stairs and toward Tony and the others, the smiling face of his wife hanging beautiful in his mind.

SARAH

The flight from Varinz carried no pursuits, no sudden screaming of found bodies, no chasing guards. Still, both Ri and Sarah found themselves looking over their shoulders as they crossed through the muddy fields and finally found themselves back across the Pearl and into the edges of the Blinded Forest. They made camp in a spot much the same as the one from the night before, though as the evening grew long and the shadows ever darker, the camp took on the anxiety and weight of the day, of the alleyway.

"No fire," said Ri, unrolling their bedroll.

"Right, yeah. I guess it's better to be safe than sorry." Sarah unrolled her own bedroll, stopping to watch Ri and the tight way they moved. "When are we going to talk about what happened?"

Dropping onto their bedroll, knees pulled up and running their hands over their face, Ri shook their head, shoulders slumped forward. "I told you, there's nothing to talk about. He was going to kill you. I stopped him."

"Ri, you--"

Ri's eyes shot up to meet Sarah's, at least some of that fire from before back. "I get it, Sarah. I get that you think I did something wrong. I get that you think I went too far, maybe I did. I was angry that he was trying to hurt you. I don't regret what I did, so you don't need to regret it for me. I don't need a keeper."

The air crackled in that brief moment, Ri's eyes catching the scant and ever fading light in a strange electric band. Sarah could feel herself begin to carry on, to push, to fight the fight she knew was needed, but she didn't. She dropped it, leaving everything unsaid fizzling in the air around them.

"We'd better rest," said Ri, filling the pause, "so we can be moving before first light. Just in case."

"Right, yeah," said Sarah, sitting down, legs crossed, hands resting over the ankles of her boots, unsure what else to say. It was in that silence that they sat, they laid, they drifted into fitful sleep, moonlight hiding the stains, now the dark color of rust, on Ri's swelling knuckles.

The night was hot and silent, and Sarah stirred in the stillness. Sleep had come only briefly, fits and jerks interrupting her, pulling her back into the dark woods. When her reaching hand did not find Ri beside her, she leaned up, eyes struggling in the night. Finally she saw them, standing along the edge of the treeline, the moonlight casting them as a dark, unknown silhouette. They leaned against a tree, back to Sarah, eyes towards the river and Varinz beyond it, searching, waiting. Beside them, leaned against one of the scrubby bushes nearby, Sarah could see another silhouette. A tree limb no more than a hand's length from Ri's grasp. Even in the darkness, Sarah could see the tense way Ri stood, as if they were ready to move, expecting. As Sarah laid back and stared up at the darkened canopy above, she couldn't help but think of the alleyway, of the starving farmers and Ri's sacrifice of their food. As a far away goatsucker called into the night, she wondered what side of Ri was most real.

CHAPTER X

A Position of Unknown Power

===

When Sarah and Ri finally came to the library in the mid-morning, its visage on the near horizon felt like an immeasurable relief. The hike from the forest back to Calarine was hung in a pained silence. More than once, Sarah had started to say something, to let Ri know that it was okay, that everything was fine, normal, routine, but she didn't. Instead, they trudged along in that thick silence, and when the Belhaven came into view ahead, Sarah felt like a great weight was lifted from her. Without a word to one another they picked up their pace. At the top of the stairs, Finch and Michael sat, the big oak doors open behind them. Finch was smoking her endless supply of hand-rolled cigarettes, and for a moment, even through it all, Sarah thought how funny it was that Finch didn't send for more tobacco.

Seeing them, Finch leaned back towards the doors and yelled out. "Tony, Bol! They're back!"

As Sarah and Ri came to the top of the stairs, Michael was on his feet, clapping Sarah on the back and giving them both his wide, wild smile. For a moment, Sarah thought she could see something wild and frantic in the edges of his eyes, and she wondered how he had been since they left. Before Sarah could say a word to him, Tony came lumbering through the door, all smiles and bellowing laughter at something Bolivar must have said.

"There you two are, I was beginning to wonder if we were ever going to see you again."

"We couldn't get the brewing gear," said Ri, their first words in what seemed like hours.

"Oh? They didn't have any of it?"

"No, they had it," said Sarah, "but they couldn't sell it to us. Apparently the empire has set out some new laws on brewing and alcohol. You have to apply for a permit."

Tony scoffed, his eyes nearly rolling all the way to the back of his head. "I'll be damned. Can't say I'm surprised, though. That's fine, I'm sure between your spells and me we can make something that'll get us close enough." Giving a big laugh, Tony patted a hand on Sarah's shoulder, his dark eyes cutting from her to Ri, and she could see the knowing on his face.

Not able to help but laugh, Sarah shook her head. "What're we going to do, play outlaw?"

"I'm not afraid of being a bootlegger, if it comes to it." Tony said, his grin now filling his whole face. "Say, two of you look road worn and near dead. Why don't we get out of this pissant sun, huh?"

"Yeah, Sarah" said Ri, "I think I'm going to go drop my pack. Get everything out of it."

"Right, yeah. I'm going to head to my office and drop my stuff, change shirts. I'll bring everything I have over when I'm done."

Adjusting the pack on their shoulders, Ri led the rest of them inside, heading for the cots in the far corner as soon as they were through the door. Bolivar lingered at the door for a minute, closing it behind them, but Sarah did not stay to see if he needed anything, how things had gone, or to deliver his request from before they left. Instead, she went to her office where she slid her satchell of her shoulder and dropped her staff as soon as she crossed through the door. At her desk, she collapsed into her chair, putting her head into her hands and exhaling, deflating onto herself. She tried to let go of the tension, but she could feel it clinging on at the base of her neck, along her shoulders. Eyes closed, she could see it playing again and again. Ri's hands bashing into the broken man's face, the blood flinging from their fist each time they drew back to hit him again. Somewhere beyond that, in the far away, she could feel the tip of the knife dig into the small of her back, the terror, the uncertainty. She felt the summoned magelight crackle in her palm, the failure of it all.

"Stressful trip?" Sibella asked, and Sarah raised her head to see that he had come to rest on the desk just in front of her.

"Something like that."

"Another of those fang walkers?"

"No," she answered, sitting up in the chair, head still resting against one hand, "do you remember when I got here, I told you that I came through Varinz on my way here. I told you that I had an, uh...altercation with some drunk."

"Right, you whacked him in the head with your staff."

"Yeah, well, we ran into him. That same guy, I mean. He put a knife to my back, was going to--fuck, I don't know what he was going to do, but...Ri stopped him. They killed him, Sibella."

"And this upsets you?" Sibella asked, not pausing, not needing any consideration.

"What the hell do you mean? Yes, it upsets me. They

beat the everliving fuck out of him, Sibella."

"They were protecting you, I thought?"

"Well, yeah, I guess. That's what they say, and I know that's how it started, but…it was bad. There was barely anything left of the guy when we left, when we ran."

"I am sorry, Sarah," said the falcon, his voice now carrying the calm consideration Sarah had come to expect from him. Leaning forward, she scratched at his head and smiled at him.

"It's all right. I'm okay, it isn't the first time I've…I'm all right. It's all just a shock, I think. I never expected that from Ri."

"Perhaps," said Sibella, his voice trailing as he seemed to try and pull his thoughts together, "they were just trying to protect you, and they got carried away. It is obvious to us all that the two of you care for each other a great deal. Perhaps they were, well, to be quite precise; perhaps they were afraid of losing you."

"I know," said Sarah, standing up and putting a hand on the falcon's head. "Thank you, Sib. I just hope I've been making the right choices."

"I trust you are, that you will. The library called you here for a reason, Sarah."

"So you keep telling me," said Sarah, giving a half-hearted laugh looking out of the open door to her office, towards the administration offices and beyond, that small pressure still resting at her back.

Later in the day, time wearing away at it all, Sarah's anxieties began to ease as they were replaced with Ri's company. The Ri she knew, that she had become used to. The gentle, laughing, nervous farmer. Together, they joined Michael in the constant shuffling and reorganization of books through the library. Ri served as the workhorse, carrying heavy stacks of books, shifting shelves, and moving tables with relative ease as Sarah and Michael finalized the library's new organizational system. Finch, who had once worked with Sarah and Michael, had become Bolivar's shadow. She spent her days following him without direction as he explored the library, chatting at him in her cigarette-tinged rasp, telling him about her current paperback excursions. Bolivar chatted back, spinning stories of espionage and noble adventure like silk, at times even asking to see the books she was reading. The two, it seemed to the others, were becoming fast friends.

"She follows him around like a lost dog," Ri commented as Sarah, Michael, and themself sat down for a break after midday.

"She's a strange woman," Michael said, rubbing at the lenses of his glasses with his shirt. "She always seems to have one foot out the door."

As she took a drink of watert, Sarah watched from across the library as Finch and Bolivar sat near the living quarters. Finch's arms were animated in excited conversation. A smile crept into the corner of Sarah's mouth. "Maybe she's in love." Ri pushed at her shoulder, smiling back. Sarah got lost in that smile for a moment, happy to see it again.

"They are spending a good bit of time reading smut together, you know," said Ri. "Hard to believe Bolivar puts up with that."

"Both of you stop it," said Michael, trying to keep from laughing himself. "Maybe she is, maybe she isn't. Either way it's none of our business." He took a drink of water, letting out a satisfied sigh as he did. "Sarah, aren't you supposed to offer Bolivar Peace Officer?"

"I plan to," said Sarah, realizing she had forgotten about Bolivar and his place in the library in the storm of Varinz. "I've just been trying to make sure I can trust him at least that much. This is all so strange to me." *Strange or familiar, leader of the merry men?* Sarah gritted her teeth against the voice in her head. "I don't want to make a mistake that'll come back to bite me in the ass."

"Everyone else seems to like him."

"Speak for yourself," said Ri.

"It's not about anyone liking him. I just want to make sure he's not up to anything. That I'm not playing into his hand, you know?"

"Don't overthink it," Ri said, putting a hand on Sarah's.

Sarah sat in silence for a moment and stared into Ri's green eyes. For the first time since The Gold Coast, she felt like she saw Ri, not the alleyway, not the rust-colored stains. Without saying a word, she whistled for Sibella, and the falcon appeared almost out of nowhere, landing on the tabletop and preening his feathers.

"Yes?"

"Let Tony and the others know that there'll be a meeting at the front desk just before dinner."

"Should I tell them what the meeting will be about?"

"No, just that it's about the Belhaven." Sarah seemed

again to get lost in the distance, and Sibella nodded just before he took flight.

Michael drank down the last of his water and stood back up, returning to the work on the books as Sarah and Ri sat together, silent. Sarah wondered if Ri would think less of her if they knew how scared she really was. If that brutality from the alleyway was the shadow of a greater hardness. If they would hate her for how much she wanted to return to the road and leave the library and its responsibilities behind. How much she wanted to disappear into a new world again. To run again.

As the evening crept around them, everyone began to gather at the front desk. They sat in the chairs Sarah had arranged in neat rows near the front doors. Nervous faces and smiles and laughter filled the air, but Sarah noticed none of it. She stood at the desk and watched with patient eyes as everyone found their seats, her heart running away in her chest, her mind cycling in and out of reality. In and out of the want, the pull, to run away. To avoid the great clawing responsibility she felt growing around her. Ri sat down with Tony and Michael. Jane squirmed in her seat, aggravated at her required attendance. Finch and Pinn sat down near the front. An empty seat was saved beside Finch, for who Sarah did not need to wonder. Bolivar was the last to file in, taking the saved seat with a sly glance toward Finch. At last, Sibella came to rest on Sarah's shoulder. The falcon preened at his feathers before looking across the assembled members of their fledgling community. Tired eyes and confused glances betrayed the anxiety of the crowd to Sibella, but Sarah's mind was too focused inward to ever see them. She was too riddled with a nervous cautiousness to see that everyone waited for her to explain the call. Bolivar sat expectant, his hands resting neat and calm in his lap.

Sarah took a deep breath and closed her eyes as she steadied her shaking hands and thought of the task that laid ahead. As she opened her eyes, it was Bolivar's smiling, foxlike face she saw first. "Thanks for taking a minute, everyone. By now, we've all gotten to know one another, so I am going to keep formality to a minimum." Sarah's words were tight, rehearsed. She worked through the thoughts in her mind, and they rolled out in a speech she knew must have seemed layered with anxiety. "There are not a lot of us, so I want us to be friends. I want us to behave like friends." She adjusted on the balls of her feet and turned to point herself toward Bolivar. "That being said, there is a need to create clarity within the roles we all fill here, and Bolivar, being the newest, has yet to find his niche. He is unique among the rest of us, with his experience as a teacher and with the military."

"Don't give me too much credit," Bolivar said. A smattering of chuckles came from the others.

Giving a thin, placating smile, Sarah spoke louder as she continued. "Due to those accolades, and his clear drive to provide his services to the Belhaven, I want to offer him a unique role. I haven't worried much with titles and designations outside of my own, but as both a gesture of good faith and to show respect towards his desire to help, I want to offer Bolivar the role of Peace Officer. I know this business about titles might not fit the idea a lot of us have for the Belhaven, but, of any role, the person charged with keeping us safe likely needs one the most."

A look of surprise swept across Bolivar's face. He turned in his seat to look at the others, their expressions a mixture of expectant apathy and quiet satisfaction. "Well," he said, running his hands over the breast of his shirt. "I thank you, Sarah."

"Don't thank me yet, Bolivar. I'm offering you the role, but if anyone here has any complaints or concerns, then those will need to be addressed." She stepped closer to the others, and out of the corner of her eye she could see Bolivar watching her every move. "Well, does anyone here have any concerns? Questions?"

The others looked at one another, whispering amongst themselves and nodding back and forth. Ri gave a cautious glance to Sarah that almost betrayed their own anxieties. In a moment, Tony straightened up in his chair and cleared his throat, speaking with a calculated precision. "None that we can think of. He seems a fine man for the job."

"A wonderful man for the job," Finch added.

Sarah nodded, and turned her attention back to Bolivar, whose face was still stuck in a confident grin. "Well," she said and crossed her arms, "do you accept the position?"

Bolivar stood up and stepped closer to Sarah. He searched her face, in long, sweeping scans. The streaks of gold in his eyes shimmered as they fought to shine out from under his heavy brow. The look in his eyes and the way his mouth seemed to hide behind his salt and peppered beard made her feel uneasy. "Of course I do, Sarah." he said, his tone kinder than she had ever heard him speak. "I must say, I'm surprised you all feel comfortable giving me this position. Trusting your safety in my hands."

When Sibella stirred on Sarah's shoulder, she reached up and scratched at his neck. Satisfied at the kind, open look on Bolivar's face, she reached out and shook his hand. "You haven't given us any reason not to trust you, Bolivar."

There was a brief smattering of applause and chattered passings of congratulations before the others stood up and came to stand with Sarah and Bolivar. Tony shook his hand, slapping him on the shoulder in congratulations and they all talked amongst themselves. In a moment, Ri came to join Sarah. The two of them stood separate from the group, watching as Bolivar grinned. He almost seemed to puff out his chest as his new title filled him with pride. In the cavalcade of congratulatory grandeur, Sarah thought to herself. She thought about how much she hoped this was enough to keep him close, to keep him where she could watch him. That nagging thought stayed in the back of her mind, refusing to relent.

Bolivar and the others sat at the tables near their living space chatting away, taking a short rest from the process of moving furniture on the third floor. He had chosen the third as his base of operations, even though Sarah had offered him space in the administration offices. He had told her that his office made most sense near the roof, where high windows looked out at every side of the Belhaven.

Sarah and Ri had watched him from the lobby as he, Michael, and Tony carried furniture to the third floor. Sarah wondered to herself if her cynicism, if her at times unsilenceable anxiety, had almost caused her to cut out someone else who did not deserve it. As the group sat in the living quarters eating breakfast, Bolivar once again began spinning stories about his exploits in the Center Line. This time, though, even Sarah and Ri became engrossed as they listened. He told of how he skulked in the night to deliver saltpeter and cotton cord to rebels on the Northern borders.

"It was a rough night on the road," Bolivar said, leaning forward and moving his hands in snapping waves as he spoke. His large frame seemed to loom over the rest of them. "Northern nights are frigid in the dead of winter, but we couldn't even risk burning a fire. By that point the guards knew that something was going on, they just didn't know who or how. But I, we, didn't care. I had one last run to make, and I intended to finish it."

"So you made these trips alone?" Michael asked. The others listened in.

"No, no, no, I had two or three people with me most of the time. The Northern Line's wilds are dangerous. Most beasts have been kept out of the rest of the Empire, but they thrive in the North. Going alone is a death wish."

"The Empire doesn't do anything about the monsters?" Michael asked as he let out an impressed sigh. "They've dealt with most of them here. From what I've seen, anyways."

"No reason to. Few people live in the wilds there, isn't that right, Tony?"

Tony shifted in his seat and nodded, "There's a reason every Northern traveler either ends up coming south or going into the Canait to trap. The Northern Line wilds are not kind.

Neither is Canait, but at least up there in the North Country the empire isn't breathing down your neck."

With that Bolivar let out a laugh of agreement and continued on. "That's about right, I suppose. Canait has its own problems, but freedom isn't one of them. I must have come close to death a half dozen times running supplies in the Northern Line, most of them from run-ins with guards."

Sarah's thoughts raced and she felt a deep, relaxed energy wash over her. Bolivar, his eyes glimmering and face bright and cheerful, told stories to the others, and in that moment, she felt certain that she had misjudged him. She felt certain that her new family, her library, was safe. Ri locked eyes with her, and they smiled together.

"Bolivar," Sarah said, "did you ever come across fang walkers?"

Bolivar grinned and started in on a new story.

MICHAEL

The next day, a gentle and forgiving rain coming down outside, settling the heavy dust along the blackstone streets Michael, Bolivar, and Finch worked on the third floor. Michael and Finch had volunteered to help him move the ever-growing mass of books, all of them on politics and history and war, that were displaced in the shifting of the third from library section to partial security office. Along the eastern wall, Bolivar and the others had moved shelves and placed tables to create a planning room. With Tony's help Bolivar had pulled a massive map of Calarine and Varinz from the wall, ripped it from its frame, and tacked to a large table at the center of the new section. As Michael worked, moving armfuls of books from haphazard stacks near the stairs to the now crammed shelves on the western side, Finch sat on top of a small side table near the new map, chatting at Bolivar.

"Oh my god, leave me alone," Michael heard Finch rasp, her smokey drawl nearing euphoria in a way he hadn't heard before. He paused when he sat the books on a table to sort them, listening and smiling at the joy he heard in his friend's voice. "I can't help it you don't like good books."

Bolivar laughed, a long, galing bellow. "I can't help it you think that reading about some alien rea--,"

"Bolivar! My god."

"Don't my god me, you're the one reading it!"

Finch and Bolivar laughed together then, and when Michael returned for more books, he saw Finch's head resting on Bolivar's shoulder, who sat in a carved wooden chair, his feet propped on the map table.

"You two behave," said Michael, his eyes squinted in a smile behind his glasses.

"You mind your own business," said Finch, her own smile in the corner of her mouth.

Bolivar adjusted in his chair to look at Michael, shrugging Finch off his shoulder as he did. "Hey, by the way, Mike, you bunch haven't happened across any books about the Great Boroughs, have you?"

Michael walked over, sat his arm load of books on the map table, and propped his elbows on top of it. He pondered for a moment, looking at the pair over the top of his glasses. "Can you be more specific? I mean, sure there's books on the second about the Boroughs. Most of them are about Goraln, stuff like that."

"This would be a more specific text. Not bound, just collected imperial scrolls. It would be about a specific Borough, I imagine."

"Like I said, there's some stuff like that. Most of the collected scrolls are in those piles by the administration offices down on the first. What Borough? I haven't read much on all of this, but I might have ran 'cross it somewhere."

"The Calling Maw."

Michael ran his tongue over his teeth and scratched at his jaw, his face twisted into a knot of recollection. "I don't remember seeing it anywhere. I'll keep my eyes out, okay?"

"I appreciate it."

Picking up the stack of books, Michael nodded and started back to the shelves, watching from his peripheral as Finch reached up and traced the edges of Bolivar's bearded jaw. In a moment the pair was laughing again, and for Michael they soon faded into the background. He whistled as he placed the books, wondering where he had heard the name of that place before. Why it reminded him of a feeling more than it did of a name.

That night, as the others slept, Michael lay tossing in bed. He gave frantic jerks and groaned against himself as his sleeping face twisted in confusion. In his dreams, or in some other space he did not understand, a blinding collage of colors devoured all that he saw. He felt himself standing in the middle of a great twisting sea of blackness, and before him stood a wall of gray that swirled and writhed against the changing backdrop of paint. As Michael stood, mesmerized by the vision, he felt a great pain in the back of his mind and spun on his heels. Behind him, towers of color clawed at the sky, shifting at random between brown and green. Near the peak of one of the towers, Michael saw a swirling mass of purple and felt cold.

PART III

TO CONJURE FEAR

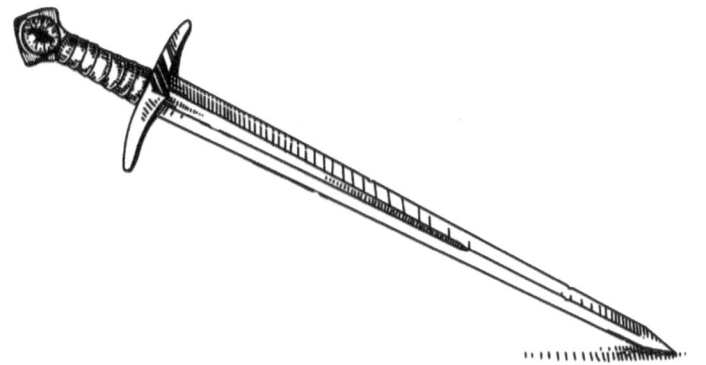

CHAPTER XI
Fox-Faced and Fidgeting

═══════════════════════════════════════

SARAH

In the week after Bolivar's arrival, no new travelers found their way to the Belhaven's doors. Comfortable with one another, the community's meager number of members settled into a routine, and life became the closest thing to normal many of them had known in years. One morning, breakfast just finished and everyone spread throughout the library. Bolivar went to Sarah as she worked on the second floor. Jane and Pinn sat at a cluster of tables talking amongst themselves, a book on magic open in front of them. They had spent their morning asking Sarah questions on magic and the varieties of Aetic arts. They sat and studied for hours, reading and absorbing in only the way kids can. As they read and Sarah worked on the stacks, Bolivar came up the steps. The steady click of his boot heels drew the attention of Jane and Pinn.

"Sarah," Pinn called out, his voice cracking in adolescent escalations as he did, "Bolivar's here. I think he's looking for you."

Sarah walked out from between two of the towering shelves just as Bolivar came to the cluster of tables where the kids sat. She nodded at him and stepped over to the table where she unloaded the books from her arms, halfway blocking Jane's view of Pinn. In his role as Peace Officer, Bolivar had begun to carry himself a little differently. He spoke to the others as if they were his wards to protect. Though no peacekeeping had been required of his new position, Bolivar still seemed focused and duty driven. A marshal with no gunfighters, a bounty hunter with no bounties.

"Why thank you kids," Bolivar said, casting a grin down at Pinn and Jane. Jane's nose crinkled at the word, but she bit her tongue and the two wandered off, uninterested in what Bolivar had to say.

"You need anything?" Sarah asked.

Bolivar scratched at his beard and thought for a moment, his face scrunching underneath the mass of hair. "Well, in my idleness today I had an idea. I am thinking about soliciting one of our members to be my deputy. Deputy Peace Officer, I guess that would be."

Sarah raised an eyebrow and picked some of the books back up, working as they talked. "Well, I don't see a problem with that. Do you have anyone in mind?"

"Bavritt."

"Have you talked to him yet?"

"No, I wanted to be sure you had no objections. This place is yours, of course."

When Sarah stopped and looked back at Bolivar she had expected the glimmer of light from his eyes and the kind face that hung his beard most days, but instead she found that familiar fox-face. That same fierce, cunning look from his first moments at the Belhaven, and she almost winced. "Well," she said, shaking her misgivings away and categorizing them in her mind as irrational anxiety, "you'll have no objections from me."

"Good to hear," said Bolivar giving a smile and a little

motion that was half-nod and half-bow and then pivoted on his heels. "I'll talk to him right away. Thank you, Sarah." At that, he headed back towards the staircase without another word. As the sound of his clicking boot heels bounced up from the wood floor Sarah chewed at the cuticle on her right thumb, her mind still stuck on that fox-faced expression. In the week since his arrival, Bolivar had grown on her. His sly aura was replaced with a kind, jovial face that often told stories that Sarah was only able to half-believe. Still, on occasion she felt a pang of anxiety when she looked at him. His teeth seemed to peek out from his beard in the hunger-snarl of a wild hunter, waiting on her to turn her back. *Well it might be good for Tony to be close to him. I still need to keep my eyes on him.*

Sarah's mind wandered to Ri, who was working in the courtyard with Tony. Knowledge of their relationship had spread through the others with relative speed, but Ri's fears were for nothing. They had no negative comments on their relationship, offering instead only feigned surprise and congratulations when Ri worked up the courage to tell them. Tony, more than anyone else, had congratulated them with a wide grin. Sarah wondered if Ri would be there when Bolivar asked Tony. She wondered if Tony's bond with Ri was stronger than any bond Bolivar might have forged in his time here. She thought about this, and the cuticle of her thumb took the abuse as she did.

"He was plain about it," Ri said that night as they laid with Sarah on the floor of her office. "He just asked Tony if he would serve as his deputy, Tony agreed, and they shook hands."

"Nothing felt off about it to you?"

Lying there, more on Sarah than on the floor, Ri adjusted to rest their head on Sarah's collarbone. Their blonde hair filled Sarah's face and she laughed, moving it out of the way. "I still don't trust him. He feels just like some of the people I used to…travel with."

Sarah looked at Ri from the corner of one eye and almost asked for an explanation, but decided against it. "Do you think Tony will keep an eye on him? I mean if Bolivar was up to anything."

"He'd tell me."

Sarah propped herself up on one arm. "How long did you tell me that you and Tony have been traveling together?"

Ri adjusted to look at Sarah. "About a month. We can trust him, Sarah."

"He just seems so close to Bolivar."

"He's not an idiot, he's just tired of conflict."

Sarah's brow raised just enough to draw Ri's attention. "What was he before? Between when he met you and Tinkret I mean."

"That's his business."

Sarah nodded, knowing better than to push it. She kissed Ri on top of the head, breathing in the soft smell of their hair and closing her eyes. "All right. If you trust him, I trust him." She pushed the thoughts of Bolivar out of her mind and focused instead on Ri, of her library, and of her mother. Her mind wandered back to *The Left Hand of Darkness*, her copy snug in her bag.

The book's words echoed in her mind. "Distrust

everything I say. I am telling the truth." She began to wonder who the villain in her story was.

As the next day whittled its way into the afternoon, Sarah's concerns over Bolivar came and went. He and Tony had chatted with everyone at breakfast about plans for building lookouts along the roof and preparing a training area in the courtyard, to train who Sarah had no idea. As the day went on, Sarah's mind finally began to ease. The sounds of harsh rains and high spring winds rattling the windows of the library, she settled into the administration offices, a worn, leatherbound novel written some time after the Rending in her hands. She lost herself in it. She read on and on until the even began to grow long, and Ri eventually found their way to the administration offices as well, lounging in Sarah's lap as the two sat on the floor. Sarah's eyes shifted from the book to Ri's golden hair. The weight of the library, of everything, nowhere to be found. It wasn't until she heard the sound of rapping knuckles on the frosted glass of the administration offices that she was brought back to reality. She opened the door to find Bolivar standing on the other side, hands behind his back and his brow pulled tight in thought.

"Sarah," he said, his tone flat and professional, "could we speak for a moment? In private."

"What is there that you can't say in front of Ri?" Sarah asked. She could not find a thought she recognized on Bolivar's face.

He gave a soft, disarming smile and glanced down at his

feet. "I'm sure that you'll tell them everything, but all the same." Ri said nothing, but a look of mild shock rested along the edges of their eyes. Deep behind them Sarah thought she saw a rage fighting to the surface. Bolivar glanced up toward the rafters, where he saw Sibella resting above. "That includes the bird. I'd like it to be just you and me."

For a moment, Sarah was quiet. She watched Bolivar's unmoving expression for any signs of the coming conversation, but when she realized there was no convincing him otherwise, she just nodded. "Ri, Sibella, do you mind giving us a moment?" Ri hesitated, but headed out of the door of the administration offices, Sibella close behind.

"Thank you," Bolivar said as the door clicked closed, his arms still behind his back in the same way Sarah had seen a hundred nobles carry themselves in the cities. His face had lost both the boisterous joy and fox-faced mischief. Instead, she saw a face of calculated certainty. She wondered if Tony knew he was there.

"What do you need?" Sarah asked. She shifted her weight from one foot to the other, her arms crossed, pushing her cotton shift up towards her collarbone. She felt vulnerable.

"I think it's time I do a little scouting in Calarine."

Sarah tilted her head. A mix of genuine confusion and relief rose up from the collar of her shirt, and she tried not to betray either feeling to Bolivar. "Then go ahead. Get Tony or whoever you want to go with you and go. You know you don't have to ask me if we're running low on supplies, just let me know when you leave."

"What I have in mind isn't related to gathering supplies. Instead, I'm looking to scout the area for...other groups.

Those 'within earshot,' you might say."

"Well," Sarah said, furrowing her brow and running a hand across the side of her face. "I had considered that it might be time to send out another call, since we haven't seen any newcomers in a while. You'd rather go in person instead?"

"My idea goes a little further. Sure, I will bring in any we come across that seem trustworthy, but I also also want to make close note of any conflict groups."

"What do you mean, 'conflict groups'?" She barely kept the shock from her eyes. Whatever weight the rain had eased had found its way back.

"Undesirables. People who, if they answered the call, might come carrying spears and swords. Traffickers, bandits. You know the type."

Sarah thought for a moment about the men who chased her off of the ridge the night before she made it to Varinz. She thought about the tip of the knife at the small of her back, the dying man in the Varinzian alley, but in the merciless swirl of her mind, she could remember her mother's words, her mother telling her to never entertain fear for fear's sake. "I don't think that's necessary, Bolivar. We haven't had any trouble."

"And you've been god damned lucky." Bolivar pointed a finger in Sarah's face, now. The tension rose between them in sudden jerks and Sarah took a step back as Bolivar's massive hand swung close to her face.

"You've been spending a lot of time up there on the third floor with all of those history books and political studies, have you taken the time to read any of them? I did while it was just me and Sibella here. You're a smart man, so tell me. How many times has 'getting ahead of the threat' been an effective strategy for maintaining peace? Because that's what your job is. You aren't Chief Military Strategist or Director of War. You're Peace Officer."

Bolivar's eyes flashed with anger, and he clenched his bearded jaw so tight that the veins in his temples stood out. "And I say that the best way for me to keep this place safe is to know what threats there are around us!"

"The only reason the Belhaven would have any threats," Sarah said in a persistent, hushed tone as she took a step closer to Bolivar and locked eyes with him, "is if you create them."

Bolivar tensed his arms, his brow sharp and crossed with an anger Sarah had never seen before. "Then let's put it up to vote. See what the others think about how their safety should be handled."

Sarah got close to Bolivar, her face almost touching his. Her mind reeled with rage. There was no anxiety, no uncertainty. In her mind was a blind, unfeeling rage that she had not felt since her journey to Calarine began. *He's going to take it all away.* "What makes you think I owe you that?"

Bolivar grinned, and for a moment Sarah started to back away, thinking she had fallen into a trap. But, as fast as it appeared, the slimy smile faded from his face. "Are you a dictator now? I thought this place was a paragon of freedom and knowledge. Maybe that partner of yours is poisoning your thoughts?"

The inflection in his voice was so clear, Sarah didn't need to question what he was implying. Ri's fears and hesitations rang in her ears, and she took a step back. She thought for a moment about lunging forward, grabbing him around the neck, and throttling him until his eyes bulged, but the difference in their strength was not lost on her. Even though she'd been on the road four times as long as him and matched his height, he still seemed to dwarf her. *I could outrun him, but I could never beat him in a fight.*

"Fine," she answered, the defeat bouncing in her mind like a child's ball. "We'll put it up to vote, and the others can decide what path they want to take on this."

He wore the satisfaction on his face like a mask. "I'll leave it to you to call the meeting then. Wouldn't want the others to think I'm staging a coup, now would we?" Before Sarah could answer, Bolivar spun on his heels and headed out of the administration offices as quickly as he had entered.

He left Sarah standing alone, her breath coming in shaky gulps. She released her tensed muscles and as the throb of anxiety welled up around her, she went and collapsed down at an empty desk just as Ri and Sibella came through the door. As Ri pulled up a chair, Sarah looked up at them. Her eyes were trembling and dark and searching.

"You okay?" Ri asked. Sibella stayed silent, watching Sarah's face with his careful, endless eyes.

"Sibella," said Sarah, offering no sign she had heard Ri's question, "go let everyone know, including Bolivar, that I'm calling a meeting at the front lobby."

"Any details I should share?"

"No, just tell them to be there in an hour."

The falcon nodded, and with a quick skitter of his talons he took flight. As he did, Sarah clenched her hands so tight the whites of her knuckles shined.

"I should have known," she groaned through gritted

teeth. "I should have known better."

"What happened?" Ri asked. "Did he threaten you?"

She shook her head and looked up at Ri. "He's too smart for that, but he's up to something."

"What's do you mean?"

Sarah started to answer, but instead just shook her head. Bolivar's comments, his insinuations, echoed through her mind. "It's easier for you to find it out at the meeting along with everyone else. Ri, I need a promise."

"All right."

"No matter what you see on my face during the meeting, don't contradict whatever decision is made. Just swallow whatever opinion you have, okay?"

Without question, Ri gave a single nod, though cnflict and simmering frustration hung in their brow. The muscles in their neck moved underneath growing tension. Sarah stood up and straightened her clothes, thinking for a minute of putting on her traveling leathers and getting her walking stick. She thought that coming to the meeting dressed as the person who had spent long years on the road alone might give her some credibility, but that thought was dismissed almost as quick as it appeared. Instead, she only reached for Ri's hand, bringing them into an embrace. They kissed, a careful, thoughtful kiss that to Sarah felt like the kind a soldier might give to his wife before he left for the front lines.

"Go ahead and go out there," said Sarah as she let Ri free from their embrace. "I've got some planning I need to do before the meeting."

"Okay, Sare. As long as you're sure."

"I am."

As Ri left, Sarah thought for a moment about the night at the creek. About the embarrassed, nervous kiss they had shared. In that moment, the alleyway was far away, no more than a lingering silhouette along the far meridian. She stood for a long while in the office, leaning on her desk, running the coming meeting through her mind over and over again. She thought of what Bolivar might say and how the others might react. She was certain, for whatever reason, that the coming argument was futile. She felt defeated before she stepped out of the office, but still she composed herself and walked to the front lobby. When she came to the front desk, the others were all seated except for Bolivar, who stood, arms behind his back, in front of them. As Sarah came to stand beside him, he looked at her with a kind, typical expression, but she could feel him smirking at her from behind his beard.

"Thank you, everyone for taking a moment out of your day," Sarah said as she turned to face the others. "Has Bolivar mentioned why we're meeting?"

"No," Tony answered, "he just said that we were waiting on you."

Sarah nodded and let out a short, sharp sigh as she turned to Bolivar. "Make your case, Bolivar." She pressed her hands hard at her side and watched as Bolivar took a step forward and cleared his throat.

"I have made friends with many of you," he said in his clean, confident baritone, "but even the few of you whom I might have a tense relationship with, I hope you at least trust me as your Peace Officer. I just want to go on a scouting expedition in the surrounding area, especially in the ruins of Calarine proper. Not just for food or to speak to any individuals who might want to join us, but also to search for conflict groups that we might need to be aware of." Bolivar turned to look back at Sarah as the others looked on at him, waiting for him to continue. "But Sarah does not believe this is necessary and suggested we put this issue up for a vote and let all of you decide."

"Why don't you think it's necessary?" Michael asked, glancing for a moment over to Tony and Ri. The tension in the room rose in steady steps.

As Sarah tried to orient herself towards the task at hand, the presence of Bolivar radiated through the room. "If we start treating other travelers as threats, we'll just end up creating enemies. It is one thing to go out and search for people to bring into this community, that I support with my entire heart, but to treat anyone like an 'undesirable' is a path that will lead us straight to conflict. A conflict our meager numbers can't handle."

"Meager numbers," Bolivar interjected, "are why we should be concerned."

In the faces of her friends, Sarah saw looks of concern and confusion. She gritted her teeth against the rising frustration she could feel sweep across her face. "Now I think you all can see why we're putting this up to your vote."

"Not really," Tony said. "This is your place, you're the librarian, not Bolivar. Not any of us." He shifted, rubbing a hand down one of his hips and shrugging. "This is your decision, Sarah."

Bolivar cut in before Sarah could respond. "If we're going to build a community then don't you all think it should be a democracy of choice?"

Swallowing down all of the screams she wanted to let loose, Sarah looked at Tony, hoping her eyes conveyed the desperation she felt inside. "Why don't all of you just tell me how you feel about this. If you're all uncomfortable with a formal vote, then a discussion will do."

"I understand where Bolivar is coming from," said Tony. He almost seemed apologetic in his tone. He shifted in his seat and rested his big hands on his knees. For the first time Sarah noticed the old, white scars that marked his dark hands. "We have no idea what kind of people are in Calarine. It's a big place, but it's sparse. We haven't explored much. There are a lot of unknowns. I'm not saying that I think there's any reason to be worried, but I understand Bolivar's point." He paused, rubbing a hang over his throat and giving a short, cut cough. "But, even with all that, I'd rather not get mixed up in anything. I'd rather us just keep our heads, if you understand me."

"I don't," said Finch. Her voice rattled in Sarah's ears. "We could have a camp of imperial guards in the middle of the city and not know it."

"Have you ever come across any problematic guard camps?" Michael asked. "Or camps of marauding raiders?"

Finch shook her head, glancing down at the ground.

"And Sarah, what about you?"

"Just a handful of bad characters." Sarah answered, thinking back to the men who came to her camp in the middle of the night, the alleyway, the small pressure at the base of her back. She had to force herself to stay in the moment. "Never anything I couldn't handle alone." The lie stung her tone, and when she looked at Ri she thought she caught the slightest glint of worry.

"So, I don't understand how this is worth talking about," said Michael.

"There's one key part to all of this you are forgetting, something I am sure both Tony and Ri can agree with. It is the stationary, established communities that need to worry about the empire, about raiders. It is communities just like this one that have to worry!" Bolivar's voice grew more and more frustrated as he watched the wary, darting eyes of the others. "We can't sit around here, singing peace and virtue. There are dangers in this world, likely in these ruins, and none of you are moving anymore. Now you can't dodge them, and this entire thing got started by sending a message out to the world that, for all intents and purposes, screamed 'Hey! I'm here! Come get me!' Someone has to have taken notice of that. All of us did, and unless Sarah somehow shielded that call from anyone with ill intent, and I doubt she did, then there's someone out there with a greedy mind and a sword in hand who has to have heard it."

Sarah's ears started to ring as blood rushed to her head. In the distance she could hear Tony and Finch talking back and forth with Bolivar, but she could not make out the words. Her eyes grew hot, her face heavy, and for a moment she felt like she was stuck on the streets of Varinz, the people bustling back and forth. Then, in a sudden swirl of the crystalline space of her mind, she was on the salted Morable coast, her one-time friends screaming at her to leave and die alone. Screaming at her for her failures, her overconfidence, her unearned certainty in her own ability. She felt her chest tighten. Her breath became sharp and shallow. Sweat creeped into the edges of her hairline. Seeing her distress, Sibella came down from the rafters and landed on her shoulder. Focusing on the falcon, his steady, drumming breaths radiating into her shoulders, she calmed. She felt for a moment that she could return to the same place she had been so many times, the screaming internal pain of panic. Instead, she took a deep breath, and her hearing returned to normal. She realized that only a moment had passed. *Tighten your grip.*

"I just don't think it's necessary," said Michael, "but I can see where Finch is coming from."

Sarah looked at Bolivar, whose eyes still shined with determination. His barrel chest rose and fell in calculated breaths, the veins in his neck stood out from the strain of his oration. For a moment, Sarah thought again about wrapping her hands around his neck and throttling him, choking the last breaths from his smug face. "All right," Sarah interrupted just as Bolivar began to retort, "I've heard enough of all this. Bolivar, we aren't going to put this up to vote." Bolivar started to speak, his face flushed and hot, but she put up a hand to cut him off. "Instead, I'm giving you permission to do whatever you think you need to do. Do your job as the Peace Officer however you think you should, but I expect every piece of anything to do with your 'conflict' groups to run through me. You don't make a move without my explicit permission, understood? Your job is Peace Officer. You are meant to keep the peace here, to maintain order. I expect you to do that."

Bolivar nodded and once again he wore his fox-faced grin. That face made Sarah's skin crawl. "Of course. You are the boss, after all."

Sarah didn't acknowledge him and instead turned back to the others. "Does that satisfy everyone?" For a long moment everyone was quiet before they shared awkward glances with one another.

Michael cleared his throat and stood up. "I think that settles it all just fine." he said, looking back to Tony for reassurance, who nodded.

"Good, now everyone get back to your own lives. This bastard of a meeting is adjourned." Sarah turned back and looked at Bolivar, her face stern. "Let me know what you decide and when you're going out."

Bolivar nodded and started to speak, but Sarah turned and headed towards the back of the library. The others all filed out of the lobby, with Ri speeding towards Sarah. Bolivar was stood alone in the lobby for a moment, seeming to survey everything around him. He smiled a soft, honest smile, put his arms behind his back, and headed towards the third floor. Sparks of satisfaction danced from the clicking heels of his worn boots.

TONY

The night heavy on the Belhaven, Tony sat in the courtyard, staring at the cold fire pit and kicking at a knot of charred pine, his hands laced and worried. When the courtyard doors opened, he looked up and saw Ri headed towards him, the doors swinging closed behind them. They carried their own look of far-off worry, and walked with their shoulders pulled in and their hands deep in the pockets of their canvas pants. When they came to stand at the burned-out fire, Tony only looked up at them and tightened his hands.

"You all right?" Ri asked. "You look about half beaten down."

"You don't look much better."

"No, don't guess I do. What's going on? I saw you and Bolivar talking on the stairs. Looked like the conversation was a little warm."

Tony raised his eyebrows and looked up at Ri from the corner of his vision. His shoulders gave a slight shrug and he unlaced his fingers, running them over his face. "Yeah, I guess it was a little warm."

Ri pulled their hands out of their pockets and placed one on Tony's shoulder. Their farmer's hand still seemed big even on the man's shoulder. "We made a deal in those woods that we wouldn't do this. Spit it out."

Unable to sit still, feeling the world moving around him, Tony stood and crossed his arms, all with his eyes still locked on the stirring ash. He thought of the evenings sitting around it, Sarah and Michael and everyone laughing and drinking his mead. Mead made in a little village in the time just before he found Ri. In that little moment of his life where he had laid his sword down and tried to claw his way back to before he had worn the Black and Red. Before he rode the borders with the Old Judge. Before he carried the thick stain of blood on his hands. Another touch from Ri, this one wordless, pulled him from the fire and he finally met their eyes. "Bolivar is taking me with him on his scouting trip. We're leaving early."

Ri relaxed, the tension falling from their face as they nodded and pushed their chop-cut hair back from their forehead. "Is that it? I imagine Sarah expects that, with you as his deputy, I mean."

Tony's eyes met Ri's again, but they were carried away to some faraway place, the red hints of violence in their dark depths glimmering in a strange nostalgic glow. "I feel something coming. I felt it when he told me his plan. I've felt it before, the hot breath of some evil thing on the back of my neck. Last time I felt it I walked away with a new name." For a moment, his voice faltered and his mouth trembled, but he swallowed and closed his eyes and when he opened them the red recollection was gone. "I took orders on faith once before, and it didn't go anywhere good, Ri. I know we made promises. I know we had, have, plans, but…I won't do that again."

Ri's face was tight and nervous. "What do you mean?"

"I mean that I'm going to watch him. I'm going to see what he is, what he's planning. I mean I don't know what this will look like when I get back. What I--we'll--have to do. What Sarah will have to do. I've felt this coming since the two of you went to Varinz. I've tried to stay close to him, to head it off, but…I don't know. I feel a fight coming."

"Tony, I told you--"

"I know what you told me. I know what I promised you. I know what we left in those trees in the hills. Ri, I will do everything I can to keep that promise. I will do everything I can to keep new blood from our hands, all right?"

Ri nodded but said nothing, and instead the two stood in the courtyard in a heavy, veiled silence. A wind stirred the ashes, beneath the cold a single dark ember rested, still holding onto the warmth of a long-gone fire.

CHAPTER XII
A New Step

==

SARAH

Still undressed and the obvious lines of sleep across her face, Sarah paced in small circles in her office, the early morning light just starting to illuminate the dust that hung in the air. Ri still slept on her pallet, bedding strewn across the floor and their shirt halfway up their stomach. Sarah stopped in her pacing and looked at Ri for a long while, the ease and beauty of the scene laid out in front of her in vibrant simplicity. *We could run. Not just me, we. I could handle just Ri. We could survive and I won't fail them. I might fail everyone else, but never them.* Three sharp raps on the administrative office door pulled Sarah from her daydream and woke Ri, who stirred on the pallet. Sarah pulled her cotton shirt over her head and walked with heavy, sluggish steps out of her office and towards the administrative office door. Halfway to it, three more raps filled the air, this time harder and faster. She opened it to find Bolivar standing on the other side, dressed in the same new traveling gear he had worn when they first met. He held out a few pieces of paper with notes scrawled across them in rust-ink.

"These are my plans, and where we'll be headed." he said as Sarah took them from him. "I'll be taking Tony with me. As long as you approve, of course. I spoke to him at the end of the day yesterday, and he agreed on the necessity. He is already aware and should be getting his own things ready right now. Again, as long as you approve, of course."

Sarah ignored the sarcasm in his voice and flipped through the pages. The documents were thrown together and filled with half finished sentences. "How long do you plan to be gone?" she asked.

"About three days," Bolivar answered, his hands once again held behind his back. "Over the past several weeks I've taken the time to learn a handful of communication spells. Should anything happen, I'll contact you."

A look of suprise filled Sarah's eyes and she looked up from the papers. The mention of spells had taken her off guard. She knew he was studying the books on magic but had not seen him actually using any. Bolivar's smug face echoed in the back of her mind. "All right, go ahead. But remember, your job is Peace Officer, not strategist." Bolivar nodded, snatched the papers from Sarah's hands, and walked away.

Exhausted from the day, Sarah put her back to the door and let the exhaustion pour out of her. As she walked through her office door, she saw Ri sitting up on their shared bedroll, their soft, pale skin shining in the early sun. She stood there for a moment, shocked at Ri's sudden nakedness. But the way the sun hit Ri's face, highlighted their hair, brought a wild, flushed grin to her face. That earliest moment, the hot-breathed night standing outside of the administration offices, had still played in Sarah's mind. Now, Sarah's stress washed away as she went back to them and laid down.

"Don't we need to get up?" Ri asked, straddling Sarah, a sly grin on their face. They ran their hands down Sarah's neck, the contrast of Ri's cream-pale skin against Sarah's traveled, sun-tanned body was almost electric. They leaned down, their chest pressing against Sarah's, and kissed her. Sarah gave a soft sigh and Ri reached down, almost ripping off her shirt. They ran their hands over Sarah's ribs, her stomach. In the briefest pause Sarah felt Ri squeeze at her hips with their legs and thought for a moment how much they really did feel like the legs of someone who had spent most of their life as a farmer. She imagined Ri carrying lumber on their shoulders, the muscles of their back standing out against a thin, sweat soaked shirt as the summer heat bore down. Sarah's face blushed as the image swirled again and again in her mind and she reached down, grasping at the taut muscles of Ri's thighs that held her pinned to the floor. In the whirlwind of everything between them, Ri held Sarah's breasts in their hands, and in a moment, they were together.

Scant rays of light catching across their forms, Sarah writhed beneath Ri, barely managing to stay on the bedroll as she did. Her hips bucked as Ri's hands found their way across Sarah's body, stopping like visitors in great cities as they did. Sarah, familiar and comfortable in their place together, started to claw at Ri's back. They pushed her hard into the floor and grabbed at her thin neck, squeezing it as she bent down to bite at Sarah's collarbone, their hand between her thighs. As she came, Sarah flipped Ri onto their back, and the cold stone of the floor sent a shock down their spine. They let out a long, uncontrolled moan, much louder than they had intended. All at once both of them realized that they were in all likelihood not the only ones awake. Sarah's eyes widened, darting around the room in a desperate search for any sign that they had been heard. She placed a hand over Ri's mouth, but when Ri bit at

Sarah's palm, all of the tension in the room dissolved. They had to fight to keep from laughing. Together they laid on the cold floor together, side by side for a long while, staring at the ceiling.

"Thank you," Sarah said, their voice cracking a little as they did. Sarah looked at Ri, noticing the way their cropped blonde hair framed the delicate lines of their dark eyebrows for the hundredth time.

"What do you mean?"

"Understanding." Sarah ran a hand down the side of Ri's face and kissed them. She wanted to tell them how much everything meant to her. How the world had been ripped away from her and she had lost so much, but now parts of that didn't feel like it mattered as much anymore. But she didn't, she couldn't, because she knew it wasn't true, not all of it.

"I am sure that Finch and the children would prefer if they didn't have another morning of Michael's burned breakfast," they both heard Sibella call out. The falcon was perched in the rafters above them. For a moment Sarah wondered if the bird was up there smirking in his sneakiness, catching them in such a vulnerable state.

"All right, all right," said Sarah, standing up. "We'll be in the kitchen as soon as we can. She heard flapping wings as she helped Ri to their feet.

MICHAEL

As Bolivar woke Sarah and Ri, Michael sat up in his cot rubbing at his eyes. It had been another night of fitful, exhausting sleep. He dreamt of the same masses of swirling colors, just as he had every night since finding the shrine. They were not always visions, but he still dreamed of the colors even if they never formed into anything real. It seemed to Michael that the more time passed, the more the horrible paintings engulfed him. He started to hate the color purple.

"Rough night?" Tony asked as he sat up in bed and stretched out his shoulders.

Michael nodded and yawned.

"You never sleep worth a shit, do you?" Finch asked, pulling on her socks.

"Not lately."

"Wanna smoke?" Finch's face was twisted up and pulled in in a thin veil of reserved laughter. Michael gave a sarcastic smirk and scrunched his nose at her, less amused than he was aggravated.

Stooping down to fish his leather ankle boots from the edge of the bed, Tony pulled them on and stood up. "Well at least you don't have to spend the next three days following Bolivar around looking for nothing." Finch swatted at him, and Tony turned to look at her. "Sure, yeah, I bet, you'd love to be out there all alone with him, huh? He could be your hero, come to save you from the Dread Pirate Rogers, or whoever is grasping heaving bosoms this week." Tony grinned from ear to ear.

Finch's face flushed crimson. "Fuck you, smart ass." Her eyes darted towards the book on the floor beside her bed. *A Ship of Ecstasy.*

Michael stood and shook his head just as the three of them heard the administration doors swing closed.

"Well, I guess that's my cue," said Tony as he pulled his pack onto his shoulder.

"You aren't staying for breakfast?" Finch asked.

Tony shook his head. "Bolivar took some time to make hard tack for the road."

Michael grimaced. He was almost laughing. "I'm sorry."

"You two be safe," said Finch.

"Don't worry, I'll take care of your beau."

Finch flipped him off as Tony started towards the front desk where Bolivar stood waiting.

Michael rolled his neck, hoping to stretch the night's stress away, and looked to Finch. "Big plans today?"

"Not at all. You okay Mike? You look like hell."

Michael smiled a tired smile and nodded. "Just having some nightmares. Any idea where the kids are?"

Finch shrugged. "They just went up to the second floor, I'm sure. You worried about them?"

"I do prefer to keep an eye on my kid, you know. I'll go get them for breakfast."

Finch started to say she would join him after a smoke, but Michael pivoted on his still-bare feet and started towards the second floor. As he neared the top of the wooden steps he collapsed and clasped his hands to the sides of his head in a sudden, agonized jerk. He found himself standing in the ethereal plane of swirling, maddening color. Stone gray and black and green and brown danced around one another as he felt the encroaching aura of purple, its horrific, black-fringed light blinded him in its brilliance, its terror. He writhed on the floor, his daughter and Pinn talking happily and unaware at the back of the second floor. His eyes stared at nothing, his mind lost in the world of his vision. A brilliant mixture of color swirled within them, erasing his irises from their plane.

SARAH

After breakfast, Sarah started back on her work cataloging the library's collection. This time she recruited only Ri, Michael having complained of a headache and lying back down after breakfast, apologizing every step of the way. His eyes were so veiled in dark circles that he looked ill. She knew, at least she thought she did, what that meant, but she did not dare bring it up. She trusted Michael to manage the issue of the shrine himself. He would have to, she had Bolivar to worry about. At times, as she carried books back and forth in the second floor stacks, organizing them into spell types, Aetic histories, and the annals of Goraln, she thought about how silly her efforts must seem from the outside. The collection seemed to go on forever, and she wondered if she would have enough time to finish it. But she pushed on, focused less on the task ahead and instead treating it as an opportunity to discover the secrets of the library. As she and Ri spent a long day in the second floor stacks, glancing at one another with the heat of the morning still on their minds, she sat down at one of the tables with a tome on the traditional Aetic arts.

"Ri," she called out, and in just a moment they came and sat down beside her. "Have you decided if you want to start learning magic?"

Propping themselves on the table with their elbows, Ri shook their head. "That just isn't something I'm interested in, Sare." Sibella came flying down to the tabletop much faster than normal, startling Ri. "God dammit Sibella, watch it."

The falcon paid them little attention. Instead, he just scratched the scattered papers that covered part of the table out of his way. "Doing some reading?" he asked, looking over the book Sarah was thumbing through. "Ah, *Tome of the Traditional Aetic Arts*, a good resource, though incomplete."

"Incomplete?" Ri asked.

"Yes, though as the title tells you it is quite substantial, it is meant to be paired with another work *Tome of the Combative Arts*. This one focuses almost entirely on passive and support magic. Things like protection runes, communication spells, that like."

"Yes, I saw that on the shelf next to this one," Sarah noted. She continued to flip through the pages, dog-earing ones that interested her.

Sibella came to rest on Sarah's shoulder. "You know, with the recent…aggravations you've had with Bolivar, it might be time to begin educating yourself on those combative arts." Sarah's hands froze, but she didn't give any other signs that she had heard him. Ri looked at the side of her face, which twitched with nervousness.

"He has a point," Ri added. "It might be time to start thinking about things like that. Either because Bolivar has something up his sleeve, or because of the small chance that he's right and we end up with our hands full."

Sarah turned to look at Ri. Her face was heavy, tired in much the same way that it had been the day Bolivar confronted her. "Fear creates nightmares, not the other way around. If I start learning that kind of magic, will I be any better than Bolivar? I'll be everything I preached at him about." If I start learning that kind of magic, will I be able to hold it together? She remembered a brief passage from a book early on in her time at the library. *Combative spells require the most focus and internal certainty of any magic. Failure can be dangerous.* All at once that small pressure was back, and she felt magelight dying at her fingertips.

"You cannot ignore the importance of intention," said Sibella. His tone was sharp and matter of fact. "If you rest on your laurels, you may find Bolivar to be a formidable problem, should he choose to become such a thing. It cannot be ignored that he has started to take up the Aetic arts himself. We do not know what kind of spells he has learned or what he is capable of."

Sarah nodded, letting out a tired sigh and stood up, slipping past Ri and getting the other tome from the shelf. She came back to the table and replaced the first with the new book, which seemed heavy in her hands. She opened it to the title page, noticing it was split into two halves, a section on "Defensive Magics" and a section on "Offensive Magics." She turned to the first page of the defensive magic section and scanned the list of spells. She flipped to the page entitled "Shield of Morine," and read. Ri and Sibella watched without speaking as she looked over the spell, taking note of its components and requirements. When she closed her eyes to focus, Sibella hopped off her shoulder and onto the table while Ri stood up to give Sarah the space she needed.

The others standing around her, Sarah closed her eyes and focused on the page, letting the words run through her as she began to form the spell in the core of her stomach. She did as she always had to do, in those earliest moments before a spell became commonplace, and pushed away her fears. She set aside her old friends standing on the Morable coast; she left the man a shadow in the alleyway. She set aside her years of running from it all. But as she did, she felt a spark of rage in the depths of her being. She thought of Bolivar, how she had wanted to hurt him. As the thought stirred in her mind, she grew bitter. She lost track of the spell, and her mind clouded. In that lost state, everything flooded back, but it was Bolivar along the cave wall, knife in one hand, severed rope in the other. It was Ri falling into the depths of the cave. On the cave floor she could see Michael and Finch and Tony and the kids mangled and broken.

Distorted with her feelings of hate and resentment, confusion and regret, she lost sight of what she wanted, of her core intent. Sibella and Ri watched as a bright purple aura emanated around her. Sibella screeched and flung himself at Sarah, sinking his talons into her arm. Ri clutched at their ears and watched as Sibella pecked at Sarah's shoulder. Her eyes snapped open, and as the aura disappeared she let out a pained scream. Sibella released her, standing back on the tabletop as Sarah clutched her bleeding arm, gasping for air.

"Go get some first aid supplies, Ri," said Sibella.

At the falcon's words, Ri darted towards the administration offices. In the wanting aftermath of the aura's appearance, the air seemed to crackle with the purple-tinged remnants of Sarah's failure. She rested her head on the table, her breath ragged and aching.

When Ri returned, alcohol and gauze in hand, they tended Sarah's wounds. Their hands were quick and sure, no trace of nervousness or unfamiliarity. "Are you okay?"

"I think so. I'm sorry, I--I'm not sure what happened. Thank you for breaking me out of whatever that was, Sib."

"It was the Calling Maw," said the falcon. Sarah and Ri could both hear the concern in his voice, even though he tried to conceal it. "It is a Great Borough about which very little is known."

"What do you mean?" Ri asked. "Why did she start to glow like that?"

Sibella sighed, craning his neck almost like he was trying to crack it. "I do not know, to be honest. All of the Great Boroughs are places where a type of magic comes from, and all of them are written about in the books scattered throughout this place, except for the Calling Maw. I am not even certain about that name. That is just what the Alchemical always called it. He claimed he heard the name in a vision one night, as he meditated. No magic is said to come from that place, but instead a type of power that seems to...coat other spells. Change them and their effects. I do not really understand it, and neither did the Alchemical."

"I went to a...dark place while trying to cast the spell," Sarah added, seeming to have gotten some of her strength back. "I let my mind wander to Bolivar and my...rage. Does that darker magic come from those kinds of feelings?"

"Not always, at least I don't think so. To be honest, this power is something I don't understand. I just..." Sibella trailed off, starting to avoid Sarah's gaze.

"What?" Sarah asked, her face grave, concerned.

Sibella cleared his throat, or at least the nearest papercrafted approximation he could manage, and shook out his feathers. "The Alchemical did not disappear. At least not... exactly. He left this place, left me here alone." The falcon stopped speaking, his small, paper face haggard. "The Alchemical left ten years ago. He became obsessed with learning more about the Calling Maw after an experience not unlike what you just went through. I do not understand why, but he said he felt drawn to it. I have not seen him since."

"I'm sorry," Sarah said. She was unable to think of what else to say.

"We aren't going anywhere," Ri added. "You don't have to worry about that." Sarah nodded in agreement.

Sibella looked to both of them and nodded. "Enough of that. Are you okay, Sarah?"

She nodded, running a still shaking hand over her forehead. "I think I'm done with this. I can't take the risk of these spells anymore. Thinking like that, getting to that place. It felt…dangerous."

Sibella shook his head, his paper feathers giving off the sound of rustling leaves as he did. "No, that is the wrong way to look at this. Though much is unknown, I do understand a little about what this power does. It isn't an inherent evil. It is not connected to these combat spells. It could infect any spell you cast. What matters is the intent."

"He's right. You can't just give up on all of this."

"Try again," Sibella urged her, "but this time let go of your anger towards Bolivar. Focus only on the purity of the words. Of the spell."

Focusing on the page, Sarah sighed and closed her eyes again. As the tome's instructions swirled in her head, she felt the magic surrounding her. This time, though, she knew she could not control where her mind went, the way it would betray her. As the slick-walled cave, the sounds of the coast slapping against its half-exposed mouth, appeared in her mind, she did not run. She instead turned her eyes to her failure, to the last friend in her life who she had let slip. The boy's face, so long shrouded in the clouded haze of her unwanted knowing, cleared and she saw him. His dark hair. His sharp, regal features. She saw the way he had held his staff--her staff--in his hands. As she tried to cling on, she saw the look on his face. A look of knowing, of feeling. For the first time, she let go of him by her own will. *Henry. Henry, I'm sorry.* The boy, a boy named Henry meant for noblehood but running with her because she promised him adventure, said nothing. Neither did he fall. Instead, the sounds of the water at the cave's mouth stopped. An endless, long coming silence like a tide perpetual in its refusal to recede. The dark stone that she had thought herself strong enough to conquer vanished. Instead, she saw Ri. She saw Tony. She saw Sibella. She saw the library, its high walls and towering shelves. *Sometimes the world issues us challenges.*

As she snapped her eyes open, a shield of crackling blue light surrounded her. From inside the bubble, she gave a somber grin.

ʟᴇᴀᴄ̧ʜᴍᴀʟɪᴄ̧

As the electric-blue shield crackled out of Sarah's hands, the cloaked figure and his shadow-veiled cat sat watching the Belhaven. The man's violet eyes shone underneath a black cloth hood, and he sat with his forearms, dark and hidden in the unnatural shadow, rested on his knees. He smiled as he saw the flash of magic in the library's windows.

CHAPTER XIII

The Capitol

==

TONY

Bolivar and Tony headed out of the Belhaven's front doors and into the Spring sunlight of the wilds. The sound of soft wind weaved around the buildings that surrounded the library. Both men were dressed in full traveling gear, Bolivar's still shining bright with its new leather squeaking as he trotted down the library's steps. Tony carried a heavy, hard-backed pack filled with gear and rations, much of his own gear left behind to make room for the new. His ax was still propped against his cot inside, and in its place on the side were three full water skins. His thick padded brigandine armor was unclasped down the front, revealing the long waisted padded cotton shirt beneath.

"A little fresh air feels nice," Bolivar said aloud, speaking more to himself than Tony. "Little wind on our cheeks and some dirt on our boots. It'll do us some good."

"What's the plan?" Tony asked as he caught up to Bolivar in the street. The pair eyed their surroundings, and Tony shifted the pack on his back.

Bolivar scratched at his beard and turned towards the heart of the city. He blocked the sun from his eyes with a raised hand and pointed towards a glimmering brass dome on the skyline. "See that dome sticking out of the middle of town?

Eagle on top."

Tony nodded and raised his hand to block the sun as well.

"That's the old capitol building from when this place was the capital of the Southern Line. We can work our way there, then see what else there is to this place. If there's anyone camped in this god-forsaken heap, they'd be at the capitol."

"What makes you say that? I figured somewhere along the fringes would be better."

"Probably find some folks there too, but I'm certain we'll find someone in the capitol. A big building like that, all made of stone? Perfect place to hold up if you're looking to weather the unknown. Better to go inward then work our way back out to the city limits, anyway."

Tony nodded and straightened the pack on his back as the two headed out. They walked at a quick, steady pace towards the city's center, where the once-vibrant capitol building stood. Its stained and tarnished brass dome shined in ostentatious objection to the city's decay. As Bolivar and Tony worked their way through the ruins, the sun hammered down on them. The stone beneath their feet soaked up the heat in reverberating waves. Tony found himself wondering how people ever managed to live in places like Calarine. How he had managed to live in a place like that, so long ago when the world was simpler. Kinder. To him, anyway.

"Can you imagine doing this now?" Tony asked. "Living in a place like this, I mean. I can't. Not anymore."

Bolivar laughed and turned back to look at Tony. His beard gave way to a light, thin-lipped smile. For a moment Tony thought he saw something strange there, but the wiling grin that often hung on Bolivar's face soon replaced it, whatever it was. "You forget, I haven't been on the road but just a short while. Not near as long as you. I still remember the smell of city streets with a nostalgic familiarity. I didn't leave out of a hate for that, you know."

"Fair, but you've been away long enough to have gotten used to dirt underneath your feet instead of this stone."

"That's true," said Bolivar. His head now looked up towards the clouds that swirled around the scorching sun. "But I miss parts of it. The art, the culture."

Thinking back to his long years as a brewer, Tony started to point out how different life was in the northern cities for those who did not hold noble lives, but as they weaved through the streets bordered by the steel towers they both stopped, their eyes searching for something unseen ahead.

"Smell that?" Bolivar asked. His eyes scanned the sky, hands twitching idly at his side. "Smoke, but I'm not sure from where. I don't see any haze."

"Yeah, I smell it too, but I don't see anything either."

Bringing his hand to his mouth, Bolivar blew a narrow stream of air through his fist. A bright spark of magic followed his breath and appeared in front of him. Tony watched as the spark darted away and weaved down the street. The tracing spell soon disappeared behind a broken fountain just ahead, and Bolivar started after it.

They followed the light a short distance before it faded out, and the sound of voices filled the air. The brief, crashing sound of clattering glass followed. Bolivar and Tony stopped and crouched beside a pile of rubble that blocked part of the street. Tony took off the pack and rested it beside him before peaking around the debris. Three men sat around a fire just underneath the eave of one of the abandoned buildings. Along the edge of their small camp, Tony saw two large swords and a metal staff leaned against the wall.

"What do you make of that?" Tony asked. He leaned back behind the rubble.

"Just travelers it seems. Those weapons are military, so they could be deserters, or they killed some soldiers at some point. But they are drunk off their asses. I can smell the brew from here."

Tony started to ask how he knew the men were not soldiers or scouts, but before he could, Bolivar stepped out from behind the pile of rubble and walked toward the camp. Tony grabbed the pack and followed after Bolivar, who hurried toward the men in a wide, confident gait.

"Hello!" Bolivar called out. "Hello there in camp!"

The three men wheeled around, the two broad shouldered ones in black linen shirts grabbed the two swords, while a skinnier one, nearly a foot taller than the other two, picked up the staff, stumbling as he did. Bolivar stopped and put his hands up and grinned a wide, mad-man's grin.

Tony stopped just a few feet behind him. His right hand went to his left hip, but all his confused fingers found there was air. He clenched his fist and wished he hadn't left his wood ax at the library. He felt as his heart started to pound in his chest, but he forced his breathing to stay still and his eyes to stay focused. No signs of the struggle within appeared on the man's dark face.

"Whoa now," said Bolivar. He was half laughing, a feigned grin on his face. "We're just travelers. Thought you boys might want to share a drink and spin yarns for a while. Looked like you were having a good time, and my throat is dry."

One of the two big men, this one with a shining bald head and knotted hook nose, took a couple of steps closer, looking Bolivar up and down. "Oi, Donny," the big man said. The skinny one grinned and walked closer. "Fine clothes on this one. Look like they're brand new, don't they?"

"Sure do," answered the skinny one. He was shifting the staff in his hands. "Hey mister, where you come up with clothes like that?"

"Let's all calm down," Bolivar answered, still holding his hands near his head. Tony stood beside him now, watching the three men, eyes still and flecked with a wild, violent red. "Let's all just have a drink together, get to know one another. Then maybe I can introduce you to my tailor." Bolivar smiled so wide it almost made Tony feel sick. He was feeling the lack of a sword on his belt. But he had left that behind, left the sword sunk halfway into a tree where he found Ri. The two broad shouldered men had begun taking calculated steps towards them. Tony knew they were preparing for a fight. His heart pounded on and on.

The other big man, this one with a long mop of hair tied in a messy knot on the top of his head, swung his broadsword onto one shoulder. "I'm thinkin' that you'll be getting on back the way you came. Fancy clothes and a big pack like that, two of you can't be nothin' but trouble."

"A'yep," the skinny one chimed in, "I think that is exactly what'll be happenin'."

Bolivar didn't say another word. Instead, he gave a

quick, sharp stomp onto the blackstone road with his right foot and shot his left hand out in front of him. A jolt of red electricity erupted from his palm, striking the bald man in the chest. The man flew backwards, convulsing as he rolled onto the ground. Bolivar took another step forward and sent both hands out and another flash of electricity flew towards the other two men. Bolivar stood straight, looking at the three men as they writhed on the ground in pain. He clenched his fists, no other signs of effort on his broad frame, and in a thunderous clap, stone shot from the ground and pierced each of the men through the chest. They all stopped moving in single, terrible jerks. Blood pooled around their bodies, the stones that rose from their chests casting the monoliths as red-stained monuments to their foolish decisions.

Tony stood still as a ghost, only able to watch as Bolivar killed the three men in a matter of seconds, having never uttered a word. The visage of blood and light and terror swirled in his mind with a glimmer of nostalgia, and he felt blood splatter his own face, there in that faraway place. He heard the Old Judge roar his name, his new name, as his brewers arms swung his sword. *Cut butcher cut! Not a brewer anymore, a butcher in the name of our War, oh yes!*

Bolivar straightened his clothes and brushed away a yellow powder that had formed on the fingers of his gloves. With an air of satisfaction, he walked over to inspect the bodies. Red scars streaked across the exposed bodies of the three men. It was a deeper, stranger red than the blood that emptied out in a hurried rush. Bolivar bent over and picked up the skinny one's staff and turned it over in his hands. With a plain white kerchief he pulled from his back pocket, he wiped the bloodied fingerprints from it and then propped himself on it. "Tony," he called out, "come grab one of these swords."

Hesitating for only a moment, Tony shuffled over to Bolivar and the bodies. He looked down at them, his eyes wandering over their scarred and mangled corpses. His mind reeled back into reality and he fought to calm himself, to hold his heart still and to push away the violence he felt behind his eyes. To stay out of old battlefields and in this new one. He thought about asking Bolivar where he had learned those spells, how he managed to learn power like that without him noticing. He saw how Bolivar looked over the scene with a gleaming eye, a shadow of the Old Judge hanging nearby, and decided to stay quiet. Instead, he bent over and picked up one of the broadswords. He held it in his hand for a moment, its weight heavy and balanced. He hated how right it felt. How it made him feel whole.

"Look around the camp and see if they have a scabbard for that thing," said Bolivar, still not looking at Tony.

Tony did as he was told, finding the scabbard under the eave of the building near the crates the men had used as chairs. He picked it up, tied it to his belt, and slid the sword into it. He was unable to take his eyes off of the dead men. For a moment he felt like vomiting. A familiar feeling rose up at the base of his throat as the memories of bodies on countless battlefields filled his mind. A crimson reflection of the moon's light on his sword. *New sword to wet now, butcher.* "Do we need to do something with the bodies?"

Bolivar took a deep, hocking breath, and spat on the skinny one. He closed his eyes and gave a prayer in a sarcastic, sing-song voice. "And so ye were born, and so ye shall lay. In the dirt with worms and dog shit, covered in snot and hay. And so you shall lay, and so you shall, until my time you can repay." He propped himself on the staff and smiled at Tony. "Ready to keep moving?" Despite the thin smile, there was no amusement on his face, no grim satisfaction. He carried the look of a man just finished with a job he had done a thousand times before.

Tony nodded, willing to do anything to get away from the dead. Trying to remember where he had heard that prayer before.

They traveled for the rest of the day, weaving their way through the city's unfamiliar streets. It took much longer for them to reach the city's capitol building than it ever would have during Calarine's thriving days. Piles of rubble and collapsed buildings sometimes blocked entire sections of the blackstone roads, and the required serpentine pattern lengthened their trip by hours. Bolivar and Tony seldom spoke to one another, only interacting when they had to work to climb over obstacles or when they stopped for water as the sun beat down, refracted and intensified through the remaining glass windows. As they came into view of the Capitol, Bolivar stopped in the middle of the road and looked at the sky. The sun creeped behind the horizon, and the shadows grew longer each minute.

"Let's make camp here tonight," said Bolivar. "No fire, since we don't know if anyone's here or not."

"No fire?" Tony's eyes scanned their surroundings for a place to sit his pack and sword. "Not worried about beasts?"

Bolivar chuckled and stuck his head into a nearby

abandoned building. "Not this close to the city's heart. Besides, I'm sure we can handle anything that wanders up. Here looks like as good a place as any other."

Carrying an air of uncertaintly but unable to find the strength to argue, Tony nodded and stepped into the building. He sat his pack and sword down before unrolling his bed roll along one of the walls. Bolivar took his own bed roll from the pack and did the same. They sat down together as the sun began to disappear beyond Calarine's skyline. Tony pulled a cloth sack from the bag and took two pieces of hard tack from it before passing it and a water skin to Bolivar. They both choked the tough, tasteless bread down and drank several mouthfuls of water before falling into a state of near-perfect silence.

After a long moment, Tony cleared his throat and shifted on his bedroll. "Bolivar, don't you think that went too far? The men, I mean."

Bolivar looked at him in confusion, and in the twilight-darkness Tony saw him cock his head.

"Those men. We didn't have to kill them."

Bolivar laughed. A real, genuine laugh that sounded like he had never heard anything quite as funny in his entire life. "They threatened us, what did you want me to do? Shake their hands? Come on now, don't pretend that's the first time you've seen anyone die. You told me about your time wearing the Black and Red."

Tony gritted his teeth against the name. "I just feel like we could've found a better way around that, you know?"

"A man who stands for a single aggression will be walked over for the rest of his life. I'm sure you know that."

Tony nodded, not caring if Bolivar could see in the darkness or not, and gave a quick sigh. He wondered what noble soldier he was quoting this time. "Where'd you learn all that anyway? I haven't seen you practicing any of that at the Belhaven."

Bolivar smiled and his white teeth shined in the growing moonlight. "Oh, I'm sure you have. You just probably haven't noticed." Bolivar paused and Tony wondered if he was waiting for a reply, but a whistling breath interrupted those thoughts as he saw Bolivar wag a finger in his direction. "As a matter of fact, you asked me about it the other day."

His head snapping to look at Bolivar, a movement so sudden he was sure Bolivar could make it out in the shadows, Tony choked down a scoff. "I don't remember that."

"Tony, a couple of days ago you asked me about some loud noises you heard in the courtyard. I told you I was just training, and you asked me what spells. We talked about that for almost twenty minutes. You doing okay?"

Tony scratched at the scraggle of a beard on his face and furrowed his brow. "Been so much going on the past few days, I guess that slipped my mind." He leaned his head back against the wall behind him, trying to search his memory for the conversation Bolivar asserted was real. Any conversation about magic or Aetics. He couldn't even remember Bolivar ever saying the word.

Bolivar settled into his bed roll and rested his head on his hands. "Oh, it's fine. Get some sleep, we'll get up early tomorrow and get to the capitol building."

Tony settled in himself and turned to his side. As the moon beams settled on his face he drifted to sleep. As his mind began to fall into the slow swells of the night, he wondered what else there was to Bolivar he did not know or understand. He lay in a twilight state for hours, thinking of the way Bolivar infiltrated their lives with his stories of heroism and boldness. He wondered, even if only for a moment, if any of it had been true. As he felt his eyes grow heavy, he prayed to his old god, asking for guidance. He asked, in that final moment before sleep took him, for the ancient and single God of the old faith to send him a sign.

In the depth of the night, the sounds of a wet, squelching slither pierced the air. The noise woke Tony, who sat up and searched through the darkness with his still sleeping eyes. The sound grew louder, and as it mixed with Bolivar's snoring it became impossible to place, seeming to move in the shadows themselves.

"Who's there?" Tony called out, but only a ripple of shocked grunts answered him as Bolivar jerked awake and raised to look at him.

"Who the hell are you talking to?"

Tony shushed him and again heard the steady slither from the darkness. From the corner of his vision Tony saw something move and reached for his new sword, hoping not to startle whatever waited in the darkness. Just as his hand touched the sword's hilt Tony saw a jerking movement and brought the sword, scabbard and all, down hard to his right. He heard a stomach-turning crunch, and a splatter of hot, burning slime landed on his arms. He scrambled to his feet wiping at it with his pants legs as Bolivar shot up from his bed roll and cast a bright ball of light from his hands. Tony's arm was whelped from the slime, his pants burned away where he had wiped at it. On the ground beside his bed roll lay a long, snake-like creature, crushed from the blow of his sword. Its oozing guts ate at the grayrock floor, leaving black scorch marks behind.

"A fucking slime-hind. So much for no beasts, huh?" He reached down and pulled his sword off the monster, his scabbard now spotted with burn marks from the acid. He held it under his good arm as he nursed at the brilliant stinging along his right.

Bolivar gritted his teeth and cast a flash of fire at the creature. The blaze engulfed the dead beast and took the dangerous slime with it. "All right, well, the excitement is over."

"Bolivar, we should sleep in shifts. If we can't have a fire there might be more."

"If you think that's necessary, sure." Bolivar had already settled back into his bedroll.

"I guess I'll take first watch, then."

Bolivar nodded and Tony propped himself against the wall, watching the night wind on as he thought about Bolivar. He wondered how many of Bolivar's stories had been the same bravado that had scarred his arm. Not once did his search for signs from the night before cross his mind. He did, though, remember Bolivar's prayer. He remembered hearing it when the creep was wiped out of Tinkret, the fires burning bodies in the streets. He sat, staring out into the night, hearing the soldiers sing their prayer.

The morning sun poured through the empty windows and onto Bolivar's face. He stirred, having been on the second watch but sleeping all the same, and stretched as he came to his feet. He looked out the glassless window toward the balconies of the capitol building. In the glare of the sun, juxtaposed against the sharp marble whiteness of the building's facade, he saw a silhouetted figure moving back and forth.

"Hey come over here," Bolivar said. The pain on Tony's burned arm had dulled to an ache in the night, and as he walked over to the window and looked out he rubbed at it with an absent minded hand. "See up there?"

Tony saw as the ant-like silhouette marched back and forth, back and forth. He could tell they were holding something in their hands, but he could not make out much more than that. "What's the plan?"

Bolivar slapped him on the back. "We walk up and say hello. They aren't anything for us to be worried about."

Tony started to point out they had no idea how many people were there, who they were, or what type of people they might be, but before he could Bolivar grabbed his staff and stuffed his bed roll back in the pack. He headed towards the capitol building and motioned to Tony and then to the pack with an impatient arrogance. Tony gathered the pack, strapped his sword back onto his belt, and followed behind Bolivar. He caught up with him just as they came out of the tangled mess of ancient steel towers and into a large courtyard surrounded by lush grass and overgrown hedges. At the center a set of ornate stone steps led to the front doors of the capitol, a towering statue depicting an ancient, bent man glaring down a thin southern face standing at their feet. Bolivar walked on towards the steps, but Tony stood for a moment and looked around in wonder at the courtyard. His mind went back to Tinkret, to his family and their visit to the city's own official buildings, the park that surrounded them in their autocratic obscenities.

All at once he was snapped out of those memories when a swish of wind ripped through the air near his right leg. He heard a sudden thunk land into the thick grass around him. He jerked and almost leapt into the air. "Holy shit! Bolivar watch out!" He stepped towards Bolivar as he heard another thud strike the ground. Two crossbow bolts were stuck into the soft clay earth. They both turned and looked to the balcony of the capitol building where they could see the once-silhouetted figure, now fully in the daylight. The man pointed a crossbow at both of them. Bolivar flung his hands toward the ground and brought a shield of blue, electric light around them.

"Wait!" Bolivar called out. He waved his hands from within the shield. "Wait! We just want to talk." Another crossbow bolt flew into the shield. As it was ricocheted away the blue field resonated with crackling electricity.

Tony crouched to keep his head from touching the top of the shield. "I told you we needed to be careful."

Bolivar ignored him and instead took a deep breath and shouted at the archer again. "I'm going to let this shield down, and you aren't going to shoot that crossbow again, all right? We're going to stop this before you get hurt." Bolivar lowered his hands and the shield dissipated around them before Tony, whose face was struck with disbelief, could protest.

For a moment, Tony thought he saw the crossbow go back to the sentry's shoulder, but instead the figure turned and disappeared into the shadows at the back of the balcony. Bolivar's tense shoulders relaxed, and he turned back to Tony, smug in the fact that his gambit had worked in their favor. Tony started to say something, but the sound of the Capitol's front doors interrupted him with a sudden, roaring groan. Bolivar looked up the massive steps of the Capitol as shadows appeared along the staircase.

"You down there!" a gruff, angered voice called out. "Come up the middle of these steps, and do it slow. And don't try any of that Aetic shit again, or we'll put a bolt through your buddy's forehead."

Tony looked at Bolivar and nodded to him, and together the two started up the middle of the steps. As the facade of the building came more into view, so too did the reality of the Capitol's condition. The old building had been left to time, and even though the forest had not yet reclaimed it, the Rending had left its mark. The moments of fire and thunder of the change had worn the stone carvings that had once graced the archways and pillars of the building away, leaving behind an indecipherable mass of stone. Many of the stained glass windows were shattered, the remnants of their once luminous art sending colored light onto the edges of their frames as light filtered through the dirt and grime. As Bolivar and Tony came to the top, they saw three figures dressed in mismatched green accented with remnants of old Crown Soldier equipment. A gruff, long-haired man stood holding a crossbow in both hands. To his right was a woman and a young boy, both holding weapons of their own. Bolivar and Tony came to the top of the steps with a deliberate slowness, their hands high above their heads. Tony's sword hung slack on his hip and Bolivar held the metal staff underneath one arm.

As they came to a stop on the top step, Bolivar surveyed the three ragged people who waited for them. The strangers, even the young boy who looked no older than sixteen, stared at them with uncaring, aged eyes. "My name is Bolivar Jackson," he said, watching the man with the crossbow tighten his grip. "We don't mean any harm. We're from another traveler group nearby, just scouting the area."

"What kind of fucking travelers are Aetics," the thin, long-haired man growled. He raised the crossbow and pointed it at Bolivar's chest. "If you're travelers, then I'm a fucking Fane."

"Don't do that," Bolivar said, his voice flat and bored. "I don't want to hurt you, and I'm sure the three of you don't want to be hurt."

"Let's just talk," Tony added. He watched Bolivar from the edges of his vision and grew nervous the longer they stood in stalemate. "Let's just take it easy and talk."

The man tightened his grip on the crossbow and widened his stance. "No interest in talking." *Interest* came out as "inturst" in the man's heavy, slurred accent.

"Realize when you are outclassed," Bolivar said. His tone shifted from boredom to frustration. "I won't ask to talk this out again. If you refuse, I'll consider the three of you a threat and will dispatch you accordingly. Child and all."

The woman gave a nervous look to the archer and swallowed. "Maybe we should hear them out," she said, looking back and forth between the man and Bolivar. "No need to let this turn into a bloodbath, right?"

Bolivar's face stretched into a grin, and he nodded.

"That's right," he said. "No one has to die today."

The long-haired man lowered his crossbow. "All right, let's step inside and have a talk. The two of you walk in front. I ain't putting my back toward ya."

Lowering their hands, Tony and Bolivar walked towards the doors of the capitol. The three strangers followed as they swung open the heavy wooden doors and stepped inside. The main hall of the capitol struck Tony as a great dichotomy. The once ornate and impressive hall, with its gold rimmed ceiling and shining brass stair rails, was hidden underneath a layer of stacked lumber and bagged supplies. At the center of the large front lobby was a ramshackle wood table with three homemade chairs. The man and young boy grabbed two wooden crates and sat them near the table before taking a seat alongside the woman.

"Have a seat," the man said, still holding his crossbow. Bolivar and Tony took their seats on the crates across from the strangers. "So, you say you're travelers from around here," the man said, "where at then? From the supermarket?"

Bolivar raised an eyebrow and shook his head. "You can't expect us to tell you where the rest of us are when we've spent the past ten minutes held at the threat of death. Just trust us that it's close and that there are more of us than there are of you."

"Number of folks never mattered before," said the woman. "We've held this place for a long while."

"How long?" asked Tony. He looked around at the amount of wear on the walls of the capitol. The three strangers only looked at him in confusion.

"Look," Bolivar said, hoping to break the tension,

"there's no reason for you to feel hostile. Isn't that right, Tony?"

For the first time, Tony saw their thin, survivalist bodies and wondered what they ate locked up in their fortress. He nodded, knowing nothing he said could ease their anxieties.

"We don't mean you any harm," Bolivar continued. "If we did, we wouldn't be sitting here having a talk, understand?"

"All right," said the man, "then what do you want from us?"

Bolivar propped his elbows on the edge of the table and grinned a wide, foxlike grin that made Tony's skin crawl. "Not a thing. Our group is pretty new, and we're just out scouting the area to see who else is around. Now, please, can you tell me how long you three have been here?"

"Long enough," answered the woman. "And we've managed to do just fine."

"That right?" Tony interrupted. "This place looks like a beggar's shelter."

The young boy shot up from his chair and stepped closer to Tony. "That right?" he asked, mocking Tony's own tone. "Want me to straighten that smart fuckin' mouth up?"

Tony looked at the boy through tired eyes, frustrated with the way Bolivar was dragging everything out. His brown eyes shined with glints of violent red from underneath the dark lines of his face as he waited for the boy to move. At that moment Tony looked more like a soldier than he had in years. *Rip butcher, rip. Rip 'em all to hell!*

"Sit down, Ridden," said the man. He gave a long sigh and rubbed at the gray temples of his hair with his thumbs. "I will admit that the ease of things comes and goes, but we do just fine."

"'Do just fine.' Famous last words, aren't they?" chided Bolivar. "We do a little better than just fine."

"Are you all Aetics?" the boy asked. He sat again, but his eyes were still locked on Tony.

"No, we aren't. The only Aetics are me and our founder, Sarah."

"So you aren't one then?" This time the boy had directed his question at Tony.

"No, I'm not. I'm just a traveler."

"I'm getting tired of this horse jawing," the man cut in. "What do you want from us? Cut the bullshit."

"What is your name?" Bolivar asked. "Let's start there."

The man swallowed and gave a quick glance to the woman "We're the Battons. I'm Jonathan, that is my wife Michelle, and this is our boy, Ridden."

"Well, Jonathan, do you know the saying 'strength in numbers'?" Bolivar leaned on the table again, and Tony could see that beneath his calm exterior his mind worked through the problem in front of him. His tone was airy, condescending.

Tony found himself imagining a snake, slithering up a tree to whisper in an unsuspecting woman's ear like the old stories his mother used to tell him. Jonathan nodded and glanced at his wife, who was watching Bolivar with a nervous intensity.

"Well, maybe it's time for you to leave this place." Bolivar gestured to the decaying scene around them. "Come with us. You'll be fed better, you'll sleep better, and you'll be safer. Strength in numbers."

"What do we need to keep ourselves safe from?" asked

Michelle. "We've been here for more than two decades. Never had more than a few stragglers come to our doors."

"There is a conflict on the horizon," Bolivar answered, his tone grave and dramatic. Tony's eyes snapped to him and he watched as Bolivar leaned in closer to the table. "We don't know how grave this conflict is yet, but it will be great. You'll need us."

"How do we know you aren't full of shit?" Ridden snapped, his shrill voice impatient and tired. "Feeding us bullshit when there's nothing coming at all. Or maybe you're planning on stirring something up?"

Tony winced at the way Ridden's words echoed in his ears.

Bolivar slapped his hands on the table and gave an exasperated sigh as he stood up. "Let's go, Tony. I'm tired of wasting my time. These three seem to be content living in squalor."

Before Tony could stand, Jonathan shot up from his chair and hurried over to block their way. He glanced back at Michelle who nodded. Ridden sat sullen in his chair. "Listen, might be that we'd hear you out, but how do we know we can trust your bunch?"

Bolivar held out his hand, and a crackling red flame erupted from his palm. It danced there, and the flickering light cast bright bands of orange light across Jonathan's face. Bolivar's voice seeped with certainty. "Because if I wanted you dead, you'd be dead." He snapped his hand closed, and all at once the flame disappeared in a burst of white smoke. He held his other hand across to the man. "So, what do you say?"

Jonathan reached out and shook Bolivar's hand, who gave a

cheshire grin and spoke in a tone so full of fiery satisfaction that Tony thought for a moment he could see smoke coming from his mouth. "So, what was that you said about a supermarket?"

CHAPTER XIV
A Growing Divide

===

SARAH

Sarah and the others sat eating breakfast at a steady pace as Bolivar and Tony woke in the shadows of the Capitol Building, the stench of the slime-hind still lingering. The day underway, Michael toiled on with the library's collection, working on the stacks of books on the first floor while Sarah watched Sibella flying in the rafters, still held down with the weight of her breakfast. She daydreamed about her days on the road, the hot sun beaming down on her as she made her way through the hills and valleys of the Southern Line. The sun came through the windows in refracted beams, casting bright rays along the lobby where Pinn and Jane sat on the floor near the desk. It cast the library in an otherworldly glow of prisms and shimmering, ethereal light. Ri came back from taking their dirty dishes to the kitchen and sat down at the table with Sarah. They leaned back on their chair, the tight, knotty muscles of their shoulders framed in the ragged edges of their hand-cut tank top. Despite the tensions that had built in steady moments since Bolivar's mention of conflict, the morning felt serene in its beauty. A quiet moment of imperceptible simplicity.

"I've been thinking about starting a garden," said Ri. They watched Sibella with Sarah. The falcon fluttered from rafter to rafter, chasing something they could not see.

Sarah looked at them, half surprised. "Really? Well, I can help you get the courtyard finished. It'd probably go quicker with my help."

"No, that's okay. I'd rather do it by hand. I've been missing it, I think. The dirt under my nails, tending crops. It has been a long time since I've done anything like that."

Sarah turned in her seat and looked Ri's face over, its soft lines marked with fading scars. She thought of the half-dozen times she had asked Ri about their past, every time the same answer. "When are you going to tell me what happened?"

In the suddenness of the question, Ri's face fell in the bright light of the Belhaven. They looked down at their feet, kicking the toe of their boot gainst the leg of the table. Thumbs hooked into the pockets of their canvas pants, they chewed at the inside of one cheek. "One day. I'll tell you about it, about everything, one day, I promise. I just…need more time."

"But Ri, I just want to--"

"Sarah."

"I told you about my friends, about Morable, I just want--"

"Sarah."

She gritted her teeth, the tanned lines of her face taut and irritated. "Ri."

"Drop it."

"Fine, fine. I'm done. I'm going to head up to the second and dig through those combat books so Sibella will leave me alone. If you want to come with me, I'm sure we can find something to do." Sarah tried to give a soft, urging smile, but Ri's eyes were still heavy and far away.

They both stood up and Sarah wrapped her arms around Ri's waist. Ri pulled Sarah's head down towards her, their lips brushing Sarah's forehead, their hand buried deep in the red curls of Sarah's hair. Sarah leaned in, relieved and calmed despite the tension she could still feel between them. As she did, she felt Ri's grip in her hair tighten.

Ri brought their mouth to Sarah's ear, their breath hot on her neck. "Your office."

Sarah pulled back just enough to meet Ri's eyes. The shades of green caught the light in a way that made them look wild. Ri let go of her, and Sarah turned almost at once towards the administration offices. Her heart raced as she walked, never looking back but always feeling Ri just a few short steps behind. As they crossed into the administration offices Ri caught the door and followed close. When they reached her office, Ri didn't give her time to close the door behind them. Before Sarah turned around, Ri had their arms around her, hands pawing at Sarah's shirt. Sarah pulled at Ri's own shirt, the tank top coming off in one easy motion, and ran her hands over their back. She felt the scars that outlined the defined muscles along their shoulders. The deep ridges between their shoulder blades. The slope at the small of their back. A single, knotted, wild scar the size of a sword blade just along their hip. As she brought her hands back up towards Ri's shoulders, she dug her fingernails in and felt Ri's breath hitch. Their grip on Sarah tightened and they picked her up, a motion so seamless and easy it took Sarah's breath away. They sat her on top of one of the tables and fell onto her, hands fast moving and hunting. There in the early morning glimmer, the light bouncing from dust hint to dust hint, Ri fucked Sarah. It was the only word she could have used to describe it. The only one that fit the raw, hungering way Ri was on top of her and in her and tasting her all in a few breathless moments.

By the time they were finished, the true finish, not one of the many that came throughout, they were both sweating and panting. They laid on the tabletop together for a moment, Sarah lying on Ri's chest, the steady rise and fall of their breath a contrast to the intensity that had come before. Sarah started to speak, to add something to it all there at the end of ends, but couldn't think of anything to say. Instead, she traced the outline of Ri's jaw with her fingers, ran them down their stomach, their slabbed muscles standing out even in their exhausted state, and rested just above their hip bone. Ri shifted their legs and looked at Sarah, still lying down, head cocked comically as they tried to get a look.

"There went the morning huh?" Sarah asked as she lifted her head to meet Ri's eyes.

"Morning? I don't remember what day it is."

Sarah's hand wandered for a moment, her finger making small semi-circles around Ri's hip bone.

"Sarah, I'm worn out."

Her hand wandered still, finding its way to their thigh, then knee, then inside of their leg, all the while the tip of her finger just barely traced their skin. "That doesn't sound like you."

Ri's head dropped down and they bit at their bottom lip just as Sarah's hand found its way to their inner thigh. They were together again, but this time in a way that only those in love can be. In a way that only young, foolish people full of vigor and want can be. When they finished, when Ri finished,

Sarah laid her head on back Ri's now heaving chest and draped her arms around their neck. They laid like that, in love and full of one another, until the dawn light gave way to the high-morning sun. After a while, they both got up and searched for their clothes, which had been strewn across the room in the early throes of their passions.

"You still going to the second?" Ri asked as they pulled their tank top on.

"Yeah, you sure you don't want to come?"

Ri grinned and Sarah's face flushed.

"You know what I mean."

"I'm going to go out and look at the courtyard. I'll come up there in a little bit."

They kissed and headed out of the administration offices, faces still warmed from the morning.

MICHAEL

After breakfast, as Ri worked the soil outside and Sara made her way through the spell books on the second floor, Michael sat on the front steps of the Belhaven. He watched the sun dip in and out of the clouds for almost an hour before he heard the doors open behind him and turned to see Finch. She carried a handful of cigarettes in her right hand and a box of matches in her left. In the front waistband of her pants she had stuffed one of her romance novels.

"Oh, I didn't know you were out here. You gonna be all right if I smoke?" Michael nodded and Finch came to sit beside him. "Good. Ri's piddling in the back courtyard. That one gives me a weird feeling."

Michael raised an eyebrow and gave a side glance as

Finch lit her first. "What's wrong with Ri?"

Finch shrugged and dragged on the cigarette. She exhaled the smoke in a long, focused stream. "Don't know, something just don't feel right about 'em. Built like a brick shit house with that short cropped hair and no last name? All those scars?" Finch shook her head and took another drag. "They're hiding something, I can feel it."

Michael smiled and kicked at a loose piece of stone. "Sounds like you're just intimidated. Plenty of farmers don't have last names these days. Plenty of farmers are stout too, you know."

"God damn right I'm intimidated. They're so fucking intense, and the only person they seem to get on with besides Tony is Sarah, and we both know why that is." Finch smiled and licked at her teeth.

Michael grimaced and choked on the air between them as the leathery smell of burned tobacco compiled into an ever-growing haze. He knew Ri didn't mind him, that they got along, but he also couldn't remember ever having a real conversation with them. As he sat there breathing in Finch's miasma, he realized he didn't really know that much about Ri. "They are intense, that's for sure, but I don't think you've got anything to worry about. Don't think we've got anything to worry about, I mean."

Finch shook her head and tossed the butt of the cigarette to the ground before she lit another. "You sure? I figure if they put their mind to it they could rip through me and you without so much as losing their breath. Probably Sarah, too. God knows that they fuck enough to build up the endurance of a full bore work horse."

Michael gave a sideways glare. He didn't want to turn his face towards the smoke. "Can you cut the vulgar shit? That isn't our business, and besides that they're young kids. Ri isn't some violent monster just because they've got a murky past. You don't treat Bolivar that way."

"Mmm, maybe so. Just call me nervous, I guess. Always have been. Staying still has always made me squirrelly. At least since Pinn's daddy ran out on us."

Michael scratched at his face. "He left you? I didn't know that. I guess I just assumed he was dead."

Finch shrugged and puffed on her cigarette. "Might be, ain't seen him for the better part of three years, but he walked out on me and Pinn by his own accord. Got an adventurous itch and didn't want to be tied down by a woman and a boy, I guess. Fuck him, I don't need him anyway. I was always the brains."

Michael gave a somber smile and nodded. "My wife left me, you know?"

Finch raised her eyebrows. "I didn't know that. Look at the pair of us. Who knows, maybe they're out there together somewhere." She dragged on a cigarette and let a long whistling breath push the smoke out. "Or dead in the same ditch somewhere, better yet."

Michael laughed and stood up, happy to have his head above the layer of pollution. "Well, I'll be inside if you need me. Don't let the big bad farmer get you before your beau gets back."

Looking up at him through the haze of smoke, Finch stuck her tongue out. "Oh, fuck you."

Michael chuckled, his stocky frame shaking as he did.

He walked back into the library with a renewed vigor, but that feeling of momentary peace was wrenched away as he collapsed to his knees just as the doors closed behind him. His vision again swirled with splashes of color and paint. He gritted his teeth and tried to will the vision away as it grew, but he failed. In a moment, he found himself in that world of color and madness yet again. He saw in front of him a mass of gold and marble splattered with greens and blacks and browns. Dancing around it were masses of red and blue and they intertwined with the scene in a way that felt dark, mischievous.

"Dad!" he heard someone call out from beyond the world of color. Michael whirled on his heels to see a figure, a silhouette of a girl, standing before him. The figure was a dancing aura of light and dark, an unusual absence of color and texture in his oil-patterned mind. "Dad, are you okay?" the voice called again.

He reached out and his hand found the figure and he realized it was Jane. "Jane, yes I'm okay. I'm okay. I'm having a migraine. It's just a migraine." His tongue stung from the lies, but he knew he needed Jane to leave, that the vision was important. "I'm okay baby. Just let me sit here for a minute."

The figure let go, and Michael turned back to the realm of color just in time to see the blue paint tear itself away from the others with what Michael could only describe as hesitance, and then as quick as it had appeared the vision dissipated. Michael gasped for air. At the lobby desk he saw Jane standing as she chewed on her cuticle with tears in her eyes.

"Dad, are you okay?"

Michael came to his feet and went to his daughter. He held her tight in his arms. "Of course I'm okay. It was just a bad headache." Jane nodded and buried her head in his embrace. Michael patted her on the head and smiled down at her. "Go play or read or whatever it is you do. I'm fine, I promise."

After a moment of hesitation, she turned and started towards the staircase. Michael stood there for a moment and ran his hands through his graying hair and sighed. It was a long, exhausted, hurting sigh. He could hear the sounds of Sarah and Ri sparring in the back courtyard, and as he realized the first floor was empty, his eyes wandered to the non-fiction shelves near the staircase.

In a trance-like state, Michael walked to the corner shelves and moved the ladder to the place where, perched high above, rested the red book. With shaky legs he climbed the ladder and pulled the book, and when he returned to the ground the hidden door was once again open. He descended the staircase and passed through the imperceptible barrier that shifted the light from natural to magical with methodical steps. He felt that this time something waited for him at the bottom. That perhaps something had been waiting for him at the bottom since his first visit to the shrine, even though he could not understand what it might be. As he came to the base of the stairs and entered the shrine, his intuitions were confirmed. A man with dark hair and a wild huntsman's beard stood near the stone table. When Michael entered the room the stranger turned to look at him.

"Ah," the man said in a soft, muted tone, "Michael, I'm happy to finally catch you here."

Michael tensed and stayed close to the stairway. "Who are you? How'd you get down here?"

"I've been popping in and out of this place for a while, but I kept missing you."

"Who are you?"

"I am a friend of Miss Silvergrove's."

"I don't think so."

The stranger smiled and a line of perfect, white teeth broke the dark color of his beard. He looked down at the intricate flooring and kicked at a loose stone. "No, perhaps not. But I am a friend. I do hope you can trust me on that."

"Then why won't you tell me your name?"

The stranger's face grew grave, and he shook his head. "I cannot."

"What? What the hell does that mean?"

"It is my penance. I can't tell you who I am, just what I am."

"All right, then what are you?"

"I am the Man of Ra' Ae. I am the Divine Force. I am the Envoy of Goraln. All I am is that, but what is beyond it I can no longer see. I cannot tell you who I am because that has been lost to me. Taken as a penance for my chosen path."

Pacing near the base of the stairs, Michael ran a hand across the sweat that had beaded along his hairline. "What does any of that mean? None of this makes any sense!"

"I wish I could explain it all to you, I do. I wish someone had been there to explain it all to me. But, that just is not possible. I only know who you are because you touched the shrine. Because you have been chosen, like I was before you."

An rage building within him, craving answers, Michael twisted into knots of frustration. "Chosen by who? For what?"

"I think you might know the answer to that already."

Michael's eyes darted to the statue of Goraln and then he clenched them shut, shaking his head in quick, frantic jerks.

"Laid out beyond me I can see your end point as clear as I see you now, but I don't know how you get there."

"Then why do I keep having these fucking visions?"

A shadow passed across the stranger's face. "Visions?"

Now Michael was close to Ra' Ae, his face harrowed and shaded by the blue mage light that hovered above. "The color. The paint. The visions. You have to know what I'm talking about." Michael reached out and grabbed the man by the collar. "I feel like I'm going mad."

Ra' Ae pulled Michael's hands off of his clothes and took a step back. His face was worried, and Michael could see that Ra' Ae's eyes searched for meaning. "That is very strange. Something much greater is happening here, it seems. I did not see this."

"I don't care what's happening, I want it to stop."

A look of regret swept across the man's face. He seemed sympathetic, if even for just a moment. "I am sorry.. Whatever this is, it will never stop. You can only learn to embrace it."

"Then help me!"

"Again, I cannot. It is your journey." Ra' Ae reached into the pocket of his brown leather tunic, its fine blue stitching highlighted by the mage light, and pulled out a small cloth bag. He held the bag out to Michael, who took it with a cautious hand. "That is a runic charm. Keep it on you, and this place will remain hidden. It is powerful magic, so you must be careful."

"None of this makes any sense." Michaels voice was

distant, thoughtful as he gazed down at the floor.

"I know. I'm sorry."

"I don't think you are. Why're you even here if you can't help me?"

"To give you the charm, and to see you with my own eyes. I am sorry I can't tell you more than that. The Song has yet to be Sung."

Michael started to argue, but when he looked up the man was gone. He let out a fitful curse and turned the cloth charm over in his hands before he headed back up the stairs.

SARAH

In the moments before Michael was taken by his vision, Sarah worked on the second floor trying to make headway on the waist high stack of books she had made since Bolivar left. Before long, she heard the flutter of wings and Sibella landed on the table, causing the scattered mess of loose pages on the table to fly off in every direction. Sarah picked up the papers and straightened them out as Sibella mumbled a late morning apology.

"Morning, Sib," she said, stacking the papers to the side and scratching at the falon's neck.

The falcon looked them over. He read over her scribbled notes on The Calling Maw, intention, and defensive magic with quick, scanning eyes. "Any news from Bolivar?"

"Not yet," Sarah sat the papers aside and laid a large, leather bound book titled Magic for the Common Man on the table. She flipped to a page marked with a scrap of paper and started reading through the list of defensive spells.

"Are you worried about him?" Sibella asked, perched on

her shoulder and reading along.

Sarah stopped and gave an exasperated sigh. "I'm trying not to be, you damn aggravation." She reached up to ruffle the feathers on Sibella's neck. He pecked at her hand as she did and made a soft screeching noise. She flipped to a spell titled "defensive aura." "Are you?"

"Progressively so, though I really cannot say why. Intuition, perhaps."

"Yeah, me too. Not sure what to do about it besides talking to Michael and Finch while the devil's out to play, you know?" Sarah marked the spell's page and leaned back in her chair, devoting her full attention to Sibella.

The falcon jumped from Sarah's shoulder to the table and faced her. "I think that is a good idea. I know tensions are high after your confrontation with Bolivar, but it is important that we understand where everyone stands. More important, though, is that they see you in your place of authority."

Sarah, nodded, the cuticle of her thumb once again under assault. "All right, I'll bring it up with them later today. Now, give me some space so I can read without you in my ear."

Sibella scoffed and flew to a different part of the library while Sarah sat and read. She went through the motions she had become all too familiar with, and as she did a soft blue aura appeared around her. It disappeared as the sound of creaking floorboards startled her, ripping her from her focused state. She turned in her seat to see Ri walking up, dirt stains on their hands and pants.

"Sorry," they said, "didn't mean to spook you." Sarah smiled and turned back around, reading over the spell again. Ri came to stand beside her and leaned on the table. What are you looking at now?"

The blue aura appeared around Sarah again, and this time she held it and stood. "It's a defensive aura." She inspected the spell's makeup from inside the strange shimmer, its blue light dancing in her eyes. "It just clings to me, instead of protecting anyone nearby like the shield. I'm not sure how it fares in practice, though." She released the aura and rubbed at her neck.

"Why don't we go out to the courtyard and find out?" Ri rubbed their dirt-stained hands on their pant leg and smiled. Sweat stains lined the collar of their tank top, making it cling to their chest. Sarah's eyes wandered to it more than once, heat of the morning still on her mind.

Sarah's voice was sing-song and sarcastic. "Practicing some of this would be a good idea, but you know, I don't want to hurt you."

Ri laughed and slapped at their own shoulder. "I think I'll be just fine."

"All right, all right. I'm surprised, I thought you hated sparring."

Saying nothing, Ri just waved her away with a dirt-stained hand, and the two of them headed out to the Belhaven's courtyard. As they stepped through the heavy french doors, the bright summer of sunlight broke through and almost blinded Sarah. Where they had made their fire pit was scorched and covered in ash, and in the corner Sarah saw where the grass had been cleared and the ground broken in several places. Mounds of dirt marked the progress of Ri's efforts.

"Any luck with your garden?" Sarah asked as Ri walked

around the perimeter of the courtyard, searching. For what, she had no idea.

Stopping for a moment to glance over at the mounds of dirt, Ri smiled. "Yeah, all I did today was some soil tests. I'm going to have to find some scraps around here and make some tools, then I can really get moving. That's going to be a good spot, though." Ri bent down and stood up with a scrap wood about three feet long and turned it over in their hands.

Out of the corner of her eye, Sarah saw Sibella perched on top of the archway that led back inside, watching. "So how do you want to do this?" she asked, a feeling of anticipation washing over her. As Ri stood with their back to her, she noticed the way that their pants were hanging on their hips, the way their calves stood out against the thick khaki canvas. She felt a familiar warmth rising up her collar and wished Sibella was inside.

Ri turned around with the length of wood, more club than anything else, and adjusted it from hand to hand. It seemed an extension of their person now, a missing limb, and Ri's face was set in a strange way Sarah had never seen before. They bit at their lip and looked Sarah over head to toe. "Well, you haven't really done any combat training. I think Sibella would be happy if we ran through some defensive sparring."

"You know I have been traveling for years now, right?" Sarah half-mocked Ri with a wide grin on her face. She bit at her own lip and glanced back towards Sibella again. *Get the hint you ass.*

Club in hand, Ri stepped closer to Sarah, and as they neared they ran a hand along her ribs. When Sarah stopped, thinking that Ri had a question or something to say, they pulled her in and kissed her. The kiss was long and warm, and Sarah felt flush knowing Sibella was nearby.

"I thought we were sparring," she said. "You'll have to get the bird to go away. And get a blanket, I don't want grass up my--"

Cutting Sarah off, Ri pulled her in and kissed her again, this time biting at her bottom lip. They said nothing else, but instead slapped a hand onto Sarah's ass, gave a wide grin, and rested the club onto their right shoulder. They motioned for Sarah to ready herself, feet wide-set and braced. Sarah, ember brows drawn in and heat rising into her cheeks, nodded and stretched her arms, but she felt at the way Ri shifted so quick from one hunger to the other. As she looked across the courtyard at Ri, she saw their sweaty form, their wide stance. Serious, despite the wanting on their face.

"Do I need to go get my staff?" She looked back towards the door and tried to remember where she had left it. Sibella still rested above the doorway.

"No, just use your magic to try and stop me," Ri said, now holding the club like a longsword, the end pointed down at their side. "I'll press you, you block."

Sarah nodded and widened her stance. The heat was easing from her face, the feeling of cold anticipation taking its place.

Ri dashed forward in two bounding steps. They swung the club at Sarah's chest, but she brought up her hands and used the quick burst of a telekinesis spell to push the club away. As it lobbed back in Ri's hand Sarah sidestepped, bringing herself opposite Ri's sword arm. Ri pivoted on their heels and brought the club across their body in a broad swipe towards

Sarah's right shoulder. Just in time, Sarah clenched her arms and the blue aura enveloped her. When the club struck its mark, the aura rippled with electric-blue energy and the club was repelled back with so much force it almost ripped itself from Ri's grasp. Ri skidded on their heels and straightened their footing almost as fast as they had lost it. They relaxed for a moment and rubbed at the wrist that held the club. Their chest heaved, their body was still tight and ready to move.

"Well I guess we know what that does now." Ri spoke in a voice so effortless, so strong, that Sarah couldn't believe it. It didn't seem like they had exerted any energy at all. As they got close, Ri reached out with the club and swung it, not an attack but a playful swing. It made a crack as it connected with the seat of Sarah's pants.

Sarah let out a gasp, her bottom lip pulled in over her teeth, and her eyes wide. This time when Sarah glanced back, she saw Sibella was gone. Either inside or along the roof of the Belhaven. Either way, he was out of sight. She lifted her cotton shirt and used the front of it to wipe the sweat off of her face. As she did, her pale stomach shone out and the edges of her breasts peeked from underneath. When she lowered the shirt, she saw that Ri was staring and bit at her lip. "Go get a blanket." Or don't, that's fine too.

Ri took a slight step forward, and Sarah relaxed her tensed muscles, thinking they were done, or at least done with sparring. As she did, Ri shot forward and swung the club hard at Sarah's ribs. She managed to deflect it at the last moment, but it grazed her side, and Ri pivoted and brought their shoulder hard into Sarah's chest. Sarah felt the air leave her lungs as the blow knocked her backwards. When she stumbled back, Ri took another step and brought the club forward. Sarah brought the aura up again and sent the club back towards Ri. Sarah's face had gone from wanting, to confused, to nervous, but Ri's had maintained that hungering, ravenous stare. Sarah dug her heels in, reached out, and grabbed Ri's tank top. With one quick motion she jerked Ri towards the ground.

As Ri stumbled forward Sarah pivoted around them and shot a blast of telekinesis into their back, shocked at the fluidity of her own motions and the way they matched Ri's. More than anything, she felt confused at the way that the tension and the lust and the wanting made her reactions quick and perfect. As the blast of energy connected with the small of Ri's back they let out a scream and the fabric of their tank ripped, leaving a black mark behind as it did. Ri hit the ground hard and slammed their mouth into the hard earth, but as fast as they fell Ri scrambled back to their knees. Blood now running down their face, Ri jabbed the club towards Sarah and missed. Sarah jumped back and slid on the ground just as Ri straightened up. All the while Ri's white teeth shone through the blood, a wide, manic grin on their face.

"You ass" Sarah spat, "I thought we were done." She was still trying to find the breath Ri had knocked out of her. Ri only smiled.

With one hand, Ri reached up to the collar of their tank top and jerked at it. The thin material gave way and Ri ripped the shirt down its front and then dropped the tattered mess onto the ground. Their bare chest heaved with each breath. Blood ran down their front, leaving trails that followed the edges of their body, Ri still smiled through it all. Sarah stared at them and for a moment felt something strange rise up behind

Ri's smile. She could feel her own body grow hot as she watched a tendril of blood trace the edge of Ri's nipple and run down their stomach. She felt confused at the way her muscles tightened at it. The way she felt ready, eager for the fight to go on. Like the fight was a precursor, a moment before something grander. She had a rising urge to rush at Ri, to push the fight further, but that thought was forced away as Ri moved first.

They swung the club at her again. This time it grazed Sarah's knee as she tried to dodge. Sarah brought up a shield, its blue-electric energy crackling as Ri brought three hard strikes down onto it. Each strike was punctuated with a raving growl. The force pushed Sarah to her knees and she watched from inside the shield as Ri battered it in bursts of three, one after the other. Never pausing, never slowing, never trying to wipe at the blood that ran in a steady trickle from their lips. Sarah braced herself, pushing everything but her intent for the spell at her fingertips out of her mind. Ri's body was tight and focused. Sarah saw in Ri's nakedness an omen, the light of the courtyard casting firelight glimmers across their bloodied body.. A moving, jerking mass of muscle that felt unstoppable. There was no beauty left in the edges of their form, but Sarah still felt the heat drawing up from her stomach. Felt the urge to move to Ri. The want of the morning was replaced with the drive to fight, but as she looked on the two felt indistinguishable. The ache in her arms was the same ache that rested in her chest. Tears formed in the corners of Sarah's eyes, but she did not know if they were from fear or frustration. Or what sort of frustration it was.

As Ri swung the club it began to crack near their grasp,

and as the seventh strike came down hard on the shield the wood splintered in Ri's hands. As the jagged shrapnel dug into their hands, they let out another scream. Not a scream of pain, but a roaring battle call. Sarah started to lower the shield, but before she could Ri brought both fists down hard onto it. Sarah felt her grip on the spell start to slip. She looked on from inside the shield at a scene that felt like a nightmare. Ri's face was splattered with blood, their teeth shining through like white flecks as they screamed and screamed and screamed. Sarah tried to find a moment to call out, to stop them. With each blow, she could see Ri in the alleyway, braced over the man's body, each swing intent on only total destruction. Each call more guttural than the last. Their bared, blood-streamed upper body moved and flexed with an uncontrolled rage. Their hands were a mess of splinters as they swung, the full force of Ri's frame borne behind them. All lust for battle faded out of Sarah, and with it so did everything else. Tears rolled down her face and she gasped in ragged breaths as she tried to force Ri back with the shield.

"Enough!" she cried. "I've had enough!"

Ri stopped and took three staggering steps back. Their chest still heaved, their face was still flecked and streaming with blood, but their eyes had calmed. Sarah lowered the shield and walked over to Ri, hands still ready and cautious.

Using the back of their hand, the one not filled with splinters, to wipe the blood from their mouth, Ri looked at Sarah with strange and glimmering eyes. Their wild expression of lust and rage had faded to one of gentle amusement. When Sarah came to Ri and placed a hand on their arm, they pulled her in and placed both hands at the small of Sarah's back. They pressed their chest to Sarah's and lifted them and held them in the air. Ri kissed Sarah, a strange, wild thing that was filled with joy and love and excitement. They half spun her around, almost laughing, until their eyes met Sarah's. Where their's were full of revelry, Sarah's were full of terror. They dropped her and as they did Sarah scrambled back, wiping the blood from her face.

Catching their breath, Ri ran their shaking hands over their face before they sat down on the ground, the exhaustion finally showing on their body. They made no effort to cover up, but all at once they appeared exposed. Vulnerable. All of the hardness had left their form. "I'm sorry," they said. Their voice trembled. "I'm so sorry."

"Ri, what was that?"

"I just got carried away."

Feeling the familiarity of it, of the same excuses given once before, Sarah sat down next to them and looked at Ri's back. The place Sarah had struck them with the blast of telekinesis had turned crimson. "Fuck, I didn't mean to hit you that hard."

"It's okay."

Sarah ran a hand over the bruise and a shock went through Ri's body. Their muscles grew tight and their breath hitched before they pulled away. Sarah tensed as she saw Ri's hands clench. A mass of splinters was still jammed into one hand.

"Don't do that."

"What is going on?" Sarah asked, pulling away from Ri. "You've never acted like this before."

"I got lost in it."

"Is that why you don't like sparring?"

Ri nodded.

"Why didn't you tell me?"

Ri shrugged.

"You need to tell me what you are."

"I'm sorry," they said. "I promise I'll tell you one day, tell you what I am, but I can't. Not right now." Sarah watched Ri struggle against the pain and reached out to touch them, but Ri recoiled.

"Tell me. I've told you about what I did now, tell me--"

"Fucking drop it! Can you just fucking stop? What the actual hell is wrong with you? Why now? Why do you need to know *NOW*? The shit I've done makes Morable look like a joke, Sarah, so please. Just leave me alone. I just want to be alone."

More from frustration than anything else, Sarah's jaw tightened and she stood up, dusted off her pants, and glanced back towards the doors to the Belhaven. "Do you want me to go get you a shirt?"

Ri looked up at Sarah, their eyes rung in dark circles. "I can get it."

Sarah stepped over to the edge of the courtyard, grabbed a metal bucket full of leaves, and dumped it out. She sat it down next to Ri and, a hand on both sides of the bucket, cast a spell to fill it with water. "Wash up, I'll be out here with a shirt in a second."

Ri nodded and closed their eyes. "Thank you."

Saying nothing, Sarah walked back into the library. As she did, Ri sat on the ground and stared at the powder blue sky, a strange nostalgia on their face.

The evening came in a single swift move and before long Sarah found herself cooking alone for the first time since her relationship with Ri had begun. When she brought the food to the table, Ri was sitting with the others, but the anxiety Sarah had expected was not there. She instead found them all talking and laughing in a way that brought warmth back into Sarah's heart. She saw how happy Ri looked. How far from the twice called beast they seemed. It was a deep contrast to their time in the courtyard. The only thing out of place was their scabbed lip and bandaged hands. Sarah sat down everyone's food before sitting next to Ri, who placed a hand on her thigh. They once again carried the same stoic kindness Sarah had grown to expect. Sarah looked into Ri's eyes and felt their tension ease. *What are you, Ri? Why can't I look away from you? What is this?* All of it reeling in her mind, she stilled herself and felt Ri's hand on her thigh and let that be it.

They all ate together and, despite the growing tensions that swirled around them, spent the time laughing. Michael, his own face tight with far away worry, did not ask about Ri's wounds, though more than once Sarah saw him glance at their hands. Finch did not even seem to see them. Instead, they all watched as Jane and Pinn bickered across the library over whose turn it was with the magic tome they had carried from upstairs. They talked of their past lives and the days, months, and years they had spent on the road. The heavy morning, the draining ache that was filling the gaps between them in the Belhaven, was filled in that moment with the food shared across the simple, wooden table. Before long, though, the food was gone and they sat in a sepia-toned silence.

Sarah shifted in her seat as the sun began to disappear beyond the horizon, the soft light of the library's windows growing ever dimmer. She knew that she had to bring up Bolivar before the night was over. She cleared her throat and leaned forward. "Finch, Michael, I have something I want to talk to y'all about." The table grew quiet, and Michael leaned back in his chair, picking at the tips of his fingernails as he watched Sarah, his glasses halfway down his face. "I want to talk to both of you about Bolivar, what you think about all this active-defense stuff. About…about militarizing the Belhaven."

Michael sighed, leaned forward, and put his elbows on the table. He pushed his glasses up his nose as he gave a side-glance to Finch, who squirmed in her seat. His eyes were tired, deep-set in dark circles, and Sarah wondered when he'd last slept. "Well, I stand with you in whatever decisions you make, but to me, it's a dangerous step. It's a step towards conflict, whether that's conflict we start or conflict someone else starts. I'm not Tony or you or Ri. I haven't served in combat, I wasn't a frontier farmer. I was just a mill worker in a tiny village, and in a lot of ways that's still all I am. I'm not cut out for that type of fighting. I don't know anything about it."

Finch scoffed and tossed her hands up in frustration. Her bronze skin shone with a crimson flush across her cheeks. She cast a scornful eye at Michael and shook her head. "What a load. If there's gonna be conflict, then it's better to stay on top of it. What if we sat around here singing songs and reading books while the empire marched up the library's steps? We'd have a hard time stopping them, wouldn't we?"

Michael's eyes cut through Finch like knives. "What are we going to be able to do against a regiment of imperial soldiers? Even if Bolivar comes back here with a hundred men, it won't mean anything against the empire. If they want this place, they'll take it, bottom line."

"So you'd rather just lay down and let them?" Finch's voice scratched against the air like a howling cat.

Sarah tried to play the diplomat to the rising tensions, but she could feel her grasp slip away. The frustrated looks exchanged between Michael and Finch made her nervous. *Slip away, away and fall.* "No, he's right, Finch. We can't do anything to stop any real threats, one way or the other, so militarizing is just going to create conflict with whatever small groups there might be in the area."

Finch stood up, her hair ruffled and messy as she paced with frustration. As she spoke she jabbed a finger at Michael. "You're an old man, and I expected better out of you. I understand Sarah and Ri here not worrying. They're too busy fuckin' one another's brains out to worry about anything besides when they can slip off, but you?" Finch scoffed again and licked at her teeth. "I hope Bolivar comes back here and talks some sense into the rest of you, because it's only a matter of time before someone comes knocking on that door not meaning to join up. What're they going to think when you stand there telling them we're just kind folks in a library while we've got an ex-soldier and a fucking war machine living here? By god, I think if it was up to the three of you, we'd all turn around and pull up our skirts." Finch stormed off climbing the stairs and disappearing in the sound of stomping feet before anyone could respond.

Sarah looked at Michael, confusion on her face. "War machine? What the hell is she talking about?"

"Ri, I think, but I wouldn't put any stock in anything she says. She's a nervous person, but kind at her center, I think. And the comments about you two…well. I'm sorry. I've tried talking to her, but it doesn't do any good."

Ri started to speak up, but just ground their teeth instead, jaw pulled tight in a grimace.

"Well," Sarah said, "thank you for standing with us." He nodded, and they sat there in a long, lingering silence, the dark of the evening filling the Belhaven.

That night, Ri in bed, Sarah sat at her desk. A ball of mage light just above illuminated the books in front of her. She turned *The Story of the First Warriors* over in her hands, a book she had grabbed from the second floor not long after Finch stormed away. As she read the stories of the Warriors Who Fought the Sun, of the unavoidable battles Goraln and the others found themselves in, she began to feel vulnerable, too comfortable. She started to feel as if, just maybe, Finch had been right. That conflict was coming, and that it was coming soon.

CHAPTER XV
Supermarkets and Sicks

=====================================

TONY

Bolivar, Tony, and the Battons left the capitol behind in the early morning light. The strange family led them to the supermarket, still not yet dedicated to the idea of joining the Belhaven but willing to show Bolivar the way all the same. Tony felt a strange sense of unease as he traveled along with Bolivar and these new strangers. Bolivar's new visage as a man capable of incredible violence hung in Tony's mind, and the idea of nights with him and the strangers turned his stomach. The family had changed their clothes into dirty, pre-Rending military garb, messy splotches of black and brown and green covering them in a way that looked like a far-off forest. Each of them carried a heavy pack on their backs crammed with equipment and wore battered, make-shift swords on their hips. The crossbow that had nearly ended Tony's life was slung across Jonathan Batton's back.

"Where are we headed again?" Tony asked. He hoped, at least on some level, to break the tension he could feel building between him and the others.

"Market," Jonathan answered in his gruff, dismissive tone. "Golden District. Some of them call it the Jungle."

"Those are pretty words. Now what do they mean?"

Bolivar slowed his pace and came to walk beside Tony,

the metal staff he had taken from the drunks draped over one shoulder. "Golden District was either a business district or marketplace here. I can't get clear answers, but they're taking us to an old pre-war supermarket that some people have made into a camp."

Tony nodded and adjusted the pack on his back. "And what's the plan once we get there?"

"Observation, nothing more."

Tony nodded again and the pair fell back into the marching silence as they came into the edge of the Golden District. The wilds had reclaimed the once shining store fronts and aging businesses. Vines and trees devoured that part of the city's ruins more than any other. Massive oaks erupted from the streets and creeping forms of green consumed some towers entirely. Halfway through the district, the sun began to set on them and they made camp, this time, at Tony's insistence, lighting a fire big enough that any beasts would stay far away. They settled around the fire and Tony passed out a small ration of dried meat, hard tack, and water. The Battons devoured theirs like they had not eaten for months, and before long everyone lazed around the campfire and listened to the quiet sounds of the ruins. The reclaimed green of the ruins around them filled the night with juniper shadows.

Jonathan propped himself up on one wiry arm, breaking the tack and putting small pieces into his mouth one at a time, the crunching sometimes drowning out his words. "So, tell me more about your library, Bolivar."

"It isn't his library," Tony interrupted. He glanced at Bolivar to gauge his reaction, but instead saw that Bolivar sat watching him, waiting. Tony swallowed and looked back at

Jonathan. "Our leader is a woman named Sarah. She's the librarian, not him. We're more like the security team, I guess."

When Bolivar shofted on his bedroll, the firelight highlighted his beard. He scratched at it, his face seeming idle and distant in the orange of the blaze. "It's as Tony said. Our leader is named Sarah Silvergrove. I am just the Peace Officer for the library. Security work, like Tony said. He's my deputy."

"A woman leader?" asked Ridden.

Bolivar chuckled as he glanced over at Tony, who was looking at the boy with aggravated eyes. "She does all right. She's a little naive, perhaps, but kind and sure headed. You won't convince her to do a damn thing she doesn't want to."

"So she's weak?" Jonathan asked. "Why's she the leader then?"

Clearing his throat, Bolivar took a long drink of water and then cleared his throat again, scratching at the back of his neck. "She's tenacious, that much no one can argue. And she is the one who found the place, who called everyone else there."

She's naive, sure, Tony thought to himself, *but she's kind. She's peaceful.*

"She was the one who sent out that message?" asked Michelle. Bolivar nodded in response. "We thought that was some kind of imperial trick. That was foolish. What if some crazed monsters came after her?"

"She was lucky," Bolivar answered. "No one with ill intent came, at least not so far. But that same concern is why Tony and I are out here. We need to know what threats are in Calarine."

Tony stood up and drank down the rest of his water before putting his cup back in the pack. He adjusted his bedroll, stretched his back, and laid down. "I'm going to call it a night. I'm sure we'll be at it early tomorrow."

Tony's sudden exit hanging a shadow even deeper than the night, the conversation between Bolivar and the Battons petered out. Before long, the others bedded down for the night as well. As the Battons slept, Jonathan's steady, drumming snore echoing in the night, both Tony and Bolivar laid awake, their eyes scanning the clouded stars above.

MICHAEL

As the stars hung high above the Golden District, Michael paced back and forth in front of the administration offices. From across the first floor, he could hear the steady drumming rhythm of Finch's snore. He had woken in the night from another dream of color and paint, this one filled with splatters of red and black and purple, fringes of black and green and brown. All of it was a knotted mess that filled him with terror in a way the others had not. He conjured up all of the will power he had and knocked three times on the administration offices' door. He stood and waited, unable to bring himself to knock again. After a long, awkward moment he started to turn and walk away until he heard sleepy, sliding footsteps from inside. When the door opened Sarah stood on the other side, her red hair knotted and piled on top of her head in a messy bun. Her clothes, catawampus and twisted around her body.

"Michael? Is everything okay?"

He looked down, hoping to hide the embarrassed exhaustion on his face. "No."

Sarah raised her eyebrows and stepped back. She

opened the door wider and Michael stepped into the administration offices. He was led over to an empty desk and Sarah motioned for him to sit down.

"I had another dream."

"What do you mean? A vision?"

He nodded.

"What was it about?"

Michael let out an exasperated sigh and rubbed at his forehead. "I don't know. I never know. It's just a writhing mass of color and nonsense. But there's a lot more to tell you. Something happened yesterday…or earlier today. Hell, I don't even know what day it is."

Sarah put a hand on Michael's shoulder. "Tell me what happened. Tell me everything."

And he did. Only stopping once to catch his breath. He told her Finch's concerns about Ri. He told her about the vision he had and how Jane had seen him. He told her about the stranger and the runic charm that now hung around his neck.

"And he said he knew me?"

Michael nodded. "Big man with a wild beard. Brown leather tunic with this bright blue stitching."

Sarah's eyes widened and she opened her mouth just enough that Michael could see the tops of her bottom teeth. Her expression was one of total, undeniable shock. "Him? I half-thought I hallucinated him."

"Hallucinated who?" a voice asked from above. Michael and Sarah realized Sibella was perched above them.

It was Michael who answered. "He wouldn't tell me his name, said he couldn't. Said he was the 'Man of Ra' Ae, the–"

Sibella cut him off and finished the sentence in a sing-song voice. "Divine Force, the Envoy of Goraln."

Michael's eyes grew so wide he almost looked insane. "You know him?"

Sibella shook his head and fluttered down to rest on the desk in front of Michael and Sarah. He let out a staccato kak and shook out his feathers. "I do not know him, but I know of him. The Alchemical named him as the man who placed the library in his care. He did not know his real name either."

"Placed the library in his care?" Sarah asked. "Does that mean he's the one who called me here too?"

"I do not know for certain, but that is a reasonable extrapolation."

"What the hell is an Envoy of Goraln?" Michael asked.

Sibella squinted in thought and almost seemed to make a face of deep, contemplative consideration. He disappeared into his internal catalog, but only for a moment. "I am not sure. The books in this library do not discuss such matters, for what reason I don't know. It could be that the empire removed them after the war for Calarine, or it could be that such knowledge has never been recorded at all. Or it could be that such knowledge was not created until after the city was abandoned, as I learned so recently." The falcon shuddered.

Sarah ran a hand through her knotted hair, her face still heavy with sleep. "Did the Alchemical know?"

"Not to my knowledge. He spoke of the man as a strange force. Why are you discussing the Man of Ra' Ae to begin with? Has he been here?"

It was then, in that brief moment, that Michael realized how close Sarah had guarded their secret. He looked to Sarah, who gave a single, somber nod. The pair of them then told the falcon everything. Sarah told him of the time she met the stranger on the rooftop, and Michael told of his struggles and his visions. As they finished, Sibella shook his head and Michael thought that if the bird would have had hands, then he might have run them through his feathers in an anxious tick.

"All very strange indeed, and even more of a reason to wonder if Ra' Ae has chosen Sarah as his next…acolyte?" Sibella groaned in aggravation and stamped one taloned foot against the desk. "I loathe this. This lack of information is going to drive me mad, I swear it."

"Great," said Michael, "just great. I'm going insane and not even the magic book bird knows what's going on!"

Sarah put a hand on his shoulder and squeezed. "Well, we do know a little. We know that Ra' Ae isn't against us, since he gave you the charm. We know he isn't responsible for your visions since he seems confused too. Whatever he is, we'll have to figure that out later, but I hope it's some comfort to know that he isn't our enemy. Your enemy."

Michael shot up from his chair and put both hands on Sarah's shoulders. His eyes were wild and desperate. "Sarah, I am going mad! I can feel myself falling apart. If we don't figure this out, I don't know how much longer I can hold it together."

Sibella fluttered to Michael's shoulder and pecked at his right hand, drawing the man's attention and ire all at the same time. "Stop fighting it."

The falcon's voice was so matter of fact it shocked Michael, who let go of Sarah, reached up and grabbed the bird. He held him out in front of him like a child. "What did you say?"

Sibella didn't fight his grip. Instead, he lingered there, his head bobbing in perfect, stationary balance. "I said stop fighting it. The visions aren't making you mad. From the way you've described them there is no evil within them. I cannot know for certain, but I believe it is your stress that is making you mad. You're fighting against a powerful force you do not understand. Of course you are losing."

Looking at Sarah, Michael still held Sibella out in front of him. The falcon's eyes conveyed an eerie sense of understanding. He sat the bird down on the desk and collapsed into a chair. "I don't know if I can stop myself from fighting it. I don't know how to explain the terror those visions give me. There's something sinister there, I know it. I just don't know if it is the visions that are sinister or what they're trying to show me."

"Maybe he's right," said Sarah. "Maybe if you open yourself up to it, it won't...I don't know, maybe it won't put so much stress on your mind? I feel like we're grasping at straws, but it's hopeful."

Michael nodded and took off his glasses. He said nothing as he cleaned at them, but his mind reeled as it tried to decide what accepting the visions might feel like. He thought it at least couldn't feel worse than fighting them. "Okay, okay. I think you're both right. I'll try to stop fighting against this, but we have to keep it between us. I don't want Jane...I don't want her worrying about me, okay?"

Sarah and Sibella both nodded. Michael stood up and wiped at the beads of sweat along his hairline. He started to speak, but instead he reached out and embraced Sarah, who patted him on the back. He nodded to Sibella before he turned and left the administration offices. As he walked back to the living quarters, he found himself hoping that this new idea would work. He hoped that they had found a way to get relief from the endless chase of the kaleidoscopic world in his mind.

TONY

The next morning Jonathan led them through the reclaimed forest of the Golden District towards their destination in a steady march. As they hiked, Tony looked through the buildings, their empty shells accented by forested alleys and new growth trees. He saw old signs that had once announced the sale of fine furs, food, and expensive clothes and found himself lost in the memory of older times. He wondered if his old home of Tinkret would ever return to the wilds like this. He wondered if vines would devour the graves of his wife and children. If they would be made part of the wilds again, removed from the control of the empire. He thought about how beautiful their old brewery would be covered in vines and Northern Ivy and hoped one day this far off daydream could come true. That the empire could be so thoroughly broken apart that even the grand cities of the North would go back to the cold ground. That he could carry on the peace he had chased since leaving the banner and the sword behind. Before long Jonathan broke his daydream as the wiry man announced that they had arrived. Bolivar came to the front of the group and joined Jonathan and Tony. Together the three sat on an abandoned wall that looked across a small hill towards a massive three-story building with a vine-edged sign that read "The Grand Golden Market."

Jonathan handed Bolivar a spyglass as he came to the

front. "That is the market I told you about. There's a lot of them that live there, but they come and go. We've never interacted with them, but we see them near the city center at times."

Bolivar looked through the spyglass at the market as people bustled in and out. Tony could see the people moving around the building carrying supplies, and wondered what was passing through Bolivar's mind as he studied them through the glass. He watched as the figures carried crates back and forth. The smoke of cook fires billowed up from nearby.

"There must be a hundred people in there," said Bolivar.

"Or more. From what we've seen they spend a lot of time sending parties out gathering supplies. Every fall they travel to Varinz. I've always figured they go to trade at the markets. As far as folks like us go, they're a rich bunch."

Tony scratched at the back of his neck and watched as the ant-like figures came and went from the market. "I don't understand why none of these people answered Sarah's call."

"I'm sure they had their reasons, just like us," said Michelle.

Tony pointed to the west side of the market where a small cluster of white canvas tents were grouped near the market. "Can you see what's going on with those tents?"

Bolivar scanned the spyglass over to them. He looked the tents over and saw that many of the people coming in and out of the market were leaving supplies outside the central tent. People wrapped in worn bandages carried the supplies inside. Bolivar lowered the spyglass and looked back to the others. "Those tents are full of Sicks."

Tony grimaced, the sword on his hip growing ever heavier. "Are you sure? Is it Sicks or just an infirmary?"

Turning the spyglass back to the tents, Bolivar adjusted his position and scanned across the encampment one more time. "They're wrapped in those white bandages head to toe. I see them stepping out, grabbing supplies. There must be at least twenty or so smaller tents clustered behind that big one." Bolivar closed the spyglass and turned back to the group. "Let's get going. We need to get back to the library. This is bigger than I thought it would be."

Tony snapped his head to Bolivar. "Woah wait, don't you think we should try and talk to these people before we go jumping to conclusions?" Tony noticed that all three of the Battons were shifting their eyes back and forth in nervous glances.

"We hermited because of the Creep," said Jonathan when he noticed Tony's gaze. "Lost our littlest to it before coming south. Won't lose anymore."

"We had no idea they were sicks," said Michelle. Ridden had fallen quiet.

Jonathan swallowed hard and looked at Bolivar. "We are with you, Bolivar, whatever you have to do. We'd prefer to be a bit further from this bunch now, anyway. At least until we come back to deal with them."

Eyes half-blazing with muted fury, Bolivar jerked his head to Tony. "Do you want to go down there and shake hands with Sicks? Because I sure as fuck don't. We need to move, now."

"Sarah told you to report back, don't you need to do that first?" *This could be war. He wants war. I can see it in his eyes.*

Pointing his finger in Tony's face, Bolivar's own filled with a shadow of anger and he pointed his finger in Tony's face. "If you question my authority again this conversation is going to change into something very different, do you understand?"

It doesn't matter where you run, Butcher! You'll always be mine! You'll always carry the banner on your back! The memories ran through Tony like a roaring flame, and he rested a single index finger on the hilt of his sword and met Bolivar's eyes. *I've killed men like you before, Bolivar. Don't make me that man again.* "Then I suppose we should be getting back to the library." He tapped at the pommel of his sword, his fingers tracing its hilt and cross guard all while his eyes stayed locked on Bolivar's.

Jaw moving beneath his beard, Bolivar turned back to the others and motioned to the packs and gear resting on the ground. "Let's get moving."

At Bolivar's words everyone gathered their gear and prepared for the long hike back to the library. As he slung his pack back over his back and adjusted the sword on his hip, Tony's mind dwelled with what waited beyond the horizon. When they started back to the Belhaven, he daydreamed again about the road, his family, and how simple things had once been. He wondered if they would ever be that simple again. He wondered how heavy the sword on his belt would become and who would wet it first.

ʃɛɅɕħɱɅʅɕ

As the threat of conflict slithered into the Belhaven's community, a cloaked figure sat around a campfire deep in the Calarine ruins. His violet eyes watched the flickering flames as a shadow-veiled cat slept at his feet. He could feel the tension rolling through the blackstone streets like a river and knew that the moment would soon come when he would return to the Belhaven. As he thought of stepping back through those heavy oak doors for the first time in a decade, he grinned.

That night, Michael dreamed a dream like a waltz, the unending waves of purple in step with his racing heart.

PART IV
THAT DARKENED PAST

CHAPTER XVI

A Boiling Pot

==

SARAH

As Tony, Bolivar, and the Battons began the hike from the market camp to the Belhaven, Sarah and Ri searched through the books on the second floor for defensive spells. The pair flipped through pages and pages of Aetic guides, a task that had become commonplace in recent days as tensions continued to mount within the community.

"Have you seen this one?" Ri asked. They handed Sarah a book on defensive auras turned to a page on deflection spells.

Sarah shook her head and took the book. "I don't know, this one is pretty similar to other ones I've already worked on. I don't want to end up just knowing a bunch of the same old spells."

Nodding, Ri sat the book down in the appropriate pile, and went back to the search. In a moment, they returned with another book and handed it to Sarah, this one titled *A Complete Discussion of Aetic Defenses*. Sarah took the book, opened it, then immediately closed it and handed it back to Ri. "That one's just theoretical analysis stuff. I wish they could get the titles of these things figured out. This is a mess." Sarah rubbed at her eyes with one hand while she pushed her mess of curly red hair back with the other. Her hair had gone uncut since before her arrival at Varinz, and now it was well past her shoulders.

Ri sat down in a chair beside Sarah and placed a hand on her shoulder. "Maybe you should take a break?"

"No, I need to keep looking. I need to keep working." Ri reached out and put a hand in Sarah's hair, who pulled away and shook her head. Ri took their hand back and gave a soft, disheartened smile. Sarah saw Ri's face from her peripheral and looked at them. "What's wrong?"

"What are you talking about?"

"Cut it out Ri, you're stiff as a board."

"The other day's still on my mind."

"You mean the courtyard?"

They said nothing, but ran a hand over their bandages.

"Stop worrying about it. It's nothing, you didn't mean it, and I haven't thought about it again." Sarah raised her own right hand, the knotted scars standing out in the light. "Besides, now we'll match."

Ri gave a faint smile, but shook their head. "You don't have to lie to me. I know that changed things. I am the 'war machine,' after all. I mean, we barely managed to fucking move on from Varinz and then...I don't know. Why're you even okay being around me?"

Without a word, Sarah reached out and grabbed Ri's right cheek and locked eyes with them. The light hit Ri's blonde hair, the ricocheting rays finding their way through the library along their own dust-beamed path. She followed the lines of Ri's still-swollen lip to the edges of their nose and along their deep-set eyes. Sarah's own hair shone a crimson red in the light and cast shadows across Ri's pale, scared face. She started to speak, to reassure Ri that nothing could ever change the way she saw them, but a beam of light broke through the mass of her curly hair and illuminated a single scar on their face. It ran under their left eye and almost reached their ear. The scar, faint but ever present, silenced Sarah. She had seen it before, a half dozen times and more than a few of them she had run her hands along it. A couple of those times it had been her lips that had traced the scars path. But still, in the long-afterwards of the courtyard, the scar looked different. It looked deeper, longer, darker. It wasn't the scar of an accident or happenstance. It was a scar of war. She leaned forward and kissed it, letting her lips linger.

"I love you, Ri. I don't care about your past. I'm not going to let this go because you have something that's there I don't understand. We all do. It's part of being alive, I think."

Ri's mouth moved as if they were going to speak, but instead they just leaned forward, took Sarah's shoulders, and pulled her in. The pair sat there in a quiet, hurting embrace for a long while. Sarah's head rested on Ri's chest, the steady rise and fall a welcome comfort. Ri's hand moved absent mindedly along the line of Sarah's spine. When Sarah pulled back and met Ri's eyes again, she saw the absent, faraway look they held. The quiet numbness unsettled her, but still she brought her hand to Ri's face and traced the delicate edge of their bruised lip.

"Ri, I know you're scared, but--"

Witihout a word, Ri pulled Sarah in and kissed her, their bruised and swollen lips not standing in the way. They ran their hand under Sarah's shirt, and then reached for the waistband of her pants. Ri's past left Sarah's mind, no longer lingering in the space between them, as they moved to a far corner, hidden by the towering shelves.

Two days after Bolivar scouted the market camp, and one day after Sarah and Ri found themselves together on the second floor, he returned to the Belhaven, the Battons in tow. He swung the heavy doors open wide as he marched in. Sarah and Ri were standing in the lobby, having just finished breakfast and planning the day. He gave them both only a passing glance before he came to the front desk and flagged for the Battons to follow.

"Sarah," said Bolivar, motioning towards the family, "this is Jonathan, Michelle, and Ridden Batton. They're prospective new members of our little community. Tony and I met them at the old capitol building near the center of the ruins."

Sarah, caught off guard, stuck out a cautious hand and shook with the three newcomers. "Welcome to the Belhaven," she said and gave a nervous smile. "If Bolivar would've let me know you were coming and I would have prepared you a space, but we'll make do." As she spoke, she cast a stabbing glance towards Bolivar, who stood unphased.

"We don't have much time to commiserate," Bolivar interjected, his face stern. "Jonathan showed us a camp in the old market district, and it poses a serious threat. We need to start making moves to protect ourselves now." Behind him, Tony shifted his weight and cast a nervous glance to Ri.

Sarah's face dropped as Bolivar's words poured into her like poison. Ri stepped closer to her and put a hand on her side. "We'll talk about this later, Bolivar. We need to let our new friends get settled. We won't be making any moves today."

He took a step closer and rubbed at the sweat on his brow. "You aren't listening to me. We need to move now, not later. This place poses a real danger to us, and we need to get ahead of it."

"I gave you very clear instructions to let me know what you found before you came back. Now maybe if you had managed to follow instructions, I could have been prepared to talk about this, but you didn't, and I'm not. So, would you please show our new visitors to the living quarters and help them get settled? We'll discuss the rest of this later."

"I will not stand by and let you put us in danger!" he shouted, drawing the attention of Michael and Finch, who were still sitting at the table enjoying their breakfast. As he went on, his theatrics grew. His voice turned to the same tone Sarah had heard politicians use in the cities. She wondered as he stood there shouting at her, if he had rehearsed what he would say. "I won't let you put this place in danger, or the people you drew here despite your lack of preparation. You behave like I am here to call us to arms! It's hundreds of people, Sarah. All I am saying is that we need to get prepared."

The heavy oak doors still standing open, the sound of spring morning winds whispering their way in, Michael and Finch came to stand in the lobby. Everyone, save Jane and Pinn, stood around Sarah and Bolivar, watching, listening. Beneath Bolivar's shouts the wind sounded like whistling steam.

"Bolivar, I won't hear another word of it." She refused to raise her voice to match his. "The issue is not violence. Like you so aptly pointed out, we don't need to draw unnecessary attention to ourselves, so we will not be making any moves until they have been planned. To do so I need time to think on this. I need all of the information." Bolivar started to speak, but Sarah raised a hand to interrupt him. "So why don't you put together a report and give it to me in the morning, hmm?"

"This camp is full of fucking Sicks," Bolivar spat.

In the heavy, stunned moment of silence, Finch gasped and put a hand over her mouth. Michael's eyes darted to his shoes. The wind continued to carry in. Bolivar's voice seemed to ride along it.

"Sicks, Sarah. You're fine with a bunch of Sicks this close to us?"

Eyes carrying some part of that raging flame, Ri stepped forward and pointed a finger at Bolivar. "You know that Sicks aren't any danger to us." They looked back at Sarah. "Sicks are just people who survived the Creep. That's it."

Sarah, keeping eye contact with Bolivar, cleared her throat. "Tony, can you hear me?"

Working his way past the Battons, the hilt of his sword brushing Jonathan's arm, Tony cleared his throat. "Yes," he answered. His voice was steady, his eyes watched both of them, snapping back and forth, and his hand resting on the pommel of his sword.

"Are these Sicks any threat to us?" she asked, not looking at him. She kept her eyes locked on Bolivar.

"Not unless one of us goes and shakes their hand. The black rot doesn't pass unless you touch it."

Sarah smirked and crossed her arms. "There you go, nothing to worry about."

"I don't like it," Finch said from behind and Sarah turned to face her. "I don't like being that close to them. I mean, that's a bunch of walking biological weapons! I don't want to end up rotting away like some plague rat." She walked over to stand beside Bolivar, shaking her head as she did. "I'm sorry Sarah, but I'm with Bolivar. We need to do something about this. I've got a kid to protect. Diseases change, and Tony hasn't been around it for a long time." Her normally defiant eyes were nervous. "Sorry, I…I just don't like it."

Michael pointed a finger at Finch and stepped up. "I have a kid too and you don't see me shaking in my boots. Starting an unnecessary fight is a bigger risk than Sicks. Don't be a coward, you're better than this. I know you are."

"We didn't come here to get in a pissing contest," Ridden interjected. His young face was covered in obvious irritation. "We came here for 'strength in numbers,' but it looks like you bunch have the strength of a herd of hungry goats."

Jonathan put a hand on his son's chest, but cleared his own throat all the same. "Bolivar, what is this? You told me on the hike here that taking care of those rotting ghouls wouldn't be a problem. The ruins don't feel safe with them there."

Bolivar shifted his weight and gave a slight lean forward on the balls of his feet. His eyes were on Sarah. "If we're going to be a place of power, then we have to assert some of that power. If you aren't capable of that, Sarah, maybe we need to elect someone who is. You hear the Battons. This place has a duty to the rest of Calarine as much as it does itself."

"You seem confused. This is a place of knowledge, not violence. And it isn't a God damn democracy." Bolivar started to speak again, but Sarah turned away. "I'm done Bolivar. I'll be in my office."

Worrying pushing further would either bring the rising

tensions to physicality or that she would lose her nerve, Sarah pivoted on the balls of her feet and marched towards the offices with Ri in tow. The sounds of argument echoed through the lobby behind them, but she never turned to see who stood on either side. As Sarah and Ri walked through the doors, they were greeted by Sibella, who sat perched on the sconce mounted on the center column. Ri stopped to lock the door as Sarah paced the floor.

"Quite the mess out there," said Sibella. He sounded almost dismissive.

"That's an understatement," Ri said. They gave a long, exhausted sigh and shook their head.

"Have they all turned on you?" The falcon's question somehow sounded both genuine and like a joke.

Sarah stopped pacing, now chewing at the cuticles on her thumbs, and shook her head. "No, I don't think so, but Finch and the new ones Bolivar brought are in his camp, that much I know for certain."

"Well," the bird said, "Finch is scared and worried about herself and her child, and the new ones were Bolivar's to begin with, so no surprises there." The falcon preened his feathers, almost seeming not to hear Bolivar's preaching echo from the lobby.

"Whatever their motivations are," Ri said, "something's got to give. It's getting tense." Sarah just nodded in response, still chewing on her cuticles.

The sound of the heavy front doors slamming shut shook dust off of the joists above, and Sibella glided down from the sconce to a nearby table as it reached him. He took on a much more serious and nodded. "I am afraid that Ri is right.

The air here has changed, I'm sure we can all feel it. Even the ones out there. Sarah, take a moment to catch your breath. I will be back soon." In a flash Sibella took flight and headed into the rafters.

As the falcon disappeared into the rafters above, Ri walked closer to Sarah and wrapped her in their arms. Together they stood there holding one another as the sounds of Bolivar's speech died out. In a moment, the lobby lowered to a murmur. The eerie silence almost seemed to fall heavier on Sarah's shoulders. Thoughts about Bolivar filled her head as she stood there, sagging in Ri's arms. She wondered what he could have said and who he could have convinced to turn against her. She thought of how foolish it was for her to start calling people to the Belhaven, how ridiculous it was for her to ever think that she could manage the responsibility. *Falling, falling, falling deep into the pits of the Morable caves. Maybe Ri's there naked at the bottom, twisted and broken, muscle wrested from bone. Maybe their naked because you've been fucking instead of tending your God damn house.* For a brief moment she felt like she was back on the streets of Varinz, surrounded by bustling crowds. An overwhelming swarm of anxiety choked her vision. The swirling feelings were quelled when Ri pressed their forehead against Sarah's and the two stood there for a moment in silence, trying to wash the worries away.

"Let's run away together," Sarah said, breaking the silence. A half-hearted grin crawled across her face as she looked into Ri's eyes.

"You know we can't do that. That you won't do it." Ri said, pulling Sarah closer.

"I know."

"This place is yours. Don't let him take it from you."

Sarah started to speak again, but in a rush of fluttering wings Sibella returned, now with a bound scroll held in his talons. "I believe I made it through the library without being seen by Bolivar or his new friends." He dropped the scroll on a nearby table, and Sarah unrolled it. "They seem to have taken refuge on the third floor, though I doubt you find that surprising. I might as well tell you that rats often take refuge in the walls."

Sarah scanned over the scroll, its plain presentation an oddity among the other books and scrolls in the library. "What is this?" she asked, reading the spell names like "Fireflash," "Sweeping Winds," and "Concussive Blow" with an air of confusion. Their descriptions were terse and plain, athletic.

"A scroll of combat spells," Sibella answered. His tone was filled with apprehension. "Offensive spells, Sarah, I think the time has come. You have taken the time to learn the mechanics and motions of defensive spells, these will be simple to you, I am sure."

"Why do we keep having to go through this? If I do this, then what makes me better than Bolivar?"

"Intent! Intent, Sarah, intent! You make me feel like a blasted broken clock!"

"Sarah," Ri interjected, "maybe he's right. We don't know what is about to happen with Bolivar. It might be a good idea to at least look at these spells."

Sibella started to speak again but was interrupted by three quick raps on the office door. Sarah turned and looked. Through the hazy frosted glass she could see Tony's outline. She walked to the door and put a hand on the lock.

"Tony? Are you alone?"

"I am," he answered, his voice hushed, "I think we need to talk."

Taking a moment to look back over her shoulder to Ri and Sibella, who both nodded, Sarah unlocked the door. Tony walked through, no pack or sword on him, but his face was haggard. His eyes were draped with a heavy exhaustion.

"Are you all okay?" he asked as he walked in. He still spoke in whispers. The others nodded and he nodded back. "I've taken a risk even coming here. Bolivar is steaming at your confrontation, and I'm done being part of his plans. I think he suspects that, but I'm not sure. If I'm being honest, he probably has since we left the market."

Sarah checked that the door was locked and turned to face Tony. "What's going on?"

Beads of sweat stood out on Tony's forehead, and he shifted his weight from one foot to the other. "When I was out with Bolivar, he did a lot of talking about how he thought you were a weak leader. It was the same kind of stuff he was spewing today. Now, I don't know about you three, but I don't think that in itself is dangerous. He's a big talker, but talk is talk you know? But…" Tony trailed off and shuddered to force himself back to the conversation, "when we were out there, we came across a camp of three armed men."

"They were drunk, weren't they?" asked Sarah. "Camped under the eave of a tower?"

Tony nodded. "That's right. They were drunk off of their asses, half out of their minds. How did you know?"

"Before I ever called anyone else here, me and Sibella ran into them the first time we left the library. We just ran, and

I've never heard anything out of them. I'm not surprised they're still there. It was a big place and they were just making camp."

"Well, they looked good and rooted when we came across them. Place was littered with bottles and trash. We could have gone around or tried to talk, but Bolivar confronted them. At first, he was playing nice, but when they started acting tough and threatened us, like any drunk jackass would've done, Bolivar just…" The images of those mutilated corpses flooded back into his mind, and he clenched at his stomach with an absent hand. "He just…tore them to pieces. I've never seen anyone move so fast. I've never seen an Aetic fight so… brutally. I don't know who Bolivar really is, but I am positive he didn't start learning magic when he got here. He couldn't have."

"Something about his story has never added up," said Ri. "That whole thing about him being a teacher-turned-rebel always sounded like dog shit to me."

Tony rubbed a hand over his bald head and shrugged. "I thought I knew him. I thought…He's a danger. Whatever he is, we can't take his show today as an empty threat. This is something real. Violence like that? It wasn't casual. Those were the movements of a man who has his mind set on a single task. I don't know what we need to do, but it needs to be done fast. I've seen men like that before, but only ever on a battlefield, Sarah."

Teeth grinding so hard that her jaw ached, Sarah's face grew solemn. She saw the spiderwebbed scars that ran along Tony's arm, and started to ask what happened, but stopped, knowing there would be time for that later. Her mind raced and her fists worked, clenching and unclenching as she tried to find a way out of it, knowing that she never could. "Go back to Bolivar, and act like we haven't talked. We'll wait for him to do what he's going to do. First, though, tell Michael to be ready. He'll need to get the kids and hide with them in the shrine when everything gets started. He'll know what I mean."

Tony nodded and left the administrative offices in hurried strides. Sarah went and sat down at the table, pouring over the scroll of offensive spells. She did not speak a word to Ri or Sibella as she did. She read quick, her mind frantic in its attempts to absorb the spells as the growing threat of Bolivar stampeded through her mind.

MICHAEL

As Bolivar's tirade petered out and Finch and the Battons followed him towards the staircase to the third floor, Michael stood at the lobby desk and watched as the children sat confused in the living quarters. He gave a somber smile, his gray-blue speckled hair catching glimmers of light that shined down from the big windows above the doors. They shined a little clearer now, the ancient dust having shaken free when Bolivar slammed the doors closed. Seeing only anxious eyes in return, he went to the children, who sat in quiet whispers together and tried to hide their obvious worry.

Michael ruffled his daughter's hair and gave a smile to Pinn. He wondered how the boy felt having watched his mother rant at the people he thought were their friends. "Why don't both of you go hang out in the courtyard? It's a beautiful day. No need in spending the whole thing in this dusty place, huh?" Jane's face faltered and then she pushed Pinn's shoulder and the pair left the library, headed into the courtyard. Michael was glad at that, glad they had left without question even though he knew that they saw through him. *Kids*, he thought, reciting his father's words, *are a good bit smarter than you're reckoning*. He sat down on the bed and ran a hand over his face. His stomach dropped, his skin grew cold and damp. As the vision started to take hold, a pang of terror ran through his heart.

But this time, he took a breath and closed his eyes. As the color and paint began to fill his mind, he thought of Sibella's words and accepted the vision as his, as part of him. This time the paint did not swirl and writhe against him. Instead, it came like a rising tide. Bright red became more and more vibrant in his mind as it clashed against a fire-tinged orange. Beyond it all he saw a backdrop of stone-gray. Michael could feel himself in his unknowable form as he stood within his own mind. He watched the colors as they acted out their roles on what he had begun to understand as his own personal stage. Still, as he watched, he felt frustrated with the abstracted world. He stood and wondered what was left of his form in reality. He wondered where the line between himself and his body remained and cursed at the complexity of what lay before him.

*I have some control now but no way to know what the shit I am looking a*t. He looked on as a familiar flash of black-fringed purple devoured the red and orange. Now no terror rose in his mind as the purple began to fill his vision. All feelings were replaced with an indecipherable abstraction. A non-euclidean, uncontrollable sense of imperceptible and total void. As the vision faded from his mind he returned to reality and found himself still sitting on the bed. He sighed and cleaned his glasses, all the while muttering to himself. "What good is a vision if it all just seems like a damn nonsense art project?"

"What was that?" Tony asked from behind. Michael stiffened. Tony put his hands up and shook his head as Michael turned around. "No need to be nervous. I'm here on Sarah's behalf, not his."

"Everything okay?"

"Relative to everything else, I guess so. Conflict is coming. I'm sure you feel it."

Michael nodded.

"Sarah sends a message. Once things get started, get the kids and hide in the shrine until it's all over. She said you'd know what it meant. Do you know where they're at?"

Michael nodded again. "How long do we need to hide?"

"Until she comes and gets you, I guess," Tony answered with a shrug. He stepped over to his cot and took the sword. As he spoke, he strapped it onto his belt with dexterous, familiar hands. "She didn't say. We don't know what he's planning, but I have a feeling it's coming soon. I'm going to talk to him as soon as I'm done talking to you."

Pushing back the hair back on his forehead, Michael swallowed hard and nodded. He thought about what a strange moment this was to realize he needed a haircut, but he did. Then his eyes went to the sword and he frowned. "All right, I'll go get them. Hopefully this all blows over faster than we think." Tony gave a half-hearted smile and Michael returned it. To Michael, that smile said what he already knew. Nothing could blow over. The storm was already there.

TONY

Leaving Michael to his duty, a duty he didn't understand but also didn't have the time to dwell on, Tony climbed the stairs to the third floor. He took each step with quiet determination, the weight of his sword heavy on his hip as he did. He thought of all the time he'd spent helping Bolivar organize the third floor into their office, all the time he'd hoped could be a friend as Bolivar plotted under his nose. He felt stupid and angry as he climbed those steps towards people he now only conceptualized as conspirators, mutineers. Furious that he had pushed his anxieties aside in the name of a feigned peace. He could taste the iron on his tongue, feel the blood wetting his sword. He could feel the tides shifting, his short peace ending. *I never wanted this. I never wanted any of this.* As he came to the third floor, he found Bolivar, Finch, and the Battons standing around a central table. Bolivar talked at them, his arms waving and pointing. The others just stood, somber-faced.

As Tony topped the stairs and came across the room, Bolivar stopped talking and turned to look at him. "Ah, Tony! Where've you been?"

Without answering, Tony walked to the table, which he saw was covered with a hand-sketched map of the library, and wondered if Bolivar's question was genuine or accusatory. "Talking with Michael and the kids down on the first. They're worried."

"Where are they?" Finch asked.

"Lobby." Tony looked the Battons over, who seemed bored and unconcerned.

"I don't suppose he'll be joining us?" Bolivar asked. He

had turned his attention back to the sketched map. "I'm sure him and Ri are going to side with Sarah in this."

"In what? No one even knows what's going on. You've got everyone scared, that's about it."

The air stiffened around them. Bolivar glanced at Finch and the others and nodded before he tapped a single finger in the center of the sketched map. "She's left us no choice Tony, we have to take the Belhaven from her."

He had expected it, had known it was coming. Tony's palm rested on the pommel of his sword. "You can't actually think that fighting one another is the answer to whatever has you worried? What the hell are you going to do with a library, collect harlequin romance?"

Finch stepped forward and wagged a finger in Tony's face. "What the hell else would you have us do? I know your weird stray is fuckin' her, but you've got to be more realistic about this."

"You leave Ri out of this, Grett." Tony had stepped closer to Finch now, but he could still see Bolivar out of the corner of his eye.

"Oh how about it? How about you go downstairs and tell everybody else you hauled a fucking Faralkin Valykrie here? A fucking cult-headed berserker!"

Tony's eyes snapped to Bolivar, who shrugged. "Did you think I didn't know what they are? I've been through the Faralt-Lands more than once, Tony. I respect you keeping their secret, but the time for that sort of thing is over."

"Yeah, so have I," Finch cut in, her face flushed with anger. "I've seen those lunatic barbarians pillaging more than I ever care to, and I'll tell you what I bet if Sa--"

The only other sound Finch could manage was a single, choked gasp. Tony's big hand wrapped around her throat, and as he tightened his grip her eyes bulged. His free hand still rested on his sword.. As he held her she looked like a child, and Tony's eyes were shining with wild glints of violent, sparkling red. He spoke through gritted teeth and tightened his grip around her throat again. "You better fucking watch it. Do you hear me?" She slapped at his trunk of an arm and struggled for what little breath he allowed her. He saw Ridden and Jonathan step forward and put a hand on makeshift swords. His soldier's eyes told him they were far enough away that he could stop them with no trouble. Those eyes he had thought he would never need again. He shook Finch a little, pulling her closer still. "You better fucking watch your mouth with me, Grett. I'm not Michael or Sarah. I'll kill you. You bunch want to make me into this again, fine. I'll gut you like a pig. Pinn won't recognize you when I'm done, do you understand me?"

He let go of Finch and pushed her forward. She stumbled on her heels and coughed a hard, ragged string of breaths, spittle flying onto the floorboards. He turned to Bolivar now and met his eyes. The two stood there for a moment, Finch's coughs disappearing into the background. "This the shit you're going to do, Bolivar? Fill everyone up with hate and pit them against one another? Whisper in Finch's ear, feed her bullshit and venom and send her after the rest of us?" Ridden and Jonathan took another step forward, hands still on the hilts of their swords, and Tony's finger twitched against the pommel of his own. "What about you three? Why the fuck are you listening to him?"

Michelle's eyes cut to Jonathan, who tightened his grip

on the wound wire hilt of his homemade sword. "Why don't you let us tend to ourselves?"

"Bolivar is going to get you all killed, you know that don't you?" For a moment Tony thought he saw a falter in Ridden's face, the hard edges of his certainty falling away to true, teenage terror, but when Jonathan half drew his own sword, the conversation dissolved and Tony matched his draw. The steel of his sword now showing over the scabbard and catching glints of light, Tony cut his eyes to Bolivar and spoke through clenched teeth. "How fast can you move those hands, Bolivar? Faster than me?" His eyes cut back to Jonathan "What about you? Think you can get to me first?"

Nothing Tony said seemed to have phased Bolivar, and the big man only raised a hand and glanced back at the Battons, who returned to their places. "Are you okay, Finch?"

"Yeah," Finch answered, but her speech was slurred and punctuated with hacking coughs.

His eyes hardened and drawn tight, Bolivar turned back to Tony. "Are you done? Jonathan and his family are scared, scared of the Sicks, the Creep. Scared of Sarah's inaction. Finch is scared you and your friends are going to get her son killed. That's why they're here, why they're trusting me to keep this place safe. So, are you done with your little show?"

"You're kidding right? Fuck no I'm not done. You need to stop this." Tony stepped forward, his chest now almost touching Bolivar's. He realized the man was breathing in steady, unbothered breaths. Drawing in and staring into Bolivar's eyes, he tried to control his own angered breathing but couldn't. Instead, he ground his teeth and tightened a hand around his sword. He heard shuffling feet and wondered if he'd find a blade sliding into his back before he could move. He wondered if it would be one of the Battons or Finch who'd kill him. But no sword came near him, as Bolivar again raised his hand to stop them. This time though, he looked at Tony with a grin that almost felt apologetic. Lightning crackled and filled Bolivar's palm. Tony's eyes widened just enough to raise his brow. He took a sliding step back, and as he did the lightning dissipated.

The stinking haze of electricity still lingering between them, Bolivar just motioned towards the stairs and sighed. "I think it's time for you to leave. I'm sure we'll see you again soon, friend."

Unable to force himself back towards Bolivar, the image of the dead men in the ruins and their lightning streaked corpses on his mind, Tony walked to the steps. He stopped, hand resting on the bannister rail, but didn't turn back to them. He spoke over his shoulder to the room at large. "Bolivar, leave Finch here. Leave her, or you'll get her killed."

"I can handle myself," Finch spat back, still rubbing at her throat.

At the sound of her rattled, bruised voice, Tony closed his eyes and nodded. He had meant what he had said to her, but he wished he hadn't. *I hope it isn't me that has to kill you, Finch. I really do.* He pulled himself straight against the rail and turned to look at Bolivar, who was leaning against the map table. "If you ever cared about her, Bolivar, leave her. If any of that was real, leave her."

"I said I can handle myself you fuck! Piss off!"

The hate in her voice sent him down the steps towards Sarah, his hand clutching the cold steel pommel of his sword, hating the feeling it gave him. The total, perfect anticipation.

SARAH

The sound of shifting paper and thudding books filled the administration offices as Sarah burned through spell books, a stack on the table nearly shoulder high, making use of them as fast as she could. The spells, despite their dangerous nature, were simple. Focused on broad and powerful emotions like rage and frustration, Sarah found it easy to focus and send the shocks of lightning and bolts of fire singing from her fingertips. When Tony barreled into the room, his heavy footfalls frantic and rattling the furniture, he drew both Sarah and Ri's attention.

"Ri," he said, his breath steady but filled with urgency, "we need to talk. Step out here with me?"

"What's going on?" Sarah asked.

"Things are bad with Bolivar, worse than I expected. He's planning to take this place from you, Sarah. I just need a moment with Ri." Tony shot Ri a glance, and they followed him through the main administration offices and into the lobby.

Left there with only Sibella, who rested on a sconce above, his eyes pensive and far away, Sarah shifted in her chair, trying to refocus herself on the spellbooks. "This all feels quite familiar," he said, never looking at Sarah. "I feel another leaving along the horizon."

"I won't leave you, Sibella. I've told you that."

The bird said nothing, resting high above. His eyes followed a shadow along the rafters, and with a single screeching kak he took flight, leaving Sarah truly alone in her office.

He's right and you know it. You've left before. Run, run, run little girl. Run because you are scared. Run because you lost track of what this place was. Because you are your failures whether you want to be or not. Sarah clenched her eyes and squeezed the edges of the book in her hands, trying to force herself to stay grounded. In a moment, her mind still reeling, she heard the administration office door fly open, the glass rattling in the frame. A few seconds later Ri barreled through, Tony close behind.

"We can all leave!" Tony shouted after them. "Ri, listen, let's talk to Sarah first, all right?"

"What're you talking about?" Sarah had stood up from the table. Ri had rushed to the corner and began rifling through their belongings.

"Bolivar's going to take this place whether we fight him or not. I told Ri we just need to leave. All of us. Get Michael and Jane and leave. If he wants this, let him have it, we can find somewhere else."

"Finch?"

"She's with him. She...she burned her bridges with me."

"Tony, I'm not leaving this place. I won't."

He slammed a fist into the table nearby and nearly sent the table toppling over as a pile of books slid off. "I don't want this! I didn't come here to be a god damn soldier again!"

Without a word, Ri swung a long leather bag onto the table. Sarah glanced at them and saw them unbuckling the clasps along the bag's edge. When she looked back to Tony, she saw that he had gone pale. His mouth was set, statuesque as if beginning to reserve itself to something beyond comprehension.

"Will someone please tell me what's going on?" Sarah asked. "Ri, you told me that was your clothes."

"I lied." They undid another of the buckles. Sarah stared at the bag now, really seeing it for the first time. Seeing that it was ornate and tooled and that two dozen tiny clasps ran along its edge. *You've been distracted.* She saw Ri's eyes too, that strange blazing rage.

With the final clasp undone and the bag laid open, Ri lifted a sword from the bag, its long scabbard wrapped in fine brown leather, its handle shining out a deep and startling chrome. The pommel was a black eye, deep and unsettling with its amethyst iris. Ri pulled the sword from its scabbard, the blade perfect and oiled, and held it out in front of them. Sarah stood speechless, looking at Ri as if seeing them for the first time. They replaced the sword and pulled the leather tie loose and tied the sword to their belt. It hung off of their broad warrior's frame as if it had always been there.

"The rest of you can run," Ri said, "but I've run enough. If Bolivar wants a fight, I'll give it to him."

The paleness gone from his face, Tony put a hand on Sarah's shoulder. His other hand rested on the hilt of his own sword. "It looks like we've got no other choice, Librarian."

Sarah looked from Ri to Tony, the two of them now new creatures. Great, ancient wolves, awakened to the hunt at the hint of blood. "We might not be enough."

"To falter is to lose the gift," said Ri. "I won't die a coward."

Sarah swallowed. The image of the Morable was again in her mind.

CHAPTER XVII
The Slipped Blade

==

Sarah and Sibella worked through the shelves of the second floor, reading through the spells the books in hopes they might find something to help them in the coming storm. All the while Ri and Tony stood by, swords on their hips, their set frames and hard eyes giving them the appearance of palace guards. *The library's guards*, thought Sarah, and for a moment she was almost sick.

"I wish the two of you would sit down and stop that."

"If you're going to be reading, we need to be watching," said Ri.

Book in hand, despite the fact that she had attempted and failed to focus on three others, Sarah sat down and ran a hand over her face. "When he gets here, I want to talk to him before anything else."

"Sarah--"

"Ri, stop. I get it, this is something more, but I'm still me."

"Yes, but--"

"But nothing. If you won't tell me what you are, where that sword is from, can you at least just listen to me?"

"Enough," said Tony. "I told you both downstairs, they'll be time enough for this when all of this shit is finished. Fight now, talk later. I won't say it again."

Rolling her eyes, Sarah threw up her hands. She felt like screaming at them, but Ri and Tony had already turned their attention back to the stairway, waiting on the sound of Bolivar and his recruits. Their friends and a family of strangers. Sarah hoped that everything would change. That Finch would see the light, and that the Battons, whoever they were, would lose hope in the grinning maniac and leave. That Bolivar would climb the stairs with his hands above his head begging for forgiveness. She knew, though, that it was impossible. Even as she thought of it she could see the bottom of the cave before her. *There's nothing left to do but fall.*

She skimmed through the words on the pages, not absorbing their content but hoping the sound which echoed up the stairs would dissipate into a different direction. That still there was a chance. That her grip on that rope might've been stronger than it was on the last. She wondered for a moment what Michael and the kids were doing, how fast they would get to the shrine. She wondered what they would do if she lost the coming fight. *Fall, of course. They always fall. This time it won't be one it'll be all of 'em.*

But that thought was forced from her mind as Bolivar topped the stairs with Finch and the Battons close behind. He stopped almost ten feet from the table where Sarah waited, his eyes dark and shaded in the faded light. Sarah still looked through the books, never giving Bolivar a glance.

"Sarah," Bolivar announced, his voice tight and focused as he stood, metal staff in hand, "As Peace Officer--"

"Cut the shit," Sarah interrupted. She still refused to look at him and hoped that cast her as stern, serious. She hoped more than anything else to hide the way her eyes trembled in their sockets. She turned to him, and Sibella came to perch on her shoulder. As soon as the bird settled into his place Ri and Tony stepped away from her side. She scanned over the group and noticed the staff in Bolivar's hand and the makeshift swords on the hips of the Battons. Finch carried a staff of plain wood in trembling hands, and for a fleeting moment Sarah wondered why she was even there. In the flickering light of the second floor, Sarah faced him but refused to stand. "One last chance to talk this out?"

"I appreciate your consistency Silvergrove, but no. I think the time for talk is done." Bolivar grinned, that same fox-faced grin he had when they met. He glanced at Ri and Tony, their swords swinging on their hips as they flanked outward from Sarah. "I see you've at least done away with the pretense."

Sarah stood up, took her staff from where it leaned beside the table, and took a step closer. At that, Sibella took flight into the joists above. "I guess so. It doesn't have to be like this."

"No, I don't guess it does. Surrender?"

Falling, falling, falling. She glanced at Ri, but their eyes were locked on Michelle. Locked on Michelle's sword. "No, I don't suppose I will."

"Pity. I liked you, Sarah. I liked all of you, but I have my own duties to attend."

A strange hesitance on his face, Bolivar tightened his grip on his staff, but whatever he was planning, whatever he had meant to do, it was too late. Ri darted forward and swung a hammer-like right hook into the back of Ridden's head. The thudding blow sent the boy, who Ri towered over and outweighed by a hundred pounds flying forward. As the boy scrambled back to his feet, Ri drew their sword. The oiled blade glinted the light as they pivoted on their heels and brought the blade to Michelle's throat. Their movements were simple, economic, practiced.

On the other side of the Battons, Tony stood, wedging them between Ri and himself. As Jonathan reached for his sword, Tony pulled his own and shook his head. "Let's stay calm," he said. The look on his face was pure, unending hunger.

Eyes darting, Jonathan pulled his hand away and looked from Bolivar to his wife. Both of them held a stern gaze, locked on Sarah.

"Leave this place," Sarah said. She took another step closer and tightened her jaw. Her heart pounded in her chest, but she did everything she could to keep it from showing. "Turn around and take these people with you. Don't do this. Don't get these scared fools and Finch killed."

For a moment, Sarah thought she saw Bolivar's face soften, but in an instant his feet shifted and he twirled the staff in his hands. Sarah clenched her hands around her own staff and brought the glowing aura around herself just in time to block a flash of electricity that bolted out of his right hand. Michelle reached for her own sword as the lightning streaked across the room, and without hesitation, Ri jerked the sword at her throat. Blood poured down the woman's front as she collapsed to the floor. Tony readied his sword just as a shriek erupted from Ridden, who had scrambled back to his feet just as Bolivar started to make his move.

In the chaos of the second floor, Tony and Ri faced the remaining Battons, and the fight erupted into reality. Framed with shrieks of child-like fury, Finch seemed to stand awestruck, the wooden staff clattering to the ground at her feet. Her unbelief was lost in the battle. Tony and Ri became a whirlwind and Sarah defended against Bolivar. All the while Finch stood unmoving, eyes wide and unbelieving.

As Sarah and Bolivar clashed, the broad-shouldered man cast spell after spell in an attempt to force Sarah towards the back wall. His spells ricocheted off of Sarah's shields, striking the shelving and columns around them as they sent papers flying in clouds of dust and splinters. As she fought, Sarah struggled to maintain her footing against the barrage of spells, but with every step she managed she pulled the fight further from the others. All the while Bolivar fought as a man possessed. He cast spells at Sarah with an intense, focused accuracy. He fought like a man who had stood on the battlefield for most of his life. The metal staff in Bolivar's hands became as a conduit. It directed flashes of lightning and fire into focused blasts so strong they pushed Sarah back on her heels each time they contacted her shields. As she clenched her own staff, Sarah damned herself for not learning to use it in the same way. All it served as now was a brace with which to defend. Sarah struggled to block the spells, each one harder than the last, but her practice had paid off. With each moment of the battle, she felt herself become more certain, more hopeful. She focused her everything and poured her intent into her spells. *Save them, save them, save them!*

But Tony only caught glimpses of the fight between Sarah and Bolivar, because his own struggles consumed his attention. Finch, freed from her stupor, screeched for them to stop in her grating, pained voice, and fled into the stacks, kicking the staff across the room as she did. It skittered across the floor before slamming with a thwack against a nearby table, unheard to anyone, lost in the cavalcade of the battle. Ridden drew his sword and swung it at Ri with the frantic, screaming horror. His face was flushed red, his eyes wide and terrified. Ri parried each of the boy's haphazard attacks with a bored ease. They played with him as a manic energy grew in their eyes with each second of the battle. The same crushing blows used in the courtyard were now levered into the oiled edge of the blade. Michelle's blood flecked off of the sword, splatting across Ri's face, but they never slowed to wipe it away. They never paused nor shifted their stance.

All the while, Tony fended off Jonathan, surprised at his ability. The man's wiry frame warped and weaved as he pressed Tony, looking for an opportunity to work in a quick, unforgiving jab with his makeshift blade. He didn't fight like a soldier or the farmers Tony had met on the battlefield so many times before, but instead his movements were the quick and practiced jabs of a snake, searching for his single moment to strike. Tony brought the broadsword up, the long blade awkward in such close combat, to block each of Jonathan's blows, trying to find an opportunity to open the distance between them. Each time he brought the big sword down, Jonathan slid to one side or the other, slashing low with the strange, machete-like blade. Once it came close enough to cut the fabric of Tony's corded denim pants, but he brought the sword around in a hard, crushing blow. Jonathan, now on the defensive, shifted back a half dozen steps and Tony finally had the distance he needed.

At the same time, Ridden rushed in, and Ri, not

wanting to end their fight so early, shifted their weight and swung hard with their left hand. They caught the boy on the jaw with a strong, clobbering blow and sent him tumbling to the ground. Blood poured from his mouth as he fell and Ri gave a twisted, excited smile and tightened their grip on the sword. They waited for him to get up, but the boy didn't. Ri's single blow had sent him to the ground a crumpled, unconscious heap.

The bloodlust still rushing through their veins, Ri darted to Tony and joined his fight. With rapid, fevered swings they pushed Jonathan until the man's sword could not move fast enough. The distance the broadsword needed finally his, Tony caught a moment of weakness in Jonathan's attacks and sent his broadsword slashing across the man's chest. A gasp of air creeped out of Jonathan's mouth as he took a final step forward and collapsed to the ground, almost split in two. The sounds of the man's final, gasping breaths were thick and drowning, but neither Tony nor Ri cast him another glance as he died. Tony wiped a band of sweat from his forehead and glanced at Ri, who still stood in a wide swordsmen's stance, hands tight on the hilt of the strange sword. Their chest heaved in deliberate, focused breaths. Their face was flushed, and a wild energy sparkling in their eyes. Flecks of Michelle and Ridden's blood splattered their sword and body, but Ri made no effort to wipe them away. Then, breaking through the heat of battle, they heard the sound of footsteps from behind. Ri spun on their heels and sent their sword darting out in a single, flying thrust. Tony lunged forward, reaching for Ri's shoulder, but it was too late.

Speared on the end of Ri's blade, Finch gasped for

breath and reached out. Hands shaking, she tried to push herself from the blade, but the oiled steel sliced at her hands and she recoiled. Finch's eyes went from Tony to Ri, her mouth sucking in wordless, gurgling gasps.

"I didn't think," she struggled, but her words were cut off and she gasped as Ri jerked the blade out and let it clatter to the ground before catching her.

"Oh fuck," Ri whispered, heard by no one but her and Finch, "oh, please."

"I didn't think...we'd fight. I told him she'd--" a bubbling cough interrupted her, and thick blood splattered her lips, "I said she'd cave." A knowing smile, one so familiar on Finch's face, broke through the blood and bile on her lips. "Fuck me, I guess. Bad taste...in--" she heaved a long breath, and as she did thick, yellowing foam rose to the corners of her mouth. "Please, tell...Pinn..." Finch's words trailed off, and she let out a final, pained rasp as her body tightened in Ri's arms and then fell limp, heavier than it had ever been before.

Ri, their eyes were wide and frantic and filled with terror, looked up at Tony through a haze of tears. As Finch's body collapsed onto the floor Tony tried to grab Ri, to pull them away in their hazed state, but Ri pushed him away. Their bloodlust swirled and mixed with the soured taste of shame, and in that pause Bolivar broke away from Sarah.

He had blinded her with a blast of white light, and as Sarah reeled and fought to retain her footing, Bolivar turned and raised a single hand towards Ri and Tony. He sent a bolt of fire at Ri, who went flying across the room and slammed into the wall as the spell exploded into a blast of roaring flames. Tony dropped to the ground to avoid the blast and scrambled to Ri as the heat cleared. Their body was crumpled against the wall, sword still clenched in a blood covered hand. Sarah screamed as she watched her lover fly across the room, and, Bolivar's attention still turned to the others, she sent a flash of fire toward him.

Managing to raise a shield just in time, Bolivar blocked Sarah's blast of fire just in time, but in the moments between casting the spell and Bolivar blocking it, Sarah covered the ground between them and brought three more fast flashes of fire onto his shield. Her face was flushed with rage, her hands fast moving and certain. From inside of his shield Bolivar grinned and blocked her attacks, little effort showing on his face, though he made no efforts to push her, no efforts to end their fight. When she paused and attempted to shatter his shield with a blast of telekinesis, the shield disappeared and Bolivar instead sent a rush of wind at her. Sarah's telekinesis broke the stream of wind, but his spell still pushed her away. As she stumbled, he brought his metal staff up with both hands and slammed one end into the floor. Crackling electricity poured out and crawled across the ground, arcing from board to table to shelf as it searched for its target. Sarah cast a defensive aura, blocking the electricity just in time. As the spell crackled over the aura and began to dissipate, Bolivar twirled the staff in his hand and sent a lightning bolt straight towards her. As the bolt of red-white lightning struck the aura, Sarah's spell gave out and exploded in a blast of energy that sent her flying. She tumbled along the ground and crashed into the bookshelves that lined the back wall. A burst of wind erupted from Bolivar's boot heels, and he closed the distance between them in a single, incredible leap.

Exhausted and gasping for air, Sarah struggled to her knees, but as she tried to stand her legs collapsed beneath her. Before she could rise again, Bolivar was standing over her, his staff still in hand. She attempted to bring up a shield to defend herself again, but it crackled and sputtered before disappearing. Her mind was broken, tired, frantic. She couldn't focus her intent on the spell and as she tried one last time to cast it, her body refused and the spell died in her mind, never even reaching her fingertips. She looked up at Bolivar as the shield dissipated, the last gasp of her magic giving out before her eyes. There was no room for thoughts of her lost friends. No room for the Morable coast or that falling, falling, falling. No room for anxieties or fears or questions. It had all been crushed out of her. Bolivar grinned a sick, fox-faced grin as he loomed over her. Sarah saw her life dwindling out and imagined Bolivar crushing her throat beneath the driven down heels of his boots. In that moment of horror, she summoned everything that remained and fought against the exhaustion that racked her body. Using all she could manage, the last of her will, her rage at Bolivar, she called up another shield. The shield stabilized and Sarah came to her feet, legs trembling with exhaustion, but knees locked and defiant. Bolivar's grin faltered and he took a half step back, less to create distance between Sarah and himself and more to take in the entirety of her trembling, exhausted form.

"Stop this, Silvergrove," he said, just loud enough for her to hear. He created a cloak of red, swirling fire around the metal staff and brought it down hard on the shield. At that single blow, the shield shattered and sent an exhausted Sarah onto her back. She had managed the shield, but she couldn't hold it. Now she was too beaten to manage anything. Bolivar grabbed Sarah by the neck and dragged her to her feet. He brought his face close to hers, his beard brushing the edges of her jaw.

He whispered to her in a voice of pure, exasperated rage. "This was meant to be simple, but you're here standing in my damn way. Complicating my life, my task, my freedom. Let this go. Let this stupid fucking library go."

Tony looked up from Ri in time to see Bolivar lifting Sarah by her neck and rushed towards them, his sword held to his side. At the sound of the big man's slamming boot heels, Bolivar brought up a shield, a darker blue than any shield Sarah had ever cast, around both himself and Sarah just in time to stop Tony's sword. Tony swung at the shield, but his sword only bobbed back in his hands as the shield crackled with a magic haze, never faltering.

His lips pulled back from his teeth, breath snarling and full of rage, Bolivar brought his hand across Sarah's face in a thunderous, backhanded slap. She squirmed in his grasp, but he held her tight. "Say you'll stop this!"

Falling. He's going to kill me. I failed again.

He slapped her again. "Say it! Say you'll stop this!"

I have to stop this. I have to do something. This is mine. This is mine.

"Say it!" A third, a fourth. Each a clap of thunder against her face.

Mustering the last of her strength, Sarah spat a stream of blood into Bolivar's left eye and his face erupted with blind fury. He dropped his staff and wrapped both hands around her throat and throttled her. His eyes grew manic as he saw the life fade from Sarah's face.

"I told you to stop this! You did this! I never had any damn choice!"

Roaring in frantic, wild terror, Tony took desperate swings at the shield, but Bolivar paid him no mind and the shield showed no signs of his strikes. Bolivar only tightened his grip on Sarah's neck. Her eyes bulged from her head, the hazy thoughts of Ri, Tony, and the others coming in and out of focus as the life was choked out of her. Tony's pained screams made their way into her mind, and she tried to look past Bolivar to see him. Instead, she saw through hazed eyes that Tony no longer stood at the shield. She didn't know where he was or where he'd gone, but he was no longer there, and the sound of his sword clattering against the shield was gone too. She felt her chest tighten and knew her final breath was near, that it was almost over. But as she looked up at Bolivar's hate-filled eyes, a flash of purple light, the edges of it fringed in a strange and ragged shade of black, shattered the shield around them, and Bolivar dropped her. She collapsed to the ground gasping for air, and as her vision started to clear she saw another bolt of energy strike Bolivar in his chest.

CHAPTER XVIII
The Master Returns

==

When the bolt of strange light struck Bolivar, he was sent tumbling back, creating distance between him and Sarah, who was struggling for breath on the floor. Seeing the narrow distance as her only chance, she struggled to her knees, the marks left by his hands still glowing red on her throat. Almost as soon as he hit the ground Bolivar scrambled to his feet, a burning mark left behind. The thin smell of burned flesh lingered in the air around them, and as the sound of heavy, striding steps filled the air. Searching for thier source without turning her back on Bolivar, Sarah saw a black-hooded man striding across the room. Purple magic emanated from his hands, and Sarah wondered for a moment if it was Bolivar or herself the man was fixated on. His own breath rattled and panicked now, Bolivar sent a bolt of fire screaming across the library, but the stranger deflected it with an effortless flick of his wrist.

His rage and frustration replaced with blind panic, Bolivar rushed towards the back wall, pressing his back against it as he watched the man striding across the room. A golden haze of magic covered one of Bolivar's hands, and with a snap of his fingers, he summoned a portal of pure light along the wall behind him. The hooded stranger sent a writhing, shifting mass towards him, but it was too late. Bolivar leapt through the portal and disappeared from the Belhaven just as the black form came near. As the portal vanished, all that remained of it were char marks along the wall.

As Sarah caught her breath and her eyes cleared, she saw a black-gloved hand outstretched. "Take my hand," a graveled voice said, and Sarah did. The voice felt both ancient and young at once, an agelessness surrounding every word. He seemed to speak from two sources, to cast out his words in waves. They cut through the air like screams but landed on her ears as a whisper. As she was brought to her feet, she saw the stranger in his entirety. He was tall and dressed in a ragged black cloak of thick and rumpled linen and violet eyes and a short mess of black hair peaked out from under his hood. The man reached up and lowered his hood, and those violet eyes flashed, lit in a way that felt like a kind of magic she had never seen before. His eyes emanated with such brilliance that Sarah didn't notice the rest of his face. She did not notice the strange, squamous marks that were scrawled on his skin. She did not notice the way they seemed to move beneath the flesh.

Sibella rushed down from the joists and landed on Sarah's shoulder. "Master?!" the bird shouted. His voice cracked in excitement and came out as a garbled screech. That excitement faded as Sibella saw the purple and black veins running along the man's cheeks, the way he looked sick. His face was a patchwork of scales and veins.

Sarah rubbed at her bruised throat as a surprised look swept across her face. Her voice was hoarse, pained from the tight grip of Bolivar's hands. Underneath the strangeness of the man's face, she saw a gentle smile. "You're the Alchemical?"

"I am, but let's tend this mess, and then we can talk." He turned on his heels and started toward Ri. A shadow-veiled cat weaved between his legs. Halfway to Ri, he stopped beside the unconscious body of Ridden and kneeled. "He one of yours?"

Tony, who had returned to Ri's body when the Alchemical entered the room, cleared his throat. Though Sarah saw that his eyes carried a wild, confused terror, his voice was even. "No, that's one of Bolivar's. The man who left through the portal, I mean. That's one of his."

The Alchemical nodded and sent out a stream of purple energy, which wrapped itself around Ridden and bound him. "Looks like he's the last one of them alive. Besides the portal-hopper, of course."

When Sarah walked over and looked down at Ridden, she saw that the boy's shallow breathing. The boy's face was bruised and bloodied, his jaw broken and twisted, mouth lolling open. The bizarre magic that bound him contracted and loosened in rhythm with the boy's breath, and inside the magic Sarah thought she could see the movement of something that felt alive. Then, on the other side of Ridden's body, near Jonathan's, she saw Finch. The world around her started to spin, and she put a hand over her mouth, eyes wide.

"Oh, god," she said, coughing against the pain in her throat. "Oh, Tony." She stepped around Ridden and came to kneel beside Finch. Tony stepped beside her, and Sarah looked over the woman's lifeless body, the blood still pooled around the sword wound in her stomach. Her mouth lay open, her eyes wide and empty. Sarah gritted her teeth and tried to steady her voice, trying to ignore the coldness she could feel creeping up inside. A familiar chill. "Why was she here?"

"I don't know," answered Tony, now kneeling too. "She was armed, but...she dropped it as soon as the fighting started, I think. I'm not sure what happened."

"I...I didn't see any of it."

Tony swallowed hard. "Ri, it wasn't...It's no good Sarah."

"Pinn."

"Yeah."

Sarah fought it, but it did matter. Her face had gone cold, her hands trembled, her mind spun into an endless whirlwind. She reached up and closed Finch's ever staring, ever accusing eyes. *I fell*, they seemed to say. *I fell and fell and fell and it's all your fault you stupid bitch.* Sarah stared at her for a moment longer, the new loss so totally familiar, perfect recollections of losses from before.

As Sarah and Tony knelt beside Finch, the Alchemical continued over to Ri. He knelt and examined them, hands brushing across old scars and new burns. Without a word he lifted Ri's limp form into his arms with an ease that surprised even Tony. He carried them to one of the few tables that had survived the battle and laid them on top of it.

Her throat ached, but her face was cold and still, Sarah came to the table. She expected to find Ri lifeless and stiff on the table, to find that she'd let another slip through. Two this time. Instead, she saw the steady rise of Ri's chest and her body eased, if only a little. She reached out and ran a hand along their neck.

"Just unconscious," said Tony. "Thank god, they're just unconscious. I don't know how that firebolt didn't split them in two." He had Ri's strange and beautiful sword in his hands, Finch's blood cleaned from the blade, and he returned it into the scabbard on Ri's belt, careful to disturb them as little as possible.

"They're hurt," said the Alchemical. "I will try to wake them soon. That Aetic did a lot of damage, but it doesn't seem he was trying to kill this one."

Not quite comprehending the Alchemical's words, not understanding Bolivar could have ever intended anything besides death, Sarah brushed a loose strange of blonde hair from Ri's face. Specks of dried blood broke free from it as she did. In her mind all Sarah could see was the open eyes of Finch, dead on the ground. *Pinn's mother, dead. Michael's friend, dead. Her watch and warrant dead again. Another slipped through. Another fell another fell, another fell.* In a swooping glide, Sibella left her shoulder and came to rest on the table, where he brushed his paper head along the side of Ri's face.

"Sibella," said the Alchemical. "It's good to see you, old friend."

The falcon cast him a dagger-like glance and then returned his attention to Ri. "Did you find what you were looking for?"

"In a way. I'm back now, though. Here to stay." His smile faltered a bit and for a moment Sarah saw one of the dark veins squirm underneath his skin. "Thank you, for keeping this place safe." The Alchemical turned to Sarah, the smile back on his face. If the strange, writhing marks did not frame that grin, it might have seemed jovial, but instead it felt like the maw of a madman. "What is your name?" he asked.

"Sarah Silvergrove," she answered. Her voice came out as a croaking whisper.

"I apologize you had to take on this responsibility. I left to find the magic that called to me, but--"

"The magic you obsessed over," Sibella interrupted.

"I've already told her that you went looking for a way into the Calling Maw. Judging by your face and that demon that trails you, you found it." Sibella's voice was sharp, tinged with his feelings of betrayal and abandonment.

The Alchemical bent down and patted the smoky cat on the head, and it purred. He made no sign of having heard Sibella's question. "This is Dirren, my friend from the Calling Maw." He looked to Tony, who felt the heavy weight of the bright eyes fall on him. "And what is your name? Since we're doing introductions I might as well know you all."

"Tony Bavritt," he answered. "Why are you here?" The question seemed to catch on the end of his tongue.

"Like I have already said, I left to search for a new magic, as I am sure Sibella told the lot of you. A magic not found in this place. I searched for answers only held in the Calling Maw. I found them, and now I am back."

Sibella shifted on the table and shook his head. "Whatever you found there was poison. That much is clear."

"Poison is nonsense. I am a conduit for the Calling Maw, and I have returned with that power better able to protect this place."

"Conduit?" asked Sibella, almost laughing. "Look at your face! You abandoned me and now look at the price you've paid. That place devoured you."

The Alchemical walked over and reached out to Sibella, who dug his claws into the table and recoiled from his old Master's touch. The falcon gave a deep, angered kak and snapped his beak twice. Sarah could feel the anxiety as it emanated from the falcon, who watched the writhing mass below the Alchemical's skin with increasing unease.

"Do not touch me," said Sibella. "Do not come near me, you're nothing now. Nothing but a lie."

For a moment something like rage flashed beneath the Alchemical's face as he held his hand out to the falcon. Something close to it, Sarah thought, but much worse. When the look cleared Sarah saw the way his eyes drooped and stared at the falcon and could feel the pain behind them. "I'm sorry. I know I left you, but I'm back now."

"How are we supposed to trust you?" asked Tony. He now stood with his arms crossed, glancing from Sibella to the Alchemical to Sarah.

The man turned to look at him. "What do you mean? I saved you, didn't I? If I hadn't meant to help you, I never would have spoken to you. I'd have killed all of you and been done with it."

"You can't expect us to trust you," said Sarah. Her voice started to return to its normal timbre. "You left this place a decade ago, so long ago that Sibella doesn't even know what you are anymore. We don't know you. We didn't know you when I found this place. Now you've shown up when…when everything has started to fall apart, and you expect us to welcome you?"

Running a frustrated hand through his dark hair, the Alchemical leaned against the table, giving Ri a passing glance as he seemed to collect his thoughts. "I understand your apprehension, but regardless of how I appear, the power of the Calling Maw is not something to be feared." His tone came off as detached, diplomatic in its cold calculations.

It was an echo of the same lecturers on the Calling Maw Sarah had heard from Sibella so many times, and it was then that she realized that the youth in his voice, the voice beneath the depth of the first, sounded just like Sibella's. Sarah closed her eyes and tried to maintain at least some form of clarity. Her throat ached. "Why are you trying to hide whatever it is you've become? It's clear that place did something to you."

"Have you seen what your face looks like?" asked Sibella. "Do not pretend that you left with a clear mind. You left this place a twisted and confused man. And now?" The bird's voice broke, and he turned his head away. Ink blots fell to the table below.

The Alchemical's demeanor filled up with that strange rage again, and he seemed to shift and move beneath his cloak. He seemed to writhe. "I am growing tired of these accusations."

"Then why don't you actually say something worth saying?" asked Tony. "I don't know half as much about this as these two, but I know that you look sick. Better than that, I know not a word that's come out of your mouth has been anything but bullshit. I'm tired, we're all tired." He paused and his eyes edged back towards Finch's corpse just slight enough to not be noticeable. "We lost a friend today, so can you please cut to the God damned chase?"

Seeing Tony's hand resting on the hilt of his sword, his body tense and ready to move at a moments notice, the Alchemical's demeanor changed. His eyes shifted back to Sarah, a thin smile resting at the edges of his mouth. "I appreciate you keeping watch over this place. I appreciate the work you had to do, the sacrifice it seems you all have made. I am back, and you are relieved of that responsibility now. I free you to grieve. That is the chase."

Sarah, Tony, and Sibella looked at one another and exchanged confused, anxious glances. The three seemed to speak to one another without saying a word. Tony tightened his grip on the hilt of his sword, but Sarah shook her head, knowing that a fight was a waste of time. Knowing that it was a fight they could not win, especially not beaten down and exhausted. She did not have the heart to see another one of her friends, of the people she called to the Belhaven, killed. Her eyes, still dry and tired and cold, glanced back to Finch.

She felt the weight of everything crash down onto her. The weight of responsibility she had taken on, despite everything she knew. The weight of Henry then, and the weight of Finch now. Loss, anger, frustration. *He's giving you another chance to run. You can run again. You should have run when Tony asked you to, but you can still run now. One dead, no different than before. Maybe this time they'll run with you.* Sibella, perhaps sensing the whirlwind in Sarah's mind, leapt up and rested on her shoulders. As she looked at him, she remembered the Falcon's streaming, ink-like tears. She remembered his story of loss, the hurt in his eyes. She remembered promising him she would never leave him. That she wouldn't abandon the Belhaven the way the Alchemical had. She swallowed hard, pushing Morable away, pushing Finch away. Not because she wanted to, the cold in her heart still panged against her, but because she had to. *Grab the goddamn rope!*

"This is my library," she said. Her voice was stern and it cut through the silence despite the way the pain still lingered. She was grateful for that, grateful it did not come out in the choking sobs she felt at the back of her throat. "It called me here. It was placed in my hands." Her battered, exhausted body struggled to hold itself up, and her eyes wavered back and forth between the Alchemical and Ri and Tony. She took another deep breath and gritted her teeth. "This is my library, and I will not let you have it.

CHAPTER XIX
Sent Away

=======================================

"You won't let me have it?" asked the Alchemical. His voice was hushed, yet his figure seemed to stretch and loom over them as he took a step closer to Sarah. For the first time, she realized how tall he was. She realized how his entire body, not just the veins underneath his skin, seemed to move with a stygian grace. "You will not let me have it? There is nothing for you to give. Everything you see is already mine."

"The Belhaven called me here. I am the librarian now." Sarah had tightened her stance, but she could still feel her knees quaking.

"You were called here?" Confusion swept over the Alchemical's face. "What do you mean it called you here?"

"I was pulled here." A lump rose in her throat, and she couldn't manage any other words, but the tight, pained expression on her face must have spoken for itself.

A short, chortled laugh escaping his strange form, The Alchemical nodded in realization. "Ra' Ae called you here, didn't he? That impatient son of a bitch."

Unable to help herself, Sarah's brow furrowed while she clawed her way through her tired, beaten mind. Then all at once an uncontrollable sense of remembrance came over her, so obvious that she knew the Alchemical could read her face. Her meeting with the stranger with the huntsman's beard, the man

Michael had met and named the Man of Ra' Ae. She tried to speak, to deny it, to say she knew him but that he had not called her there, but she couldn't. A thick mix of anxiety and uncertainty overwhelmed her and instead she only gave a single, pained stutter that contained no discernible words. *What did he want from me? He didn't tell me.*

The Alchemical laughed, this time louder. His chest heaved as he regained composure. "You are here trying to lead these people, and you don't even know what brought you here? You don't know what he wants from you, do you?" He gestured to the destroyed second floor of the library around them, and Sarah realized how much damage her fight with Bolivar had done. "Has Ra' Ae even explained any of this to you? Sarah, you're following a man who will leave you to flounder here until the last moment, trust me on that. I have been where you are now, a long time ago." He stopped and ran his hands through his hair as he smiled a wild, mocking grin. "Can we stop this? I came here to relieve you from this, Silvergrove. To give you a chance to walk away from that bearded buffoon's nonsense. If you're half as wise as you seem to think you are, you'll pack your things and run."

"She has been a good leader," said Sibella. The falcon was defiant in his tone and adjusted on Sarah's shoulder as he watched his old master in his strange, new form. "At least she has been here. At least she is not twisted and broken into some unnatural, unknowable thing."

Spinning on his heels, The Alchemical spun marched toward the far wall where Bolivar disappeared into the portal. He slammed a hand into the wall where the portal's burn scars remained and turned his intense, violet gaze to Sarah. His eyes flashed with anger so intense it frightened all of them. "Do any of you know what kind of magic that was?"

Sarah looked to Tony confused, but Tony wore a knowing, almost embarrassed look. "Crown magic," he answered. His memories of his time in the North, of the robe-wearing soldiers who marched in to purge the Creep from his village, filled his mind.

"And what does that mean?"

"It means he was a Crown Aetic."

His eyes blazing, the Alchemical pointed a long, veined finger at Sarah. "I was halfway to Varinz when I heard your foolish call. I spent years carving the runes on this place, hiding it, and you ripped all of that down in an instant. Then you welcome a Crown Aetic into these walls? Who knows what information he sent back to the empire, or where he went when he hopped through that portal. You think you can protect this place? You couldn't protect an empty field, Silvergrove."

Unable to withstand the accusing gaze of the Alchemical, Sarah's eyes drifted to the ground. She didn't know if he was wrong. Sibella hopped from her shoulder to the table and lowered his head, hoping to offer at least some comfort. "At least I've been here,"

Without any sign of movement, the Alchemical was standing with them again, his stance as if he had never crossed the room. His face did not betray a single moment of sympathy. "The Belhaven would be better off if you had never come at all."

She clenched her eyes and fought at the feelings that swam in her chest. Everything that had happened since she found the place whirled in her head, a kaleidoscopic barrage of her new life. Her love with Ri, her new friends, and her responsibilities compounded like blinding explosions. Then, the words of the Alchemical flooded in, and she realized he had asked for her name when they first spoke. He had asked for her name, but now he claimed to have heard her call. She heard the lies that had layered his words, the subtle misdirects, and wondered what else had been a half-truth. Her mind wandered back to the man on the roof, the Man of Ra' Ae, who had served as her reassurance and as Michael's guide. His words *sometimes the world issues us challenges we do not understand,* echoed in her mind.

"I won't do this," she said, tightening her jaw and struggling to stay centered.

His cloak showing no signs of movement, the Alchemical took a step forward. "Do not make a mistake you do not under--"

"I won't do this. I won't just roll over, not after everything else. We can find a way to work together, we can-- you can help us."

At that, the Alchemical's eyes flashed, the violet light in them growing brighter as a scowl filled his face. The marks on his face writhed beneath the lines of his jaw. "The only thing I want from you is for you to get out of my library."

Sarah watched the squirming masses beneath the Alchemical's skin, the way his eyes rose and faded as that strange, unearthly rage grew in him. His lies, his misdirections, his secrets, they all came together and Sarah tensed, trying to look strong despite her beaten state. Seeing that cave in Morable, her friends falling. Henry and Finch and all the others. She reached out and grabbed the rope.

"I will not give this place to you."

Tony's head snapped to her, his anxious expression clear in the corner of her vision, his hand once again on the hilt of his sword.

"I will not let you take this from me."

Almost seeming amused, the Alchemical shook his head and smiled. But the longer he wore it the sicker, the stranger, that smile became. The thin lines of his lips began to melt and fade as his form shifted. The second floor of the library grew dark, despite the day outside, as all the light was sucked away. His body twisted and stretched, and as it did he seemed to grow taller and taller, towering over Sarah. His face loomed over her own, feeling both a thousand miles away and as if it almost touched her. As his smile grew with him, the space beyond it felt infinite. The hidden form beneath his cloak writhed and fought against the fabric.

"Do you think you have a choice?" his voice asked, but any youth had drained away. It was the voice of eons. Books rattled on their shelves, and papers scattered. A purple glow emanated from the twisted, writhing forms that used to be his hands, but now they seemed like tentacles, long and black in their terror. "Do you think you can stand in my way? I will squash you like the child you are."

All at once Sibella launched himself from Sarah's shoulder and let out an crying screech. Sarah watched, stunned and cowering from the monster before her, as the paper falcon dug his talons into the Alchemical's unknowable form and sent his beak into him. The beast that had once seemed a man let out a scream as a black-tentacled hand shot at the bird, sending him to the ground. As the falcon struck the wooden floor, the thud seemed to break through the sounds of the slithering and moving, and the darkness around them began to fade. The Alchemical, where he had just stood a towering monster, now appeared just as he had before. He stared at Sibella, saying nothing. For a moment, Sarah thought she saw his eyes fade to a hazy golden-brown. No one said anything, their eyes all shifting from the falcon, brave and still on the floor, to the Alchemical. When Sibella stirred, the man turned back to Sarah, his eyes once again that color of a near-gone sunset.

"You do not understand the wrath you ask for," he said. His voice was once again a thing of youth and agelessness and eternity. "Let go of this, before another one of your friends is taken away."

Sarah, who still stood stunned beside Tony, looked at the falcon, who now crouched on the floor, his paper form struggling to find breath. No thoughts of running came to her mind, no thoughts of letting go. Instead, she swallowed hard, raised her chin, and lifted her hands. She stood, still shaking and unsteady, in a spell caster's stance. "Tony, take Ri and Sibella and run."

Hands on the hilt of sword and brow drawn tight, Tony shook his head. His eyes again held the whispers of violent red patience. "I won't run, neither would the bird. We'll--"

Long, full-bellied gales of laughter erupted from the Alchemical, so strong that he clutched at his chest and almost began to double over. "You impress me!" he said and flicked his wrist, sending out streams of purple energy. Bands of magic wrapped around the wrists of Tony and Sarah, binding them where they stood. Dirren, his black, shadow-cloaked cat, leapt and tackled Sibella. The living shadow pinned the falcon to the ground as Sarah and Tony struggled against their bindings. The man came to stand between them, his face a mournful, terrifying visage of purple and black, but the corners of his eyes were still crinkled and shining with laughter.

"You're all so brave. A little foolish, sure, but fearless. Destiny is a nonsense concept, an idea fabricated by people with a lot more time and patience than I have, but you seem to have bought into it wholesale. I admire such blind optimism. I think I must have had something like that once, even though I can't remember when that might have been. That's the type of person he craves."

"Let us go," said Tony. He had stopped fighting against the magic bindings and instead rested on his knees. His sword hilt dug into his ribcage, but he didn't move. His voice was level and calm. Practiced. "You know we aren't a threat. There has to be another way to settle this."

The Alchemical ignored them and continued on as he paced in a circular path between them. He stopped for a moment to look down at his feet where Sibella struggled against Dirren's paws. "And maybe you are right and I'm wrong, but I can't take that risk. That Crown Aetic's presence here, Sarah's call into the world. There's no telling what attention it has brought on this place. I can't trust you to keep it safe. Even if he truly has seen something in you. Perhaps you do serve the chords of fate, but I cannot pretend to know the Song." The Alchemical stopped and looked at Sarah with somber, almost apologetic eyes. They would have seemed apologetic, at least, had they not seemed so endless. "I have to take matters into my own hands, and to do that without distractions from any of you...well, I'm afraid I have to send you all away."

The coldness left her body, the resistance, the strength. Her grip had given out, but this time they would all fall. Tears ran down her face, sobs punctuated her words, and her body trembled in her bindings. "No!" Sarah shouted. "You don't have to do anything! You know what's right. We both want to keep this place safe!"

"I can't risk you distracting me from the work that has to be done here. If you make it back here before the end, then you will have your opportunity to prove me wrong. You have every chance to prove your place in the Song."

Sarah squirmed in her bindings and looked beyond the Alchemical to Ridden's still unconscious body on the ground. She looked at the lifeless corpse of Finch, the battle-battered remains of Jonathan and Michelle beyond even her, and the realization of her failures settled in.

"Sarah," the falcon called out, "do not worry. Wherever he sends us we will find our way back. We will stop him."

The words caught in Sarah's throat and she closed her eyes, the tears now rolling from her cheeks and falling to the battered wood floor.

His cloak spilling across the floor and pooling around him, he crouched and ran a thumb along the top of Sibella's head. "I really hope you do. May we meet again, Sarah Silvergrove. Bring the falcon back to me, we all still have much to discuss."

The room erupted in a flash of brilliant, purple light. The spell blinded Sarah and the others as it engulfed the second floor of the library, leaving no corner untouched. As the magic faded and the light returned to normal, the

Alchemical stood among the destroyed remains of the second floor, with only Ridden remaining

EPILOGUE

Castle in the Dark

===

Her vision returning in slow, spotty glimpses, Sarah groped out to the half-visible world to get her bearings. She could tell that she was lying down, but was unsure of where she was, what she was lying on. The ground was thick with leaves, but underneath was a strange, unfamiliar texture. It somehow felt both like fresh tilled soil and as impenetrable as stone. As she came to her feet, her vision returned enough to see that they were surrounded by a dark, windswept forest. The trees were laid bare. Their twisted and knotty forms weaved in impossible figures above their fallen leaves, all set against the silhouette of a red-black sky. She looked around and saw Tony and Sibella coming to as they regained their vision. To her right, Ri laid on the ground, still unconscious.

Tony stretched his back and ran his hands over himself. He felt his tattered brigandine and his sword before he rubbed at his eyes, the last of the spell's effects wearing off. "What is this place?"

Eyes locked on the dual-toned sky, Sarah shrugged. Her face was haggard and bloodied. For the first time she noticed that much of it was swollen. She felt emptied.

"Well, we don't need to keep standing here."

"Where are we supposed to go?"

"Anywhere is better than here," added Sibella. He shook the stiffness from his paper feathers and preened at the ends of his wings.

The falcon's wings were spotted with tears from the cat's claws, and as he came to Sarah's feet, she bent to pick him up. She held him in her hands as she looked him over, realizing how much the fragile thing had given for her, and all of the coldness left her face. She could see him clawing at the Alchemical's horrible form, a bird of prey to the letter. But now, he looked as fragile as an origami ornament. She noted the delicate folds and lines of his enchanted pages, the words of the Belhaven still there on him, even in that alien place. She ran a hand over the wounds, focusing on the paper and the mending it needed. As she did the marks began to fill and close, her magic healing the wounds the cat had left behind. Not as perfect as they had once been, but at least whole. That which the Alchemical had created, Sarah had mended. As she finished, the bird brushed his face against hers and came to his place on her shoulder.

A far off wind sending the trees rattling against the sky, Tony bent down and picked up Ri. He draped them across his shoulder and was surprised at the weight of their limp body. He thought back to the Alchemical and the way he had lifted Ri's body with ease. Tony adjusted Ri on his shoulder and pushed the thoughts from his mind. There would be time for everything else later. "Lead the way."

They all watched the twisted forest as they started out, and for a moment Sarah thought the ground moved on its own beneath their feet. But just as quick as the thought had entered her mind, it disappeared. The disoriented, confused, ageographic nature of this new place clouded all of their minds as they took it in. Together they walked through the strange forest, the ground half-lit by the off-color sky. The woods seemed to twist and move around them. They wandered through the bare trees and listened as the sounds of the forest grew louder with each passing moment. The sounds of crunching leaves, squelching earth, and howling voices filled the stiff air as they walked in near-total silence. At the edge of the forest light peered through the knotted woods, diffused through the tangled mess of empty limbs.

"Head towards the light," said Tony. Eagerness radiated from his voice as the pain in his back and bled into his words.

Stopping to wipe at the nervous sweat on her forehead, Sarah nodded and looked back over her shoulder at Tony, seeing Ri. She saw their steady breaths and heaved a sigh of relief. Then, for the first time since the battle with bolivar had begun, she thought of Michael. "I hope Michael and the kids are all right. We shouldn't have left them. Pinn…" She trailed off, seeing Finch's eyes.

Sibella nodded. "I do not like it either, but we had no real choice in the matter. The Alchemical does not know of that place, and that will give Michael the upper-hand."

A howl echoed across the forest and Tony shuddered. "I'm worried about him too, but there's nothing we'll be able to do for him if we die here. We need to keep moving. Let's worry about Michael and Jane and…Pinn," he stopped. Stopped speaking and stopped walking and stood in the whispering forest as Sarah looked at him. "Oh God, Pinn." He snapped himself back into reality and adjusted Ri on his shoulder. "We'll have to worry about that when we know what we're dealing with here. Let's go."

Sarah said nothing and started forward again and

worked her way towards the tree line. Her body ached from the fight with Bolivar, but she pushed on and hoped that beyond the forest laid answers to her questions. "Watch yourself. We don't know what is going to be on the other side."

Together they continued on, and as the tree line grew nearer, the light became brighter and brighter, its purple hue clashed with the red-black sky behind them and cast strange, dancing shadows on the ground in front of them. Sarah paused and turned to look at Tony, and the two shared a moment of quiet realization.

Sibella adjusted on Sarah's shoulder and spoke in a near-whisper. "I think that we are somewhere very dangerous."

Her hand shaking and uncertain, she reached up and gave Sibella a reassuring scratch on the crown of his head. In the moment, she was unsure if it was meant to comfort him or herself. As they stepped through the tree line, the light grew brighter and cast them in an aura of black-fringed purple identical to the strange magic the Alchemical had flung from his veined hands. In front of them, across a vast field of black-blue grass, was a massive castle, its stone as dark and the night and framed in a brilliant aura of white light.

"This place feels unnatural," said Sibella. The awe poured from his words like honey. "I...I believe we are in the Calling Maw."

As they all stood, awestruck and terrified of the bizarre place they now found themselves, Ri stirred on Tony's shoulder. They let out a soft, tired groan and pressed a hand against the middle of Tony's back. As Sarah helped Tony lay the waking Ri on the ground, an unnatural screech echoed from the woods behind them.

AFTERWARD

=====================================

I've thought a lot about what to say in some sort of potential afterward during the long three years that I've spent working on this novel. For most of that time, probably close to two years of it, I wrote under the assumption that I would go the traditional publishing route, and that this afterward would be, at least in some way, directed towards some facet of the publishing industry. That I would have agents and industry editors to thank. Obviously, things didn't quite turn out the way I thought they would.

Of course, seldom few things turned out how I thought they would when I started this project in November of 2021. At first, the idea for this whole thing began as just a one-sentence prompt, "What if a librarian ruled the world?", and from there I wrote blind, no other ideas for a plot. Early on in that first draft I realized that, whatever this story would eventually turn out to be, it wasn't going to be any of the frameworks I started out with. Over the course of the ensuing months and years, a lot happened. I made some incredible writer friends through the Mississippi NANOWRIMO Discord. Nothing here would ever have been possible without them. This novel was my first fully-completed manuscript. The first one I dedicated myself to editing. It means the world to me, and I want to thank each and every one of you for reading it.

As a matter of fact, there are a lot of thanks that are in order. Thank you to my wonderful friends who listened to me talk about this thing for three years. Thank you to my cavalcade of beta readers, who all helped me turn this into something real. A special thanks among them to Ray Wright, my friend, and neighbor, who had to listen to me more than anyone else and likely knows this novel better than I do. A special thanks to Hannah Jane Costilow, my friend who also happens to be a brilliant and talented editor, without whom this thing would be unreadable.

Special thanks should also be directed to my friend J.A. Wellings, who made the cover for every edition and all of the beautiful interior illustrations. She really helped bring my vision into the real world.

Finally, I owe a great deal of thanks to my wife, Miranda, who has been with me through so much strife, at least part of it coming from my seemingly perpetual drive to write. If Hannah Jane and my beta readers have read some truly rough pieces of this novel, she has read things no person should ever have been forced to read. For that, I owe her more than I can ever repay.

Thanks are also owed to you, reader. I do hope we run across one another again somewhere along the path. Remember, The Song has yet to be Sung.

Billy Don Loper
September 5th, 2024

Billy Don Loper is a writer and native Mississippian who tells stories, primarily, about Mississippi. He received his BA and MA in History from the University of Southern Mississippi with a focus on Mississippi Cultural History. He utilizes that background to write about the dark and hidden aspects of life in small town Mississippi. Loper writes in a wide array of literary forms and genres, all of which focus on the life, story, and culture of Mississippi and the American South.

www.ingramcontent.com/pod-product-compliance
Lightning Source LLC
Chambersburg PA
CBHW030227120726
47903CB00005B/1390